Volume 1

by

Graeme Smith

Print ISBN 978-1-77145-747-7

Books We Love, Ltd.
Calgary, Alberta
Canada

Copyright 2015 by Graeme Smith

Cover art by Michelle Lee Copyright 2015

All rights reserved. Without limiting the rights under copyright reserved above, no part of this publication may be reproduced, stored in or introduced into a retrieval system, or transmitted in any form, or by any means (electronic, mechanical, photocopying, recording, or otherwise) without the prior written permission of both the copyright owner and the above publisher of this book.

Shadow Dance
Volume I

Jack Shadow
Shadow Dance Book 1
Acknowledgements

There are three quotes I use at the front of 'Jack Shadow'. To the best of my knowledge Mr Herodotus has no issue with me using his words. Jack's are Jack's, and since he hasn't killed me yet I guess he's OK with my quoting him. But John Leonard's were a different matter.

One of America's best loved literary, film, theatre and television critics, Mr Leonard passed away in 2008. The quote of his presented here is used by kind and generous permission of Sue Leonard. I cannot thank her enough. Jack would have been less without John's words.

Characters come from strange places. Where they finish isn't always where they were going when they set out, and it isn't always all the writer's doing. Jack is no different. So:

To Sher Reese. Who was the first one to tell me Jack wasn't all Bad – because he was funny. My thanks indeed for you telling me to keep him going.

To Lady Cheryl – who proved Jack really was a Bad Guy. She hated him :-).

To the real Prowess Rayna – who may not really (at least as far as I am aware) be a Shapeshifting empathivore, but really is an amazing concert pianist. My thanks for letting me use a little bit of you here. And, as ever, to my long suffering pre-release readers, both alpha and beta. I owe you no small debt:

To Kaptain K, to Lady A, to the real Kohkoh, to the real Sonea, to Lady Leanna, Lady Talon, Lord Jim and Lord Tranq, to the long suffering Bright Fantastic of InWorldz who come to the Blarney to hear me read, to Lady Tanya, my thanks. And don't go away. The not-summer night sky is screaming.

And to Lady Gail. For Vladivostok –and the Rickenbacker Falls!

Shadow Dance
Volume I

Very few things happen at the right time, and the rest do not happen at all: the conscientious historian will correct these defects.
—Herodotus, The History of Herodotus

Isn't it amazing the way the future succeeds in creating an appropriate past?
—John Leonard

History. Just a big damn pot, and sometimes it needs stirring. Me? I'm a spoon.
—Jack Shadow

Prologue
Lead Guitar in a Lead Zeppelin

The name don't matter none.

Jack Shadow. ShadowJack. Like the lady said in the song, the name don't matter none, 'cause it's all the same. I do my job right, you ain't never heard of me. Never met me. And them that do meet me—mostly they don't tell anyone.

Ever.

If it can hurt you, I likely used it some time. I'm the guy you passed in the street, the guy you never saw. Maybe I bummed a cigarette. Maybe I dropped some change in your tin. Maybe you were my friend. Maybe I killed you.

Maybe both.

Yeah, yeah. I've heard 'em. Every one of 'em. They all start out the same. The jokes. "See … this guy walks into a bar…." Well, that's not me. That guy, I mean. The guy who walked into a bar. I'm the guy who walked out.

No. It's not amnesia. Or at least they don't say it is. Near as anyone knows, I just don't have a past. Near as anyone knows—or admits to. I don't walk round a corner, and some guy from a car shoots at me because long ago I—well, sure. Guys shoot at me. Hell, women too. But not for long ago. Mostly for last week, where 'last week' is any week you choose. No, I just walked out of a bar. Or so they tell me. The Dragon.

The Dragon? Look it up. It's all out there. 'Order of the Dragon'. Hell, 'Sárkány Lovagrend' if you speak Hungarian. Which I don't. Yup, the Internet's a wonderful thing. Guy who had the idea was Dragon. The Dragon loved it so much, they gave him a Special Commendation. I know that for a fact. They sent me to deliver it—the Commendation.

See, you can't have good ideas being talked about. Ever.

Mind, I said it was out there, about the Dragon. Never said it was true. It isn't. None of it. That's the Dragon way too.

Oh, they looked, the Dragon. They really looked for me. Me before the bar, that is. And there isn't much the Dragon can't find if they want to. But there it is. What they told me, one day I walked out of a bar. Were there piles of dead bodies behind me? A stacked deck I was dealing, or one I was dealt? I don't know. I walked out of the damn place. I never walked back in. Just … just away.

But they were waiting, and they took me. The Dragon. They tell me they do that a lot. Wait. Till the time a beat of a gnat's wing can topple an empire. Me? I guess I'm a gnat.

I walked out of a bar. The rest … the rest will be history. Some day. Not that I'll be in it. Nobody remembers the gnats. Not if they did their job right.

What's a gnat? It's like they say: if you gotta ask, I can't tell you. But maybe a story would help. Not that it ever happened, of course. You comfy? Of course you are. I took care of that.

As airships go, it flew like a lump of lead. That might have had something to do with me shooting the Captain and both deck crew, and locking the hydrogen release valves wide open.

The ship had taken off with some big-ass ceremony. A guy with more money than sense had paid some guy with more sense than money to try to do what the Hindenberg had told people not to do. So the guy with no money had done some thinking, then some other guys did some making. Now the guy with no money had money and the guy with lots of money had an airship. Big-ass airship, big-ass launch ceremony. So with all the smoke and mirrors, it hadn't been hard to get on board. The flight from London to New York meant the blimp had to go real high, to catch the jet stream. I figured there'd be time.

OK. So you're thinking the big shot, right? Hell no. He had the smarts to think maybe being on the maiden voyage wasn't such a hot idea. So he'd got on with all the cameras flashing and then sneaked off out the back. Left some dumb look-alike stand-in with the reporters to make happy faces and tell them funny stories. No. There was a band on board, to keep things poppin'. The Dragon wanted to make sure the bass player never made it to New York.

Why? Damned if I know. They don't say, and I don't ask. It's a job, that's all. Just another job. That's the Dragon. Some say it's all about the balance. Some say it's the harmony. Some say Dragon's just a bunch of mean sons of bitches out to rule the world. 'Course, most of them as say that won't say it any more.

Not ever.

Me? I say it's just a big pot, and sometimes it needs stirring. Nobody needs to tell the spoon nothin'. I'm a spoon.

So I did what needed doing, and now the ship wasn't going anywhere but down. Along the way, some people got brave. So they got dead. No big. At least it was quick for them. But the chute I had was only good at low altitude and the damn ship was dropping real slow. Time to kill. So there I was. Sliding down the sky jammin' real bad *Nobody's Fault But Mine* on a dead guy's axe, till I could pop a window and open my chute.

Real bad? Hell. I never said I could play.

That's what it's like in the Dragon. Sure, they tell you you're a hero. Saving the world. And if you believe it, what do you get? Well, you get to play bad lead guitar in a lead zeppelin.

I ain't no hero. Like I said: I'm a gnat.

So there it is. Let's try that joke again. See, this guy walks out of a bar....

I can tell you're wondering. Why we here, you and me? Why we talking? Why am I telling you all this?

Well, see, every job needs that moment. The moment you bang the side of the pinball machine and rock the ball, without ringing tilt. A distraction. So. Consider yourself distracted. But don't take it personal. It's just a job. I'll make it quick.

Oh, and don't worry. I won't feel a thing.

Chapter One
36-24-36 Caliber Pistol

If this was some comic book, I'd have a secret radio transmitter hid behind a fake bookcase. Right. Like I live anywhere long enough to collect books. But that's the movies. Yes, or the comics. The Dragon? Dragon ain't like that. The Dragon, you're in a cab, and suddenly the driver starts tellin' you about a job. And when you look for the driver again, they ain't never there in the taxi rank. Or maybe you get home and take your jacket off, and there's a bit of paper in it that wasn't there when you went out. One you never noticed being put there. One I never noticed, and I'm real good at noticing.

So I can hear you askin'. What if somebody wants something done, and they can't do it themselves? What if they just make like they're Dragon and try to get someone like me to do it? Sure. Someone could do that. But anyone smart enough to know about the Dragon had better be a bit smarter. Smart enough to know if they did something that dumb, the Dragon would look for them. And find them. And—well, and.

I get back to the dive I'm staying in for now, and there's no bookcase and no secret radio transmitter. I didn't take no cab, and there was no piece of paper in my jacket when I took it off. Or I guess there wasn't. Because I never got to take it off. Because what there was, was a blonde. A blonde with a glint in her eye, a gun on the table next to her and legs that should have needed a passport for how long they kept going. She got as far as 'Jack'. As in 'So you gonna shoot me, Jack?' Probably because my gun wasn't on no table. That wasn't good. The guy on the desk would have told her Steve Metcalf, up in room 14, was a nice enough guy. The Dragon would have been and gone before I got there. So I answered her question.

Dead bodies are a bitch to get rid of. Or they should be.

I figure this one shouldn't be too hard. The jerk in 17 had so much skirt walking in and out, no one was going to notice one more. Or wonder why they hadn't noticed this one. She had a bit more class than his usual hook, but the fire would take care of that. So I take her gun, go down the hall and put a bullet in his head. I turn the gas on a crack, put his fingers all over a cigarette, and light it. I leave it lying in an ashtray then go back for her. I figure I give him my gun, put hers back in her hand and take a walk. No big. Another boom in the Big Apple.

Should have worked out fine.

Like I said: if this was some comic book, there'd have been some Clue. A lipstick kiss on the mirror. A note. A little tape recorder that said it would blow itself to bits five seconds after it was done saying something dumb. But like

I said: this ain't no comic book. All there was, was what there wasn't: the blonde.

Most people I shoot, they don't get up. But most ain't none. The ones that don't, they're trouble. Dragon trouble. So I slipped her gun in my pocket. I went back to 17 and stubbed the cigarette, dropping that in my pocket too. I cleaned 14, which mostly meant making sure what was there was all Steve Metcalf and none of me. I took the clothes he'd had on when I started being Steve and he stopped, washed his shirt in the sink and hung it out to dry. Dropped his shorts on the floor. The job I was in town for was a quick one, so the Dragon hadn't had to do anything clever. Steve was still in good condition in the bag. I dragged him out and put him in bed. Then I went back to 17 and lit another cigarette. Or rather, the jerk that lived there did. I pulled my own gear out of its sterile bag and dressed. I did the check—pockets, boot, jacket collar, belt. The rest.

Emergency kit. I never go anywhere without it. Mostly so I get to be the emergency.

I checked 17, and sniffed. Time to leave.

Yeah. I know. Boom. Hey, I never said I was nice. Here's a quarter, call someone who cares. See? I'll put it here. Oh, right. You can't reach it. Nerve paralyzers will do that—like the one I put in your beer. The Dragon say they make it from some tree in the South American rain forest. It acts quick. You just won't be able to move none.

Chapter Two
264 String Sidekick

When someone tries to blow your head off, stopping them is a good place to start. But stopping them ain't enough. It's generally a good idea to find out why they wanted to give you a blow job in the first place. And there's two ways to find out. One is to take a walk and see if anyone else has the same idea. The other is to go ask someone who might know.

I did both.

Walking down a street to see if anyone wants to give you a .357 headache isn't generally considered a smart thing to do. But pulling the emergency cord and runnin' to the Dragon to tell them some broad knows too much and you didn't drop her makes the walking thing look like genius. So I walked. I walked Broadway and I walked Lexington. I walked Central Park and I dropped by the Queensboro' Bridge on 59th. No, Simon wasn't there. No, not Garfunkel either. And nobody with an AK-47 wanting me to slow down—dead. So I took the A train like Ella said, and walked by the Apollo. But nobody played. Nobody took a shot at me at all. Which made a bad thing look worse. Most days, somebody wants to shoot me. If they can find me, at least. And today I wasn't trying not to be found. Someone had the word out. And the word was 'hands off'.

Damn. I hate the bloody piano.

I didn't need to practice. I knew how to get to Carnegie Hall. She wasn't playing 'til later, but that didn't matter. I knew she'd be there. A C-note persuaded the guy on the door he hadn't seen me. After that, she wasn't hard to find. I knew she knew I was coming when the notes changed to 'Dragonstar'.

Prowess was sat at the piano in silk that probably cost more than the guy on the door would earn in his life. She smiled. "Good evening ... oh. Who are you this week, old friend?"

That's P for you. It wasn't evening, and as far as I know I don't do the 'friend' thing. Not that Prowess ever listened. She'd rather hit a bad note than be impolite, and Prowess never hits bad notes. You get used to it. "Blonde. Legs like a long, cold glass on a hot day." Like I said: I hate the bloody piano.

"I changed this a little. Can you hear it? Just here ... like that?"

I sighed. "Blonde. Legs. Bad habit of not staying dead." I slapped the prop and two hundred grand of grand piano lid dropped hard on the rest of a million dollar piano.

"You have no soul, Shadow!"

A claw ripped through the air where my head was supposed to be, but I knew Prowess. I ducked, I rolled, and I jammed my gun into a mouth with more teeth than a chainsaw. "Blonde. Legs. Not dead enough. And Prowess? This one knew my name."

You may have heard of her. Prowess Rayna. Finest concert pianist you'll ever hear—if you give a damn about piano music, which I don't. Oh, and Shape-shifter. And empathivore, which I do give a damn about.

Ever wonder why you go to a concert, and you walk out feeling tired? Well if it was Prowess, that's easy. She ate you. Not your flesh. Your thoughts, your emotions—she ate you. The energy keeps her fed, and the information she gets keeps her in silk. And pianos. So when I need to know something, I ask Prowess. Mostly with a gun in her mouth. That's just how we are, her and me. Well, most people and me. She's not really my side-kick. I just tell people she is when I want to piss her off. Which is mostly.

Prowess grew another mouth. She knew I wasn't taking my gun out of the one it was in. "You really don't, you know, Jack. Have a soul, I mean. A girl has to eat, and you just don't have a scrap about you." Prowess looked over my shoulder. "Oh, and you should probably duck, Jack."

The bullet slammed into the piano. Prowess screamed. I wasn't sure what pissed her off more—the damage to the piano or the noise the lead made as it hit the strings. I'd ducked, so I rolled again and came up, my gun aimed at the blonde. She grinned. "Jack. Didn't your mother ever tell you it's rude to point?" Then she grinned again. "Ah. But then you wouldn't know, right?"

I put three in her chest. Not because I thought it would do any good. More because there was a lot of it and it was an easy target. The blonde pouted. "Now Jack. That's just not nice. Oh, and Jack? You'd better run. They're coming for you." She winked. "I'll be seeing you, Jack."

I pumped another into the space she'd stopped occupying, just in case. But nothing screamed, nothing started dripping blood and everything was just another lousy part of another lousy day. I figured things probably couldn't get any worse, which is normally the time they start doing just that.

"She right, Jack. They're coming." Prowess wasn't looking to unhappy about whoever it was.

"Who's coming, P?"

"The Dragon."

Prowess was right. The not-dead broad was right. I was right too. Things really were getting worse. "I'm Dragon, Prowess."

"Yes you are. And so's she. But which Dragon?" Prowess looked like the question didn't make sense to her either, and she was the one askin' it. But eating thoughts can be like that. Emotions too, she told me.

I don't do those either. Emotions.

See, sometimes it isn't the answer that's the problem. It's the question. We're not there yet. The question, I mean. But the thing about being Dragon is, you don't ask questions. Not if you're a gnat. Not if you're a spoon. So just you sit tight. We'll get there. Get where?

The Question.

Chapter Three
Jack 2 Jack

Yeah. I could've run. After all, if the blonde-who-wouldn't-stay-dead said it, it must be good advice, right?

Sure it was. And there's a whole load of dead bodies would agree with you.

Ever tried to outrun a bullet? It can be done, but this wasn't the time. Besides. If they used bullets, there wouldn't have been anything to worry about. Bullets is patty-cake. They'd smack me round some, then patch me up and tell me not to go doing again whatever it was I'd no idea I'd done. That's the Dragon way. The way this was shaping up, there wouldn't be no….

The cut on my throat stung as it bled. Riftblades. Sharp enough to draw blood before they even touch you. As mine dripped red down my neck I knew I'd need a new shirt. I had an idea it wasn't going to pass expenses.

Prowess kept on playin' Dragonstar, but I figured the Claw wasn't a music lover. His shimmersilks did what they did best, which was to make you look at anything in the room except them. Chameleons blend in. Claws grab the corner of your eye and wrap it round themselves. Prowess didn't break a note, but one of her eyebrows raised. It's hard to fight when you don't have a thought in your head she hasn't eaten, so there isn't much she can't take down if she wants to enough.

Except me.

When I didn't raise an eyebrow back, Prowess just went on playing.

Claws are who the Dragon send when they're serious. They don't talk much. Mostly because after the Dragon pick them for training when they're three, their tongues are ripped out. So this one told me where to go the same way they all do, by making sure the riftblade was everywhere he didn't want me to be. I just went where it wasn't.

Outside, the car was waiting. The door swung open. The sap I'd been expecting slammed into my head, so I just let everything go bla—

* * *

An hour later

—ck. My eyes cleared, and I returned from sap-land. The room was still black. It could have been empty. It could have been full of Claws. The only way to find out was to do something stupid. I was already way past stupid and heading towards 54th-and-couldn't-give-a-damn. But then, I never had. Given a damn, I mean.

The long table stretched away from me. At the other end was the high-backed and carved chair. I'd seen it before, after I walked out of the bar. Seen it once. You were only ever supposed to see it once—when they recruited you. He's always the one you see—at least he is if you're a guy. You see him just that one time. Unless you get neck deep in some gardener's dream birthday present. I figured sniffing would be a bad idea. So I sniffed. The only smell was old wood and the musty only a really old room can must. But that's what upwardly mobile deep-shit smells like.

I waited.

Sure enough, I didn't have to wait long. Just like last time the slow tap of the cane was getting closer. Even before he came into the room, I could see him in my head. The cane lifting. The slow step. The cane hitting the ground. The slow step. The tap. He'd been good once. One of the best. But he'd started to enjoy it too much. Doing extra jobs, just because. So they kicked him upstairs. That made it OK, doing it for fun.

I don't do fun. Like I said, it's a job. Just a job.

He came in and sat in the high-backed chair. Just like last time. The top hat. The silver topped cane. The black cape, the velvet waistcoat. He's like the Dragon. There's a hundred stories. A hundred theories. They're out there: books, the 'Net. One of them's got it right. Actually, that's a lie. None of them tell the truth. Not about him and not about the Dragon. But I'm Dragon. I'd say that anyway.

I nodded down the table. "Hey, Jack." That's not his name. It's just what you call him if you want to piss him off. A muscle twitched under his eye, but he didn't say a word. I wondered if he'd said any words to the others, those nights in Whitechapel. I tilted my chair back, and lifted one leg up onto the table. That was to piss him off too. But that wasn't the only reason I did it. It got my hand nearer the top of my boot. He didn't look up, but his hand slammed the silver topped cane down onto the table. Before the first echo had died the walls shimmered and twenty Claws stood with riftblades ready. Jack still didn't look up, but his other hand waved irritably. The Claws vanished, as though they'd never been there.

Maybe they hadn't.

"Jack. Jack, Jack, Jack." Jack sighed. At last, he looked up. "You know, I offered. You do understand? To retire you, I mean." I shrugged. I didn't say anything. If I got lucky, he'd say. After all, just about anything he said would be more than I knew. Jack frowned. Well, the other Jack did. I just smiled. He frowned some more. "Sadly, they didn't accept my offer." Jack's teeth bared briefly. He probably thought it was a smile. "A shame. It would have been a worthy challenge." The teeth bared again, no more than a split second. "One, of course, you would have lost."

I tried to look knowing. If I got lucky, it would piss him off again. I reached back and scratched my neck, brushing the collar of my leather on the way. Jeans come and go, but apparently I'd had the jacket on when I walked out of the bar. The Dragon wanted to issue me a new one. I threw it away. It wasn't sentiment—I don't do sentiment. But the one I had fitted me like it had been custom made. I'd almost died a few times finding out how custom made it really was. Then there are my own modifications. My emergency kit. The mage who made it owed me, so he promised never to tell anyone else what he'd done.

I believed him. And saved him the effort of keeping his promise.

"Who is she, Shadow?" Jack glared down the table.

I shrugged again. "Someone told me she's Dragon." If I hadn't already turned the old apartment to matchwood, I'd have been getting a new one. Because the Dragon hadn't found out about the blonde when I went to see Prowess. From what Jack had just said, they already knew. Which meant they either knew about her being in the apartment, or they knew about her before. And didn't tell me. "So you tell me, Jack."

The silver cane lifted up, to slam into the desk. Then it stopped, hovering in mid-air. Jack lowered it to the table, gently. "They thought about kicking you upstairs, Shadow. But I helped them see it was a bad idea. If she's coming after The Mast...." Jack stopped, his lips twisting like he'd just bit into sour with a capital S. "I mean, if she is a threat to our organisation, then no doubt you can resolve the matter. But if it's just you she's interested in, then your position will indeed ... change." Jack grinned. I could see he was happy about the idea. Looked like I wasn't a gnat any more. Now I was a goat. The one you leave out to attract the tiger. Thing is, whatever happens to the tiger, it doesn't tend to go well for the goat. Jack smiled. "Shadow? Don't disappoint me, now. Don't die too quickly." He got up. He picked up his cane. As he left, the slow tap-tap-tapping echoed through the room.

Just like Whitechapel.

The others in here? Oh, don't worry about them. They ain't part of this job. Well, not part of your part. Not anymore. Call them decoration. They can't see a thing. Or hear it. So go ahead. You can scream. Scream all you want. You've got reason. Not that you know what it is. Not yet.

You just think you do.

Chapter Four
350 And Down

There wasn't a car outside. Which wasn't good. Because it meant they'd stopped caring if I knew where I was. Where Jack was. Because they figured I wouldn't be telling anyone.

No. I'm not telling you.

The team was good. Real pavement artists. They didn't just change—a reversed jacket here, a hat there. They didn't just rotate—the little old lady in front, then across the road, then the guy with a briefcase. They were Shifters too. I saw the little old lady turn into the kid on the skateboard in a shop window reflection. And that was the problem. They were good. Real good. And I caught them. So either they weren't quite good enough, or….

There was no 'or'. They were faking it.

I figured I was supposed to be so pleased with myself for seeing them, I wasn't going to be looking for the real deal. So I didn't. I ducked in stores, making sure it looked casual. I went down alleys that didn't have exits. Not unless you knew which door to knock on, which fire-escape to pull down. And it worked. One by one, I lost them. All of them. Which made it worse. Because I shouldn't have been able to do that. To lose them. They were a team, and for sure they was talking to each other. Either they all stayed, or none of them. So they were either dumb, lazy, or they wanted me to be. And it was OK for them to be dumb. Or lazy. But not me.

Sometimes, things can get on top of you. This time, it was Fifth Avenue. 350 Fifth Avenue, to be precise. 350 Fifth Avenue and one thousand four hundred and seventy two feet of straight-up. OK, plus the fifty five feet of straight-down foundation I was at the bottom of. No, they don't take the tours down there. They don't even know there's a 'down there' to take them to. Best I could manage, not even the Dragon know. But I'd paid someone a lot of money to make sure there was one. A down there. One I knew about. Now I leaned against a wall that hadn't been touched since I built it in 1929.

Like I said. It's out there. On the 'Net. Bloomfield. July 30, 1975. See, sometimes the best time to finish a job is before you even start it. There's ways, if you know the right people. She wasn't Dragon, but she could get me where I needed to be. Or when. And could tell me how to get back. Of course, she had to learn to keep her mouth shut. But I'm a helpful kind of guy. I put her behind the wall, right next to Jimmy.

I waited. Maybe whoever it was would just stay upstairs, waiting for me to come out. If I was right, they'd be able to tell. But if they were smart, they'd work out there might be another exit. One they wouldn't be able to watch. And I was right. She came out of the shadows. I had a feeling she'd have liked to slink, but—I glanced over—being about sixteen she wasn't quite up to it yet. I raised an eyebrow.

She tried for a menacing smile, and got as far as a curled lip. "Call me Madame Death."

I sighed. "Kid, I ain't calling you Madame. Not in here and not out there. You can be—" I thought a moment "You can be Twinkle." I grinned, waiting some more. I didn't have to wait long.

"Twinkle? Twinkle?" She took two steps, and launched herself at me. Which told me the first thing I'd been right about. She wasn't human. As she shot through the air towards me I twisted sideways and raised one foot, then kicked her in the head. Her skin smoked a little where the silver blended into the steel strip on the bottom of my shoe touched her. But I could see it healing quick. Twinkle hit the ground and rolled back against a wall. The growl growing in her throat wasn't all that was growing.

Some girls take bad hair days just a little bit too far.

I shook my head. "See, I don't do partners." It wasn't going to make a difference, but it made sense to go through the motions.

Twinkle smiled. "I'm not your partner, Jack."

I shrugged. "Figured it was better than goatherd."

Twinkle spat. It didn't sizzle where it hit the floor. Likely she'd have preferred it if it did. "You're mine, Shadow. When the time comes. When we know what ... who ... when you're girlfriend's taken care of."

Now I knew why Jack had been so unhappy. He'd been passed over. "So you're my retirement plan, huh?" Twinkle grinned. "Big bad ass, huh Twinkle?"

Her eyes went cold. "None badder, Shadow. I'm going to eat your heart. If I can find one."

I sighed. "You stone, Twinkle? Put many down? Got many of their friends comin' after you?"

"Enough, Jack. Enough. And they don't come after me. Not for long, anyway." She was getting herself back under control. The growl was gone, and so was the hair. So I shot her. The slug ripped into her, the soft silver nose spreading. Even while the hit was throwing her back against the wall, the wound was closing over.

Werewolves are like that. But not when the bullet's silver. Or, they're not supposed to be.

Twinkle laughed. "Silver, Jack? Can I call you Jack? You think the Dragon would send me after you if that was all it took? You don't know what you're up against, Jackie boy. The Master...." She stopped. She didn't look happy.

"Master, Twinkle?" She didn't say nothin'. I grinned. "You're right. Silver—well that would be too simple." Now she didn't look quite so certain. "So it wasn't just silver."

Getting answers out of a werewolf isn't easy. They're tough to hurt, and anything you break mends real quick. And there's no fix. No cure for what werewolves got.

Or almost none.

The mage who turned 'none' to 'almost' was on the other side of Jimmy. But he hadn't gone there before he told me how to make bullets that weren't just silver. Like the one I'd put in Twinkle. The one that made sure she'd never have a bad-hair day again. So I told her she could tell me everything she knew, or I could throw her ass out on the street. And put the word out to everywhere that Little Miss Bad Ass wasn't quite so bad no more. And that hunting season was open. So we talked. It took a while, but it turned out if Twinkle knew anything, she still wasn't sayin'. So we talked some more. My way.

Then I built a new wall.

Oh, don't worry none. I ain't here to make you talk. You only got one thing to tell me anyway. We'll get to that. Right now? All you got to do is listen.

Chapter Five
A Walk in the Park

I hoped they thought Twinkle was as good as she thought she was. They'd pulled the pavement team so I'd think I'd lost them, knowing Twinkle was on my ass. If they were still watching, and didn't see her, maybe they'd think it was because she was good.

Right. And maybe they were just too dumb to have a tracker mage on her. Sure.

I knew they couldn't see her under 350 Fifth. I had that place warded up the wazoo. So they'd have lost her there. But they'd have waited. To see her reappear. And they wouldn't see a damn thing. Not of Twinkle anyway. Me? Me they'd see. So they were going to be coming. And this time they'd mean business. Wet business. I was out of time and out of....

As I turned, I saw it. Her. Twinkle. Ducking into a store behind me. Which was all sorts of impossible. Or, since I'd given up on impossible after walking out of a bar I never walked into, a damn close second. So I did what I'd been going to do anyway.

I ran.

Now, when you're running, 'specially if you're running from a smart-ass were-kid with a bad habit of not staying dead (I was getting kind of tired of that), you don't actually run. You walk. You hop cabs. You do the subway shuffle, you go to places your tail can't go, and leave ways they shouldn't be expecting. You know how many men's rooms there are in the Apple? I do. And I used near every damn one. But it didn't make a blind bit of difference. Everywhere I went, there she was already. Which was interesting. In fact, it was so interesting, it was why I was right back where I started, at 350 Fifth. Or rather, under. Under and staring at what was behind a wall I was getting real tired of rebuilding.

"That was fun, Jack. Let's do it again!"

If there's one thing I hate, it's a girl who giggles. Well, along with having my fingernails torn out by the roots. And root beer. And ... OK. One of the things I hate is a girl who giggles. But even girls who giggle are better than girls who don't stay dead. And even if I'd never know about the giggling part, the wall I'd just ripped down was busy telling me Twinkle had the staying dead down pat. So I put a slug through the blonde's chest, more out of habit than hope, and I wondered who I'd been seeing behind me all day.

"Why, Jack! I didn't know you cared! Me, of course! You needed some time, and I wanted you to have it. So I thought it best if the Dragon thought their little pet was still on your tail. Wasn't that nice of me, huh Jack? Taking care of your—" Blondie grinned, and winked, "—ass, and all?"

Blondes who don't stay dead are bad enough. Blondes who can read my mind, I can live without. And according to Prowess, nobody could read my mind. But it looked like Prowess never told Blondie. Still, like the kids say these days, there's a hat for that. And I had one. I got it made when I did the Nixon job. I grabbed my Stetson off the shelf and jammed it on.

Nixon? Oh, he was a real nice guy. Straight as an arrow. Dragon didn't like that, so we did a switch. We had to get Lucy a sex-change, but she said it beat the crap out of the Papal Palace.

As usual, Blondie didn't seem bothered by the fatal chest wound she was busy not having. She grinned. "Nice hat, Jack." Her eyes narrowed, and focused. After a while she raised an eyebrow. "Damn, Jack. That's a very nice hat."

"You never hear the stories, Blondie? How Nixon always wore a Stetson?"

"Nobody ever saw Nixon in a Stetson, Jack."

"Oh, they saw him, Blondie. They just never got to tell anyone." I didn't wink. I didn't grin. I didn't give out some evil laugh. That's for the comics. For me, like I said. It's just business.

"Yes. I guess there'd have been times young Lucrez—er, I mean young Richard—would have needed a hat like that." Blondie must have liked comics. She winked again. For the wink, I could care less. But I was beginning to see why the Dragon were so hot on her. She knew. And I didn't know what she knew, but it was already too much. "Jack.

Unless you're going to shoot me again—and do feel free to try—we really need to talk."

Central Park. They say it's nice in spring. Of course, it wasn't spring. A cold wind was blowing up off the lake, and standing in the middle of a hunk of metal didn't make it any warmer. But Blondie said that was sort of the point. Bow Bridge. Sixty foot of cast iron over water. Not flowing water, but Blondie said the cold iron would make up for it. Standing in plain sight on the middle of a bridge while the Dragon had every Claw, mage and anybody else who wanted to make a name for themselves after my ass wasn't my first choice. But Blondie told me all those guys were busy watching me and her run all over New York. And that nobody could see us where we really were. It seemed being not dead wasn't all she was good at. And I was beginning to get an idea that whatever Blondie was, she was real good at being it. So if she wanted to talk, I was going to listen.

"You know they made movies here, Jack?"

Thing was, small talk wasn't what I wanted to listen to. I said nothing.

"Manhattan. *The Way We Were* ... you ever see *The Way We Were*, Jack?" I said nothing. "I guess not. You don't even know the way you were. Right, Jack?"

"This the part where you make me a deal, Blondie?" I was starting to get some ideas about Blondie. I didn't like them much. "Like, I do something real dangerous for you, and you tell me about me? Guess what. I pass. Go to hell, Blondie." I figured it was worth a shot.

"Hell? Nice try, Jack." Blondie looked out over the lake. "No, I'm not Mr L. Though I won't say we haven't met...." She looked at me and winked. "No, I thought of offering you a deal. But I knew you wouldn't take it. So I went for Plan B."

"Plan B?"

"Yup. You see, somehow The...." I could hear the capital letter "...The Master heard you were after him, Jack."

The Master. That was what Twinkle had said. And since Blondie liked the comics, I guessed I'd better stick to the script. "The Master?"

Blondie just carried on. "And he really, really wasn't happy about it, Jack. You've got—well, a reputation."

"So when someone told him I was after him, he…?" Comics. Bleh. But sometimes you have to stick with the script to get people to say what you want to hear. I figured this was the part where one of the Bad Guys told me everything I didn't know. Then tried to kill me. There'd probably be sharks. And frikkin' lasers.

"Oh, he sent just about everybody he had after you, Jack."

So far it seemed to be working, so I stuck with the script. "And why would you want that, Blondie?"

At least she didn't waste any time on the 'who, me?' thing. "Mostly so you'd have to kill the bastard, Jack. A— let's say, a friend—told me you're just about the only one who can. Kill him, I mean. Before he kills you. Or has someone else do it. He's not big on the personal touch." Blondie grinned. "Well, not these days, anyway." Blondie paused. "Oh, Jack?"

"Yes?"

"Can you swim?"

This time it didn't look like there'd be any sharks. This time the crews either end of the bridge just dropped their invisibility spells and opened up with their AKs. And totally against the script, Blondie pushed me over the side of the bridge.

Some days, whatever answer you've got is the wrong one. A bit like yours is going to be, I guess. But don't worry. We're not there yet.

OK. So I lied. You should probably worry.

Chapter Six
Goleta A-Go-Go

There's good fishing in the lake. Good fishing, and in summer you can get a rowboat and row under Bow Bridge. Not that I fish. Or row. But, fish or rowboats, the damn thing's still only about six feet deep. And no sharks, with or without lasers. So the guys with AK-47s running on to the bridge shouldn't have had any trouble at all. And I shouldn't have still been swimming down with Blondie ten minutes after she pushed me over the edge. And if I had been—I should have been drowned. I wasn't. Which was good. What wasn't so good, not if I wanted to have one single idea about what was going on that is, was what I was. Stood on a beach in—I checked a nearby sign—Santa Barbara. Dripping wet. With a blonde in a two-piece that would have been an arrestable offence if it had about twice as much cloth. Which it didn't.

"Hey, Jack! Gonna get me a popsicle?"

I pulled out my wallet and peeled a fifty. I squished it in my fist, the water dripping from my fingers, then flicked the ball of useless paper at Blondie. "Keep the change."

"Spoilsport." Blondie narrowed her eyes. My leather vanished, along with most everything else I had on. The Speedos were—or more accurately very much weren't—all that replaced them. I was on a beach, my ass saying hi to the wind with a near naked blonde. Who probably wasn't a blonde—not a human one anyway. The Dragon wanted me dead, and I didn't have a gun. Or anything else my leather kept close to hand. Some days, you just shouldn't get up. And that's supposed to happen to other people, not me. It was time to get pissed at someone, but the whole no-gun, no emergency kit thing made that a little difficult. So I did the most dangerous thing anybody can do. I shut up. And thought. Blondie waited, one eyebrow raised. I looked round some more. The sun hung low, creeping close to the wet horizon. It was probably going to be a fantastic sunset. Which was kind of interesting. See, one thing a lot of people don't know about Santa Barbara: the beaches pretty much all face south. The fishing pier made it Goleta—which meant the setting sun was kind of lost.

"Smartass." Blondie didn't sound happy. Nor was I. Because that made it twice she'd read my unreadable mind. And I was fresh out of hats. "Look, Jack. Just roll with it, huh? You really don't want to see where you are right now."

"Didn't have to be here at all, Blondie. What you do? Take out an ad? Centre page of the Times?"

"You know, Jack, sometimes you're just no fun at all." The beach disappeared. The rocky cave walls weren't any real improvement. My leather was. Blondie seemed to think her two-piece was fine, assuming she was responsible for the absence of beach. If she was what I thought she was, the beach would have been cake. "Thing is, Jack—what if it was the beach that was real, and this is the illusion? Or maybe this is an illusion too, and what's real is—" the rock walls disappeared. The inferno of flame crisped my leather in an instant. The other instant—the one where my flesh burned from my bones in searing agony—seemed to last a lot longer. "—this?" The flames vanished. The waves rolled onto the beach. "So Jack. Be a good boy. Get me the damn popsicle, huh?"

At least she let me keep my leather.

The Beachside Restaurant on Goleta Beach is a little unusual. For one thing, unlike a lot of things 'Beachside', it's on the beach. The sun was setting where it should be, beyond the university. And if my Mango Absolute Martini had an olive in it, I could live with that. Mostly because the olive wasn't shooting at me. Oh, it happened once. But that's a different story. On the other hand, I figured it wasn't a good time to be taking risks. So I ordered a beer, and threw the olive out onto the sand.

It didn't go bang.

"You got a problem, Jack." Blondie didn't sound too unhappy at the idea.

I waved a waiter over. "You got any more olives?"

"Jack. Are you listening?"

The waiter came back with my beer. It had an olive in. I gave him a ten. When he'd gone, I took the olive out and held it up in front of Blondie. Then I flicked it out onto the sand. This time it went bang. Mostly because of the slug I'd put in it. The crowd in the restaurant just carried on like nothing had happened. Which was also interesting. So I shot the waiter.

Blondie sighed. "You're just going to be a pain in the ass, huh Jack?"

I shot a woman playing 'maybe, baby' with a guy in a suit. I shot the suit. I raised an eyebrow at Blondie. A kid in ruby slippers came through the door, so I plugged her. And her little dog, too.

"Jack!"

I dropped the eyebrow I had up, then raised the other one. Hell, if she was going to mess with me, she could at least have let the place have decent beer.

"I don't know, Jack. I try to be nice…."

The restaurant walls faded away again. The rocky walls were as little improvement as last time. I put a bullet into the rock and wasn't really surprised when it didn't ricochet. When the flames roared round us again, things started to make sense. When they didn't burn me to a crisp, they started to make sense-er. I didn't turn round to look at Blondie. Mostly because I was pretty sure she wouldn't be there.

The blast of fire that rolled over me told me I was right.

Some days—well, some days, being right is just about the worst damn thing you can be. Like, right now. Because pretty soon you're going to have to give me an answer. When I ask you the Question. And whatever you say, you'll be right.

You'll just wish you weren't.

Chapter Seven
Blonde Bombshell

"Bloothy hell, Jack. You really pisth … pith…." When you've got as many teeth as a dragon, talking can be tricky. Dragon mouths are designed with different priorities. The huge golden dragon, who'd been behind me until I turned round, spat. "Damn it."

If she'd wanted me dead, I'd be dead. And there wouldn't have been any talking first. Dragons are like that. It looked like Prowess had been right—Blondie was definitely dragon. Just not Dragon. So now I had a Dragon who wanted me dead, and one who didn't. At least not yet anyway. I shrugged. It let me check a particular little lump on my left shoulder was still there under the leather. "Everybody's got to be good at something, Blondie."

The dragon shimmered until it wasn't a dragon any more, and went back to being a near-naked blonde. The flames crisped the swimsuit Blondie was almost wearing until she wasn't wearing it at all. It was clear none of her blonde came out of a bottle. She looked down, then grinned. "Oh, Jack. Whatever there is, I'm just the best damn thing there is at it. Wanna find out, huh?" She did a bump and grind in mid-air that would have done Vegas proud, floating with not a damn thing supporting her. Not that she needed any support. I remembered the huge golden dragon. Then I told my head to stop thinking. And to stop drawing pictures. To really, really stop drawing pictures. I didn't say anything. Blondie seemed to like the sound of her own voice, and people who talk can say things they don't really want you to hear. "Like I was saying, Jack. You really piss me off." Blondie waited. I waited. Blondie waited some more. "Actually, Jack, you piss just about everybody off. You know that?"

I shrugged. Hell, everybody's got to be good at something.

Blondie winked. "Shall we slip into something more comfortable?" She waved her hand. Well, it looked like she waved her hand. I tried to avoid thinking what she might really be waving. The flames shivered. The bedroom walls they shivered into were probably more dangerous. The bed Blondie was sitting on, patting a space beside her? I'd be safer back with Jack, and a hundred Claws. I raised an eyebrow. Blondie sighed. "Spoilsport." The bedroom walls shivered. The candlelit table in the corner of the quiet little restaurant was probably just as dangerous. As far as the silk in the dress Blondie had on was concerned, the candlelight was just passing through. So it did. Me? I checked the lump on my shoulder. And my gun. I raised my other eyebrow. "Do you like my dress, Jack? I made it just for you." Blondie did her version of a shrug. I had an idea it wasn't a gun she was checking—or 'a' anything. Blondie winked, and shrugged again. If I was supposed to get some point Blondie was making, I was on overtime. And from the look of the points she was making under the silk, double time. So I did what I always do when it's time to move things along. I wasn't surprised when the bullet went right through the head waiter. And the two at the table behind him. And the wall.

Blondie sighed. "Now really. How can anybody bring us dinner if you keep shooting them? Aren't you hungry, Jack?" She shrugged again. Slowly. She raised an eyebrow. I shrugged as well, and looked for someone else to waste my time not shooting. Or at least, not killing. Blondie sighed again. "I don't know. Men. Well, boys. But dinner's not ready yet." Which was interesting, since we hadn't ordered any. "So maybe I should tell you a story. Just to, you know, pass the time, Jack. Not because it's true or anything. Are we clear on that, Jack? About it not being a true story?"

It was my turn to shrug. "So long as there's no dwarves. And nobody sings. One hi-ho, and I'm out of here."

Blondie smiled. "No. No dwarves, Jack. Not dwarves. But—what do you know about dragons?"

Now we were getting somewhere. Time to see where it was, and who would be damned for getting there. "Dragons? Big-ass, mean...."

Blondie flushed. "What? My ass isn't...."

I grinned. "Like you said, Blondie. This ain't no true story, right?" I grinned again. "So. Dragons. Big-ass trouble. Meaner 'n snakes, and nasty with it." Blondie's flush was running down her throat, running down to make points of its own. Or at least to say hi to the ones that were already there. Which was fine by me. If you want to get even, get the other guy mad first. It clouds their thinking. "Pure bad-ass magic. Impossible to kill. Though...." I let myself look pensive. Whatever pensive is. "...though I've got some ideas on that."

For a moment, Blondie looked worried. "Ideas? What...." she shook her head. "Damn you, Jack. Not that you can be. Damned, I mean." I filed the 'not that you can be'. I had a feeling it was important, though not right then. "Let's just stick with 'impossible to kill', huh Jack? And there's another thing about dragons. You know want that is, Jack?" I waited. She was going to tell me anyway. "YOU DON'T STEAL FROM THEIR BLOODY HOARD!" The thing with dragons, they got real fiery tempers. Even when they're busy being blondes with 36 inch—for want of a better word—guns. So the first thing a dragon does when it gets mad is burn anything in sight. I smashed my chin down on the lump on my shoulder.

See, it's always a good idea to have a back door. And if you can't guarantee one will be around, to carry your own with you. The lump crushed, and I made like a flower. I faded.

Oh. Right. You could use a back door right now, huh? But it's damn good stuff, that Dragon juice. You couldn't use a door right now if you had ten of them and an hour to get running, right? But it's OK. In the end, there's always a way out.

In the end.

Chapter Eight
Kiss-story

I looked round. The head waiter was still pretending I hadn't shot him. The couple behind him were pretending all they were thinking of was dinner. Oh—and my hair was on fire.

The thing with back doors is it's a good idea to know where they go. This back door wasn't like that. It just took me where I needed to be. That's what the mage who makes them for me said. Yes, makes. No—I didn't kill him. I don't kill everybody. Especially not people I might need around again. I made a mental note to give him a call. I like my jacket lumpy. This time? This time it seemed I needed to be sat in an intimate little restaurant. With my hair on fire.

"Oh, I'm sorry Jack." Blondie waved something that probably wasn't a hand. The fire went out. "But…."

I figured either I had to change my policy on not shooting some people, or the mage who made my lumps was still on his game. I shrugged. "So. Where were we? In this totally not true story you're not telling me?"

Blondie spat. Then she waved her hands over the ball of fire that came out of her mouth, before anything else started burning. "But Jack! It wasn't my—er, I mean, in the story. It wasn't her fault, right? He was so cute! And a girl's allowed to have fun, right?"

Right. I put my boots up on the table. I leaned back. I figured it was going to be a long night.

* * *

1446, Sighișoara, Transylvania

She could tell everybody in the room hated her. Well, the women at least. It was, she thought, quite wonderful. The shape she was wearing felt a little strange, but the men around the room didn't seem to mind. Especially….

He walked over. "Good evening, my lady. Or is that Grófka? Or…?"

She felt every woman hate her just a little more. She shrugged her shoulders, slowly. Various other parts of her moved. The gorgeous young man in front of her smiled.

She smiled back. "Oh, whatever you choose, my lord. Titles are so tiresome, don't you think?"

He shrugged. "They impress my father." The man looked towards an older one across the room. "But then, he is *Voivode*."

She stroked her necklace. It had taken a lot of power to make. Her heart and soul. Not, she thought, that her kind had hearts. But it had been worth it. What she'd used had grown back, and it helped her keep in shape. She grinned. The huge emerald hanging from it drew his eyes back where she wanted them. "Well, sir. Perhaps we can discuss things to—to call each other—some place more...." she looked round, smiling. "More discreet?"

* * *

"And when I, er, I mean, when she woke up, he'd stolen it!"

I grinned. "Her virtue, you mean?"

Blondie spat. Again. "Screw virtue." For a moment her eyes went distant, and she smiled. "And he most definitely did." The smile made like a flower, and faded. "No. I mean the bloody necklace, Shadow!"

"In the story, you mean." It was my turn to grin. The look on Blondie's face made me almost mean it. "So somebody really did it. Stole from a drag—"

"Hush your mouth, Shadow! If that sort of thing got out, I'd, er, I mean the dragon in the story would have every dragon that ever was on her ass for screwing up. We've got a reputation to keep up. NOBODY steals from a dragon. And lives, at least."

"So why did he? Live?"

"Why did who what?" Blondie wasn't grinning anymore.

"The guy. In the story. Why did he live?"

"Story, Jack? Did I tell you a story? It must have slipped my mind." Blondie still wasn't grinning. Very definitely not grinning. I made a mental note of how not-grinning she was. "So how come the Dragon's after you, Jack? I hear they want you real dead."

It looked like we were finally getting to the night's main event. I shrugged. "Damned if I know. Someone told me it was your fault, Blondie."

"Mine, Jack? Mine? All I did was hang around you."

"Hang around, Blondie? First time I saw you was—"

"In your apartment, Jack? Sure. Just because you never saw me though, didn't mean I wasn't there. Maybe—maybe some other people saw me."

"Right. Because you made damn sure they did, huh? Why would you do that, Blondie?"

"Maybe because you're cute, Jack." Blondie grinned again. She shrugged. "Think that was it, Jack? Because you're—" she shrugged. Again. "—because you're cute?" I waited. Then I waited some more. Blondie stopped grinning. "But, just so we're clear Jack, I never actually did anything. Right? Nothing at all. And absolutely nothing that could be seen as threat to anyone, right? Anyone not you, that is. I just, like, hung around. Anything anybody—any anybody—might have assumed, that's nothing to do with me, right?"

Not a threat. To anyone. Apart from me. Because for some reason, the Dragon wanted me dead. But that's how it is for gnats. Sometimes they get squished. "I guess not, Blondie."

"No guessing, Jack. Nothing. To do. With me. Right?" Blondie shimmered—into Twinkle. "So, Jack. I guess you have things to do, huh? Things to find out? Questions to ask? Maybe you ought to go ask someone who might know some answers? And we can't have anybody getting, um, worried. While you ask your questions. Any anybody. Not yet, right Jack? So I'll keep them off your back. While you—while you do what you do so well, huh?" Not-Blondie waved what was probably not a hand. The Fifth Avenue traffic roared by. Blondie took off—though not literally. She was being Twinkle, and Twinkles don't have wings. Me, I took the foot-train to Harlem. It's easier to spot a tail that way. There wasn't anything to spot, so I picked a new no-questions-asked dive with a flickering neon sign and took a room. That's what I was doing—a new room every night, and nothing left behind. You sleep on your own plastic sheet, and put their bedding back in the morning. That way, there's less to trace. What you mostly don't do is blow the place to matchsticks just before dawn. I didn't. But someone did. See, dawn is good. If someone's asleep, round dawn they're in deepest REM sleep. Sound and sounder. So it's a good time to make that someone dead. To squish them.

I don't squish.

See, that's the other thing I do. Round midnight, I took off out a window. Places nice folks don't go, they're squashed close up. Which is good. Out a window, up a wall, over a roof—there's always another window open. You grab whoever's there. A needle, and Mr Sandman couldn't keep them deeper asleep. They get to use your bed, and you use theirs. In the morning, you switch back. It works. Makes you harder to track. And it works especially well if someone wants you dead. They get to blow some sucker not called you into whatever passes for glory.

The matchsticks that used to be the GoodNight Motel said someone probably wanted me dead.

Blondie was trying as hard as she could to tell me something, without saying what it was. Maybe she couldn't tell me. So maybe it was time I found someone who could. And make them tell.

See, that's how it is. Sometimes, you got to find someone who can give you some answers. But before you can get the right answer, you have to have the right Question. So that's why we're here. Why you're here.

The Question.

Chapter Nine
Fay-Tal Attraction

Boxing Day Night, 1887. Whitechapel, London

If you have to make a professional's life miserable, don't ever try it while they're working. Whether you're their target or not, they're looking for you. Because they're looking for everything, looking for everyone. At least, the good ones are. So the best time is when they're playing. Because even professionals stop looking properly when there's a ball involved. Or, as it may be, a foggy night. If, that is, their thing is foggy nights. Which is why I was stood in an alley off Commercial Road.

There's nothing really difficult about time travel, though the ingredients are a bitch. Virgin's Tears are getting real hard to come by. Not so much the tears—more the virgins. Which is mostly why there's a crowd of unicorns hanging round near every street corner, looking hopeful. It's not generally a problem. The few people who can see them are normally locked up pretty quick by the large number of people who can't. Who are told to lock them up by the ones who know the unicorns are really there. So it evens out—Unicorn's Horn is a lot easier than it used to be. And unicorn steak takes some beating.

I'd followed her from the pub at Mitre Square. I made a mental note to take care of it. The pub, I mean. She'd made her way through the alleys the way she had every one of the last few nights. Sometimes she'd stop on a corner, say hello to some other girl on the night shift. They all knew her. Or enough, anyway. Too many would just make more work later.

"'Night, Fay. You get home quick now!" She smiled at the latest one. I followed her as she slipped into another alley. That was when I heard it. Tap. Tap. Tap….

It was time.

If nothing else, he was thorough. He'd been keeping his pattern random, backward and forward. That was going to confuse the heck out of historians. This one was a backward, and he was a long way down his road. The stake through her stomach. The cut open chest. His knife careful and precise, the liver and heart extracted. Like I said. If you're going to make a professional's life miserable, do it when they're having fun. So I stepped out from the shadows. "Hey, Jack." Then I shot him.

No. I didn't kill him. He had questions to answer. Besides. He was Executive Suite. Dragon would have him tagged from zipper to zatch. I killed him, they'd smell it on me in a minute.

* * *

350 was tight. Wasn't the first time I'd stashed someone there so we could chat a while. But I couldn't have him running out on me while I did what needed doing. It's kind of hard to run without legs. So I cut his off. It gave knee-capping a whole new meaning, except he didn't have any anymore. Knees, that is. I sealed the ends of his legs in hot tar, so he wouldn't bleed to death. And so it wouldn't look out of place when I got rid of him later. Not yet though. Like I said: he had questions to answer.

* * *

1888. Whitechapel, London
I was a little short on Virgin's Tears. So when I got back to Whitechapel, a few weeks had passed. I figured that wasn't good. I was right. When I broke into the morgue, Fay was gone. So I went to the pauper's graveyard. Good job nobody was going to pay for cremation. I dug. When I opened the casket, she wasn't happy.

"Bloody hell, Jack. Took your time, didn't you?" Yup. She was pissed.

"Hello to you too, Prowess." That's the thing about being a Shape-shifter. Having your heart and liver cut out is more an inconvenience than anything else. "So. Who do we have to fix?"

The cop was easy. Even police Inspectors take an occasional drink, and Edmund Reid was no different. First, Prowess fixed him so he got rid of all evidence there'd ever been an investigation. After he was done she sucked a bit harder, and he forgot everything. Like it never happened.

An evening or so around Whitechapel, and nobody there remembered Fairy Fay. A little gasoline, a match, a little of Prowess, and nobody remembered there'd ever been a pub at Mitre Square either. Or the people in it when it burned down.

The easiest person to get rid of? Somebody who was never there in the first place. So Fairy Fay went back to the land of the never-was, and a whole new set of web pages got a reason to exist. But that was OK. Web pages are like unicorns. Everybody knows people who believe them, or in them, are crazy. Which suits the Dragon just fine.

That left Jack.

* * *

Back at 350, Jack wasn't happy either. "Shadow. This time—this time you've really gone too far. You know you can't kill me. And you know you can't hold me here forever. When I get back and tell The Master...." He stopped.

"Yes. The Master. I've been hearing a lot about him recently. Who is he, Jack?"

Jack laughed. "A nice try, Shadow. But you don't sit at any table high enough to know about...." He stopped again. "Yes. A nice try indeed."

Damn. I was going to have to rebuild the bloody wall. Again. A few strokes with a hammer I kept for occasions like this, and Twinkle greeted the world. As in, not greeting. Being dead will do that. You didn't need Jack's surgical training to see she'd been dead for a while. "Nope. I don't. Know any high tables, I mean. But she did," I pointed.

"But she's ... we've been tracking her for ... I saw her yesterday!" If Jack hadn't been happy before, he was even less happy now.

"Yup. You've been keeping tabs on her, right? While she 'followed' me?" It was my turn. I grinned. "Well, we had quite the little chat, Twinkle and me."

"Twinkle?"

I sighed. "Twinkle. We didn't exactly get down to names, Jack. Anyway. We had quite a little chat. I'm good at chats. Right, Jack?"

"Do at least try, Shadow. I don't know how you did it, but it doesn't matter. She was just a Cleaner. There's nothing she could have told you about—about matters." Jack didn't grin. I guessed he figured he was about to find out how good I was. At chats. Which was fine by me, because he wasn't.

I grinned. "I guess you're right, Jack. I guess there's no chance those high tables thought your … amusements … were getting risky. That you were getting sloppy. That they put one of their best in your pocket, to maybe find out. No chance, right Jack?" Getting Jack on edge would make things easier. So I pulled a knife from my boot, and put him on edge. Throats aren't any good if the mark knows you can't kill them, but stomach wounds bleed big, and you can always sew them up. "So, Jack. Since you don't know what I know, you won't know when I know you're lying. You know?" I stopped, just to check if my 'knows' were in the right place. They were. "So. The Master. What do you know, Jack?" I lit a flame under the tar I'd used to seal his legs. I grinned. Normally the grin was just for effect. Normally, like I said, it was just a job. It was this time as well. But this time was different. This time, I was working for me.

I figured the grin should have just about done it. So I hit him. Hard. He went out like a light. Which let Prowess stop being the extra layer of wall behind me. She grimaced as she slithered down. "Damn. I hate that. You get used to legs and—" she shuddered. Or shivered. "—and bits."

"Is he ready, P?"

A bit of Prowess oozed over to Jack. Then it stopped. "Ready for what, Jack? What do you want?"

"Everything, P. Hell, I don't even know the right questions yet. I need everything, and I need to be able to ask him stuff I don't know."

Prowess' face went hard. As though she wanted to make a point, she grew another face and that one went hard as well. "That's big, Jack. Damn big. You see...." She looked at me. "Well, no. You probably don't. What do you think memory is, Jack?" I waited. She was going to tell me anyway. "You see, memory—it's not all that chemical nonsense they talk about. It's your soul, Jack."

Which was interesting. Because I remembered things. Which meant....

"No it doesn't, Jack." Prowess apparently couldn't read my mind. Blondie was different. Of course, most people couldn't walk out of walls either. Not that Blondie was exactly people, so that's just what she did. Walk out of the wall. Prowess' brow furrowed. Her eyes started to glaze. "I wouldn't do that, if I were you." Blondie sounded amused.

"Powers above! She's a dragon, Shadow! What the—" Prowess stopped. She thought a moment. "Yes. I do believe the moment is appropriate for this sort of thing. What the fuck have you got me into, Jack?"

Blondie grinned. "He's a little puzzled, my dear. You told him he has no soul. But he remembers things. So he thinks you're lying. Are you lying, dear?" She grinned wider. "Oh, don't worry. I'll take care of it. No, Jack. She isn't lying. Yes. What people call memory is really their soul. Little bits of their soul that get scraped off at different times, in different places. Little bits of their soul the rest of their soul is always connected to. But you? You have—something else. And no. I'm not telling you what it is. Not yet." She grinned again. I had a feeling there were a lot of things Blondie wasn't telling me. But we'd get to those. Whether Blondie knew it or not. She winked at me. Which meant she probably did. And didn't seem too worried.

Prowess pursed her lips. "Whatever, Jack. But what it means is, I can't do what I do. Eat. Bits of him, I mean. I have to take it all, Jack. All of it. I have to take his soul. And I'm not doing it. Unless...."

That's how it always is. In the end. There's always a price. Always an 'unless'. "Unless what, P?"

"Unless I get you too, Jack." Blondie smirked. Me? I waited. Prowess spat at Blondie. "Don't be so tiresome."

She looked at me. "No, Jack. Not that. Not that it wouldn't...." for a moment, she looked thoughtful. Then, "No. Not that. You're the only person I've never been able to read, Jack. So that's what I want. To read you."

I shrugged. "Nothing to read, P. What you see is what you get. I'm just a guy who walked out of a bar."

"That's what you are now, Jack. But it's not what you were once. So if ever you find out, I want it. I want it all."

"You'd better agree, Shadow." For some reason Blondie sounded excited. Which probably wasn't good. But I still needed what Jack had. And Prowess? The wall had a lot of space left behind it. If I needed it. "Sure."

"And done!" Blondie wasn't just excited. She was on fire. Literally. A ball of flame sprang into life round her. "Oh. Sorry. Never mind me." I had another feeling. That something important had just happened. And I had no idea what it was.

* * *

September 8th, 1863. Baie Sainte Marie, Nova Scotia, Canada

A cold wind blew along the beach. I dropped Jack from where he'd been slung over my shoulder. Prowess' smile was as cold as the wind, and then some. "So what do we do, Jack? He's empty now. You going to kill him?" I told her about the tag. Told her how the Dragon would smell it on me if I killed him. Prowess frowned. "But—but he'll be dead anyway, won't he?"

I could see P's lips moving as she tried to work out how a guy who was going to have been dead for a hundred and fifty years wasn't going to be dead when we'd taken him from. And if that sounds confusing, you're right. It is. Lucky for me, that's not how it works. "He's Tagged." The look on P's face said that didn't help. I shrugged. "The Tag's in his head with him. Say I Tagged you yesterday, at Carnegie Hall." Prowess looked pissed. I sighed. "OK, I didn't. But say I did. Tag wouldn't know you was here in the Back-Along. Just know a day was gone and you wasn't dead. But you die? The Tag wouldn't know when. Just that it happened so many days after they was set on you. But they'd get a print of every soul near you the moment it happened." It wasn't like that at all. But it was close enough.

"So what do we do, Jack?"

"Can you put anything in him? Anything at all?"

"There's always a bit left. A fragment. A scratch of his soul. So yes. A few words, maybe."

"Well then. Not Jack. Jason. John. Something beginning with J."

Prowess eyes looked far away, across a distant horizon of years. "I knew a boy once. Jerome...."

"Where was that, P?"

Prowess smiled, her eyes still distant. "What? Oh. Trieste. But...." Her eyes focused back on the here and now. "But no matter." Her eyes focused on Jack. "There. It's done." We left, the same way we came. Someone would find him. Soon enough.

See, that's the way it is. There's always something somebody wants. And there's always a price. The trick is to make sure somebody else pays. Like now. I guess that's a question for you. Who's going to pay?

But it's not the Question. Or maybe ... maybe it is.

Chapter Ten
Neck-Stacy

I had a Dragon that wanted me dead, and a dragon who wanted—well, one thing she wasn't getting for sure and certain. And something else. I had an idea about what the something else was, but not the why. And of all the letters in the alphabet, why's the one you need most. Blondie was real good at turning up where I didn't want her, but not so hot at coming when I called. Then I realized. I'd never called.

I figured 350 was as good a place as any. So I got me a chair, sat down, and I did it. I called. "BLONDIE!"

"No need to shout, Jack."

She walked out of the wall. Again. I made a mental note that putting her behind it one day might not be the smart thing to do.

Blondie grinned. "Probably not, Jack. But it might be fun if you tried."

I pointed to the Stetson on the table next to me and raised an eyebrow.

Blondie sighed. "But my way's quicker, Jack!"

I sighed too. And put the hat on. "So tell me about the necklace."

* * *

1446. Sighișoara, Transylvania

"And this is…."

The red velvet, she thought, was a little over-done. And there was too much gold. She'd never understood why they were so in love with it. After all, it wasn't hard to make. One the other hand, she wasn't here for his gold. Though making it hard was—she grinned. "Drágám! It certainly is!" She smiled wider. "And, perhaps, not only is it—" She threw herself back on the bed "—what it so clearly is, but might it not be a little warm as well?" She reached up and grabbed his shirt, pulling him down. As he fell towards her, she tugged harder, tearing his shirt open. "Perhaps we are wearing too much?"

Clothes, she had always thought, were such clumsy things. However, there was an art form to removing them. One, she thought as she watched him, their females were much better at than males. But the end result was—her eyes ran over his chest—quite satisfying. When he reached to remove her necklace, she stopped him. "Oh, *kedves*. Let it lie. Surely you don't begrudge a girl her…." She ran her hands over places she thought he might find interesting, "…her decorations?" From there, things went exactly where she'd intended them to. Until she woke up, and he was gone. Which was, after all, so much more convenient.

On the other claw, her necklace was gone also. Which most certainly wasn't.

* * *

"So that's what this is about? A necklace?"

"Jack. I told you. It helps me keep in shape. You like the shape I'm in, Jack?" Blondie ran her hands over, well, over Blondie.

I shrugged. "You seem to be keeping it just fine."

Blondie grinned. "Oh, this is easy, Jack. I'm not—" she winked at me, "—I'm not distracted. That's when things can get, shall we say, out of control. When I'm…." she tried to look coy. It didn't work. "When I'm 'distracted'." I made a point of looking blank. It felt safer. Blondie spat. For a moment, the room flared with fire. "Oh, bloody hell Jack. He took my bloody necklace! And I haven't had any in…." Blondie's brow furrowed. Her lips moved, counting. "…in nearly six hundred bloody years!"

I had a Dragon that wanted me dead, and a dragon who'd set me up to be dead because she wanted—well, a lot more than her necklace. And from the fire washing round me, it looked like I'd been elected to solve her problem. One way or another. With emphasis on the 'other'. Whoever had the necklace was powerful enough to stop a dragon getting it back. Getting the damn thing back was probably going to put me at risk of certain death. On the other hand—I looked at the naked blonde floating in mid-air, staring at me with a look that hung 'hungry' out to dry—on the other hand, it was probably safer than the alternative.

See, that's the way it is sometimes. When all the choices are bad, sometimes whatever you choose puts your feet on the same road to hell. It's just that one doesn't get you burned to a crisp right away. Like now. But like I said. We'll get to that.

Chapter Eleven
Back 2 Jack

"You mean all this is because...." Prowess blushed, "because a dragon isn't getting any...." She blushed deeper, "Any you-know? With humans?"

I shrugged. "Looks like it."

"But what's wrong with, I mean, other dragons? Don't they, um, 'you know'?"

"Yeah. I asked her about that." I brushed my fingers over the singed part of my jacket collar. Again. "She called me a racist. She was—" I tugged at the singe, "—she was quite intense about it. Seems humans are rather more inventive. Creative. Energetic." Blondie hadn't stopped at 'creative'. Or even energetic. Mostly, Blondie just didn't stop. Hell, even I'd thought about blushing. But Prowess didn't need to hear all that. If she did, she'd need to make more blood. For extra blushing.

"And now she can't. Can't you-know. Because...?"

"Because of the necklace. The one she doesn't have. Because turning into a dragon halfway through, um...."

Prowess flushed. Again. "Ah. Right."

I tried to stop my mind drawing pictures. It didn't work. "And dragons, turns out in some ways they're just like people. They get, well, excited. And when a dragon gets excited, things can get hot." Prowess flushed. "No, not that." My mind drew some more pictures. "OK. Probably that as well. No. The whole 'breathes fire' thing."

Prowess stopped going red. I could see her mind drawing pictures as well. Probably ones similar ones to the ones my own mind was working on. "Wow. Hot sex." Prowess went back to flushing. "I mean, hot you-know." Her eyes twinkled. Shifters are good at that. "It gives fire insurance a whole new meaning, Jack." Her eyes got distant. "Maybe I should try it." Her eyes focused. "What do you think, Jack?" They focused more. On me.

Prowess making jokes was bad. Prowess drawing pictures could get a whole lot worse. "I think I need to find that necklace."

Prowess poked her tongue out. "You're no fun at all, Shadow."

Fun. I'd heard of that.

"So why didn't she just go get the damn thing, Jack?"

"I asked her that too."

"And?"

"She asked me how Jack was doing. Asked me if he'd recruited any new girls yet."

* * *

An hour later

Isaac knew what he was talking about.

Isaac? Oh. Sorry. Newton. Isaac Newton. He worked out how once things start moving, they tend to carry on. Moving, that is. Whether you like it or not. Apparently nobody had stood in front of an avalanche until he came along. Or maybe it was just that nobody who did survived. And I was starting to feel like I was in front of an avalanche.

Thing is, Jack was gone. The Dragon wouldn't get any loud ringing bells saying he was all over dead, because he wasn't. Not where he was, anyway. But he wasn't going to be turning up for work either. For a while, nobody would care. But if he didn't turn up for long enough, people would start. To care. And to dig. So I had to fix it. Without knowing what 'it' really was, at least not yet.

"I'm not doing it, Jack." There's always a solution. But it was fairly clear Prowess didn't like this one. "I'm not doing it."

When somebody who doesn't seem able to tell you something tells you something else, it's often a good idea to listen. And do something about it. And if you've got a Shape-shifter who can look like anybody they choose, and who has all the memories of someone else, then asking them to impersonate the someone else might seem like a good idea. Especially if it keeps people thinking he's still around.

"I'm not bloody doing it, Jack!" Apparently, to anybody apart from the Shape-shifter, anyway.

"Look. Blondie set the Dragon on me, P. And Jack asked me about her. And she asked me about Jack. If he'd recruited any new girls yet. So I figure maybe Jack knew something, or someone who could give him orders did. So I need someone who can find out who the someone…." I stopped, mostly to check my 'someone-s, "who the someone is."

"Shut up, Jack." Prowess' brow was furrowed.

"P, I'm out of options here. I need to…."

"SHUT UP!" Prowess never shouts. She told me once. She said the notes don't work right if you shout. And she was shouting now. I shut up. "Jack. I don't have to do it. He didn't."

Now it was my turn to furrow. "Didn't what?"

"Recruit any girls. He only did boys, Jack."

It made sense. Sending girls to Jack to be recruited would be like asking a fox to raise chickens. So why had Blondie asked me if he had? Then I got it. Because it wasn't the question she wanted to ask. And asking me the wrong question was just a Blondie being dumb, not a Blondie being a threat to anyone. But maybe she figured it would make me ask the right question. So I asked it. "Then who did, P?"

"Did what, Jack?"

I sighed. "Recruit the girls. Did he know?"

"Oh." Prowess' brow furrowed again. "Oh." It wasn't a happy 'oh'. I guessed Jack had known. I was right. And Prowess told me who.

I should have known too.

Answers are like that. It's not that you have to find the right answer. If you ask the right question, the answer's there. Right in front of you. So that's my job. Asking the right Question.

The Answer's your problem.

Chapter Twelve
Cherry Pop

"But ... but I thought all that was just stories!" Strange? Strange is just a day at the office when you're Dragon. But having your skin speak to you, even whispering, makes for a whole new page in the dictionary. "Eeew! She really does. Yuck! But isn't it, well, sticky?"

Jack had known where girls were recruited. Even been there once or twice. But only by invitation. Otherwise, there were only two ways in. One was to be a new recruit, and female. The other? The other I didn't qualify for. I'd taken care of it the last time I was here. Because I'd been there before too. I just hadn't connected the dots. But after a great deal of blushing and not-talking-about-it-because-it's-well-you-know, it turned out Prowess did. Qualify. So Prowess did her thing, and I got all wrapped up in a new skin. The guards were well trained. They'd been given a little Sight, just enough to sort out the qualified from the non-qualified. But first impressions count, and their first impression of me was all Prowess. And it kept them distracted long enough for me to make them guards the woman we were watching bathe used to have, rather than guards she did have.

Everyone has to be good at something. Me? I'm the best there is.

So we watched a woman people tell me is beautiful take a bath. And every now and again she'd use a knife—and top it up. The screams hadn't changed. They were just like last time. And what interested me was that she really was beautiful. And what she wasn't wearing.

* * *

Five years ago. Somewhere in New York

What they do, when you're new Dragon, is they give you a partner. Someone with more experience at Dragon work. Someone to tell them how good you really are. Or take care of you, if you aren't. 'Take care of' as in 'don't worry about it. I took care of it'. Without any need for a pension plan.

I didn't figure on being taken care of.

So when they told me I was getting a partner for the next few jobs, I asked around. Of course, nobody wanted to say anything. People who say things don't last long in the Dragon. So I just kept asking. Until they answered. But I'm a nice guy. I made sure they didn't have to worry about the Dragon finding out.

Ever.

As introductions go, a woman naked apart from an emerald necklace might be high on most guys' dream lists. And if they knew they were going to end up in her bath with her, maybe even higher. Because that's what happens when people meet Liz—they end up in her bath. One way or another. I knew I didn't like one way, even if I didn't know if I qualified. So I chose the other. I made Liz's guards into guards she used to have, flipped over her into the bath, smacked her head against the wall—and made sure I didn't. Qualify, that is. As bath water. I'd even brought my own custard. Then I took her knife and grabbed one of the spares she kept chained by the bath. The carotid is always good. They scream a while. I figured the screams might wake her up. So I waited. While the blood flowed.

* * *

"You—you raped her?" I couldn't tell what made Prowess most disgusted. What I'd done, how I'd done it— or who I'd done it to. So I gave P the signal we'd agreed on. As my skin slithered off and went back to being a shape-shifting concert pianist, I ceased to be a sweet and, apparently, virginal woman and went back to being me. I nodded to the woman in the bath. "Hey, Liz." Then I flipped over her into the bath, and slammed her head into the bath wall. Again. And for a while, Erzsébet Báthory lost interest in proceedings.

She always hated me calling her Liz. Countesses can be like that.

"You raped her?"

Of course, the stories are—well, just that. Stories. I knew, mostly from having been in it, Liz's bath was about five feet square by four feet deep. Which is one hundred cubic feet. Or about six hundred and twenty three gallons, if you think George Washington was ungrateful rebel scum rather than the Father of the Republic. And the average human body has about one and a third gallons of blood. So if Liz really was in the habit of 'bathing in the blood of virgins' she'd have needed maybe four hundred and eighty spares every time she wanted to wash her hair. So she didn't. But the virgin thing—that was straight. Because blood is power, and virgin blood—well, Liz never settled for second best. So Liz was the biggest reason there were so many unicorns on street corners. On the other hand, she was always good for Tears if you needed to take a trip. And the first time I met her—I didn't know if my blood would qualify. So I made sure it didn't.

"You raped...?"

"P, it was just tactics. Liz—they told me she was big on virgins. And me? I didn't know if I was. Virgin, I mean. So I took care of it. Made sure I wasn't." I sighed. "I was short on time, P. Had to make things up as I went. And we're short on time now. Nobody'll worry if they find the guards—Liz does that every now and again. But—"

"She kills her own guards? Is she mad?"

"Oh, no. It's a prophecy thing. She told me once. She...." Suddenly the story she really had told me once looked like it might make sense. Which it never had before. I had an idea Prowess wouldn't like the sense. "But that's not important right now."

"What aren't you telling me, Shadow?"

"P, we'll get to that." Pretty much whether she liked it or not. "But first we need Liz to tell us things, right?"

51

Prowess sighed. "This might take a while." Her eyes focused on Liz. It must have been a tough read, because she made some more. And some more. Then fifty six eyebrows raised. "Oh." It wasn't a happy 'oh.' "Oh dear." Prowess' brows furrowed. All of them. Apparently she reconsidered. "Jack? What's a good swear word?"

"There sort of aren't any 'good' ones, P."

"Then what's a really bad one?"

I shrugged. "How about—"

"Never mind, Jack. Whatever it is, it isn't bad enough." A new strand of Prowess whipped through the air and wrapped round my head. "I think you'd better see this."

That's the thing with asking someone a Question. Sometimes they give you an Answer. And every Answer is bad for someone.

Maybe everyone.

Chapter Thirteen
Deal-Nightful

It wasn't the first time Prowess had shown me what she could see. But it was the first time I'd got quite so wrapped up in her work. So I figured it was bad.

Being right's a bitch.

* * *

1610. Csejte Castle, Hungary

"Of course, the peasants do not matter. But when one's equals turn against you? Then they prove only that they are peasants."

As the walls had been built across the doors of her rooms, the once beautiful Countess had tried sweet words. She had tried threats. And as the cement round the stones walling her in had set solid, she had tried screaming.

The screaming had lasted longest.

But even screaming comes to an end—and then she had slept. And even though in her time she had woken in the company of many beautiful young men—to do so while walled inside the rooms of her own castle was a little unusual. "You impress me, Erzsébet. And I am not easily impressed." And when the beautiful young man addresses one as an equal, as one familiar, and when one has done what one has done not only for pleasure, but to try to attract just such a one as this may be? Why, naturally one responds in kind. The once beautiful, once powerful, now imprisoned Countess smiled. "<u>Üdvözlet</u>, my lord." She paused. "Or perhaps I should say—*Voivode?*"

The young man smiled. "Not, as I think you know *Grófné* Erzsébet, for many years. But then, what are such titles, or indeed what need such years be, for those like us?"

Us—she savored the word. The old woman had, it seemed, spoken truth that day. And while the things Erzsébet had done had been delightful, they were also a means to an end. She smiled. "As you say, my lord. I regret we must meet in such...." she waved her hand disdainfully at the stones round them.

"Do not let it concern you, Erzsébet. Though indeed I think we might best talk in more conducive surroundings. *Gyere ide!*" At the young man's words, a second person appeared beside him. Dull eyed and blank faced, the arrival looked identical to the once beautiful Countess. "This ... servant ... will serve your purpose here, my lady. And perhaps this," the young man tossed a necklace of sparkling emeralds to the Countess, "...may serve as token of my intentions?"

The once beautiful Countess raised an eyebrow, but slipped the necklace around her neck. Then a beautiful young Countess smiled, and took the hand of the beautiful young man. "Oh indeed it may, my lord."

Dull eyed and blank faced, a single figure stood in the walled rooms ignoring the food around it. Soon it would serve its one remaining purpose—and die.

* * *

So far, so meh. If Blondie's necklace thief got around, so, I guessed, would Blondie. Given half a chance, anyway. But that didn't explain why P didn't think I knew any words bad enough.

"Shut up, Shadow."

"I didn't say anything."

"Shut up not saying it then." The bit of Prowess she thought was going to give me a headache wrapped tighter round my head.

* * *

Sunday September 2nd, 1666. London, England

"And so this Dragon of yours, Wladi my dear." The beautiful woman lounged, ensuring suitable parts of her beauty came into contact with the young man holding her.

The young man chuckled. "Of mine, *kedves*? Perhaps I should buy you a history book, no? Surely it was the creation of that *ostoba*, Sigismund? I was five when I learned of it. Was made a member." The young man smiled. It was not a warm smile. "Or so the books say."

"Yes, my dear. Of course. As if dear Sigismund could even spell such a thing without moving his lips. Or without someone whispering in his ear? Some trusted courtier, perhaps? A courtier who knew of unicorns?"

The beautiful young man's smile was flat. "Indeed. Unicorns—and emeralds that are not emeralds." For a moment, the young man's eyes were distant, and the smile real. "And dragons who are not dragons...." His eyes went distant again, and he shook his head. "And that, *kedves*, is the point. That to achieve the future which is my right, I must first establish a suitable past. Just as it had to be Sigismund who established the Order and not I. And that it had my—" he grinned, sourly "—my benefactor's name."

"Quite. And so...." the Countess smiled also.

The young man interrupted her, his smile gone, "And so if I am to live forever, my dear, the future cannot include a past wherein my beloved Erzsébet successfully plotted to have me assassinated. So she might take my place."

"Ah." The beautiful woman pondered. "But we are so much alike, my lord. We desire...." Her hand wandered, slid lower, "...many of the same things. So what might convince me otherwise? For it might strike me that, since I still live, the ambition alone is not terminal in nature."

The young man smiled. "Ambition is good, my dear. But so is wisdom. And since those you have drawn to your cause are now dead meat ... did you enjoy dinner, my lady?" The young man smiled. It was not a warm smile. "I had thought to offer you a story. One that might, perhaps, bring wisdom."

The Countess pondered the well-roasted meat on which they had dined. She shifted slightly, so her lover's hand fell somewhere more interesting to them both. "A story? Delightful, my lord!"

Wladislaus smiled. "It was long ago. Well, these things do not always fit the words we use. But suffice, it was when I was younger than I am now. You see, there was a party at my father's castle. One I had spent no little effort arranging for him to set forth." He paused. "No, my dear. I think, perhaps, it is better if you see." Wladislaus grabbed his lover's head. As he stared deep into her eyes—she began to scream....

* * *

1446. Sighişoara, Transylvania

He could see every woman in the room hated her. Let them hate. It had cost him—or at least others whose lives he could afford to spend—much to learn of her. Of her, and of her tastes. Tastes he had taken steps to ensure he fitted to perfection. He walked over. "Good evening, my lady. Or is that *Grófka*? Or...?"

She shrugged her shoulders, slowly. It was, no doubt, intended to arouse his interest. The emeralds round her neck were all the interest he had, but he smiled. He allowed his eyes to stray to those parts of her current form she no doubt thought fascinating. She smiled back. "Oh, whatever you choose, my lord. Titles are so tiresome, don't you think?"

He shrugged also. "They impress my father." He looked towards an older one across the room. "But then, he is *Voivode*."

She stroked her necklace. The huge emerald hanging from it drew his eyes, but not for the reasons she no doubt assumed. She grinned. "Well, sir. Perhaps we can discuss things to—to call each other—some place more...." she looked round, smiling, "more discreet?" She showed no hesitation in following him to his rooms. He had always thought the red velvet a little over-done. And there was too much gold. But then he was so rarely here, even when others thought he was. The woman who was not a woman threw herself back on the bed. She reached up and grabbed his shirt, pulling him down. As he fell towards her, she tugged harder, tearing his shirt open. "Perhaps we are wearing too much?" Another time, he might have called the servants. For custard. Custard and—and other things. The toys he found most pleasing, even if his companions did not. But on this occasion screams were not his purpose. He merely let matters take their course. And when the woman who was not a woman slept, he slipped the necklace from her. Then he took his clothes, and left the room. His horse was ready and he would need it. He had little time until she woke. He sent word to those who must know, and made for the hunting lodge. Then he waited. It didn't take long.

"Get your bloody ass out here, Tepes! Before I burn your little hut to the ground!"

The words were strange. But the sentiment was not. He smiled, but did not get up. "And my greetings to you, *Grófka*. Or should that be my lady lizard?"

"Lizard? LIZARD? I'll roast your hide, thief! Where's my bloody necklace?"

"Your necklace, lady lizard? Yes. Perhaps we should discuss it. The door is open...."

The door he spoke of blew from its hinges in a blast of fire. Where it had been, his companion of the evening stood, naked save for her long, golden hair. "No discussing. Where's. My. Necklace?"

He grinned. He was going to enjoy this. "Lady dragon. Your necklace is—well, let us say, the soul of my desire. And, for now at least, not yours." The blast of fire that washed over him suggested the dragon was not impressed. That it did not kill him suggested she wasn't being quite as impulsive as it might seem. "I have, as you say, stolen it. And I have taken steps. If I die in some, shall we say, unfortunate accident, others will hear I have stolen it. Stolen a dragons's craft from a dragon. And if such a word got out—that a mere human can steal from your kind—well. There would be, no doubt, consequences."

"Consequences? You know what they'd do. Bloody kill me." The naked woman who wasn't a woman paused. "How do you stand it? Being dead, I mean?" The naked woman who wasn't a dragon almost looked scared. "And they'd do it very slowly, With extra screaming. And no custard." She paused again, then sighed. "OK. So you didn't get me here to talk about the weather. You want a deal. Talk."

"A deal? Now why did I not think of that?" The young man grinned.

"Cut the crap, Tepes. Talk."

He stopped grinning. "Quite simple, lady. It is a thing of great power, as you are. How could it be else? I want power. I shall have it studied. I shall gain power. And one day? One day I shall die. And when I die, the necklace is yours again. But until then, by your name and your power, you swear you will do nothing to threaten me, my deeds or my intention. Nothing. Or your name and your power are mine, and your kind will learn of my theft."

The dragon laughed. "Until you die? You humans. Dead already, you are. And you do not see it. Pfah. So. A few years for you to study what you will never understand, and none I need fear ever learn of your theft? Very well." The woman raised her hand, and one of her nails dug deep into her arm. Green ichor welled. Vlad Tepes drew his dagger, and cut his own arm. The woman leaned over him, and their arms pressed tight. In a flare of light, the contract was sealed. The woman grinned, if a little sourly. "I'd kiss you, Tepes. But I don't do leftovers. Your loss." And she was gone.

Vlad grinned widely. He loved those who thought themselves clever. He took the knife, and cut his arm again. He drew the triangle on the floor, and the symbols. While it was still wet, he called, as he'd been instructed. He had expected some sign—perhaps thunder, or demon cackles. But perhaps the great Lion that appeared was enough in itself. He spoke the command, and the Lion was a man. "I have it, Great One."

The man who was not a man grinned. "Well done, mortal. I have often pondered their power. My Lord knows much of it, of course, but now I may study it also. And who knows. One day ... but no matter. You have done all you offered, and I shall do the same. Come. Kiss me." Vlad steeled himself. He stood, and did as he was bid. As he did, he felt a wind rushing through him. "There, mortal. It is as I promised. Your soul is in me, though I have not taken it. And there it shall stay, and I be thy phylactory. Of course, you will have to feed. But until I am broken, never shall ye die. And thy enemies will fail, and all ye seek shall be thine." The man who was not a man grinned. "And save the One who cast us down, there is no Power that may break me. Ever." He laughed. Then he wrapped the necklace in his hands. For a moment, black light burned. "And here—take these. For your study also. My power, and the lizard's. Beauty, after all, should not pass, no?" The man who was not a man flicked a nail, and two emeralds flew from the end of the necklace into Vlad's hand. Then Barbas, Great President of Hell, was gone.

***

Sunday September 2nd, 1666. London, England

"Barbas? Ye dare to reach so low?" The beautiful Countess blanched. The young man's eyes were cold. "There is nothing I do not dare, *kedves*. And no price I will not pay. It might serve you well to remember that." He smiled. "But come, my dear. The night is a little cold, no? Perhaps we should so something about that."

* * *

Barbas. Damn. Prowess was right. I really didn't know any words bad enough.

That's how it is sometimes. You spend all your energy looking for an answer—then wish you didn't have to ask the damn Question. But it's OK. I'll ask it. It's just a job.

And don't worry. I won't feel a thing.

Chapter Fourteen
Fixer-Upper

"She's looking well for...." Prowess' lips moved as she counted, "what is it? Four hundred years?"

She was. As far as my experience of totally naked women went. I was getting some ideas about that. But they'd take a while to, um, work out. And we had things to do. Or rather Prowess did. So I told her.

"I'm not doing it, Jack." It could have gone better.

"P. You've already done it." Sometimes logic works.

"I'm not doing it." This wasn't one of those times.

Liz's guards were all dead. But bells weren't ringing, and new guards weren't beating down Liz's door. Because, like I said, Liz did that now and again. Killed them. Every one of them. And now I knew why. She'd told me why one time, but it had never made sense.

Not until now.

"I'm not bloody doing it, Jack!"

"P, you sort of have to. Because I still remember."

"Remember what, Shadow?"

"Remember Liz telling me you did. And if you hadn't—I wouldn't. Remember. Or I'd remember her not telling me as well."

It took a while. But I told her. What we do. They do. The Dragon. They fix things.

* * *

An hour later

"But—but you can't!" Prowess wasn't pissed. She'd gone past pissed a few shouting matches back.

"Can't what?" I wondered if we were headed for another one.

"Can't go changing the past!"

"We don't."

"We?"

I figured the Dragon weren't likely to be inviting me to any more staff dances. Not that they had any. "OK. They. They don't."

"But you said…."

"They don't change the past. They just fix it. To match the future."

"What future?"

"The one they've got."

"But…."

Unicorn Horn and Tears won't do it. They only take you into the past. Your past. But someone else can use them. To take you to your future. So long as it's their past. Or present. So they do. Every new recruit. Just once. One night someone comes. Maybe someone you know, maybe someone you never saw before. But they know things. Things nobody else should know—about you, what you've done. And when they've convinced you, they take you. Up-Ahead. Tomorrow, and a hundred, hundred tomorrows more. They show you the 'why'. They show you all the happy, comfortable people. All the people busy not being hungry, not breaking laws. All the sensible, not-crazy rational people not believing in madness like Unicorn Horns and Virgin's Tears. Or Shifters. Or dragons. Or The

Dragon. Nobody asking any questions, because everybody was taken care of. And then they bring you back. They bring you back and tell you if you ever tell anybody, they'll kill you. And that now you're a gnat. A spoon. And they really will—kill anyone who talks.

Or someone will.

I was getting an idea. Why they come, and who they come to. But it hadn't quite worked itself out yet.

"But...."

See, that's what you do. When you're a gnat. You fix things that don't fit. And when they're fixed, that's how they always were. And if people remember it being something else, they forget, and remember it right. Sure, it doesn't work on some people. But it's like the unicorns on the street corners. The few people who remember things as they aren't anymore are normally locked up pretty quick by the large number of people who don't.

"But ... but I can't, Jack! I really can't!"

So Prowess told me why she couldn't. And it made sense. And I had a feeling I'd still be needing P, because things weren't done yet. So she was right. It probably wouldn't be smart to take someone back who qualified for Liz's more personal attentions. For her bath water. So I took care of it. Of course, I offered to knock her out. For some reason, she didn't think that would be necessary. She even found where Liz kept the custard. Things got a little complicated when I told her I was a leg man. But P was OK with it. After a while, she stopped making new ones.

When things were done, I mixed up some Unicorn's Horn. Liz was always good for Tears. And I took P back to do her thing. I wondered why Liz never mentioned the giggling.

Even though gnats remember all sorts of things that never happened any more, I still remembered the story Liz had told me. How her Sight had told her the little old woman was telling the truth. And the alarm bells still weren't ringing, and new guards still weren't banging on the doors—and at last it made sense. It made sense that one day an old woman looking for work had knocked at Liz's castle, before she was walled into her rooms. How the old woman had told Liz she would rise to greatness on a sea of blood. How she would be betrayed, but how it wouldn't matter because a greater fate awaited her. And how one day she would fall, because her guards would bring her doom.

It all made sense. Now, at least. And most of all, the one thing that had never made sense made sense. Why an old woman looking for work would be a piano tuner.

That's often how it is. When the Answer doesn't make sense—you just don't understand the Question right. Not yet. But you will. Just not for long.

Chapter Fifteen
Right-Now

"Bastard!"

For someone who normally froze into a fit of blushing at 'you-know', Prowess seemed to have got her hands on a whole new vocabulary. The razor teeth, multiple jaws and tentacles wrapped round my throat suggested she was interested in getting her hands on other things. Without wasting her time on hands.

"BASTARD!" I had a feeling she was pissed at something. At someone. OK. At me. I'd have explained, but the tentacles wrapped round my throat weren't letting me get a word out. They were also starting to sprout razor edged spikes of bone. "You made me make her! The Countess of…." The tentacle relaxed a little. "Jack, what's a good word for blood? That starts with a C? I love alliteration."

"Cruor. That's a good one." You get to learn all sorts, in my line of work.

"Cruor? That means blood?"

"Well, red stuff. Leaky red stuff from people, anyway."

"Thanks, Jack." The tentacle tightened. The spikes of bone bit. "You made me bloody make her! The Countess of Cru—" The tentacle relaxed. "Cruor? Countess of Cruor? That's just silly, Jack."

"Claret? That any better?"

"Oh, I like that! Claret!" The tentacle tightened. "You made me make her! The Countess of—"

This wasn't going anywhere useful. My arms were wrapped at my sides, but I could reach. I ran my left hand over my leather. P wasn't a dragon, so the back door might work. On the other hand, we still had things to take care of. So I made do. The first spell wrapped round me and threw anything touching me across the room. Like Prowess. The second wrapped her up in a block of ice too thick for her to break. "P. It had to be done." I got some rope and made sure Liz wasn't going to be making any trouble if she woke up. "Thing is, starting over would be a bitch. See, I remembered her. Liz, I mean. Telling me the story. If you hadn't done what you did, I'd have remembered something else. But I'm a gnat. That's what we do. Fix things—and remember it both ways. But you remembered. Remember. What she was. So if you hadn't done what you did, you'd have forgotten. And if she hadn't been what she was, we wouldn't be here, because she wouldn't...." Damn. Dragon stuff's a bitch. "Look. If she hadn't been the...." I stopped. But I couldn't see any way out. But it was still a terrible name. "If she hadn't been the 'Countess of Claret', she wouldn't have been able to show us what she did. So we wouldn't know what we know, right?

Prowess shrunk a tentacle and used the space it made to tap on the ice block round her.

I shrugged. "Be my guest. But no hitting, OK? Or strangling."

The ice block exploded. The razor teeth, multiple bones and tentacles morphed into a shape-shifting concert pianist with a frown. The concert pianist looked down, then blushed. A little more shape-shifting, and they changed to a concert pianist with a frown—and clothes. "I never thought of lit like that." A tentacle flashed out and smacked me round the back of the head. "But you're still a bastard, Jack."

I shrugged again. "Maybe. Damned if I know."

"No, Jack. Not damned. You have no soul to damn, remember?" Prowess was still frowning. "So your girlfriend here—"

"Partner. Ex-partner. Ex-ex-ex partner. In Dragon work."

Prowess raised an eyebrow. I had a feeling it spoke volumes in the secret language women never teach men, but blame them for not knowing. "Right. Your ex-girlfriend here had to be what she is so we could know what we know. Did I get that right?"

"That's about it."

"And the...." Prowess looked round the room. At the spares. At the stains. At the hooks and blades and other toys. "And the this? The however-many-hundreds of those?" She pointed at the spares.

"Collateral damage, P." I shrugged again. It was becoming a habit.

"Ah. Right." The Shape-shifter looked at the humans. Then she shrugged too. "Oh, well. So what do we do now, Jack?"

"I think...." I walked over to Liz where she was sat tied tight and gagged. I'd cut the seat out of a chair and bound her to it, over a bowl. For necessary functions. "I think we wait."

"Wait?"

"For things to work out."

"Work out? Jack. What am I here? Your straight-man?" Prowess looked down. "Er, woman?"

"P. Look at her. Would you say she's beautiful?"

P looked. "Well, not bad. The nose could do with some work, and her, er ... those ... well, she could maybe use a few inches of...." Prowess flushed. "Yes, Jack. She's beautiful. So what? It's the necklace, right?"

"What necklace, P?" The thing with naked beautiful women is, they're naked. Not 'naked apart from', for some variable value of 'apart from'. They're naked. And Liz was naked. "See, I wondered about that." I looked round for a knife, then pulled one from my boot. At least I knew where mine had been. And in who. "How the necklace she doesn't have on was keeping her from looking about three hundred years past her use-by date. So I figured...." I slit a line down Liz's arm. The blood spilled red—but it glowed. Glowed green. "I figured she was trying something new."

Horn and Tears wouldn't work. They only take you back, and this was in our future. So we waited. And waited. Until matters took their course. From the look on Liz's face, it hurt. I figured it was new. Well, Liz-new. She'd still been wearing the necklace when I first saw her, five years ago. I wondered what it took. Once a day? Twice? I had a feeling Liz didn't have to worry about fiber in her diet. But eventually it was done. And I was right. Things really were a whole lot messier. But once I'd fished round some in the bowl under Liz's chair, and washed it clean, I had it. Worn, and rather more rounded than most. Almost smooth. As thought it had been sanded down. Or dissolved.

A single emerald.

Prowess wrinkled her nose at the stone. She sure wasn't going to sniff it, and even more sure wasn't going to lay a finger on it. "Eeew. As beauty treatments go Jack, that one's never going to catch on. So now what?"

I tossed the emerald in my hand. "Now we wait. Some more." It didn't take long—a day. And the beautiful once-a-Countess was quite clearly not quite so beautiful. The hair, greyer. The skin, duller. So I got my knife and the emerald, and sliced. This time, the arm was my own. I let my blood flow over the emerald. It sank in, soaked deep into the emerald's heart. I brushed the gem over Liz's lips—and nothing happened. Which was pretty much what I'd expected. So I grabbed Prowess, and sliced her arm.

"Ow!" Prowess wasn't impressed. But her blood flowed, ran over the gem. After the stone absorbed it, I brushed it over Liz's lips—and the emerald glowed. In a moment, the grey fled from her hair, her skin tone fresh and rose.

"Very clever, Shadow. Very clever indeed." The voice was familiar. Too familiar. "Oh. And by the way. That hurt." A rope of shifted muscle flew out from Prowess and smacked me round the back of the head. The only problem was, it wasn't the Prowess I'd slashed. Because now there were two of them. The new Prowess who'd appeared in the corner of the room grinned. "No hard feelings Jack? Never mind. You've got work to do. Say hello to Berlin for me." She winked at me. "Be seeing you, Jack." Then she was gone.

A bad day was getting worse. I just didn't know for who yet.

* * *

February 27th, 1920. Berlin

On the Bendlerbrücke, the Landwehrkanal flowed beneath us. The timing was going to be tight, but I figured it was do-able. "Can you take enough, so we can ask any questions we have to later?"

Prowess' eyes were wild. "Jack? Who was that?"

I sighed. Some days, all the answers do is make more questions. "Far as I could tell, P, it was you."

"Me? But I'm me!"

I sighed again. Time's a bitch. Especially when it's not me bitching it. "P, I figure we'll get to that." I had an idea. Making it make sense could come later.

Prowess shook her head. Maybe to clear it, maybe just to say none of this was happening. She swallowed, then squared her shoulders. "So is this flat rate, or am I on commission? Never mind, Shadow. What do you want her as? Another vegetable?"

"Not this time. More meat, less potatoes. This one's going to be a mix." I could hear someone coming onto the bridge. It was time. The woman walked onto the bridge and climbed to the edge. She readied herself to jump. I slugged her, and grabbed her. "Some of this—not too much. And…." I ran what I remembered through my head "…and Nicholas."

"Nicholas?" Prowess looked puzzled. Then light dawned in her eyes. "Ohhh. I get it. Clever Jack."

I shrugged. I'm a gnat. A spoon. It's what I do.

Prowess focused on the woman I'd slugged. Then on Liz. She looked at me, and nodded. I switched Liz's clothes with those the woman had been wearing and threw Liz off the bridge. I knew the patrol was close enough to hear the splash.

* * *

At least 350 had a table. I pulled my knife from my boot again. If you do it quick, and in the right place, they don't even get time to scream. I grabbed a bottle of Horn.

* * *

1984. Charlottesville, Virginia USA

Some more Unicorn Horn and Tears, and a teleport dropped me in Charlottesville. The locks at the Martha Jefferson Hospital weren't any trouble. I found the right file and checked where I needed to look in the lab. I switched what I found in the lab with a bit of Franziska's intestine she didn't need any more. Not that she needed any of it—not now. Then I took me across town. The locks at Jack (I was starting to wonder if I should change my name) Manahan's were even easier than the Hospital's. The house lights were dark. I slipped in, slipped the envelope with the hairs into the book, and slipped out. Which left just one thing to do. I drank.

* * *

1616. Ecsed, Hungary

More Horn, to make sure the age was right, another teleport, and I was there. I cleared out the dried clay—all that remained of the golem Vlad had created—and put Franziska to her final rest. And for the first time, there really was a body in the Báthory family crypt.

* * *

Sometimes that's how it is. When all the things you thought you knew turn out to be wrong, you have a choice. You can either change what you think you know—or change the things that make you wrong. It's a decision. A choice. An Answer. And either way, everything is different. Everything—and everyone.

We're nearly there. And then? It'll all be over. One way or another.

Chapter Sixteen
Time to Why

Prowess knew how to get to Carnegie Hall. Maybe she just didn't need the practice. When I got back to 350, she was still there. "Talk to me, Shadow."

I was pretty sure I knew what she wanted to talk about. I even thought I knew some of the answers. But I was pretty sure it wasn't the right time for answers. On the other hand, tying a Shape-shifter to a chair and waiting for something to happen so it could be the right time didn't seem like a good idea. Ropes don't really give Shape-shifters many problems. So as the air shimmered behind Prowess, I did the only thing I could think of. I kissed her.

"What? Jack! Mmph...." She was either going to beat the crap out of me, or kiss me. Either way I figured she'd be distracted enough for the Prowess appearing behind her to do whatever she'd come here to do. Which turned out to be slipping a needle into the neck of the Prowess I was kissing. Or not kissing, as she froze solid.

"Damn." The new Prowess looked at the frozen one. "I wish I hadn't had to do that."

I discreetly ran my hands over my leather, just in case. "Why not?"

"Because if things work out, I'll never know what kissing you is really like, Shadow."

I shrugged. "So. Who the hell are you?"

Prowess ran her hands over her body. Half way through, they changed to feet. "You know damn well who I am, Jack. But we're wasting time."

I shrugged again. "Guess we are. So who are you, then?"

The look on Prowess' face was unfamiliar. I'd seen her angry, I'd seen her lost in her music. But I'd never really seen her sad. "I'm dead, Jack. Or at least—I am if things work out." She slipped something between the lips of frozen Prowess, and held her hand out. I took what was in it and drank.

* * *

Up-Ahead

They do it to you once. After you join, and after they're done training you, they do it. One night someone comes. Maybe someone you know, maybe someone you never saw before. But they know things. Things nobody else should know—about you, what you've done. And when they've convinced you, they take you. Up-Ahead. Way Up-Ahead. They show you the 'why'. They show you all the happy, comfortable people. All the people busy not being hungry, not breaking laws. All the sensible, not-crazy rational people not believing in madness like Unicorn Horns and Virgin's Tears. Or Shifters. Or dragons. Or The Dragon. Nobody asking any questions, because everybody was taken care of. And then they bring you back. They bring you back and tell you if you ever tell anybody, they'll kill you. And that now you're a gnat. A spoon. And they really will—kill anyone who talks. But they take you so you can see it's worth it. What you do. So you can care.

Caring. I've heard of it. Me? Like I said, it's just a job.

So Up-Ahead wasn't all strange. I'd been here. Once. And now it was twice. At least this time we were in 350, so we had some time. I raised an eyebrow at the Prowess who wasn't frozen, and nodded at the one who was. "I guess it didn't work. The other times, I mean."

Not-frozen-Prowess was still looking sad. She shrugged. "I always knew you were smart, Jack. No. I tried it with just you, but apparently I'm—er, she's…." Not-frozen-Prowess looked confused. "Damn, Jack. How do you keep all this straight? Well, it seems I'm stubborn. When you came back, I didn't believe a word of it. I wouldn't do what…." Not-frozen-Prowess clammed up. But she wasn't doing bad, for someone who hadn't been trained for it.

"No sweat, P. I get it. So you came back a bit further. For both of us, this time. I'm being nudged, right?"

"Well I don't get it!" Whatever Not-frozen-Prowess had hit Frozen-Prowess with, it was wearing off. Ropes of Not-frozen-anymore-Prowess (I made a mental note to come up with better names) spun out and twisted round the other Prowess. "And what did you do to me, bitch?" Not-frozen-any-more-Prowess blushed. "Oh, sorry Jack. That's a Bad Word. I mean…."

"Don't sweat it, P. But do me a favor?"

Prowess' neck stretched and her teeth grew. Her head flew over to her other self and began to bite. A new mouth appeared in her left leg. "What's that, Jack?"

"Stop beating yourself up over it, huh?"

It's what I do. I'm a spoon. And if you're a gnat, a spoon, you wonder. If anybody ever did it to you. This time, I didn't have to wonder. "This is you, P. But it's not you. Because this is you from Up-Ahead. From your future."

"From my future." Now-P looked at Up-Ahead-P. "Then I've let myself go to heck, Jack."

I couldn't see a hair's difference between the two of them. But I figured Now-P was just trying to find her feet. I winked at Up-Ahead-P. "Guess you'll have to remember not to next time, P."

"At least my taste in clothes improved." Up-Ahead-P maybe hadn't seen the wink. Or maybe being more stylish than yourself is a big thing for women. Even if they're not women.

"Ladies?" If I didn't get them distracted, 350 was going to be full of more mouths and more hitting than there was room for. I looked at Up-Ahead-P. "You didn't bring you here to talk dress sense, P."

"No." Up-Ahead-P was looking sad again. That probably wasn't a good thing. I just didn't know for who yet. "She has to … I have to … to see something."

There's a reason The Dragon spend so much time training gnats. It saves time later, when the words get difficult. I figured I'd give her a hand. Or some words, at least. "Me too, huh?"

"Yes. Well, no. I mean, I remember you were there. But it's me. Her. If I—if she—doesn't see it, that's it. It's over, Jack. Or rather, it never…."

Damn. Sometimes I hate being right. "Hold it, P. Do you remember telling me?"

Up-Ahead looked confused. "No, I … but…."

"No buts, P. See, if you change what you remember, then this won't be happening. It'll be different. Does it need to be different, P?" That's how it is. When you're stirring the History pot. You nudge. You change—but not the big things. So history remembers Gavrilo Princip shot Archduke Ferdinand. Nobody remembers Ferdinand's driver, who took a wrong turn at the Latin Bridge. Of course, before I slugged the real driver and took his place, he didn't.

"No, Jack. It needs to be just like it is." Up-Ahead-Prowess was still sad, and she was looking at me. And Up-Ahead-Prowess told us where we had to go. It was like most things I got to do. Just a walk in the park. Up-Ahead said it was going to be easy. Dead easy.

Sometimes, the best way to lie is to tell the truth.

If you're going to get mugged or shot in New York, make sure you're in Central Park. If you can, make sure it's on the east side. We weren't there to get mugged, but 100th and Fifth Avenue was still where we were going. Just not the parts of Mount Sinai most patients saw. Or maybe they all did, in the Up-Ahead. In the end. All those well cared for, comfortable uncomplaining people who would have told me they lived in the best of all possible worlds.

All those cattle.

The beds stretched as far as I could see. The tubes ran red as the machines sucked what they wanted from the occupants. Every so often, a wall panel would open, and a bed with a now shriveled occupant would trundle back into the hole. Then it would come out again, and the occupant would be different. Different, and juicy. Full. The smell of burnt flesh rippled from the holes each time they opened.

"What the hell...?" Now-P didn't seem as upset as she had been by Bad Words.

I pulled Liz's emerald out of my pocket and showed it to her again. "Think about it, P."

"But there were only two of them!" I knew Now-P got it. She just didn't want to.

I shrugged. "It probably takes more." Another bed trundled back into the wall.

"More?" Now-Prowess wrinkled her nose as the smell of burned person rolled out. Then she turned her head. I was almost impressed. It takes a lot to turn a Shifter's stomach. From the retching sound, Prowess might have to make herself a new one.

"More blood. Or bigger baths." I looked at Up-Ahead-Prowess. "So what did he do? Grind the stone down? Little specks for his followers? And—" I nodded to the endless rows of beds.

"You are clever indeed, whoever you are." He didn't look a day different from the last time I'd seen him, in Liz's memory. Wladislaus Dragwlya, *vaivoda partium Transalpinarum*. Vlad Dracul. I guessed he'd never heard of Freddie Mercury, because I had a feeling living forever was pretty high on his personal agenda. But what was interesting was, for someone with strong ideas about me being dead in my Now, Up-Ahead-he had no idea who I was. "Very clever. Maybe that's why Lord Barbas told me to be here today." He shrugged. "Never mind." He shrugged, and gestured to the guards with him, each with a glowing green speck embedded in their forehead. "Do feel free to kill them, my friends. All three of them. In fact—I insist on it." Vlad turned, and left the room.

"Jack?" If Up-Ahead-Prowess' eyes weren't crying, her voice was making up for it. "I can't keep them off long."

I ran my hands over my leather. I shrugged. "There's only ten of them, P."

"I know." Up-Ahead-P could have done sad for the Olympics. "But we tried that, Jack. It … it didn't work. So this time … it's time for you to leave, Jack."

"We can't leave you here! You'll … I'll … they'll kill you!" Now-P wasn't sad. She was furious. "Do something, Jack!"

"He can't. Or he can. Or rather, you can. You'll know. We'll know. When the time comes." As Vlad's team started to advance, Up-Ahead-P started to bulge. There were teeth. There were tentacles. "You see, if either of you die I never exist anyway. And if you don't? This now never exists. And they never kill me." Up-Ahead-P looked at me. "Damn, Jack. How the hell do you keep this stuff straight?" And as Prowess broke the link holding us to the Up-Ahead, a tornado of shape-shifting fury tore into Vlad's guards.

* * *

I keep a calendar on the wall at 350. The day doesn't matter, but I change it every year. The one on the wall this time said we were back. The look in P's eyes said she was scared stiff—and pissed. Me? I still had a dragon who wanted a necklace, and a Now-Dragon who wanted me dead. And an Up-Ahead-Dragon who'd never seen me before. Who didn't remember me. I'm a gnat. I know how that happens. But whoever wanted me out had forgotten something. Because even if it's just a job, I do my job right. I'm the guy you passed in the street, the guy you never saw. But anyone I look for, I find. Find them—and the rest's history.

Nobody nudges Jack Shadow.

A bad day had got worse—but at least now I knew who it was going to be worse for. Because I didn't know forever from donuts. But Dragon, Fallen Angels, Hell or high water—if anybody was going to die, or even never to exist, it wasn't going to be me.

That's how it is. It's not blood. It's not hospital beds. It's not the smell of burning. It's you, or someone else. And sometimes, just sometimes, there's that moment. The moment you bang the side of the pinball machine and rock the ball, without ringing tilt. A distraction, the flicker of a gnat's wing, when everything holds its breath. So. Consider yourself distracted. But like I said. Don't take it personal. It's just a job, even if this time I'm working for me. I'll make it quick.

Oh, and don't worry. I won't feel a thing.

Chapter Seventeen
Haures-Ticked

When someone tells you something's impossible, but it's happening anyway, things are normally already in a bad place. Someone's probably already in the brown and smelly. And most times someone's in the brown and smelly, it's generally safest to assume whoever's going to suffer, it's probably going to be you.

Things were brown. And smelly.

"But how can there be two futures?" Prowess had a point. Because according to everything the Dragon told gnats, there couldn't. There weren't. Because if there was....

"There can't, P. Because if there was, there'd be an infinite number of them. It wouldn't be the unicorns on every corner. It would be Prowess-1 trying to fix the past so she didn't get in the wrong cab and miss the concert at Carnegie Hall. And Liz-239 going back to make sure she never got walled up in her castle, and Liz-856 stopping Liz-

239 because otherwise she'd never get to meet Vlad. It would be—well, a mess."

"So it's a good thing things aren't in a mess then, right Jack?" Prowess didn't waste her time with sarcasm. She did sweet, understanding, compassionate, cut-your-throat-out-with-kindness sarcasm.

What I thought I knew, the Dragon had told me. So it was time to ask someone who wasn't Dragon. "Blondie! Get your ass in here!"

"Don't you have more important things to focus on than my ass, Jack?" Blondie wasn't big on doors. Walls were more her thing, like the one she'd just walked through. She did an exaggerated six-check. "Though I can understand your distraction. Maybe we should discuss it somewhere?" I didn't know a bump from a grind, but Blondie did. So she proved it.

"You want your necklace or not, Blondie?" I was pretty sure time was getting short. And whatever I had time for, it wasn't being bumped.

"You're damn right I do, Shadow. Or you and I are going somewhere more … more private. Whether you like it or not. A girl's got her needs, you know."

"You're not a girl, dear." Prowess was being sweet. Which probably wasn't good. "I think Jack can do better than a—er, how old are you again? Than a lard-ass thousand year-old lizard, anyway." Apparently sweet didn't last long. Though I had no idea what Prowess was so pissed about. And even if I did, I was going to make damn sure I didn't.

"Lard ass liz—"

350 was getting warm. And it wasn't because there wasn't any air-conditioning. "Damn it, P! And you, Blondie. There's a time and a place, and I ain't being in either of them. OK?"

"Your loss, Jack." Blondie winked. Again.

"I have absolutely no idea what you're talking about, Jack." Whatever Prowess didn't know I was talking about, her tone told me she was damn sure it was my fault. Whatever it was. And that she'd discuss it with me later.

Probably when I wasn't there to interrupt, so she could use more Bad Words—without blushing.

I knew if I mentioned Vlad, Blondie would have to clam up. So I didn't. "I was thinking, Blondie. How come it's only unicorns?"

"Unicorns?" Blondie looked puzzled. Off balance. Which was a good start.

"On street corners. Like, I nudge things. So how come there's not all sorts of people nudging back? How come some Jack from when I've kicked Vla—" Damn. "How come some Liz I didn't drop off the Bendlerbrücke isn't here making sure I didn't drop her?"

"Don't be more stupid than you have to be, Jack. Because she can't, of course."

"Why not?"

Blondie grimaced. "Because she can't."

"Why not?"

"Because you can ask the question."

Blondie's lips were tight, her throat trying to close up. But I figured so long as I could steer clear of anything that might be a threat to Vlad, I could push a bit. "So if I can remember it, it can't be changed?"

"Of course it can. It just hasn't been changed yet. You're just in a Now where it didn't happen."

All the books say there's supposed to be some sort of sign when someone who wasn't there before decides to be there. Which just shows what books know. Because there wasn't a noise, or a crash of lightning, but he was there. If he hadn't been shaped like a man, he would have looked like a leopard.

"You know, it's really rather fascinating. Of course, Jack can remember. Mostly because he, well because he can't remember. But Mistress Prowess—she's different. Or rather, she's not. Jack's different." The leopard man stopped. He shook his head, his lips moving. I had a feeling he was repeating what he'd just said. He sighed. "Bugger. That doesn't even make sense even to me, and I know everything." The man-leopard drew a block of arcane symbols on the floor. He stared at them, then rubbed one out. He stared some more, then disappeared, reappearing with a huge book. He shook his head. "Bloody Modern Glyphs. Never could get my head round it. Now in my day—" He leafed through the book, then redrew the symbols, and two lines at an angle. "Oh. I'm sorry. Could you do me a favor, Jack? Just join these two together." He handed me the chalk. I drew another line to join the others together. He took the chalk back. "Thanks. That makes it yours. We could do the whole 'drawing in blood' thing, but that wouldn't be much good with you, would it? Oh. I'm Haures, Great Duke of Hell. Now do be a dear, and tell me to get in the damn triangle."

* * *

An hour later
"...So that's it, really. All rather simple."

"That's it? The future's just what souls remember? Including the dead ones, and the ones that haven't been born yet? And what the hell...." Prowess flushed. "What the heck is a soul that hasn't been born yet?" Apparently Prowess and the leopard man didn't share the same dictionary.

Haures, Great Duke of Hell darted a look at Blondie. "Ah. So you haven't told them then." He sighed. "At least that helps me know when I am. No, my dear Prowess. Outside of this triangle, I'd be delighted to lie to you. But since Jack ordered me into this mystic triangle—"

"One you drew! It might be fake!"

Haures sighed again. "Look. If it were fake, you'd all be dead. Yes. I know all things, past, present and future. I know them because I know what souls remember. All the souls. Ever. Because souls—you can't destroy them. They can only...." Haures stared meaningfully at Blondie. It would have helped if I had any idea what the meaningfully actually meant. "You can only change them. So I knew Jack was going to order me into a triangle. I knew because you were here. Because Ashftghyersygthyz...." Haures nodded towards Blondie. I figured I'd stick with Blondie.

"Never mind. Just saying all of it would take a week. I know because she was here. It just seemed pointless to waste time while Jack learned how to summon me and draw the Binding, was all."

Prowess looked at Blondie. I watched her Shifter lips try to twist round the dragon's name. Then she looked back at Haures. "But you can't know the future. Because there isn't just 'a' future. There's two of them! So which one's real?"

This time Haures wasn't sighing. Leopard eyes burned, and leopard claws shot out from leopard paws. "My dear, stupid Shifter. There are a lot more than two. But only one of them can ever actually happen. At least, that's how it's supposed to be. That's the point. It's why I'm here, un-summoned, in an amazingly powerful triangle I drew myself . A triangle I told Jack to command me into. Because Barbas' bloody games are giving me a bloody headache!"

It was starting to make sense. Why I could nudge, be a spoon. Why Vlad stole Blondie's necklace. Why Up-Ahead Vlad had no idea who I was. Because when something's impossible, it never happened. So either Vlad was impossible, or I was. Which was fine by me. All I had to do was kill him. Kill someone who as far as I knew couldn't die unless I killed a Fallen Angel. Maybe Vlad reached the same conclusion. Because that was when the room under 350 exploded.

That's how it is sometimes. When it's you or someone else. Like you. Like you, here.

Like me. Like me, now.

Chapter Eighteen
No Soul-A-Mio

It wasn't just that it made sense. It should have made sense a long time ago. Which wasn't good. This wasn't a good time to start getting sloppy. Like being blown to pieces by an exploding thermite charge. It was either that, or hell-fire. Either would have done the job of killing us all just fine. Or they would have, if the triangle Haures was standing in hadn't expanded to surround us all. "It's a good job you noticed that hell-fire pocket going off, Jack. Oh, and ordered me to protect you all."

It probably was. A good job, that is. Except I hadn't done it. "I didn't—"

Haures hand smacked over my mouth. I felt a sharp leopard claw pressing into somewhere Blondie might have been interested in. "I said—" the claw pressed a little deeper "It's a good job you noticed the bomb, Shadow. And told me to protect you all. Right?" The claw retracted. An open bottle appeared in Haures' hand. I could smell the Unicorn Horn. I grabbed the bottle from an enslaved Grand Duke of Hell who was clearly so much in my power he was going to do exactly what he wanted. I drank.

* * *

Two minutes ago

"Because Barbas' bloody games are giving me a bloody headache!"

It was starting to make sense. But making sense would have to wait. "Haures?"

"Yes, Jack?"

"There's a bomb. Make the bloody triangle bigger!"

* * *

The inferno outside the walls of the triangle raged. I didn't think I'd have to worry about Twinkle being found. Or Jimmy. Or—I did a quick count. It's amazing what you can fit behind a wall.

"That was close!" Prowess tried to touch the flames. People do that. I've never known why. "How did you know, Jack?"

Prowess. Prowess-now, who one day would be Prowess-Up-Ahead. Prowess, who one day would nudge me. Unless I had things totally wrong, she wasn't going to be very happy. She'd probably find some way to blame me for it. So what else was new. I nodded at the Grand Duke of Hell. "That's it, right, Haures?"

Haures nodded. "Right." He waited.

Prowess stamped her foot. "Either someone tells me what's going on, or...."

"Or what, P?" I grinned. I could see a little vein pulsing in Haures' forehead.

"Well, or something! You just see if I don't!" Apparently that was what passed for gaining a tactical advantage in Prowess world. I sighed.

"Stop playing silly buggers, Shadow. You have to bloody well say it. Or I'm going to get another migraine." The little vein in my maybe-not-captive Grand Duke of Hell's forehead was getting bigger.

Prowess stamped her foot. Again. "Say what Jack? You know, that's a really, really big vein, Mr Haures."

I sighed. "Souls."

"Phew. That's better." The vein in Haures' forehead stopped pulsing. "Indeterminate temporal flux flows. Give me gas, they do." He looked meaningfully at me. "And bloody migraines."

If you could answer a question someone was going to ask you before they asked it, because you knew they were going to ask it, and then they didn't ask, you'd probably get migraines too. But there it was. "Souls. It makes sense."

"Shadow. If I have to stamp my foot again, it's going to be on your damn ... er, your bloo—" Prowess stopped. "Jack? What's a Bad Word that isn't really Bad?"

I shrugged. "Blasted?"

Prowess lips moved as she tried it out. Then she smiled. "Blasted. Thanks, Jack." She straightened her back, and glared at me. "Shadow. If I have to stamp my—"

I patted her on her head. People don't like that. Probably why I do it. "I get it, P."

Prowess flushed. "Well?"

"See, it's like this, P. Or I think it is." And I told her. Told her how, if you're going to go round nudging things, you have to be able to know not just what you're changing, but what you're changing it to. If the future is just the memory of all the souls there are, and if changing things just changes what souls remember, then it probably helps if you don't have one to remember with. To be changed by. A soul, that is.

I've always been more a jazz man anyway.

"But that doesn't make sense." Prowess' brow furrowed. She must have thought it needed help, because she made four more eyebrows and furrowed those too. She looked at Haures. "If it's the soul that remembers, and Jack hasn't got one, how does he...?"

Haures shrugged. "Remember? He doesn't."

"Don't be ridiculous. Of course he remembers." Blondie shook her head at Haures. "He's the best there is, and he'd hardly be that if someone had to remind him how to dress himself every morning."

"Trust me. He doesn't. You can't change things if you can remember them. If you have a soul. Otherwise you'd be changing yourself. Like lifting yourself up with your own bootstraps." Haures looked down at bare leopard feet. "Well. If you wear boots, anyway. No. You need to stay the same. But you still need to keep track. So you need something to remember them for you." Haures snickered at Blondie. "Something to keep you dressed, perhaps. Not that you'd know a lot about dressing men. Right, lizard?"

"Lizard? Lizard! I'll...."

"Right. Of course you will. But you'll what?" Haures walked over to Blondie. "Here I am, lizard. Show me what you're going to do." He waited. "Right. I thought not." He turned back to me. "Look. We really don't have time for this. If Barbas is lending Vlad hell-fire, he's close to getting involved himself. And—"

Things were getting out of hand. Which is mostly about the time they get out-of-hand-er. This time was no different.

"*And* what, Duke Huaras?" The hell-fire was gone. The Lion that had taken its place was another matter.

"Haures?" Prowess' voice was strained.

Haures grinned. "Are you certain, Shifter? The choice must be yours."

Prowess scribbled on the ground. "It's the thought that counts, right? Now get in the damn circle, Fallen." Smiling, Haures stepped into Prowess' Binding. The large one still round me and Blondie fell. As it did, Prowess screamed. A sheet of Shifter flew through the air and wrapped itself round the Lion. The Lion Shifted, twisted—and a bearded man fell to the ground. The man rolled, crouched, and raised a hand. I had an idea the sparks glittering at the tips of his fingers weren't what he was expecting. "Oh." He backed against a once again undamaged wall. "Crap."

I recognized the voice. "Hey, Jack." All it needed was a tapping cane.

See, some days you're just not yourself. And some days, you're not even sure who 'yourself' is supposed to be. But it doesn't matter. Because whoever you are, you'll be someone else soon enough. That's just how it goes.

Or how it's going to.

Chapter Nineteen
Angel Down

The thing about Fallen Angels is, they can't be killed. Which is a real bitch if you have to off one so you can off someone else, so they don't get to off you. It was time for Jack's First Rule. If you can't win? Change the victory conditions.

Maybe I should start again.

* * *

"Remember? He doesn't." Haures shook his head.

"Don't be ridiculous. Of course he remembers." Blondie shook her head at Haures. "He's the best there is, and he'd hardly be that if someone had to remind him how to dress himself every morning."

"Trust me. He doesn't. You can't change things if you can remember them. If you have a soul. You need something to remember them for you." Haures snickered at Blondie. "Something to keep you dressed, perhaps. Not that you'd know a lot about dressing men. Right, lizard?"

If this was going to work, I'd have to move fast. I swallowed some more of the bottle Haures had given me, and grabbed Prowess. I had no idea when we were, but the walls of 350 were in one piece.

* * *

A month ago

"Jack! What—" Prowess looked round wildly. Not half as wild as I figured she was going to be though.

I hit her with my left, hard enough to make the skin split. Her blood soaked into my fist. Most women stop talking when you do that. "Not now, P. We have to talk." Of course, Prowess wasn't most women. There were teeth. There were tentacles. Mostly there was screaming, and a great deal of trying to kill me. It wasn't the first time. I had no idea if it was going to be the last. Or if it was never going to happen at all. "P! Stop messing around!"

The tentacles relaxed. "Or what, Shadow?"

"Or Vlad won't know who the hell I am."

Prowess shifted back to being Prowess. "What?"

"I think I've got it." I knew I had. I just didn't know how. "Vlad-y-lad wants me waxed. Which means he can't." Prowess was looking confused. I knew how she felt. "Or rather, it means he won't. Because the Vlad we saw? He didn't know who I was. And if he'd put me down, he'd know, right? So the only way he could not remember me isn't because he killed me."

Prowess face went flat. I figured she was getting it. Which was more than I'd been doing, at least until now. "It means you never existed. Right, Jack?"

There wasn't much to say. So I didn't say it.

"Keep talking, Jack." P wasn't looking confused any more. Now she was thinking. Which was better than her trying to kill me.

I shrugged. "Not much to say. Never existing doesn't really fit into my plans. Mostly because having plans means I pretty much have to exist to have them. So if it's me or Vlad, it's not going to be me. I kill Vlad, right?"

"But—"

"No-no-no. I kill Vlad, right? Because of you."

"Of me? Why?"

"Because you said so. Or not you. The other you. She said if either of us died, she'd never exist. But if we didn't die? Then that place we were, that Wlad-y-louse, he never gets to exist. So she—you—didn't die." Never mind Prowess. I didn't know how I was keeping it straight. It felt like all I had to do was think of a question, and I knew the answer. "Which means there's a way. Even if Vlad's got Barbas. Even if Barbas has to die so I can kill Vlad. There's a way. So that's the question, P. How do you kill a Fallen Angel?" That wasn't it. It felt wrong. Wrong because.... "Because you can't. Because, Fallen or otherwise, Angels, they're perfect. That's how they were made." I wasn't going anywhere near who made them. "So if you can't kill an Angel, because it's perfect, how do we kill Barbas?" And there it was. Right there. And only P could do it. But I was betting she couldn't. Not on her own, at least. She'd need help. And it wasn't going to come cheap. "P. We haven't got long. We have to go back." Who wants to live forever, huh? Pretty much everybody. Until they find out what it costs. "Or Vlad wins."

Prowess sighed. "So that's it, is it Jack? The beds, and the machines, or—or what, Shadow? Because there's always an 'or-what', right? And if anybody's going to pay, it isn't going to be you, is it Jack?"

84

I shrugged. "I didn't make this game, P." I was getting an idea maybe I did. But Prowess didn't need to know that.

"Can it, Jack." I'd seen the look on P's face once before. But it was a different Prowess. Just like the one I'd seen before. Before she died. Died saving my ass.

Dumb broad.

Prowess sighed. "I swear, Jack. One day, you'll be the death of me." Either I would be—or I wouldn't. It's just what I do. So I told what had to be done. And why she had to do it. Then grabbed her, and swallowed some more Horn.

* * *

"Right. Of course you will. You'll what?" Haures walked over to Blondie. "Here I am, lizard. Show me what you're going to do." He waited.

"Can I stop being distracted now, Shadow?" If this was a comic book, Haures' voice would have echoed in my head where nobody could hear it. But it wasn't a comic book. So it didn't. It echoed in my jacket. Now, at least, I knew why I had it. Why I never remembered my dreams.

You don't wear a jacket to bed.

"Never mind, Jack. We can get to that later. Focus. Can I stop being distracted?" I knew a few tricks, but talking to my leather wasn't one of them. As far as I knew. "Oh. Right. Bugger. Now I remember. Left collar for yes, right collar for no." I straightened my collar. My left collar.

"Right. I thought not." Haures turned back to me. "Look. We really don't have time for this. If Barbas is lending Vlad hell-fire, he's close to getting involved himself. And…."

"'And' what, Duke Haures?" The hell-fire was gone. The Lion that had taken its place was another matter.

"Haures?" Prowess' voice was strained.

Haures grinned. "Are you certain, Shifter? The choice must be yours."

Prowess scribbled on the ground. "It's the thought that counts, right? Now get in the damn triangle, Fallen."

85

Smiling, Haures stepped into Prowess' Binding. Then the large one still round me and Blondie fell. As it did, Prowess screamed. A sheet of Shifter flew through the air and wrapped itself round the Lion. The Lion Shifted, twisted—and a bearded man fell to the ground. The man rolled, crouched, and raised a hand. I had an idea the sparks glittering at the tips of his fingers weren't what he was expecting. "Oh." He backed against a once again undamaged wall. "Crap."

I recognized the voice. "Hey, Jack." All it needed was a tapping cane.

You can't kill an Angel. They're perfect. Made that way. So if you can't kill one because it's perfect, what do you do? You make it imperfect. And there aren't many less perfect things than a human soul, never mind Jack's. But even Prowess couldn't smash her way into a Fallen Angel to drop Jack off. She needed help for that. And there's always a price. Especially when the help's another Fallen Angel. But there's nothing wrong with prices—especially if someone else is paying. And Prowess—Prowess had nudged me.

I wondered how she'd sound, playing jazz.

That's how it is. There's always something that has to be done. A thing to be done, a choice to be made. And don't think I don't know you can feel it wearing off. The Dragon juice. It's meant to. And when it's done wearing off?

Then I'll do what has to be done.

Chapter Twenty
Double-O-Fallen

The first thing was to shoot the Fallen Angel who wasn't Great President Barbas right now. Killing him wasn't the plan—not yet, anyway. Prowess just thought it was. Mostly because I'd told her so. Not that killing him wasn't a good plan. But it had one small flaw—it wouldn't work. So I shot him in the leg, so he couldn't run. Then I shot him in the arm, so he couldn't hit anyone. Then I shot him somewhere that might interest Blondie. Because I could. And to put him in the right state of mind.

"Jack? He's still alive. Why's he still alive, Jack?" Prowess' voice was weak. Having your soul ripped out, even if you gave it away to a Fallen Angel as part of a deal to get the power to corrupt another Fallen Angel, probably does that.

Me? I wouldn't know.

I was busy, scribbling symbols I didn't know on the floor with a piece of chalk. That's emergency kits for you. I drew a triangle round the symbols. "Haures? Er—Grand Duke of Hell, great wise one, knower of all things...."

"Cut the crap, Jack. Just tell me to get in the triangle." I was getting used to my leather talking to me. And I was getting an idea why it could. Not liking it was just part of the job at hand. Which was mostly making sure I walked out of this alive.

"Get your ass in the triangle, H." Haures got. "Now tell P why killing Barbas is a really bad idea."

Haures shook his head. "Not yet, Jack."

"You're in my bloody triangle. You have to do what I say. So say. Tell Prowess—"

"Not yet, Jack. It's not time. Don't screw things up now we're this close." I was either going to have to get a new jacket, or the one I had was going to have to go back to not talking to me. My jacket must have heard me. Or Haures did, which seemed to amount to the same thing. "I will—I mean, it will—just not yet. Ask me, Jack."

"OK. So what's so important?" I looked at Haures, to make sure he knew I wasn't talking to my jacket.

"How about saving your life?" Haures spat. "Damn. This is going to make a migraine feel like a day at the beach ... not that I like beaches much. Right. Let's get on with it, Ms Rayna. Thanks to Jack lying to you about what he was going to do to Barbas—" Haures shot me a look that would have turned milk. He probably thought he was smiling. "Well, thanks to Jack, you are now a soulless undead. Which will not only play merry hell with your pension plan—"

"Pension plan?" Prowess was sounding like confused had waved goodbye to buggered-if-I-know a long time ago.

"Hell-fire. Don't they teach you people anything these days? People don't die. Their souls just reach a point where they have to go somewhere else. No soul-ee, no die-ee. OK?" Haures wasn't going to wait for any discussion. Not unless he was prepared to wait for hell to freeze over before it was done. "Anyway. That's not important right now."

"I'm not going to die? Ever?" I knew Prowess. She'd make a great ice-maker.

"I SAID THAT'S...." Fallen Angels can shout. But from the look on Haures' face, it wasn't him making the walls of 350 shake. "Look. I'm sorry. But we have to move quickly. My dear Brother in Evil here—" Haures waved at Barbas-Jack "—went a bit too far. Or he didn't. That's sort of the point. The temporal flux is so far past manufacturer's specification." Haures sighed. "Look. Why do you think I'm here? To save your sorry asses? Hell, no. Not my job description. 'Sower of Discord'? Sure. 'Walking smart-ass on all things Divine'? Absolutely. 'Grand Protector of anyone who Summons me'? Definitely. 'Kicker of Ass'? Well, mostly just for fun. But it's like you said, Ms Rayna. Or rather, it's nothing like what you said at all, but it'll do for now. There's two futures right now, and that's not supposed to happen. They both think they're real. And it can't bloody be that way." Haures spat at Barbas. "For a Great President, B, you're a putz-head."

"The human is mine. Mine, and our Master's. And he will do what he will do, and a million, million myriad souls will come to me, and to my tool, and time itself will be remade! And when it is done, our Master's armies will storm the very gates of Heaven!" The hissing voice wasn't Jack. If I didn't kill him soon, Barbas would be back. And then it would be over. The only problem was, I had no idea what 'it' was. The good thing was, so long as I got out alive, I didn't give a damn.

"Great Jesus." There were two things wrong. The first was the way everything had stopped, apart from Prowess, Haures and me. The second was that a Grand Duke of Hell was saying words he probably shouldn't be able to say. Haures kicked the unmoving form of Barbas. "The little shit's going to get away with it."

Prowess sighed. Then a rope of muscle flew out from her and smacked me back of the head. Then another flew out and smacked Haures. "So. Is someone going to tell me what's going on?"

Haures shook his head. "Do you know how long it takes to build a good legend? Oh, well. Bugger it. It's like this…."

* * *

In the Beginning

As desks go, it wasn't big. The room was a little warm, probably because of the flaming sword leaning in a corner singeing the paintwork. The Angel at the desk made some marks on a piece of parchment. There was a knock at the door. Michael looked up. Good. This one was on time. That was going to be important. "Come in."

The Angel who came into the room wasn't particularly impressive, as Angels go. His feathers were frayed, and his Great Sword of Justice was more of a 'Can-Opener of Convenience'. "You sent for me, Archangel?"

"Yes, Haures. I did. How would you like a promotion?"

* * *

Haures sighed. "I should have known better. He's a right bastard, that Michael."

Prowess raised an eyebrow.

Haures blushed. "Oh. Right. Sorry."

* * *

In the Beginning

"Promotion, Archangel?"

"Yes. A promotion. We're going to make you a...." Angels aren't supposed to get irritated. Michael shook his head in irritation anyway. He reached to a shelf and took down a huge book. He leafed through a few pages. Then he nodded. "A mole. We're going to make you a mole." He shook his head again at the picture of a small brown animal with large, spade shaped claws. "Buggered if I know why."

"NEVER MIND. JUST GET ON WITH IT, MICHAEL." The Voice echoed through the room. Probably through all Creation.

Michael shrugged. "You see, there's going to be a little trouble."

"Trouble?"

"Oh, don't look so worried, Haures. It's all part of the Plan. It's the whole Free Will thing. You see, they have to have a Choice." The ragged Angel called Haures wondered if he looked as confused as he felt. Apparently, he did.

"Oh, it's nothing much. There's going to be a Rebellion. Lou's behind it all. Not that he's got a lot of choice, of course." The two Angels nodded respectfully to where the Voice had come from. Which was everywhere, so it took a lot of nodding. "Anyway. Just in case, we want a man—well, an Angel—on the inside. So thank you for volunteering."

Haures sighed inside. He hadn't known he'd volunteered for anything. But that was the thing about omniscience—it knew before you did.

Michael pursed his lips, as though sour had come to stay, and brought its bigger brother too. "You're going to be a Rebel. You're going to Fall, and be condemned to Hell forever. Or until pensionable age. Whichever comes first. And you're going to keep an eye on things. Just in case anybody gets too clever for the Boss's own good. Or Plan. Right? Of course right. Now. Let's get you fitted out. You're going to need some upgrades. Let's see. Knowledge of the Past, Present and Future—I think we'd better give you the new version 666. Hmmm. It's still got some bugs in—headaches and such. But you'll live. Or at least, not die. Now. What else...."

* * *

"See, the thing is, Barbas got too smart. And he broke the Rules. All those souls, going to Hell's armies courtesy of Vlad Tepes and a dragon who couldn't keep her pants on. And all without Choosing. And an army that size? Not a good idea. So I had to do something."

Prowess looked at Haures. She looked at me. "But you've done it! We can kill Barbas and...."

Haures sighed. "That's not how it works. Yes, Jack can kill him. But the only soul we—well, you—had was the Ripper's. So he'd go to hell, and when he got there ... well, blowing my cover would be the least of it. No. It's like Michael said. The whole Free Will thing. Someone has to Choose. But we can get to that. First, you have to do something."

"I gave you my bloody soul! What more do you want?" Prowess wasn't happy.

"I want you to die. To save Jack's life. So he can die. Well, and live." A familiar looking syringe appeared in Haures' hand. "You know, you Shifters are a right bugger. But this should put her—er, you—to sleep for a while." A bottle appeared next to the syringe.

Prowess took both of them. "She tossed it in her hand. "Well. I guess this is it, Jack." She looked round. "Damn. Never a piano when you need one."

I had to think, and think fast. A dead Prowess wasn't going to be any use to me. "Hold on, P." I turned to Haures. "Wake them up."

"They're not asleep, Jack. I've frozen time is all. But she has to go. Or you die."

"No. I don't. She has to go because you're a lying scumbag. She has to go, and she has to die, so I believe you. Right here, right now. Right?"

Prowess waved the syringe at me. "Jack! What are you talking about? This is how it happened, remember? I came, and I used this on me...." She frowned. "How do you keep track of all this, Jack?"

I shook my head. "Looks like I don't, P. Looks like someone's been doing it for me. And—"

I'm not sure Fallen Angels are supposed to blanch. Haures did it anyway. He blanched. "Jack. You're confused. It has to be this way. You see, the future's just—"

My right's better than my left. I smacked Haures hard. His head bounced off the invisible wall of the Binding. "I get it. I don't remember. My leather remembers. I guess it was real lucky I've got it, huh? Like those goons of Vlad's. With their little bits of emerald. Right?"

"Well, crystal makes a really good memory store. That's why...."

I smacked him again. "Right. That's why Barbas wanted the damn necklace. Not to study it. To make Vlad what he needed."

"Jack?"

"Yes, Prowess?"

"Why are you hitting a Fallen Angel, who could probably burn you to ashes where you stand?"

"Because he can't. Because right now, if I'm dead, he loses. Right, Haures?" The Not-Really-a-Grand-Duke-of-Hell nodded. He didn't look happy about it. So I smacked him again. I had an idea I was going to need the practice. "And mostly—mostly because none of it's true. None of it happened." I smacked Haures again. Now it all made sense. All of it. And one way or another, liking it wasn't really going to matter.

That's the job. And that's all it is, a job. And whether I like it or not—whether you like it or not—it doesn't really matter. You do what you have to do.

And so do I.

Chapter Twenty One
Dealer's Choice

What do you do if you know the future? If you know all the futures, and none of them look good? If you're a Fallen Angel, you make sure everybody downstairs can see you cheering along. And if you're a Fallen Angel who isn't really Fallen? What you do is, you find a sucker, and you make it his problem. My problem.

You cheat.

Haures broke whatever spell he had over the room. He didn't want to. Said it was important Prowess go save my life. I wasn't against my life being saved—in fact, I was going to insist. But like Frank told me once. It was going to be my way.

As the room woke, I ran over to Barbas. He was still bleeding from the slugs I'd put in him. Which was fine by me. I pulled one of my knives from a boot, and put the point to his eye. "You know, I bet this would pop right out. If I wanted it to."

"You are dead, Shadow." The voice hissed with ice and fire, both at once. I wondered if Fallen Angels went to some special school for that. "He's right, Jack. You're dead." Jack's voice wasn't much different. I could almost feel the cold Whitechapel fog.

"I guess we'll just have to see about that." I dug the blade in deeper. I twisted. The eyeball popped out. The face it had popped from screamed. Twice. "Well, well. I never knew Fallen Angels screamed." I could hear Prowess being sick behind me. "I wonder what else makes them scream. What do you think, Jack?" I wrenched open Barbas' mouth. I slid the blade inside, setting the tip against a tooth. I slammed the flat of my hand against back end of the handle. The tooth popped out just as neatly as the eye. The knife slid through Barbas' cheek. The screams were louder. "You know, I rather think that proves it."

"Proves what, mortal?" This time the hissing was clearly Barbas.

"Proves you can kill a Fallen Angel." I put the knife point over Barbas' heart. "At least—you can if they have a soul." I pushed on the knife. The point sank into Barbas' chest.

"That's right! Kill me! Er—him!" Jack's voice was excited. "Kill me! Then...."

I grinned. "Ah, yes. Then. Then what, Barbas?"

Barbas said nothing.

"Because you know what I think? I think, then you'll die. Or rather, Jack here will. Ripper Jack, who killed so many. Who most certainly doesn't have a ticket to the Pearly Gates. Right, Barbas?"

Barbas said nothing.

"And where Jack goes, you go, right B? Down, down—well. Maybe not down. Where is Hell these days?"

"Actually, Jack, that's rather interesting. You see, the Divine and the Profane are really just—" I got up. I walked over to Haures. I smacked him, hard. His head bounced off the wall. Since I really shouldn't have been able to do that, I figured he was rolling with my plan—whatever my plan was. I wondered if he knew, because I sure as hell didn't. I hit him again. "Keep," smack, "your mouth," smack, "shut." I raised an eyebrow. "Got it?"

"Yes, Jack. I got it." I was getting used to my leather talking to me. I just hoped nobody else was.

I went back to where Barbas was lying, his mouth pouring blood. "See, the way I see it, you might be able to talk your way out of it." I slid the blade into his mouth, and popped another tooth. The gaping slashes in his cheek crossed over, flesh flapping as he breathed. "But maybe you won't. Because I figure there's a whole load of...." I looked over to Haures. "Hmm. What do they call them? Hell-ions? Hell-izens?"

Haures shrugged. "Well, there are the Damned, of course. And those who Damn them, and those who Torment and...." He saw the look in my eyes. I wondered what it looked like. He, clearly, didn't. Wonder. Or like it. "Whatever, Jack."

I turned back to Barbas. "Like he says. Whatever. So. I bet there's a whole load of folks who'd love to make your life—or your death—very interesting. For them, at least.

Right, Barbas?" Barbas sounded like he was trying for the Olympic gold in saying nothing. Or rather, he didn't. So I popped another tooth.

"You are clever, mortal." The hissing wasn't quite so fiery. But the ice was still there. "Too clever." Barbas looked over at Haures. "Too clever for you I see, you sniveling worm."

"I may be a sniveling worm, Barbas—" Haures drew himself up, "but I'm not the worm on the end of a knife."

"You make a valid point, worm." Barbas looked at me. "So. Since I am not yet dead—perhaps we may bargain."

"Bargain?" This was better. "You ain't got nothing I need, B." I popped another tooth—on the other side, or Barbas wouldn't have any cheek left.

"Really? I did not know you were a gambler, Shadow."

"Gambler?" If in doubt—keep them talking.

"If you kill me, then as you say there will be many wishing me ill. But, Hell is not a good place to make wishes. My Master knows my value. Perhaps he will intervene."

"So what? You're suggesting I don't kill you?"

"Indeed. And if ye do not, then by my power ye shall stay whole, and by my power—"

I shook my head. "I'd love to oblige, B." Behind me, Prowess gasped. "But, see, I can't. Because there's Vlad-y-boy. And I remember what you told him. I was sort of there. How did it go? 'There, mortal. It is as I promised. Your soul is in me, though I have not taken it. And there it shall stay, and I be thy phylactory. Of course, you will have to feed, but until I am broken, never shall ye die. And thy enemies will fail, and all ye seek shall be thine.' Did I remember it right, B?" Barbas spat. The spittle sizzled where it hit the floor. "So either you can break your promise to Vlad, to protect me, or you can break your promise to me, to keep yours to Vlad. But either way, you'd have to be able to break your promises. And since you're not in a Binding right now, I suppose you can lie through your back teeth as well, right? Oh. That reminds me." I got busy with the knife. Soon more teeth lay on the ground. "Well. Metaphorical back teeth, at least."

Barbas screamed. "Ye shall die, mortal! And I shall feast on thy heart!"

I shrugged. "Maybe. Maybe not. But not maybe both. And that's the real problem, right? To keep your deal with Barbas, sealed by your power, Vlad has to live forever. And I've been there. If he lives, I die. Or maybe I never exist. But if I live, and believe me I'm going to, Vlad has to die."

Barbas spat. "There cannot be two futures. And so it is simple. It is as it must be. You must never exist, mortal."

I kicked him where I'd put the last bullet. He screamed. "Barbas, you may be a Great President of Hell. You may be a Fallen Angel. But I'm Jack. I'm Jack Shadow, and I've got a job to do. I'm here, and I ain't never not being here. And you're going to help." I got up and walked over to Haures. "And you will, too." My left smacked into his head. "So how did it go? When this happened before?" My left smacked him again. A wound opened. Fire began to drip from it. "When you sent her to the Up-Ahead? When you sent her to my past? You told her to lie, right? To tell us somehow she survived?" My left smacked into him again.

"Er—Jack? I'm bleeding." My leather sounded worried. "You can't do that."

When someone says something's impossible, and it's already happening, someone's in trouble. And this time it wasn't me. My left smashed into Haures again. "Was that it?"

"Stop it, Jack. It's alright. I'll go. I have to go. Otherwise … well, otherwise we're already dead. Because that's what happened. Right, you son of a…?" Prowess spat. For once, it wasn't at me. "You son of a whatever you're a son of?"

"Yes." Haures voice was soft as he lied. "Yes. That's how it happened. You see, I sent you Up-Ahead. Because you were there already, you could find yourself." He looked at me. "She chose it, Shadow. It's how it has to be."

I grinned. The little vein was pulsing in Haures forehead. I asked the question I knew I was supposed to ask. "Does it hurt, Fallen One? There being two futures?"

The Fallen Angel who wasn't really Fallen winced. "You know it does, Jack. But it'll be over soon."

I grabbed him, and threw him over to where Barbas lay. "Do Angels have mothers, Haures? Fathers? I don't think so. Or if they do, nobody married them. Because you're a bastard. A lying bastard." And Haures screamed.

It's that moment. When everything stops, and you know you can do it. But if you miss—it's game over. So you do it. You smack the side of the table, and rock the universe.

You cheat. My way.

Chapter Twenty Two
Blood Music

Haures screamed. My left hit him again. I felt the surge in my fist. One more. For luck. His head hit the wall. I spun round. "P?"

"Yes, Jack?"

"Do you trust me?"

"Heck no, Jack."

I grinned. P wasn't stupid. Well, not too often. "See, we're not dead, P."

"Not yet."

"And Haures here wants to save me. By sending you to the Up-Ahead. By sending you to die."

"That's now how it happened, Jack. We were there."

"No we weren't, P. Because there isn't any Up-Ahead. Not yet. That's really it, isn't it Haures?" I clenched my left tighter, to check. I felt the hard pulsing. It was enough. So I kicked him instead. "Or rather, there's lots of them. Just like there's lots of pasts. But there's only ever one Now, right Haures?" I kicked him again. Because it was better than kicking myself. "So what do you do if you don't like what you see? All the what-you-sees?"

"Jack. Don't say any more. Barbas will—" Now Haures looked scared. Really scared. Which was fine by me. I had a job to do, and at last I knew what it was.

I grinned. "So what you did was, you hired me. You just didn't bother telling me I was hired." I turned to Prowess. "Oh, P?

"Yes, Jack?"

"You really are a stupid bitch." A rope of Shifter tentacle whipped out from Prowess, teeth hungry for my throat. It was a good job she was predictable. I twisted, and it flew past me. My knife slashed—and the tentacle dropped to the floor.

"Ow! Damn, Jack! That hurt!" The tentacle twitched. Prowess leaned over to grab it.

"Sorry, P." I wasn't. But that's what you say to women. Or so I'm told. But I had what I wanted. I looked at Haures. The vein was swelling, fit to burst. "Did you do it to all of them, H? In case I ever talked? Or just to me?" I remembered the night. Or, I guess, my jacket remembered it for me. The sudden waking. The dark figure. The smell of Unicorn Horn—and the Up-Ahead. The Up-Ahead that never really was. Haures would have been a wow in Hollywood—I could have used him on the Apollo 11 job. The first one, anyway.

"Don't be stupid, Jack. All of them. Otherwise something would have gone wrong. Like it has now." Haures was past scared, into losing and shaking hands with beaten. Which was just how I wanted it. "I hope it's worth it, Jack. Winning. Winning, so the whole damn world can—well. Can be damned."

"Well indeed." Barbas spat. He was losing blood, but apparently a chance to laugh was worth a bit more. "I wondered how young Wladislaus seemed so sure of what he wanted—so sure of what would happen."

Haures shot Barbas a look that would have made lemons taste sweet. Then he gave me its twin, for good measure.

I grinned. "He knew what would happen, Lord Barbas, because someone told him. Someone who knew everything." I raised an eyebrow at Haures. Then I raised the other one, to keep it company. I shrugged at Barbas. "And that's why you wanted the necklace. I've read the Ars Boetia. You can already change men's shapes, so it wasn't anything to keep them looking young, was it? So I figured it must be because it was dragon." I looked at Blondie. "Isn't that right?" This time it was Blondie's turn to spit. "Because there aren't any dragons, are there Blondie? Or rather—they're not really dragons. They're souls. Souls who decided never to be born. Untouched souls. Raw power."

"The UnBorn, Jack. That's who we are. UnBorn, and in-bloody-visible. Not on Heaven's books, and not Hell's either. And we like to keep it that way. So we're not supposed to do anything to get noticed. Never mind steal let people steal bits of us! I need that damn necklace, Jack. If The Council find out—" The sparkling cloud that used to be a dragon shimmered as it spoke. "It's not bloody fair, Jack! I just wondered what all the fuss was about. Then I found out. Damn, you humans are lucky!"

"Sure, you wondered, Blondie. What was it? You woke up one night, and you weren't alone? And you had all sorts of interesting extra bits to…." I grinned again. "To play with? Or be played?"

"What are you saying, Jack?" Blondie didn't gasp. But I could see the light beginning to dawn.

"I'm saying Barbas screwed you too, Blondie. Just like Haures screwed me."

If anybody can wink furiously, it's a beautiful woman who isn't a woman, because she's a dragon. Who isn't a dragon because she's an unborn soul. The sparkling cloud shifted back into Blondie. She winked. Furiously. "Well. Not quite like he did you, Jack."

"They screwed all of us, Blondie. I'll get your necklace for you. But first, I have to be alive. Which means—"

"Which means I have to die. To save you." A rope of Prowess slammed into Haures. "So why do I have to die, er...." Prowess looked at me. "What's a really Bad Word, Jack?"

I shrugged. "It doesn't matter, P. He was only doing his job. And you had to die, so you didn't come back. So you'd believe in it now—the Up-Ahead. So I'd believe in it. Why do you think mister Past, Present and Future over there has such a headache? We're screwing him now." I nodded at Haures. "Him—and every future he knows." I crouched in front of Barbas. "No. It was the crystals, wasn't it. In their heads. Did you show him how to absorb the emerald? Make it part of him, like Liz was trying to?"

Haures groaned. But he couldn't resist. Some people are like that. "It's the lattice structure. It's like ... like memory. So it can store—"

I smacked him one more time. Then I took Prowess' tentacle to Blondie. "So what do you think?" I dropped the tentacle. And I opened my left fist. Liz's emerald was burning, soaked in the fire of Haures' blood. But the fire was singing. Singing Dragonstar.

"Jack! Is that my ... my soul?" Prowess reached for the crystal.

I pulled it away. "Remember when I smacked you?"

"Damn right, you bast—" Prowess stopped. And it wasn't because she was going to say a Bad Word. "You hit me. And you made me bleed. And—"

"And the soul is in the blood. So I primed it. Figured it might come in useful."

"So you hit Haures to—"

"Soul's in the blood, P. And he doesn't have one. So I figured the only one I'd get would be yours." I grabbed the tentacle. "So what do you think, Blondie? Can you put enough of P's soul in this? So it can...."

"So it can what, Shadow? Be Prowess, and save you?" It wasn't Barbas. This time it was Jack. And he was laughing. "And how will it get there?"

I'd been wondering about that. Wondering—and hoping I'd work it out before now. Which I hadn't. "Well, maybe Haures—"

"I wish I could, Jack." Haures sighed. "But it would only be a part of Ms Rayna. It can't be her."

Prowess laughed. "But I don't have to die! You can send me—well, wherever you sent me." Prowess stopped. I could see her lips moving as she tried to apply good grammar to time travel that wasn't time travel. She gave up. "You can send me anyway!"

"Only if he kills you, P."

"Kills me? Why?"

"Did you believe her, P? When you were there? When she saved us?"

"Of course I believed her! I read her, Jack. She was telling…." Prowess' face turned to stone. "Oh. Right. She was telling the truth, Jack. She knew she was going to die."

"And now?"

Prowess looked at me. "Was it good, Jack? While it lasted? You and me?" Prowess never could read me. I shrugged. "Damn you, Jack. Couldn't you just lie? Oh, the heck with it. No. The bloody, damned, why-me hell with it. So I guess I go. And he kills me anyway."

P pissed at me, and a job going to hell. Just another day at the office. I looked at Barbas. "Well, maybe…."

Barbas grinned. Or I thought he did. The blood made it hard to tell. "Oh, of course I can, mortal. Give me the gem and I will—"

"He'll vanish into yesterday and make damn sure you never get the Ripper's soul inside him, is what he'll do." I kicked Haures. He got the message. My leather shut up.

"Jack?" Blondie grinned. "Do you promise, Jack? To get my necklace?"

I shrugged. "I sure as hell won't be letting Vlad keep it, Blondie."

"And give it back to me, when you have it?"

Damn. You never know when something like that will come in useful. "Yes, Blondie. And give it back to you."

"You know, you're such a sweetie, Jack." Blondie grinned at Prowess. "Don't you think he's a sweetie, piano lady?" The emerald in my hand swirled, and a cloud of sparkling glitter floated over to Prowess. It settled—and sank into her. Blondie grinned even wider. "You taste pretty good, Prowess." She winked. "And I don't think jazz is your thing." Blondie swirled back to a cloud, then swirled again. Prowess hung in mid-air. She looked over at—well, at Prowess. "Damn, girl. You're fine. And now I've tasted you, you'll never know the difference."

Prowess looked at me, looking at her. Or, not-her. "Sweet. Right." She flushed. "Close your eyes, Jack. And, um, dragon lady?"

"Yes, dear?"

"Could you put some clothes on?"

Not-Prowess sighed. "You people. You take all the fun out of things." She winked at me. "Be seeing you, Jack." And a clothed Prowess vanished.

See, everybody lies. And everybody tells the truth. So I'll tell you a truth. Sometimes, just sometimes—someone actually does get out of here.

Alive.

Chapter Twenty Three
Tilt

"You can't do that!"

I wasn't sure who sounded less happy—Haures or Barbas. I was quite sure I really didn't give a damn. "Do what?"

"What you just did!" Haures was clutching his head. Barbas-Jack was ... what Barbas-Jack was doing was looking worried. Concerned. Or, to put it another way, terrified.

When someone tells you something can't be done, and it's something you just did, things are probably in a bad place. The looks on the faces of two Fallen Angels were saying we were there. Which just meant I had to work out who it was going to be bad for, and how it wasn't going to be me. "What can't I do?"

"Oh, god." Haures looked up. "Oh. Right. Sorry—oh, God. My bloody head."

"God, Haures? I begin to think there are things my Lord should know about you." Apparently Barbas-Jack wasn't too weak to raise an eyebrow. So he raised one. At me. "And I think that should relieve me of any ... concern ... regarding my Infernal reception when you kill me, mortal. So. If you wouldn't mind getting on with it?"

Haures clutched his head. "And just how are you going to get there, Barbas?"

Barbas-Jack looked puzzled. "Get where, traitor?"

"Any-bloody-where! He broke the Rules!"

Barbas-Jack stopped raising eyebrows, and went back to looking worried. His brow furrowed, and a sullen red glow began to spread from him. It reached the walls of 350—and stopped. "What? It cannot be!" He tried to glare at me. The glare took one look, and gave up its seat to fear. "What have you done, mortal?"

"IT'S A RIGHT BUGGER, ISN'T IT?" The old man in the red overalls and a blinding white t-shirt wasn't anyone I'd put behind a wall. That didn't stop him walking through it. "OH. HELLO, JACK."

Haures blanched. "Er ... you're ... aren't you?" He dropped to one knee.

Barbas-Jack laughed. "Fool. It is my Prince! He has come for—" He stopped. "Er—you are my Prince, are you not?" He dropped to one knee as well.

"YES."

"Hah!" Haures and Barbas both laughed. Then they looked at each other. Then at the old man.

"But...."

"But...."

"YES." The old man grinned. "LIKE I SAID. IT'S A RIGHT BUGGER." The old man looked at me. "Look, do you mind if I don't keep doing the whole 'do you mind' thing?"

I shrugged.

"YOU SEE—er—you see, they're a little miffed with you, Jack."

I shrugged again.

The old man grinned. "Mostly because you just destroyed the universe."

Chapter Twenty-Four
Nudge

What do you do when an old man in overalls tells you just destroyed the universe? Most folk either laugh at the poor crazy guy, or panic. Me? I tried the door. Well I would have. If the one I'd come in by had still been there at least. Since it wasn't, I raised an eyebrow at the old man and grabbed the pick I kept near for when someone else needed a new home behind the wall. I swung it—hard.

I was going to need a new pick.

"Jack?" Prowess was starting to look pale.

"P?"

"I'm ... I'm kind of hungry, Jack."

Prowess doesn't eat. Not people food. When she isn't gorging at concert, she grazes on the scraps of soul people leave behind them and call memory. And there's always soul for her to feed on. So long as there's more people than two Fallen Angels, a guy without a soul and an old guy I was pretty convinced qualified as old, but that was probably about it. I looked at the old guy. "So what happens now?"

The old man shrugged. "BUGGERED IF ... I mean, buggered if I know, Jack."

Haures gasped. "But...."

The old guy shook his head. "I know. Omniscient." He sighed. "Look. If I know everything that's going to happen, how can...." he waved at Prowess, me and Blondie, "how can they have Free Will? How can they Choose?" He looked at me and shook his head. "They just don't think." He grinned. "Of course, they were made that way. You see, Jack, I messed up. I made a deal" the white t-shirt glowed bright, "with, well, with me." The red overalls burned sullen red. "Of course, neither of me told, um, me about it. That's what happens when you delegate. I don't know what I was thinking." If I was looking as glazed as Prowess was, the eyebrow he raised made sense. Which was more than he did. He sighed. "Look. Part of me agreed to look the other way while the other part of me gave poor Haures there a new job downstairs. Or what was going to be downstairs. And part of me agreed not to notice when Barbas over there tempted one of the Unborn, and gave young Tepes a way to create an army of un-souls to storm the Gates of Heaven. That was the deal."

"The deal?" I didn't mind poker. Just this time it looked like I was one of the cards. We all were.

The old guy shrugged. "See, you just can't get the staff these days. Even when you are the bloody staff." He stopped, frowning. "Oh, bugger. Is that a Paradox again? Damn. Well, and bless I suppose. I was going to leave that out this time. Oh, well. Let there be, like, Paradox." He waved his hand vaguely at the wall and tilted his head. Whatever he was listening for, he seemed to think he heard it. Which was more than I did. "Lucky for you my tongue slipped there, Jack. Accidentally, like." For some reason, he winked. At me.

Haures looked at me. He looked at Barbas. "Oh. Ohhh...."

Barbas was looking as scared as Haures was. And I hadn't even hit him recently. "Please, Haures. Allow me. I am not quite so ... restricted." He looked at me, still scared. "Oh shit. Oh crap."

If it was my turn, I had no idea what it was my turn to do. So I didn't. I waited.

The old man waved a hand again. "Let there be chairs." A chair appeared behind everybody, including him. He sat down. "That's better. All that standing. Plays merry hell with my knees, it does. Well, it would if there was, like, a Hell right now." Everybody sat. Me, I leaned against a wall. If the room we were in was all there was, I figured I could trust it for a while. I wasn't so sure about the old guy.

There series of thuds as various rears hit floor where chairs used to be told me I was right. The old guy sniggered. "Heh. Sorry. Couldn't resi—"

The end of what I figured would be 'resist' lost itself in the smack. The smack that came when he hit the wall. The wall I'd thrown him into.

"Jack! You can't!" Prowess blanched.

"Mortal! You will doom us all!" Barbas sounded like he was giving up on scared and trying to remember how to be terrified.

"Oh crap." Haures seemed to have forgotten about any restrictions. "Barbas. I think you missed the point."

"What point, Traitor?"

"He's still here."

Everybody looked at me. Me, still being there. Still being there and not, I supposed, being blasted into not-being by the old guy I'd just smacked. Which was mostly why I'd done the smacking. To find out. I yanked him up. "Chairs."

"What? Tough guy, huh? Hitting old men like me?"

I smacked him into the wall again. "Chairs."

The old guy shrugged, and waved his hand. "Alright, already! Just my little joke, it was. So you want chairs? Let there be chairs!"

I threw him down into the chair I'd smacked him out of. I waited.

The old guy grinned. "Damn, boy. You're good. I did alright when I—" He stopped. "Let's pretend I didn't say that, shall we?" He waved his hand. "Since they won't REMEMBER IT ANYWAY." Prowess, Heuras, Barbas—they just froze solid. Stopped moving. The old guy raised an eyebrow. "YOU GONNA SMACK ME NOW JACK?" Someone once said there are more questions than answers. That's mostly because people don't answer the easy ones. This one was easy. So I answered. He picked himself up from where I'd smacked him to, and nodded. "GOOD ANSWER. SO. LET'S TALK."

A chair appeared. I leaned against the wall. Sometimes, you just gotta take your victories where you find them. "So. I broke the universe, huh? I must have missed that bit."

The old guy grinned. "Well, early model, see. Couldn't get the parts." He blushed. "Mostly 'cos I hadn't made 'em yet. Nope. Left. Right. Up, Down. Dark—and light. Even Noah! Not that he listened to me. I told him, I did. Bloody gills! You'll thank me later! So what does he do? He goes off looking for cedar wood." He sighed. "You just can't help some people." He shook his head. "Sorry, Jack. Where were we?"

I pointed. To the door. The one that wasn't there.

"Oh. Right. Universe. The one you broke. See, it's all your fault, Jack. It's fine if it's only got two ways to go. Then you came along. Heh. Wonder how that happened, huh?" He grinned wider. I figured any grin that big wasn't likely to mean good news. Not for me, at least. "See, you cheated. Ain't supposed to be able to do that. Ain't nobody supposed to be able to do that. Universe knew if you had to bloody exist at all, even if the jury was still out on that, there was only two things you could do. Go with Haures' plan, or let it slide. Game over, right? But you went and did something else. Damn universe was still keeping one eye on Door A, one on Door B. Never saw you coming. Slammed right into the wall and...." The old guy frowned. "Well, it ain't like it's really a wall. It's—"

Sometimes, making a point is enough. Or a hole at least. The old guy put his finger into the hole my bullet had made in his forehead and pulled out the slug. He grinned again. "Boy. Are you going to piss people off. Well, you will if you get to exist, anyway." He waited. I figured I was supposed to say something dumb, so he could say something smart. So I didn't. He grinned. "I almost feel sorry for me. Er, both of me." His face turned serious. "But I don't, Jack. That's why you're here. If you're here at all, that is. Bloody pains in the asses, both of me. See, they—um, I—er, both of me—well, they got bored, Jack."

I raised an eyebrow. It beat the heck out of anything else I could think of.

"Look. It wasn't like I didn't do all the hard work. So I delegated! I made, well, me. Both of me. I mean, heck. I figured I deserved a vacation!"

Raising one eyebrow works. Both just look silly. So I didn't raise the other one. "So?"

"So they got bored! I go to all the trouble to make them—me—so neither of me can win—and they got bored! They cheated! They figured, they cheat, one of them comes out on top, winner takes all. AND THAT'S AGAINST THE BLOODY RULE."

I figured I'd give him a break. "Rules?"

"Not Rules. I tried that. Nearly put the bloody chisel through my thumb, I did. Of course, it didn't work. So I fixed it. Rule, Jack. Just one. One even I can't break."

"Why not?"

He looked unhappy. "Because I made it, Jack. Or it made me ... one or the other."

"So what is it?"

The old guy hunched over in his chair. "I already told you, Jack. You just weren't listening. Anyway. I'm not telling you again. It's a riddle, and it's my best one. But they're cheating. So I'm going to cheat too. Or I already have. Or I didn't. One of those, anyway. But they cheated real good. There's just nothing as exists can stop 'em."

I shrugged. "Guess you're screwed, then."

The old man looked sly. "Guess so, Jack. Unless they get stopped anyway."

"But you said nothing that exists can stop them."

The old man winked. "Guess I did. Guess it's one of them pesky Paradoxes. Know where you might find one, Jack?" He waved his hand. What little there was left of the universe decided it was still around and started happening again. Prowess threw out a tentacle. It wrapped round me, clamping my arms to my sides. She gasped. "No hitting, Jack! There's got ... got to be some way...."

Of course, there was. I wondered if that was another of the old guy's Rules. That there was always another way. "Let go, P. I won't hit anyone." The tentacle relaxed. I raised an eyebrow at the old guy.

He pouted. I knew he was just playing to the gallery, but I filed the image under 'never think of this again'. "Oh, if you insist." He waved his hand. "Let there be, like, um, stuff." He cocked his head as though listening. "Oh, bloody heck. Yes, and things. Things and stuff...." He looked over at a still-pale Prowess. "Right. And souls." He listened some more. "So look in the big box. The one under the...." He looked at me and shrugged. "You really can't. Get the staff, I mean." He sighed. "Oh, bugger it. REBOOT!" There was a deafening crash. Or there would have been, if it hadn't stayed totally quiet. My ears still hurt though, from the sound there would have been. The old man looked down at the shiny, well-polished black leather boots he was suddenly wearing. He looked at me. "You know, I'd bloody fire them. If they weren't, like, me."

I nodded towards his blinding white vest, and the red overalls. "You mean...?"

He sighed again. "No, not that me. Er, those them. No. Different union." He looked up at the ceiling. "Stop messing about. If I have to come out there ... now bloody REBOOT! Oh. And add some of those Higgs-Bosons. They're in the jar by the—yes. Those. A friend of mine's going to need them. Or not...." He winked at me. "Call it a field upgrade, Jack." And he was gone. On the other hand, the door was back. I opened it. Then I closed it. Then I opened it again.

"Er—Jack?" Prowess sounded worried.

"Yes, P?"

"What are you doing, Jack?"

"Seeing if he's still outside, P."

"Er—if who is, Jack?"

That saved a few questions I'd been wondering how to ask. So I didn't ask them. Because it was past time for questions, and into time for answers. Somehow, something that nothing that existed could stop had to be stopped. The massed powers of Heaven and Hell had to be kicked where they couldn't be kicked.

I grinned. This was going to be fun. Or it wasn't. either way, it was just a job. Even if it looked like I'd never really known what my job was.

Or who I worked for.

What do you do when someone's picked you as the sucker who's going to fix what he can't fix? Who's going to nudge things the only way that stops them going to hell?

You cheat.

Barbas-Jack was almost gone. There really wasn't much time. "Barbas?"

"Mortal?"

"Maybe there really is a deal we can make."

* * *

Now

The thing about cheating, it's only cheating when the other guy does it. On the one hand, things could go the way it looked like they was supposed to go. Which meant one way—I never existed. Vlad got to build an army of undead and storm the gates of Heaven. Or the other way. The way Prowess got to die in a dream that never happened, just so I'd get motivated to go kill Vlad myself.

And then there was my way. Door C, but this time I didn't destroy the universe. I know I won't, because the old guy over there behind the bar told me so. And there we are. Or rather, here we are. And that's the problem. Because we can't be here.

At least, not both of us.

Barbas saw it my way. Not just because he knew I wasn't going to stop hurting him until he did. More because I was offering him something he'd never get if he won. And Haures? He wanted Barbas to get what I was offering. Mostly because that was the only way he was going to avoid getting burned. And you can do a lot with two Fallen Angels. Trust me, I know. After she got back, Blondie spent most of her time trying. But if Diogenes had it bad just looking for an honest man, what about one totally innocent? After all, there ain't no such thing, right?

Right. There really ain't no such thing. So I cheated.

Seems when the old guy made things start over, he accidentally-on-purpose missed a bit. Kind of careless, huh? A little bit of nothing much. But off the books. Off anybody's books. A bit just big enough to make this place. Sure, it's a bar now. It just wasn't always. Remember fifth grade? Blondie over there was the girl you almost lusted over. Barbas—he was Bennie Walters. The guy who got there before you kissed her. This innocence thing. It's tricky stuff. Keeping you straight for—well, I'm sure if felt like twenty years. It wasn't. Not quite. Or not even near.

Where did you come from? You didn't. See, you don't exist. Well, you do. But just like this place, you're not on their books. Not on any books. But everything has to be on the books. So just as soon as the old guy behind the bar stops being accidentally absentminded, this place will be too. On the books. Real. This place—and whoever's in it. Right now, they're waiting. There's a huge boiling spiral of Paradox in the stuff people who can see unicorns get locked up for seeing. So the Dragon, they're out there, waiting. To see what it's about. And what they don't know is, they're part of what it's about.

So are you.

So am I.

See, Blondie—she's UnBorn. Dragon. So she's not on the books yet either. It's tough to cut a dragon. To break one. But like I said. It's amazing what you can do with two Fallen Angels. Especially if the dragon's helping. So we broke a bit off her. That's you. Then? Then we raised you. Innocent. Clean.

Call me dad, I'll kill you.

Actually, I won't. I sort of can't. Because you're not just you. You're me as well. Or you might be. See, right now, there's two futures. Only two. I didn't like the one where Prowess died. Not because she died. But I might need her some time. If I exist, that is. So I'm going to cheat. Door A, you walk out of here. You'll live your life, you'll be happy—you'll die. And you'll go to Heaven. But Vlad will take the world to Hell. Because I won't be here to stop him. Haures knows. He's seen it now. He argued a bit, and he's got some holes in him he didn't have before, but he saw things my way. Eventually. Door B, you don't. Walk out of here, I mean. Door B, my friend Prowess over there rips your dragon soul right out of you. Because I need it. So she can put you into Barbas. But don't worry. You ain't staying there.

You'll just wish you were.

Barbas, he knows all there is to know about being good at what I do. He'll make sure I do too. Of course, I can't remember, not having a soul and all. So I'll need some help. A bit of Blondie—that's why she can read me, see?—a Higgs Boson or ten—and Haures over there makes a new leather jacket. And I get to kill Barbas. He'll even help. Because once you're inside Barbas, he'll have a soul. He'll be mortal. And that's why he made the deal. What's in B will be you. Innocent. Pure. And after I've killed him, Mr B'll go back to Heaven. And they'll see all that innocence, that purity—and they won't be able to kick him out. But it's OK. They've got a great PR team up there. The books'll change—all the books. He'll never have Fallen. And if he never Fell, he never made a deal with Vlad. Blondie never lost her necklace. The Dragon waiting outside? They'll never have been there. But I will. Because you made me. Then I drink some Horn. There's a road, or there was. Somewhere between Bucharest and Giurgiu, I'll do what I do best. And Haures knows that's true. He's seen that as well. So yay—well, just yay. Someone wins. Or at least—they get to keep not losing.

But there's always a price. And this time, you're it. Because a man without a soul will walk out of a bar. And none of this will ever happen, because we'll have stopped it before it did, you and me. No Dragon. No Vlad. No—no anything I remember. A Paradox. Because unless I walk out, I was never here. And Haures knows that too. He's seen it.

He's seen me walk out.

I sort of have to. Because if you do, if you walk out, I never exist. Because I'm you. Or I used to be. And you're me. Or you might be. And if I never exist, I can't kill Barbas. And if I can't kill Barbas? Then Vlad wins. The world goes to Hell, so you can go to Heaven.

No. it isn't fair. Nobody ever said it would be. But I'm betting it's one of those Rules the old guy wouldn't tell me about. That there has to be something. Someone off the books. Not on Heaven's side, or Hell's. And not on yours, either. Just—someone. Someone who can break the Rules. To screw up the un-screwtable.

That's me. Or at least—it is if I exist.

So here we are. Here it is. The Question. And you get to choose. The Answer. And one of us is going to die. Or never have existed.

Take your time. Just—not too much.

Epilogue

See—this guy walks out of a bar....

Dedication:

To Sam, even if you'll never read this.
Thanks for being Maya!

Coda
Primo Movimento

1971, Washington D.C.
The White House is one of the most secure residences in the Western world. That had become even more so under Richard Milhous ('Lucy' to her friends – not that she had any) Nixon. There wasn't a door could be unlocked, never mind opened, without lights somebody was always watching starting to blink and alarms someone was always listening for starting to ring. Which didn't seem to bother the owner of the hand unlocking this one. He twisted the pick – and the lock released. Somewhere in a distant room, lights didn't blink and alarms didn't ring. He might have grinned, but he wasn't big on grins. This wasn't fun. And it wasn't just another job.

He stepped into the room, followed by the figure behind him. The sleeper was extremely well trained, her senses fine-tuned and her reactions hair-trigger. She was good. Better than good. But the man wasn't just good. He was the best there was. He stepped silently over to the sleeper's bed. His hand didn't seem to move, but now it had a gun in it. From behind him something wrapped tight round his arm, pulling it down. Or trying to. "Do we have to? There's got to be another way."

The man shrugged. "Only two, P. Only two." He waited.

The tentacle released from his arm. Not that it would have made any difference. The gun hadn't moved from its position over the sleeping woman's mouth. The second figure sighed. "You're a bastard. I hate it when you're right."

Jack Shadow's gun settled on the woman's lips.

Prologue
Sixteen with a bullet

You know how it is. New girl, new school – and the cute hunk in the third row over was giving me weird looks. I figured if I gave him so much as a smile, in ten minutes I'd be finding out how his Dad had a mysterious underground lair and was gonna take over the world. That was how it was in my last school, anyway. But the afternoon was double History, and it had been a bitch of a day. Not only that, Mom had made me memorize faces my first week. Then what the hallway scuttlebutt hadn't told me, her files did. And Cute Guy hadn't been one of the faces she gave me. Surprises like that aren't generally good news. So I made sure he was toast by lunchtime. Well, not toast so much. But he was sure history.

School Farm is great. Every school should have a compost heap.

Perhaps I should explain.

See, Mom works for – well, if I told you, I'd have to kill you. Which was mostly what she did for them, before she got kicked upstairs. Kill people, I mean. But it was OK. They're government. Well, sort of. That was why we were on our own. The wrong sort of people were always trying to find things out about Mom. That was why my most recent Dad left us. Mom found him sleeping late. Thing was, he wasn't alone. Like Mom said, she could live with him doing his secretary, just that he couldn't. It wasn't that the skirt Mom found him in bed with was his secretary so much. More that her vodka and rye was kinda short on rye, if you know what I mean. So Mom gave Dad a 357 express ticket out of town and the secretary got to show some of Mom's friends she could sing more than 'Несокрушимая и легендарная'. But there it was. Dead Dad, newspapers sniffing round. It wasn't like it was the first time. The Organisation's got a whole Department for it. So here I was, and this was me. New name, new town, new school.

Of course, that one wasn't my real Dad. Mom burned through men like an AK on full auto. Me, I was the one time some guy burned *her*. Back in the day she was on Presidential Protection. Tricky Dicky. Thing is, something smelled wrong. So she was doing what she does best, and digging. One night she wakes up, there's a gun in her mouth. Which is strange, because nobody sneaks up on Mom. The guy tells her to stop looking. Tells her she's stirring things up, and that's his job. So she smacks the gun out of his hand, and they get to fighting. That's how Mom said it started anyway. One bust room later they're sweating rivers and somehow it ain't fighting any more. Nine months later there's me. And Mom got transferred. Up. To people who think 'Rules of Engagement' are for wimps. So I asked her where Dad was, my real one, I mean. It was the only time I ever saw Mom look scared. She said she didn't know, and she didn't look. I got mad, told her I deserved to know my real Dad. She said "You don't know jack, girl." But it worked out. She got me my first Glock to make up.

So that's how it is. New girl, new school - oh, and a dead jock. Well, a girl's gotta keep in practice, right?

Chapter One
Dead hunk talking

It started out like any other day. Mom was big on homework, even over breakfast. But her idea of homework wouldn't suit most classrooms. Things like where to find an unregistered M15 in Denver. Or the best place in Cleveland for C4. I told her we'd done that stuff when I was six. She told me it wouldn't matter if the one time I forgot, I was fifty. I'd still likely be dead. She had a point. I have this weird memory thing. Important stuff, I'm OK - Mom makes damn sure. So I can field strip my Glock with my eyes closed. But other stuff I forget. Like whether it's Tuesday or Christmas. Or what I did on my birthday last year. Once I looked for a book for half an hour and it was in my damn hand all the time. That's why Mom never lets up. So every morning we do stuff again. And again. And again.

Before I left for school, we did the car check, like Mom said I had to every day. Lights, brakes – smart kids did those. But Mom made me do other stuff. Not the James Bond shit – rocket launchers and oil slick sprayers. That's for the movies. The real stuff. Nitro levels and running a glass underneath to check for things that might go bang. Most kids don't do those. But most kids aren't Mom's. Once we were done, I kissed Mom and lifted her purse. Like, there's more things than one a girl's gotta keep up on after all. As I slid in the car, she held her left hand out. Her right had the Glock that was supposed to be – I checked – in my thigh holster. I grinned, and traded her. Mom grinned too. "Bye, SWAB. Don't kill anyone I wouldn't kill." It's a Mom joke. Not the kill thing. SWAB. 'Sixteen – with a bullet'. Every year since I was seven, she just changed a letter.

Why seven? That was my first wet job. Mom had to do PTA and she had some unfinished business for the people she worked for. Even Mom couldn't be in two places at once. So we traded. I took out her mark – and Mom went to talk to the bitch who'd given me a Fail in Math. I got a new Math teacher after Miss Mathews left town all of a sudden.

Well, that's what people said she must have done. They sure never saw her again.

I gunned an engine that would have given a 455 Rocket things to think about if I wanted it to, but looked lemon Popsicle if anyone lifted the hood. Then I flipped a quarter. That's another of Mom's tricks. Never drive the same route. Never have a pattern. So the first few turns, I flip. And I watch. You always watch. Because the one time you don't is gonna be the one time someone's there. But that time wasn't this one, and I pulled into the school lot.

"Hey, Maya baby." The lot was empty. I was early. But so was someone else. The mouth was Steve Logan - Quarterback of Middle-of-Nowhere-High Football. Six foot three and two twenty pounds. Most of it ego. I smiled, and walked over. I reached out, and I grabbed some bits he bragged a lot about using on every chick in town, even if Mom's files said the only tail he'd ever got was some his Dad bought him on his sixteenth birthday. "It ain't May-a. 'Cos no, you may not. And I ain't your baby. I'm the chick with your balls in my fist, so it's My-a. As in I own your ass. Got it?" I made my smile a little sweeter, in case anyone was looking. Then I clenched a little harder, in case he wasn't listening.

"If he hasn't, it sure looks like *you* have. Got it, I mean. Or them, maybe?"

I didn't know the voice, but I sure knew the face. Mostly because I'd put a 357 hollow-point in it yesterday. I looked at Cute Hunk Guy. "Aren't you supposed to be dead?"

He grinned. I had to admit, he was pretty good at it. "I guess you missed." He grabbed the hand I wasn't using and raised it to his lips. He kissed it.

I snatched my hand back. Or I would have, if he hadn't already dropped it. "Missed? *Missed?* I..." But he was gone. Which was also kind of strange. Apart from him walking round all not-dead I mean. Because we were still in the parking lot and there wasn't anywhere for him to hide. He must have hid in some place that wasn't there, because he was sure gone. So I smacked a left hand that could still feel Cute Guy's kiss into Logan and dropped him flat. I probably should have let go of what I still had in my right fist first – but I figured it might let the lesson stick longer. "Like I said. M-a-y-a. My-a, jerk. So if you don't want me to do this again, somewhere your buddies can see, remember. My-a." I smiled. "Later, slick. Like, a lot later. Like, never. Got it?" I let go, and got up. I had more important things to do. Like kill a dead guy.

* * *

I don't do sports. Well, not ones that involve short skirts and jumping as high as possible so guys can see what they ain't going to get. Or shorts that would give a can of spray paint a run for its money. Skirts or shorts, they play merry hell with a thigh holster - even one like mine. And don't even talk to me about changing rooms and showers. I had to make two girls with rather more curiosity than was good for them 'leave town' just as suddenly as Mom had done with Miss Mathews. I told Mom it was a choice between me being a good school citizen and getting with the program, or me wearing hot and heavy. Mom? Mom got me a bigger Glock. And a new holster. Brand new and secret Organisation gear. Said she got it from one of the guys in their lab who thought he was cute. Mom never missed a trick, even if her tricks didn't know that was all they were. It was a combo armpit and thigh holster. Wrapped round me real close, like a best friend with great benefits. But it had different kinds of benefits. Knives wouldn't cut it. And you couldn't tell it from skin. Mom called it 'trans-dimensional chameleon skin'. She said how it wouldn't just look like me, like my own skin colour. She said it was high-tech. Opened up a space in, well, space. One my Glock would fit in real sweet. Waterproof, and only I could get it open. So no gun bulges, and my stride would still glide. She said once I put it on, nobody would ever know I was carrying. Which was the good news. The bad? Bad was, it was bio-tech. *Integrated* bio-tech. Once it went on it was never coming off. It would grow with me, but it would *be* me as well. I said, fuck bad. Anything let me wear my Glock in the shower or a swimming pool was cool. Damn cool. And how did I put it on?

But still, the type of Phys Ed Mom had on her agenda didn't come in schools. So the ones I went to got letters from big important doctors saying I had something totally invisible but I might drop dead if I saw a playing field. And the Principals got late night phone calls from untraceable numbers about whatever dirty secrets they had and how they could stay secret. The Principals mostly figured I was a good Family girl, the other kids figured I was either a wimp or a lucky bitch, depending. Me? I got to go for long walks. Like this one. Thing was, the walks were supposed to be alone. Like, it turned out, this one wasn't.

"Hi." As Cute Hunk Guys go, he had it down pat. The tree he was leaning against was just a frame for his Olympic Gold in 'cool'. But I'd spent a long time at the School-of-Mom, and Cute or otherwise, nobody follows me without me seeing them. Apart, it seemed, from this Cute. I pulled my Glock. As my skirt dropped again, he grinned. "Nice... holster." Since mine was damn near invisible, I figured he wasn't talking about any place you could put a Glock. Not unless you made kink look straight, anyway. Oh, and it sounded like he was big on one liners. Me, I let my Glock do my talking. A clip later he raised an eyebrow. As opposed to spouting blood. Or looking surprised. Or being dead. So I swept his ankles, yanked his arm and dropped him flat. My foot on his throat held him down while I checked the tree. The splinters round the holes and the buried lead told me nobody had been messing with my clip. But 357 slugs aren't supposed to go from Glocks to trees without messing anything in between real bad. And – I looked down – Cute Guy was a lot of things, but a mess wasn't one of them. Right now what he was mostly doing was looking. Like, up. There was a small chance he was looking for the buckle on my thigh holster, but a much bigger chance he wasn't. Which was fine. There wasn't any buckle anyway, so if he wasn't going to play nice and be dead at least he could play guy and be distracted.

I moved my foot, maybe to get a better hold on his throat. But mostly to give him a better distraction. "Thing is" I ground my foot into his throat a little harder, letting my thighs 'accidentally' spread a bit wider "Thing is, if it was a vest, there'd be no slugs in the tree. So it ain't no vest. But if it ain't no vest you're all dead already. So what gives?"

"Well, maybe we should talk about that." He was still grinning. And looking. Then he looked up. At me, not my skirt. "Or maybe we should do the whole small-talk thing, if we're going to get all personal. Like – do you like poetry?"

Poetry? Poetry wasn't good. Poetry could make a bad day a lot worse.

He grinned some more. "Like my favourite. I wonder if you know it? Robert Frost. 'I must go down to the sea again...' He waited.

Poetry. Right. Frost. Who never got closer to any lonely sea and sky than 'Sand Dunes'. Riiight. But there was still a chance. I grinned as well. "Sure. I know that one. 'And all I ask is a chance to see the Catcher in the Rye.'"

Now he wasn't grinning. "And a Boojum, and a Bandersnatch, and a Snark soft waiting."

It was my turn. And it was this week's code. The Big One. The Emergency One. The one Mom made me memorise every Sunday. The gun Cute Hunk Guy hadn't had in his hand until he did said I'd better get it right, unless I knew his trick with bullets. And I didn't. So I pulled him up. Now I wasn't grinning either. "And a Walrus, and a Carpenter, and the oysters quaking." Because dead or not, Cute or not – Cute Guy and Mom went to the same staff dances.

Chapter Two
Girl on a wire

There's something you should know about the people Mom works for.

They don't exist.

I mean they really, really don't exist. Really-really, like in 'click your heels three times before you go to sleep and tell yourself they don't exist' don't exist. The ruby shoes-day thing is optional. Because if they ever think you think they *do* exist, the red isn't going to be your slippers. It's going to be your you. It's going to be your you while you bleed out and someone like Mom makes sure they were never there to start you bleeding. And there's something else to know about them. Apart from them not existing, I mean. Because while they're real busy not existing, they're everywhere. Like, when the first rocket lands on Mars, someone in a little Martian office with lousy Martian coffee and great phone lines is going to be watching and phoning home. Probably while they keep a laser sight on some dumb astronaut's ass. So when I tell you Cute Guy took me to one of their offices, which I'm not going to tell you because then I'd have to kill you, you can bet we didn't have to go far.

No. I'm not telling you where it was. Maybe it was an old abandoned farm. Or the local library, where the librarians carry silenced Magnums to reinforce that thing about being quiet. You choose. Because they don't exist, right? So Cute Guy didn't take me anywhere. But we went there anyway.

There's only two kinds of people get into the type of place Cute guy didn't take me. The ones They know are on their side, and the ones They know aren't. Well, there's a third kind. The ones in between. But still, only one kind ever comes out. After they'd taken every weapon I had on me –and gone into some very personal places to find some of them (they make stun grenades real small these days) – I was figuring I'd better be one of the first kind.

Mom had told me about this stuff. Back in the day I'd have been strapped to a chair, plugged into wires while somebody asked me if my name was Minnie Mouse. But that was the old days. It's called 'fluttering' now. The chair I was in didn't have wires – none I could see, anyway. But I'd bet the allowance Mom was always forgetting to give me it was stuffed with vibration sensors, temperature probes and mikes. The room I was in would be a mess of ultra-infra-geek-speak light and sound intended to let people know not just what I'd had for breakfast last week, but whether I was lying about the calorie count. That's why they hadn't given me my clothes back after they'd done the weapon search, though they'd left my holster on. It was all partly to keep me off balance and partly so all the tech they didn't care if I knew about got to know more about me. Me? I was trying to work out whether to be worried or pissed. Because even if every tech toy in the room was making the hot, naked chick its sole focus of attention, Cute Guy wasn't. Which either meant he was gay, or it meant I was in deep shit.

Cute Guy put down his coffee. They hadn't offered me one. Hot liquids running round inside the target screw up the tech toys. He shook his head. "You've got an interesting file, Maya." At least he got my name right. "Actually, you've got two interesting files." He raised an eyebrow and waited.

I figured if he was going to be a smart-ass, mine was smarter. I raised my own eyebrow and waited right back. I figured I had nothing to lose, so I concentrated for a moment. I smiled, while I felt my nipples turning into bullets. If that didn't distract him some…

It didn't. He picked up a clipboard, made a tick. "Ah, yes. Sven. And Maria." He shook his head, made some more ticks.

Sven. And - I'd have smiled, but I wasn't going to give him the satisfaction – and Maria. Mom had brought them home last year. Said too many jobs got screwed up by hormones. Two months of pyjama parties, without the pyjamas. I ended up sore in places I hadn't known were worth getting sore in. But by the time the two of them were done, Mom was satisfied none of *my* jobs were going to get screwed up because some cute guy – or girl – smiled at me. Or didn't. And that I was more than capable of, um, screwing anyone else up if necessary. I shrugged, and let my nipples relax. "So I guess you've been watching, huh?"

Cute Guy shrugged. "It's what we do." He paused. "Well, or part of it." He sighed. "Shall we get this over with?"

I shrugged too. Apparently it was in style this week. "Sure. Whatever." I thought for a moment. "My name is Kaitlyn. I'm fat. I worry about my math grade. I've killed six…" Cute Guy looked down at his clipboard. I sighed. "OK, I've killed eleven…" He raised an eyebrow. I shook my head. "Look, that guy in the parking lot doesn't count! He stole my space!" Cute Guy waited. I sighed. "Alright, already. I've killed *twelve* people. I like marshmallows, walking in the rain, and my Glock 357. Oh – and I want my fucking clothes back." See, that's how it's done. They have to see some lies, and some truth, so they can tell the difference. Before they get on to the real stuff. The stuff they really want to know. It's called base-lining. So I figured I'd save some time.

Cute Guy made some more checks on his board. He looked up at the wall mirror I knew was one-way glass. A light above it flashed twice. He nodded, then looked at me. "Ah, yes. Your, um, fucking clothes." He didn't sound sixteen. He sounded older. He sounded hard ass, and professional. He sounded like – like Mom. He pressed a button. The guy who came in had my clothes – and my Glock. Cute Guy nodded at them. "So, Maya. How would you feel about blowing your fucking Mom's fucking head off?"

Preludio
Primo Movimento

December 1475, Near Bucharest

The target battled on. The Turks threw themselves on the blades and arrows of the Moldavian, determined the target was going to fall. Which was exactly what the man wearing the black leather duster and aiming the Barrett M82A1 had in mind.

He steadied his sight on the target.

At five thousand feet per second the seven hundred and fifty gram shell would go through Vlad Tepes like a knife through butter. The man in the leather duster knew there'd be no trace anyone would find that he'd been here. Gently, his finger began to squeeze the trigger.

As the girl in the leather jacket stepped from behind the tree the man turned, his eyes locking hers. She was amazed. Nobody ever saw her coming – *nobody*. Not that it made any difference. Her trigger finger tensed – and a 357 slug hammered into the man's head.

The Barrett fell, the man slumped over it. The girl slipped the Glock back into her thigh holster. She moved in to clear the site. L would be real pissed if there was so much as a scrap of evidence. She looked up as the handsome sixteen year old stepped from behind a rock, a gun in his hand. "Hey, CG! I didn't know you were riding shotgun!"

The boy looked round. He shrugged. "It's a good job I am, I guess. We've got a problem."

"What problem? I don't miss. Like, ever. He's dead, CG."

The sixteen year old shrugged. "That's the problem, M. Or rather, you are. See, you're supposed to be dead now too. Or gone. Or never here. One of those. But we can fix that." His gun came up. There was a single crack, red fire burning from the sixteen year old's gun. A second flare of red fire erupted from the girl's thigh, and the girl slumped to the ground. The sixteen year old put another Hell round into the girl's head, just to make sure. He walked over to the corpse and looked down. He lifted her skirt and ran his hand up inside it. He sighed. It was just too bad. If he hadn't been over a thousand years old, or if he'd ever actually reached puberty, he might have had a different reason for doing what he was doing. Well, if she was still alive anyway. Which she wasn't. For a moment, he thought he felt a flutter of life in her spirit – but then it was gone. He shook his head. His hand found what it was looking for and pulled. Even though she was dead, it wasn't easy. If she'd been alive it probably wouldn't have been possible at all. But she wasn't and the thigh holster came loose from her leg, dripping blood. He drew a crystal dagger from the sheath on his leg and kissed the blade. For three minutes his lips moved, his words a harsh whisper on the wind. When he was done the dagger blade glowed a sickly yellow. He cut into the thigh holster, slicing it open. Red fragments spilled out, a once-gem shattered by the boy's hellfire slug.

The boy took the fragments and put them carefully into the rune-box She'd given him. L was going to be pissed, but there was no way in Hell he was going to try to carry it with – he looked over at the dead man in black leather – the other thing as well. He'd come back for it. He grimaced. Come back. Like getting home wasn't bad enough. He pulled a sheet of paper out of his pocket and wrote on it in thick black marker. Then he pulled a red gem, filled with a dull red glow, out of his other pocket and held it tight. He began to chant again – then to scream. As he screamed, the red gem began to glow brighter. Eventually he stopped screaming. Dull, dead eyes read the paper, holding the now burning gem tight in the same hand. With his other hand, he took a flask from his pocket. The smell of Unicorn Horn filled the air. He drank - and was gone. The sheet of paper drifted in the wind – then flared into flame, leaving only ash.

* * *

The slumped figure in the leather duster coughed, a hacking, rasping gasp. Above him the Paradox Storm twisted the sky. Nothing not Summoned was going to get in. He grinned raggedly, blood bubbling between his lips.. He knew there was no way he could draw a pentacle. But - he grinned again, even though it hurt - that's what emergency kits were for. His hand jerked. Slowly, so very slowly, the hand struggled to a pocket in the duster. Reaching in, he dragged out a folded sheet. The man coughed again, more blood spurting from his mouth. He rolled, and dragged himself to one knee. He unfolded the sheet and laid it on the grass, a black pattern visible on the surface and a monogrammed *H* in one corner. He fell to his side, twisting to land away from the sheet. After a few moments of exposure to the air the sheet flared red fire and white lightning. The flames and lightning vanished, but the heat didn't. The air seared, the grass shriveled, and the earth fused to rock under the sheet as it burned away. Rock scribed with a black pattern. The man in the black leather duster struggled to his knees. He pulled a small glass vial filled with a red fluid from a patched slit in the shoulder of the duster. His hand slammed down over the vial, smashing it into the center of the pattern. With his last breath, he cried a long and complex name, then fell face down over the pentacle.

The sky opened.

Chapter Three
9 to 5 to 357

"Sure."

The thing with fluttering, Mom told me, is they sometimes throw stuff in to shock you. To surprise you. To get a reaction. But the other thing is, when someone like the people Mom works for asks you how you'd feel about blowing someone's head off – they're probably not kidding. I ignored my clothes, and reached over to my Glock. Mostly to see if Cute Guy (I was really going to have to do something about knowing his name) did anything to stop me. He didn't – and the machine guns or lasers or whatever else they had buried in the walls didn't start stopping me either. The Glock's clip was in, and the weight was right to say the clip was hot. I raised an eyebrow at Cute Guy. He shrugged. I aimed the Glock at the mirror on the wall and pulled the trigger. The bang was loud, and the ricochet made a hole in the wall. The mirror was just fine, with a blur where the slug had smudged whatever they were using as armour glass. So they'd given me a loaded gun – and didn't seem worried if I was going to use it.

I slipped my gun into my thigh holster. As I did, I ran my fingers over a 'fault' in the leather that looked just like my skin. Whatever they'd done, they hadn't found the lump under it. Mom once said it might be the last thing I needed some time I had nothing left. She never said what it did. Of course knowing Mom it could just as easy kill me to cover her back trail as save me. But at least it was still there. And my leg sure felt better with the weight of my Glock where it should be.

I ignored the rest of my clothes and leaned back, crossing my legs so my Glock was near my hand. Mom had told me this would happen one day. I mean, sure. I'd done some stuff like the PTA thing for her. And other things. I wondered if the fluttering had picked me up. I'd hit twelve before I hit eleven. But it was all off the books. Mom said it was like 'take your kid to work' day, even if it was a lot more often than a day and mostly she didn't come with me. But there's a limited number of employers in Mom's field – and only one where she wouldn't have to blow *my* head off if she found out I was working for them. So it looked like it was time. At least I wouldn't have to worry about Career Day at school – not that I ever had. I pointed my index finger between Cute Guy's eyes, and cocked my thumb. "So where do I go for your trick with bullets?"

"You don't."

He didn't look amused. Which was fine by me. If I was reading it right, I wasn't amused either. But the game's the game, and there are Rules, even if I knew I'd break them just as soon as it suited me. But now wasn't then. Not yet. "Look, CG..."

"CG?" Cute Guy and the electronic voice that could have been male or female, from speakers I couldn't see, could have had Siamese tongues. I shrugged. "CG. Cute Guy. But don't let it go to your head. I eat..." I grinned, remembering Sven's face. Then I grinned some more, remembering Maria's. "I eat Cute for breakfast."

"Is this absolutely necessary?" Cute Guy's face had gone from 'not amused' to 'can I hurt someone?' as he looked towards the mirror.

The voice behind the speakers laughed. It wasn't a pretty laugh, but if it was laughing at Cute Guy I figured I might like whoever owned it. "Just get on with it..." the voice paused a moment. "... CG."

Sometimes you really can hear a smile.

I leaned back a little. It gave me an opportunity to adjust specific bits of my me and maybe make CG's life, or at least part of his anatomy, a little harder. "That's not how it goes, CG. If you're going to be my…" I looked over to the mirror. The light flashed. Twice. Damn – I was right. "My case officer, aren't we supposed to do that whole 'trust me' thing?"

Cute Guy sighed. "The first time you saw me, you did your best to blow my head off."

I shrugged. "Hey! I waited 'til lunch. At least you died with a full stomach." I frowned. "Or didn't die."

CG shrugged too. "You missed."

"I never miss." If there'd been a glass of Jack in the room, nobody would have needed ice. My voice would have frozen it on the spot. I don't miss. I point, you're going down. So I was pissed, and I didn't give a shit who knew it.

He shrugged again. But this time it was more to cover the flinch I'd seen him flinching. Which was better, but not enough. He put his hand out. I let mine drift closer to my Glock. He shook his head, and sighed. "So what do you know about magic?"

"What, you're going to make the Empire State disappear? Or do I get to pick a card?" I wasn't in the mood for dumb-ass jokes.

"Not exactly." Cute Guy turned his hand palm up. The air over it began to glow, to burn. Then the fire flickered – shifted. And a girl-shaped flame with a tiny face I'd seen in a mirror danced in his palm. "Let me tell you a story."

* * *

The Treasure Room, Court of King Alfred the Great, 890 AD

In what would one day become South America the Maya Indians were writing books. In Rome a baby was being born whose bastard son, grandson, great-grandson and two great-great grandsons would all sit on St Peter's throne and who, with her mother Theodora, would rule Rome in what would one day be called the Pornocracy.

And in the newly rebuilt London, an eight year old boy eased an iron spike into a lock.

The boy sighed. These new metal locks were, he thought, a right bastard. The locksmith who had generously told him their secrets, mostly while screaming and bleeding, hadn't seemed very happy with the boy's devotion to his trade. He grinned as he eased the metal spike between the bolt wards and gently twisted. The locksmith had stopped screaming too soon. But he'd got what he wanted. People who didn't know they were being paid by an eight year old boy had told him about the King of Gwynedd's (whatever a Gwynedd was when it was home) visit to the court. The boy had been getting into places he shouldn't get since he was five. Getting into the treasure store wasn't the problem. But these new bloody metal locks…

The spike caught. The bolt shifted. The boy smiled.

Whatever a Gwynedd was, the word was he was bringing treasure. And as far as the boy was concerned, the only important thing about treasure he hadn't stolen yet was how and when he was going to take it. As the bolt slid back it looked like that time was now. But as he eased the chest's lid open the boiling black cloud inside was no treasure he'd been looking for. His eyes glazed, and he fell to the floor.

The cloud boiled, then shifted. A young girl stood where it had been. The Fallen Angel, named Belphegor by those who knew names they'd be better off not knowing, smiled. This one would serve his Prince well, and for long. And the Stealer of Children had had her eye on it for… well, for what the child might think was a while, anyway. The brat would make a fine gift for her. But it was only fitting said brat should know its place first. Besides. Eight was a fine age. The boy should keep it for – Belphegor grinned wider – what it at least would think was rather more than a while. The Fallen Angel waved his, or currently her, hand. Let it be so.

* * *

CG spat. "So I've been eight ever since. A thousand years. Never even made bloody puberty! And now I have to babysit a *girl*! Eeeew!"

He didn't look happy. I knew I wasn't. I just didn't know what I was least happy about. That he was giving me this demon-curse magic bullshit or – I remembered the fire girl dancing in his hand – or that it might not be bullshit. I stood up, grabbed his hand and yanked him up. "You're a pretty big guy for eight, CG"

"Glamor." He shrugged.

I grinned. "Glamour? I don't see no stockings and lace."

"Eeeeeeeew!" CG looked over at the mirror. "Do I *really* have to?" The light flashed. Twice. I was willing to bet whoever was behind it was grinning too. He sighed again. "G-l-a-m-o-r." I did my best blank look. He sighed. He was getting quite good at it. "Magic, you…" He looked over at the mirror. The light flashed. Once. He winced. "It's magic. Eyes, touch – all the senses. That's why you missed. You were aiming at what you saw." He shimmered. An eight year old boy stood where he'd been. An eight year old rather shorter than CG had been when I'd blown his head off. Or thought I had. "Not at me." He shimmered again.

I turned to look over at the mirror. "So I'm hired then?" The light flashed twice. "Paycheck, pension…?" The light flashed three times.

CG grinned. "We're not big on pensions. Most of our… employees… don't make it to collect." He looked down at the him that wasn't himself. "Or never get to bloody retire."

I shrugged. I looked at the mirror. "OK. So maybe no pension. But benefits, right?" Medical? Dental?" The light flashed twice. I grinned inside. My face never twitched. I stepped sideways and bent. As I lifted my leg and cocked, I swung in a half circle and released. My foot planted in what looked like CG's crotch. I almost wished it was his crotch –

but what it was would do. CG flew back and slammed into the mirror. An eight year old boy slumped to the ground, his mouth full of broken teeth and blood. This time my grin was on the outside. I looked at the mirror. "Dental. That's good." I looked at CG. Now I wasn't grinning. "I. Don't. Miss."

I grabbed my clothes. Apparently I had a new job. Now I had to find out how I was going to get screwed doing it.

Preludio
Secondo Movimento

The burning gem crumbled to dust in the hand of the handsome sixteen year old boy with dull and lifeless eyes. A red fire leaked from it, and seeped into his skin. He screamed. When the screaming stopped, the boy's eyes were bright with life. Bright – and aware. He dropped the body slung over his shoulder and looked at the one way mirror on the wall. "It's done, L."

The hidden speakers crackled. "Excellent. Now give me the jacket."

The boy cursed inwardly. Damn and… "L. I figured you'd want hers first. If I'd tried to carry both of them together – no way. The Storm was… I'd never have got back, boss. And I knew you wanted…"

"So you didn't bring the jacket, dear?" The vocoder may have hidden the speaker's gender, but somehow whoever it was managed to make the crackled words sound sweet. Which, the boy knew well, was about as bad as it could get. "Then I will tear every limb from your body." The words were still honey and soft. "I will make you scream for a hundred thousand years. You will…" The sweet voice sighed, and paused. Then it was no longer sweet. "We'll talk about this later, Ealdric. For now – GET ME THAT JACKET!"

The boy winced. He took another dull glowing red crystal from his pocket and clenched it in his fist. A red haze seemed to rip from his body, soaking into the gem. Again he screamed in agony. As the haze faded into the gem, the gem glowed – and the boy's eyes were once more dull and lifeless. He put the now burning gem in his pocket, and pulled out a flask. The smell of Unicorn Horn filled the air. The mirror sighed. "You've forgotten again, haven't you Ealdric? The other pocket, fool." The boy took a sheet of paper from his other pocket. He read it – and drank from the flask.

* * *

December 1475, Near Bucharest
The Angel's wings were battered, feathers broken and twisted. Above him the sky twisted in a way that hurt even his eyes. It had, he thought, been a right bugger breaking in through the Paradox Storm, even with the Summoning's power. He shook his head. Fuck it. He shouldn't have thought the 'bugger' word. Adjusting to white wings wasn't easy. He looked up. "Er, sorry boss." He sighed. Two dead bodies. That wasn't unusual for anything Jack was involved in. Jack being one of them was pretty much a first. He looked up. The Paradox Storm was getting even stronger. It was going to be a right bug… er, rather a problem flying out again. Only the pentacle's Summoning had let him find a path through. He sighed. "We'd better be bloody…" He looked up again, and almost apologized. He didn't. "We'd better be bloody even after this, Shadow." The Once-Fallen Angel Barbas leaned down and ran his hand over Jack's leather jacket. His fingers stopped on a lump other jackets wouldn't have had. "Damn…" He looked up. "Sorry, sir. Old habits." He looked down. "You really are a sneaky bastard, Jack." A fingernail sliced at the leather. Emerald fragments fell from the tear into his hand. Barbas' hand tensed, and he crushed the fragments of gem. A cloud spilled from his fingers and settled into the leather. The body coughed. Barbas' wings flapped, and he landed

by the other corpse. At least Jack had taken her with him. Then Barbas looked at the corpse again. Something was wrong. The dead girl was lying with her head towards Jack. She'd fallen his way. If Jack had shot her, she'd have fallen back the other way. Which meant someone else had been here. Barbas sniffed. The air reeked of magic. And it was a smell he knew. It was Her. Stupid woman. Well, stupid not-woman. He'd never liked her anyway. But it looked like she'd found a new way to kill Jack now Barbas had never stolen the dragon's gem and - the Not-Fallen Angel winced. Remembering things that had never actually happened made his head hurt. A lot. It was almost enough to make him feel sorry for Haures – but only almost. As Fallen Angels go, the little bast... He looked up again. It was getting to be a habit. "Sorry, boss."

He grinned. "Bad call, Lil. You can't kill what isn't alive." He stopped. The Stealer of Children wasn't that stupid. And anyway, he wasn't supposed to know about her plans, now he'd never been Fallen. But if She-He-Wasn't-Supposed-to-Remember wasn't stupid, maybe her Agents sometimes were. Which meant someone had screwed up. If they'd taken the jacket, he'd never have been able to bring Jack back. But they hadn't, and the Paradox Storm was really boiling now. Which meant someone had killed Jack – but Jack wasn't dead. Which meant he'd lived, and stopped himself being killed – and hadn't. Which for sure meant he was going to be pissed when he woke up. And Paradox Storms were a bitch. Nobody was going to get into this moment until Jack had done what he did best – or didn't. But In was one thing. Out was easy. Barbas took the flask from a pocket he didn't have, and the smell of Unicorn Horn filled the air. He set it by Jack, where he'd find it when he got round to not being dead. The Not-Fallen-Anymore Angel extended his battered wings. They flapped once - and Barbas was gone. The maybe-dead-but-always-Jack's body coughed.

The battle raged on. The Turks threw themselves on the blades and arrows of the Moldavian Guard, determined the one who led them was going to die. Jack frowned. It would have to wait. Right now, he had business to take care of. He just had no idea what it was. He opened the flask and drank.

***

The burning gem crumbled in the handsome boy's hand, the fire seeping into his skin as it did. His no longer dull eyes looked round. He looked at the flask in his hand. He read the sheet of paper again. He took another dull glowing crystal from his pocket and clenched it in his fist again. The gem filled with fire, and his eyes dulled. His scream would have made it clear to anyone who was listening that it hurt just as much as last time. Again, the gem crumbled, the fire passing into him setting life in his eyes. They cleared – but they were frightened. It wasn't just the severe absence of anything resembling a rampaging Turkish army. It wasn't even the lack of a convenient dead body. Mostly it was the fact that nothing had changed at all. By all the Rules of Magic, still being where he was, in the office, was impossible. And since he was, in fact, where he was, that meant – well. He had no idea what it meant.

In front of him, the mirror shattered. Behind him – the bullet ploughed into his head.

Chapter Four
Kissy, kissy – bang, bang

Different day, same old same. As I kissed Mom goodbye, I lifted her watch. She went for the knife I keep in my boot. Which was cool – because I'd moved it into a sheath on my back, between my shoulder blades. I grinned. Any day I start out a winner is a good day. She grinned back – and waved my car keys under my nose. I grabbed my keys and pulled a face. We did the kiss-goodbye thing, and I turned the key. Mom didn't know it – but today I wasn't the only one going to school.

The thing with High School, you want to bump into somebody, you don't do it in class. You don't hang by their locker, unless you're either desperate or everyone knows you're both already an item. But the Lunch Room's cool. Besides - it gives you more flexibility. It gives you options. The Mystery Meat my 'bump' had transferred from my plate to CG's chest was, if not elegant, satisfying. As my 'bump' threw the rest of my tray into his face I tried to stop it with my right hand. Not that I tried very hard. It was just a good way of slipping the note I was hiding down his open collar without being noticed. My foot hooked his ankle, and his jerk-back turned into more of a splat-flat as he hit the ground. I smiled. "Oh, I'm so sorry. I guess I must have missed you there." I looked down at the Mystery Meat. "Or maybe I figured your dress sense needed some camouflage." Then I took off. Anybody looking would figure it was just me territory marking. Like dogs, but – I remembered the look of the Mystery Meat nothing on earth was going to make me eat – wetter.

Recess bell rang, and I made tracks. CG was right where the note had told him to be. Anyone saw us sneaking behind the bike rack shed would draw their own conclusions. Now I knew he was old enough to be my multi-great grand-pop, and young enough to be my kid brother, the thought was faintly eeew. But since no lips were gonna to be locking I shrugged it off.

Like any guy, CG started off with dumb questions. My knee reminded him why dentists get to take so many holidays, and he switched to smart answers real quick. He wasn't keen on the deal, but I told him it was the only way it was going to work. I figured if my new boss – and his – wanted Mom bad enough, he'd fold. When he made like wet paper I knew I'd figured right. He pulled a red-gold ring set with a ruby out of his pocket and muttered over it. Then he gave it to me. "This should do it. Just don't let it fall off."

When things go easy, generally it's time to get worried. "So you, like, just happened to have that ready, huh?" I scratched the back of my neck, just low enough to grab my knife.

He sighed. "Idiot child. I've been casting spells for a thousand years. Hells, I could teach *you* to..." He must have seen me start to look interested. "Not, you understand, that I'm going to." He sighed again. "Just don't lose the bloody thing. And I mean bloody. That gold was yellow when it was dug out of the ground. Now if you're going to throw that knife, would you like to get on with it?"

I shrugged, and let go of the knife hilt. I slipped the ring on my finger, and blew her a kiss. It was game on – and momma was the ball.

* * *

The thing with following a pro is, they're going to see you. Not maybe see you. Not probably see you. They are going. To see. You. Unless you've got a pavement team, and a real good one, it's a done deal. And Mom was a pro's pro. I'd followed her all over town and she hadn't twitched. So I knew she knew I was there. Anyone else, she'd have wasted them or lost them, depending on how bored she was. But me – with me behind her she should have stepped out of an alley by now, and made me feel dumb.

It wasn't like I hadn't followed her before – heck, that was part of why I'd planned it this way. We did it for training at least once a week. But I was supposed to be in school, and Mom was kind of big on at least pretending to be normal. And that wasn't all. Because Mom wasn't making it hard enough. She wasn't stopping near store windows at bad angles, so the glass made like a mirror to check her six. She wasn't doing the street car shuffle, she wasn't – she wasn't being Mom. She was being just about as ordinary as Mom never was. And that rang bells. Real bad alarm bells. Because that meant she was trying to put me off guard – or at least off balance. And that wasn't all. She'd been trade-crafting. The blob of gum on a store window. The empty soda can thrown into the paper recycle, not the cans. Just the way she'd taught me, but in a code I didn't know. Which meant – well, I had no idea what it meant, but whatever it was, it spelled t-r-o-u-b-l-e.

Every trade, it has its little secrets. Like, how the store puts a rack of jeans out at some crazy high price, and nobody buys, and everyone says the store's dumb. Then a week later, the same rack is there with a huge sale markdown and everyone buys them. Even though they're the price the store always intended to sell at. And the store smiles to itself, and knows just how dumb to be. Well, momma's trade was no different. When there's Bad Guys around and you want to let your friends know, that's how you do it. Like, if you put the blob of gum on the low end of the store window, then throw the soda can in the garbage, you're saying everything's fine. But if you put it, say, on the upper half of the window, and put the soda in the paper recycle, maybe you're waving your friends off because you're hot. Or maybe you're telling them to load up and come running. But the code Mom was using wasn't the Organisation's – not the one she'd told me was theirs, at least – and it wasn't our own private one. Which meant she was either playing with my head, or talking to someone else. And if talking to someone else was bad enough, what was worse was, I hadn't seen them. The Someone. Or Someones. Suddenly today wasn't looking as pretty for me as it had started out. Which would have been bad news with a capital oh-shit, if it wasn't exactly how I'd planned it.

Mom wasn't doing what she should be doing, wasn't using store windows as mirrors, wasn't jumping buses, wasn't making sudden changes in direction – nothing that would help her tag a tail. So either aliens had stolen my real Mom in the night and left an imposter, or she knew she had a tail already. Like I said. A pro's always going to see you. Or in this case – see me. Because I'm good, but this wasn't my best me. And anyway – once they've tagged you, the target always has the edge. So either Mom had given up on whatever she had been intending to do today and turned it into Shadowing 101, or – or she hadn't. And a Bad Day was about to get a lot worse. For someone, anyway. If things worked out, that was going to be me. If they didn't – well, it would still be me. But with a lot more blood. And the way Mom was tracking, today wasn't a training day. If today had been a Jim Croce song (so sue me – I like grandma music), 42nd Street would have been way behind us, and we were headed places Big Jim Walker would have shat in his pants before going. The Middle-of-Nowhere Mom had brought us to this time wasn't big on much. Even the train tracks held their noses passing through. And on the other side of those tracks were dark alleys even the night didn't like going down.

Alleys Mom was going into now.

Mom had made me read maps of town until my eyes bugged. Maybe it was standard training. Either way, knowing where I was wasn't anywhere near as good as knowing if anyone *else* was there, or round some corner. So I was checking my six, my ten – every number on the dial. So busy checking, in fact, I missed the alley Mom ducked down. And now really wasn't the right time to get stupid. The alley she'd ducked into had to be one of two. Of course, the first one I looked in wasn't it. Time was getting wasted, and that wasn't part of the plan. Even though wasting definitely was.

The other alley was right. Maybe too right. "Hey, SWAB. Shouldn't you be in school?"

I shrugged. "Double math, then Games."

"So you decided to play a different game, huh?"

"Well, you always say you can't ever be trained enough, right?"

"Why, I suppose I do." Mom grinned. Then she didn't. "Bad move, honey." Mom's hand didn't move much, but her gun was in it, pressed against my temple. "Real bad." Then she pulled the trigger. Once – twice. I fell to the ground.

That was when the me not lying dead on the ground stepped into the alley. The real me. My hand went under my skirt. I pulled my Glock – and I blew my fucking Mom's fucking head off.

Sonata
Esposizione - Primo Movimento

Washington D.C. - 350 And Down
"I'm telling you, P. I *knew* her!"

The woman in an elegant evening gown extruded a tentacle and tapped her teeth. "So who *is* she then, Jack?"

The man in the leather jacket grimaced. "That's the thing, P. I knew her – but I've absolutely no idea who she is. I've never seen her before in my life. And that's not the problem."

The woman with a tentacle raised an eyebrow. "It isn't?"

"No. It isn't. The problem is – I didn't know she was there. And I *always* know, P. Always. Comes with the package."

"So how? How do you know?"

"What?" The man in the leather jacket looked confused. He wasn't very good at it.

"Jack. So you didn't know she was there. So she killed you. Which is bad – but you're still here." Prowess paused. "Hmmm. That's two questions. Why are you still here, Jack? I mean, instead of being dead?"

Jack shrugged again. "That's the easy one. I can feel the Paradox Storm from here. I must have nudged me. Which is another problem entirely."

"Why you, Jack?"

"Because he's supposed to be the only one who can. And he must have, because he's here. Alive. And I know that's true. But since that's absolutely impossible, he can't have. So he's not here. He's dead. Really, totally dead. And I bloody well know that's true too. Oh, my head!" The man with the skin of a leopard spat. "Damn you, Jack. If you weren't already dead, I'd bloody kill you." Haures, Great Duke of Hell and undercover agent for Heaven, clutched his temple, and looked down. "Bugger. Jack. Do be a dear. Go back and draw this damn triangle I'm standing in?"

Prowess looked at the floor under Haures. "Er – what triangle?"

Haures sighed. "Exactly, woman. Or not-woman. I'm here. So someone must have summoned me. And we'd all be a lot bloody happier if that was Jack, yes? As opposed, say, to some mysterious secret enemy who knows all about his secret hiding… Ow! My head!"

The man in the leather jacket sighed. He pulled a bottle from a pocket. As he opened it, an acrid smell filled the air. Any nearby virgins might have known what it was – but they were getting hard to find. He swallowed from the bottle. For a moment, he seemed to shimmer, then he was solid. A mystic triangle surrounded the Great Duke of Headaches. Haures grinned, if only weakly. "Well. That's better. A little bit, anyway. One down…" his lips moved, as though counting "Well, one down, and rather too many to go. Headaches, I mean. So, Jack. Where do you want to start?"

Chapter Five
Dead girl talking

"It's a bloody good thing she likes head shots."

The dead me lying in the alley shimmered, and CG went back to looking Cute. As opposed to looking like me. Not that I'm not cute. Hell, I'm the cutest damn thing there is. CG wasn't bad either, but I wasn't going to tell him that. Not unless he bought me dinner. Or at least dinner. "Oh, don't be a wuss. I know" I looked down at dead-mom "Ok, so I *knew* Mom. She does great head." As I slipped off the ring on my finger I did my own shimmering, and the nondescript guy I'd been looking like so I could follow CG-me and Mom was gone. "Here." I tossed him the ring.

CG snatched the ring out of the air. "Don't be a smartass."

I smiled. "I'm glad you noticed." I did a bump and grind that would have made Vegas proud.

He flushed. I made a mental note to make him do it more often. "Never mind that. You screwed up!"

I raised an eyebrow. "Typical male. If screwing's what's on your mind, I'm the best there is. But in this case – things went exactly to plan."

"Plan? The hell it did! We needed – L needed – to know if your mother was selling us out! You said we'd follow her and find out, and you'd take care of things if they went wrong!"

"Oh. That plan." I grinned. "So I lied."

"What?"

"Look, CG – hey. I know it's fun and all, but I can't keep calling you CG. What's your name?"

He flushed. Again. "Ealdric."

"Er - ?"

"Look! It's a perfectly good name!" He flushed some more. "Or at least, it was in eight bloody ninety AD."

I shook my head. "Maybe. But it won't work in a High School hallway. What do they call you in class?"

"They don't."

"What?"

"They don't. I was only there to tag you. Nobody else saw me." He grinned. "Well, apart from Logan. That was a real nice move you put on him."

I dropped a mock curtsey, making sure he got some thigh. "Why, thank you, kind sir." I thought a moment. "But you might have to be seen. So…" I thought some more "So look, Rick…"

"Rick? I think I prefer CG." Rick didn't look happy. Which was fine by me.

"Rick. Well, maybe CG if we're" I winked. "alone." CG might be a thousand years old, but he was still male. He flushed. I grinned some more. "So look, Rick. OK. Maybe the Organisation figured Mom was a threat. But you're big girls and boys." I winked again, and let my eyes drop a little. "At least, I hope you are." He flushed some more. I grinned some more. "You can take care of yourselves. But all the time Mom was training me, she was always big on the Organisation. So if she was lying to me back then, I figured maybe she was a threat to me too. And if the nastiest, bad-ass bitch in this town or any other's a threat to me, I'd better know about it. And put a bullet in her head before…"

"Why, thank you, dear. That's the nicest thing you ever said about me."

If there's one thing Mom wasn't good at, it was losing. And it looked like this time was no different. CG was grinning. Not-dead-Mom was smiling. But at least some things were starting to make sense. L. Riiiight. We'd always laughed about it, Mom and me. We kept McGill, but Mom said she hated her real name. So Nancy was all she ever admitted to - to anyone else.

So there it was. Different day, same old same. And family or Organisation - Mom was still boss.

Sonata
Esposizione - Secondo Movimento

Washington D.C. - 350 And Down
"Start? How about we start with who killed Jack?" Prowess looked over at the man in the leather duster. "And, um, why he isn't dead." Her brow furrowed.

"Oh, he is." Haures clutched his head. "And, of course, he isn't. And she's dead too. OW! And, apparently, she isn't either!"

"She? Which she? What's he talking about Jack?"

"The she who killed him." The Grand Duke of Hell nodded nervously at a Jack who appeared to be rather inconsiderately continuing to breathe. "Or, um, didn't. Her employers killed her after she didn't. Or after she did. Or rather, they killed her, but she's..." Haures clutched his head again.

Prowess' brow deeper. "What?"

"I said, well, he..."

"Shut up." Jack's voice was flat.

The nervous look Haures was wearing decided it needed a vacation. It's sudden replacement showed that whatever it took to scare a Grand Duke of Hell, apparently Jack was it. "Oh hell. This is where you... But you can't! You c...!" Haures collapsed to the floor as one leg gave way underneath him, black and red smoky blood pumping from the fresh bullet wound. He looked up. "You know, you really can't. Do that, I mean. It's impossible. I'm a Grand Duke of..."

"We'd better be even now, Shadow. I just..." The man in the leather duster raised one eyebrow. The gun in his hand spoke again. The Angel with bright shining wings who had just appeared in the corner of the room fell to the floor, his kneecap shattered. He looked up at the man in the leather duster. "Bloody Hell..." Barbas stopped, and looked up "Er, I mean, bloody Heaven..." The Angel sighed. "Damn. Er, I mean Bless. This takes some getting used to." He looked at the man in the leather duster. "What was that for, Shadow? I just saved your life! And anyway. You can't _do_..."

"Can't do what?" If this had been a movie, Jack would have been delicately blowing the smoke from the barrel of his gun. But it wasn't a movie. And he was Jack. So wasn't doing anything of the sort. What he was doing was keeping a gun two Angels clearly thought shouldn't have been able to hurt them pointed at two Angels he didn't seem to have any problems hurting at all.

A thick rope of Shapeshifter flesh flew over Jack's head, dropping to the floor behind the Angels. As Prowess reformed, tentacles bulging teeth that would never be able to play a grand piano wrapped tight round each Angel's throat. Prowess shrugged. "I'm sorry." The tentacles sprouted more teeth, and tightened. "I really don't understand what's going on." The teeth began to bite. "But, well..." She looked up at the man in the leather duster. She flushed. "But there's only ever two sides really." She looked back down at the Angels. "There's Jack's." The tentacles tightened. The teeth got sharper. Prowess looked up at Jack. "And the one I'm not on."

The room flared bright. First red, then white.

The old man in the white vest and red overalls sighed as he looked at the frozen Prowess and two Angels. "HELLO JACK. YOU CALLED?"

Chapter Six
Wrong Number

"Right. To business."

We were back at the ranch. Which wasn't really a ranch. And like I said. If I told you where the Organisation's offices were, or what, I'd have to kill you. But whatever it was, somehow 'back at the ranch' seemed to fit. So that's where we were. Back. At the ranch. Mom was pulling a file down from a shelf in an office larger than some small countries. She'd always told me not to take chances, so I didn't.

The bullet hole in the wall opposite the business end of my Glock would have been perfectly normal – if Mom's head hadn't been between me and the wall.

Mom sighed. "Don't do that, dear."

I dropped my Glock lower. This time the bullet hole was in Mom's desk. The desk just the other side of the ass I apparently hadn't shot my Mom in.

Mom sighed again. "No, dear. I'm not like Ealdric." She turned round, leaning back against the desk. She looked at me, one eyebrow raised. "Well?"

The Glock kicked in my hand. It kept kicking as I emptied the clip. I looked at the splintered, bullet riddled desk Mom was very clearly not being dead on. I raised my own eyebrow. "Magic."

"Yes, dear."

"I mean, like – <u>magic</u>."

"Yes, dear."

"Like, bibbity-bobbity, abracadab…"

"No, dear. No magic words. No bibbity, no bobbity. Magic." Mom sat down behind the desk. Or rather, Mom didn't. I could tell, by the change in her voice. Mommy wasn't home right now. My new boss opened the file in front of her. "Did you ever wonder why the world is the way it is?"

"What? A mess?"

My new boss smiled. It was the sort of smile made sharks wish they had more teeth. "It's not a mess. It's just exactly the way we want it to be. Because we made it this way."

"We?"

Mom smiled again. Sharks would have grown wings, just not to be in the same room as a smile like that. She nodded towards the door. "You can always leave, dear."

Like I said. There's only two kinds of people got into the type of place I was in. The ones the Organisation knew were on their side, and the ones they knew weren't. But only one kind ever came out. And even if this was my new boss, it was still Mom. *My* Mom. I knew if she thought I wasn't on her side, she'd put a bullet in me and not even wince. Just like I would. I slipped my Glock into my thigh holster, pulled up a chair and sat down. "So?"

Mom slid the file over to me. "Your first job, dear. This is Margaret Spencer, New York. Three weeks ago she went to the store near her apartment. She bought a carton of milk, some eggs, a loaf of bread – and one lottery ticket. She didn't have her numbers with her, so she took a Lucky-Pick. She has a new apartment now. Three hundred and sixty million dollars will do that for you."

"So what's the job, Mom? You want her dead?"

"Dead? Damned if I care, dear. No. I want her not to win."

"Oh." I thought for a moment. "So. Fraud, maybe. Rig the lottery company's files? Run up some photos showing she was playing hide the salami with one of their systems guys?"

"No dear. You're not listening. I just. Want. Her not. To win."

Mom smiled. Somewhere far away, I could hear sharks screaming.

Sonata
Sviluppo - Primo Movimento

Washington D.C. - 350 And Down

The man in the leather duster shrugged. "It's not like you've got a cell phone." He checked the wall calendar. "Not that they've actually been invented yet."

"CELL PHONE? WHAT'S A... Damn, Jack." The old man raised an eyebrow. "DO YOU... I mean, do you mind?"

Jack shrugged – again. "It's your universe."

The old man winced. "Not exactly, Jack. But that's... never mind. We'll get round to... I mean, you'll... er..." the old man shook his head. "And Haures thinks he knows about headaches." He sighed. "Excuse me?" The old man walked over to the Grand Duke, and waved his hand.

Haures woke with a start. He looked at Jack. He looked at the old man. Then he looked at the old man again. "Oh. Bugger."

The old man sighed. "I think that's my line, Grand Duke. Now. Cell phone. Apparently I haven't got one. What is it, and why would I...?"

"Cell phone? But... but they haven't been inv..." Haures winced, clutching his head, and a gentleman who had up until that moment been buying frozen shrimp to cook dinner for his wife suddenly found himself standing on Sixth Avenue, talking to his hand. "Joel? This is Marty..."

"Oh. I see." The old man sighed. "Jack. Jack, Jack, Jack. You work for me now, remember? You know you don't need a cell phone to call me, Jack. You don't have to say anything, and you don't have to do anything. Not a thing. Oh, maybe just think. You know how to think, don't you, Jack? You just put your lips together and..." The old man stopped, a confused look on his face.

The slam of the gun in Jack's hand was not, unusually, accompanied by the sound of a scream or that of a body hitting the floor. Not that the absence of either seemed to disturb the man in the leather duster. "<u>For</u> you? Let's just say I'm not working <u>against</u> you. Yet." He raised an eyebrow and nodded at the Grand Duke.

The old man waved a hand, and Haures stood, once more frozen in whatever wasn't passing for time in the room under the Empire State Building. "So why the bullet holes, Jack? In the - the Fallen?"

The gun in Jack's hand disappeared somewhere into his leather. "Like I said. You don't exactly have a cell phone. So I figured Angel blood – you'd notice. And maybe come find out why they were bleeding. Since it's..."

The old man smiled. "Since it's impossible to hurt them at all, Jack? Like, a Paradox maybe? Yes. Of course I'd notice. So how's your friend?

"My friend?" Jack didn't play Poker. He'd found it too easy. So the wary look he wasn't wearing stayed in the wardrobe he didn't have, and as far away from his face as possible.

"Yes, Jack. Your friend. The one you make sure nobody knows about. The one who makes your toys for you. Like your nice new gun. Your friend with the limp. How's Heffy, Jack?" The old man sat down on the chair that hadn't been there a moment ago. He raised an eyebrow.

Chapter Seven
It could happen to you

"Eeeeew!"

Mom had told me to go find CG in one of the little lab rooms the Organisation keeps for purposes best not enquired into, and to do it before I grabbed lunch. She said it with one of those 'Mom' smiles – now I knew why. CG looked up from the thing in his hand that might have been a pestle, if I had any idea what a pestle was. Which I didn't. So 'thing in his hand' was probably close enough. He shook his head. "Sorry. Unicorn Horn. That's unicorns for you. Great PR – lousy personal hygiene. Not that that's the problem." He picked up a very tiny bottle of liquid. It shone a faint green. "Virgin's Tears."

I ran my mind over my less-than-dear fellows at Middle-of-Nowhere-High. Off the top of my head, I could think of a few I'd seen crying – mostly the football squad when some smart ass teacher was dumb enough to expect them to do something hard, like spell their names maybe. Or the cheer squad when someone didn't try to look up their skirts. But I couldn't think of even one who'd be worth tapping to fill the little glass bottle. This was Small Town USA. Everybody in town was practicing to be everybody else's relative. It's not like there was much else to do on a Saturday night – or any other night come to that. So nobody qualified. On the other hand, I hadn't actually noticed any unicorns either. So I did the smartest thing I knew how to do at times like these. I said nothing, and waited.

CG sighed. "I know. No unicorns. But that's normal. They're big city hunters, mostly. More lost and lonely types in cities. Folk who never had so much as a friend, never mind..." CG flushed "Well, never mind anything else. It's not like here, where half the town are their own grandparents. So cities are where you find them. Unicorns. Hanging round near every street corner, looking hopeful. It's not generally a problem. We get the few people who can see them locked up by the people who can't."

"So how do you...?"

CG flushed. "I... well. When the boss needs supplies, I go get some."

I grinned. "CG! So you're a...? You should have said! I could have taken care of it for you any time!"

He flushed again. "Look. I may be a thousand years and change, but I'm still eight. Sort of." He flushed again. "Well. Where it counts, anyway." His face went flat. "Besides. It's one less to worry about."

"Worry about?"

"Weren't you listening? I said cities are where they hunt. And a unicorn without its horn is a dead unicorn." I dropped the eyebrow I had up, and raised the other one just for practice. CG sighed. "Look. You ever meet one? A virgin, I mean? Who's met a unicorn?"

"CG, I don't know if I've ever met any virgins at all. Well, apart from you." I winked. "But like I said - we can talk about that."

"No we bloody can't. You have any idea how many pacts I've signed with demons? There's a price to pay, and being eight makes it a lot easier to pay it. OK? Anyway. You never will."

"Never will?"

"Meet one. A virgin who's met a unicorn." CG reached onto a shelf and took something down. He tossed it to me. The spiral twist on the horn sparkled like mother of pearl. The point was sharper than my best knife. "People never ask why unicorns want to hang out with virgins. You ever get horny, Maya?"

I grinned again. "Why, CG. I thought you'd never ask."

This time it was CG's turn to raise an eyebrow. "Riiight. Ever wonder where the expression came from?" He nodded at my hands. "Pretty sharp, you think? But it makes getting the tears easier. Still, you've got to be quick. They don't last long."

"The tears? Or the girls?"

CG raised an eyebrow. "Girls? Unicorns don't gender discriminate. Where there's a way, there's a horn." He nodded at the tip of the horn in my hand. "And unicorns aren't exactly known for, um, taking their time. So if you want Tears, you gotta be quick. And we've got a squad in most cities. They clean up."

It wasn't like any of the fairy tales Mom was supposed to have told me when I was a kid. Though Mom's stories weren't ever short on blood, or even horn come to that, they tended to have a lot more lead in them. "So that's unicorns, huh? Getting their honey's for nothin', and their kicks for free?"

CD sighed. "Remind me to assign you some more reading. Why do you think I've signed my bloody soul away to..." his lips moved for a moment "... sixty three different demons? Though that's demons for you. Big on power, lousy at book-keeping. Look, unicorns are magic, right? Hells, there's nothing much more magic. Well, apart from..."

"From what?" If I didn't know about it, it was a possible threat. That's what Mom said.

For a moment, CG looked frightened. "Never you mind. If you ever have to go up against one of the Unborn, you're dead already." He shook his head. "No. Unicorns are more than bad enough. We don't need drag..." His eyes went to the mirrors. "Right. So if you're a unicorn, you need power, just to keep being one. And there's nothing with more power than a soul. Especially the fresh ones. The pure ones. Capiche?"

I looked at the blood still oozing from my thumb where I'd touched the point of the horn. And I told myself if I ever came across any unicorns, we were going to have a nice little chat. And it would be my Glock doing the talking, even if I hadn't 'qualified' for unicorn interest in a long time. Which made me I wonder if Mom had had more than hormones-not-screwing-missions on her mind when she brought Sven and Maria home. I shrugged. "Point..." I tossed the horn back to CG "... taken. So what's the big deal then?"

CG raised his other eyebrow, as though I'd done something clever. "Big deal?"

I had no idea what I'd done right, but wasn't going to boost his ego by asking what it was. I nodded at the horn. "Horn. Tears. Deal?"

"Oh. She didn't tell you. Figures."

"Tell me what?"

"Your new job."

Sonata

Sviluppo - Primo Movimento

Washington D.C. - 350 And Down

The man in the leather duster shrugged. "Heffy? Never heard of him."

"YOU'RE A LOUSY LI... er, I mean, you're a lousy liar, Jack." The old man paused. "Actually, that's not true. You're damn good at it. But there aren't many who can get their hands on Chaos – never mind make it into bullets, and a gun to fire it. Or all the other nice toys he's fixed you up with. Heffy's about all there is."

"Like I said. I never heard of any Heffy. But if I had, I guess I'd be thinking about paying him a visit. He said those slugs would take care of anything."

"No he didn't, Jack. He said they'd take care of anything you needed to take care..." The old man stopped. "Very clever, Jack."

Jack raised an eyebrow. "So you know whoever it is you think I know. And whoever it is, they tell you what they say to me. <u>Exactly</u> what they say to me. Maybe I'd better remind them who they're working for."

"Oh, he's working for you, Jack. It just might not always seem that way. Not yet, anyway." The old man shook his head. "So why are we here, Jack?"

"You mean you don't know?"

"Of course I know, Jack. But you have to tell me. There are Rules – and even I can't get round all of them."

The old man winked. "So humour me, Jack. Why are we here?"

"Someone tried to kill me."

"Ah. Well, you don't look dead Jack. So that's alright. Isn't it?"

"No. It isn't. They got me. Got me cold. And I never saw them coming. And I always see them coming. And I was working. The fourteenth century wasn't big on 357 Glocks, but that's what she hit me with."

"She? So you're busy taking care of unfinished business, and before you can put a bullet in Vlad's head, some young girl you didn't even notice steps out from behind a tree and puts one in yours?"

"Interesting. I never told you about…"

"So I'm a good guesser, right Jack?" The old man tilted his head, nodding slightly at the shadow of an old woman Jack knew had no reason to be on the wall it was decorating. Not that that seemed to stop it being there. The shadow raised what looked like the shadow of a stick. "I mean it's not like I'd risk any trans-temporal-quantum-irregularity, universe fucked up and ending paradox stuff by telling you stuff I'm not supposed to know. I'm just a bloody good guesser, right Jack? I mean – RIGHT JACK?"

Jack made a point of not looking at the shadow on the wall. "Guess so." He made equally sure he didn't watch as the shadow faded from the wall it should never have been on.

"Phew." The old man wiped his forehead. "She can be a right bugger, Moira."

"Moira?"

"Never you mind, Jack. So. You ever wondered how you do it, Jack?"

"How do I do what?"

"What you do. When you… fix… things?"

Jack shrugged. He took a bottle from his jacket, and threw it to the old man. "Damned if I know. You tell me."

"No, Jack. You tell *me*." The old man tilted his head towards the wall that was busy not having any shadow on it.

Jack's gun echoed – and the wall had a new bullet hole. There was a faint scream that might have been an old crone – or even three of them. He nodded to himself as green ichor oozed from the wall. "Right. So I get a job. I read all there is to read on the target. It's best if I can find things they wrote themselves – but whatever I can get. I drink my medicine – and I fix it."

The old man gave a worried look to the bullet hole. "Right. Right – yes, Jack. But how?"

"I go back. I go back to when the target needs fixing – and I fix it."

"So how do you know? How do you know where you have to go, Jack? And how do you get there?"

"I told you. I read stuff. And I know. The rest? Unicorn Horn and Tears."

"But how do you _know_, Jack?"

Jack sighed. "Because I remember. Because once I've done it, it's in the past. Well, my past. So my now-me can remember doing it."

"So Jack. You remember. And you remember things that happened, and things that never happened, even if they did once, because you stopped them. And maybe – just maybe – sometimes you even remember things happening that never happened at all. Because you haven't 'nudged' them yet, but one day you might. Right, Jack?"

"Right."

"So you ever wonder what memory is, Jack?"

Chapter Eight
Stop making sense!

"Time travel."

There are some things you just have to say twice. And I'd only said it once, so I figured I'd try it again, just to see how it sounded.

"Time. Travel."

The second time didn't really help.

"Well, it's not really time travel." CG didn't look like he liked what he was saying either. Not 'not like' in the sense of 'dear god, unicorns smell bad'. More 'not like' in the sense of someone who rather liked things making sense, and was having to get used to the idea that they really didn't.

"Oh. That's alright then."

"It's just that – well, it's like, there are things that happened. Like, in the past. And they're true, and everyone remembers them, and they've always been true – but some people can do - well, things..." for a moment a look of almost fear flitted across CGs face. I made a mental note to find out what caused it. Knowing what scares people can be useful. CG took a deep breath. "Some people can do things so that the things that definitely happened, and have always been true, never happened at all, and nobody remembers them. Er, apart from the people who did the things to..." CGs brow furrowed. He was probably trying to keep track of his things. I made another mental note to check his things out some time – just to be helpful. "I mean, the people who changed the things that never happened remember them happening. And..." CG shrugged. "Oh, bugger it. It's magic, right?"

Magic. That made it OK. Sort of. In a not-really-OK sort of way. "Right. Magic. Which is something perfectly normal, and reasonable, and follows a definite set of rules – even if we don't really understand what they are, and it looks like cheating."

"Magic isn't cheating!" CG looked rather upset. "It's an art!"

I couldn't see why he was upset. Being good at cheating was pretty much everything the Organisation was about, so I didn't see that calling magic cheating made things any worse. But that was artists for you. All mouth and 'look at my big paint brush'. "Whatever, CG. So I drink the Unicorn Horn, and I very definitely don't travel in time, but I go make sure Little Miss Spencer doesn't buy a lottery ticket. So that somehow she'll never have bought a ticket, and I won't have to go back and fix it. Right?"

"Right. Well, no. not right. Otherwise, since you won't have to go back and fix it, you won't, and so she'll buy the ticket and... well. That would be a Paradox. And the Universe gets really, really pissed off at Paradoxes. I mean pissed off in a sort of 'bugger this, I'm picking up my marbles and going home and not existing' sort of way. That's why you get to remember, so you know, and the Universe knows, that it all makes sense."

"Sense. Riiiight." I shrugged. "What<u>ever</u>. So why?"

"Why what?"

"Why what what?"

"Why bother? So some stupid bitch won the lottery? Why do we care?"

That's when he told me. And if I told you, I might sort of have to kill you – so it might be a good idea to check behind the curtains when you get home. Or are you there already? Don't worry. It's not too late.

Well. Probably not.

See, there's a thing about Lotteries. Pretty much everywhere has them, and pretty much everyone knows some story about someone who won a ton of money on one. But you know what?

Pretty much nobody actually ever met anyone who did.

Oh, sure. Once or twice, maybe. Or your aunt's kid's friend's baby-sitter's uncle once won a hundred bucks. But the Big One?

Right.

And there's a reason for that. See, people like the People I worked for now – we spend a ton of cash. And, or so CG told me, there's only so much you can get away with using magic to transmute lead into gold, or junk bonds into stock market fireballs, without starting to look suspicious. So one day some genius came up with the idea. The Lottery idea. And now we need a lot fewer votes in secret committees for black budgets. Because every week a whole load of folks give us all the cash we need.

No. Not the 'charitable donations' bit. Don't worry. The hospitals and the old folks and the kiddie play parks get that. Well, after we've taken our 'collector's fee'. No. The Big Ones. Because that's what Lotteries are all about. Sure, we put some low-grade operative up on TV to pretend to collect. But next time you're buying a ticket? Buy two. It's your patriotic duty – plus it means I might not have to kill you just yet. And while we don't put it in the ads you see on TV, every one of those tickets helps us do – well. Pretty much anything we want. Which is just how we want it. And that was why I had to drink the result of really bad Unicorn personal hygiene. Because someone had screwed up. They'd screwed up, and Little Miss Spencer had got a whole load of money that really should have gone towards getting high ranking foreign politicians killed accidentally-on-purpose. Of course we do domestic ones too. But those aren't tax deductible. Not that we <u>pay</u> any taxes. Mom told me the IRS sent some accountants to see us once, to collect. The IRS is still looking for them. They won't find them. See, people who tell you the pen is mightier than the sword never met the Organisation's Accountancy section. <u>They</u> say there's nothing like an AK47 to fix an unbalanced balance sheet. Or a too-curious auditor...

Anyway. It was my new job to make sure Little Miss S didn't win. Or rather – it was my job to make sure I didn't have to do my job at all, because she'd never won in the first place. And, apparently, to do it without the universe getting so pissed off with me none of us ever existed. And, if that wasn't more than enough of a pain in the ass, according to CG Mom wanted it done loud and invisible. Which is Trade Talk for 'something big enough that the right people know it happened, but slick enough that nobody who isn't supposed to knows who the target was'. But even with my flaky memory, Mom's homework sessions hadn't been wasted. I had an idea. So I checked the load on my Glock and grabbed the bottle in CG's hand.

He didn't let go. "Hey! Not so fast! First, you get your homework."

"More homework? Who do you think you are? Mom?"

"Hell, no." Now CG looked <u>really</u> scared. "No. But the orders are hers. Anyway – how do you think you're going to get where you have to go?"

"Isn't that what magic's for?"

CG sighed. "Yes. And no. You have to tell it where to take you."

"And how do I do that? I'm no magician."

"Sorceress."

"What?"

"Sorceress. We don't call ourselves magicians. That's for idiots with top hats and disappearing bunny rabbits. No, you don't know how. Nobody does."

"So how…?"

"Oh. Right. Well, you're trying to find someone. So we use something called the First Law of Contagion. Which means getting as close to your target as getting can get, without actually spooking them. But don't worry. We have people for that. If you ever want the note Napoleon wrote to the Comte de Montholon asking if he could borrow the Comte's wife, just before arsenic mysteriously appeared in his food (or didn't – we make damn sure nobody believes a word of it), we've got it. Bloody man was in real danger of creating a united Europe. We couldn't let that happen. We figure we hit him. Or we figure we will one day. One of those, anyway. So we grabbed the note. We grab lots of notes. And things. Anything we might need one day to lock on to a target."

That's when he gave it to me. The file. Not the one Mom had given me. The other file Because apparently a large part of my job was going to be reading rather sickly hand-written letters to prospective boyfriends who didn't give a damn, and sniffing used and unwashed items of… well. Let's just call it clothing.

I bet you never thought being a member of a Secret Organisation was this glamourous. Guess what. It isn't.

Sonata
Sviluppo - Primo Movimento

Washington D.C. - 350 And Down
"So memories are souls."

"DAMN, JA - I mean, damn, Jack. You're getting better. It only took me three tries this time before you got it."

The man in the leather duster raised an eyebrow. "This time?"

"Never mind, Jack." The old man looked nervously at the bullet hole still oozing ichor. "That's not important right now. But yes. What folk call memories? That's what they are. Little bits of soul, scraped off and left behind. And you, you've got a thing for souls, Jack."

"Oh I don't know. I've always been more of a jazz man." Jack smiled at an old memory. Or maybe, he thought, an old soul.

"Old soul is right, Jack. A lot older than…"

"That's interesting." Jack's gun was back in his hand. "Not even P can read me. Well. Blondie could. You blond, old man?"

The sound of Jack's gun was loud. The old man's sigh was somehow louder. "Jack. We already did that bit, remember? Now pay attention."

Jack's finger tightened on the trigger. "Girl. As in, one I can't see."

The old man waved a finger. The shocked look on his face suggested something should have happened. He waved his finger again. When the thing that hadn't happened stubbornly carried on not happening, he looked even less happy. "You know, by all the Laws of Magic your gun's supposed to be a petunia right now. I swear Heffy gets too carried away for my own good sometimes. Never mind. So yes. Memories are souls. Or bits of souls. And the thing with souls is - well. You ever been sailing, Jack? No. Of course you haven't." The old man looked nervously at the shadow forming on the wall. "I mean, not yet." The shadow got larger, somehow more solid. "I mean - oh, bugger it. So if you did..." The shadow grew. "NOT THAT YOU HAVE, I MEAN," The old man winked at Jack, carefully ignoring the shadow, "YOU'D USE - I mean, you'd use a compass, right?"

The explosion from Jack's grenade threw the old man off his feet. The wall where Jack had thrown the grenade didn't come through anywhere near as well. For a moment the shadow hung in the empty air. Then it was gone, just like the wall. Jack raised an eyebrow.

The old man got back to his feet. "BLOODY HELL, JA..." The look on the old man's face was fighting a war between fury and terror. One look at Jack, and both apparently decided being somewhere else was a good idea. The old man gulped. It didn't look like he was used to it, and he must have needed the practice – he did it again. "Yes. Right. Of course, since I'm, like, a god and everything, you do know that's impossible don't you Jack?"

"What's impossible? You mean the thing I just did?" Jack's voice was flat.

"Yes, I mean..." The old man patted his head. The flames sputtered under his hand. "Jack! My hair!"

If Jack had been someone else, he might have grinned. But he wasn't, so he didn't. "What hair?"

"Exactly, Jack! I mean..." The old man looked down at Jack's other hand. The one holding a new grenade. "I'm really going to have to have words with..." Jack's thumb twitched on the grenade pin. "Ah. Right. Yes. Where was I?"

"Compasses." Jack's hand was empty. The old man had a feeling it might not stay that way.

"Compasses. Compasses? Oh. Right. Yes. So these bits of soul, you can feel them. Like a compass, Jack. And when you feel them, you can find them – and go to them. Because they pull you, do you see? Compasses – well, they're just magnets, Jack. Getting pulled by a bigger magnet, right? And ordinary people feel them too, Jack. The memories. The bits of soul. They'll go someplace and they'll feel like they've been there before. And maybe they have. Or some part of their soul did when it was... Dammit, Jack! What do they teach you people in schools these days?" The old man sighed. "Anyway. They'll maybe feel some event that took place long ago, and it was like they were there, and they'll suddenly cry, or laugh. But people, well, they're heavy, Jack. So the little bits of soul they're feeling can't move them back to when the bit was scraped off. And why are they heavy, Jack? Heavy like you're not heavy?"

Jack's nodded. "Because..." his hand drifted towards a lump in his leather "... because they've got soul. Real souls. Souls of their own."

"Oh, your soul's real, Jack. It's just got some grow..." A shadow started to grow on a wall that was busy being a pile of rubble, so couldn't possibly hold a shadow. The shadow didn't seem to care, and grew anyway. The old man grinned nervously. "Er, right. We don't need to worry about that right now. Anyway - that's what you sense, Jack. Souls. That's why nobody can ever sneak up on you."

"Blondie did." Jack's brow furrowed a moment.

"Yes. But it wasn't because she didn't have a soul, Jack. Hers just was so damn big you couldn't see where it wasn't. It was everywhere. But that's the Unborn for you."

"So the girl with the gun. If I didn't see her, or the kid, then..."

"Then if they weren't dragons – and they weren't – they didn't have them, Jack. They didn't have souls."

Jack shrugged. "I don't know from souls. Bullets in the head – those I know. But like the man said, I figure it's better to give than to receive. So just tell me how to find her, and I'll take care of it."

"Yes, Jack. That's what you said last time." The old man's voice was flat.

"Last time? You said that before, old man. Thing is, I don't remember ever being here any 'last time'." The grenade in Jack's hand would probably have looked better with a pin in it. The pin lying on the ground said the grenade wasn't going to win any beauty contests.

"Yes, Jack. Last time. Lots of last times. Times we had this conversation. TIMES I KILLED YOU, JACK. KILLED YOU SO YOU WOULDN'T DO SOMETHING I'D REGRET." If a sigh could be sighed in capitals, the old man sighed one. Jack's grenade hung where he'd thrown it, but not where he'd intended it to arrive – it was hovering in the air halfway between his hand and the old man. It was also steadfastly refusing to explode. For some reason, the air smelled faintly of petunias. "I don't want to kill you, Jack. I keep hoping I'll remem…" The shadow not hanging on the wall Jack had blown to pieces got larger – got blacker.

The shadow of an arm reached out, and a very not-shadowy iron rod smacked down on the old man's head. He fell to the floor. The old woman with the iron bar in her fist sighed. "You know what a trans-temporal quantum irregularity is, Jack? No. Damned if I do, either. But much as I hate to admit it, the old bugger's right. You can't kill her, Jack. And you're right too. Someone has to, if you're going to stay alive. And you have to stay alive, Jack. You really do. So I'm going to tell you a story." Outside the room, the Universe imploded. The old woman sighed again. "And then you're going to forget I told you a damn thing, Jackie boy."

Jack raised an eyebrow. "And who's going to make me, old woman?"

The old woman grinned. "Why, pretty much the only person who could – and make it stick. You are, Jack. You are." A chair appeared behind Jack. "NOW SIT YOUR BLOODY ARSE DOWN. Once upon a time…."

* * *

The old woman sighed. She was good at it. "So that's how it was. Well, or will be. Or won't be… or maybe both. Unless…"

"Right." Jack's voice was bleak, his eyes cold. "Unless it gets fixed. Which it can't. Because it's impossible to fix it."

"That's about the size of it, Jack." The old woman waited.

Jack smiled. The smile was colder than his eyes. "I guess I'd better get on with it, then. I'd just better not…" Jack's head nodded to what was currently busy not being outside the room "… know why. So you'd better make sure…"

The sound of the old woman's iron rod smacking over Jack's head echoed through the room. The old woman crouched down, her hand running over the lump in the unconscious Jack's leather. A faint mist seeped from her hand into the jacket. The old woman looked at the man on the floor, and smiled – a very, very old smile. Then she bent over, and kissed Jack's forehead. She winked. "Towonda, Jack. Towonda!"

Where the old woman had been was a shadow – and where the shadow had been, was nothing.

Outside the room, the Universe heaved a sigh of relief, and exploded. By an amazing coincidence, everything ended up exactly where it had been before. Which probably wasn't a coincidence at all. Inside the room, Jack got up from the floor. One hand rubbed the bruise on his head – the other brushed the lump in his jacket. For some reason, he smiled – a warm smile his face wasn't used to wearing. Then it was gone. "P?" He looked over to where Prowess had tentacles tight round the throats of two Angels who were busy trying to remember they didn't actually have to breathe. "Let 'em go. We've got work to do."

Prowess relaxed the teeth in her tentacles. "Work, Jack? What work?"

Jack shrugged. "Damned if I know, P."

"So what…?"

"Don't know that either."

"Then why…. Er…?"

Jack's hand brushed a lump in his jacket. He smiled. "Why? I guess… why not?" He paused. "Damn. You think that girl's a cheer-leader?"

"Cheer-leader, Jack? What's that got to do with anything?

Jack shrugged. "Oh, nothing I guess." He paused again. "Save the not-a-cheer-leader, save the…" He shrugged. "No – never catch on. Let's go, P."

Chapter Nine
Ready to Rumble

"OK. So I'm going to need some stuff." The reading had been the usual crap. Not that it being crap meant I didn't need to know it – but once you've read one target file, you've read them all. Works here, shops there, friends, lovers – not that little Miss Target had any of those. But the usual grind's about the only thing you get to make sure you're not the one who gets ground. Like, that time in Vladivostok. If I hadn't known the security guard was left-handed, and how he never ate peanuts – but that's another story. This one, like I said. I had an idea. But like I said as well, even if it looked like CG wasn't listening, I was going to need some stuff. So I said it again. "Hey. Q-tee. I'm going to need some stuff."

"Cutie?" Apparently CG-s ears were fine, even if he didn't look too happy about it. Or, at least, about what he was hearing.

I sighed. "No. Not this time." I winked. "OK. So this time too. No. I mean Q hyphen t and a couple of e-s. Like, Q-tee." CG looked blank. If he'd been an agent, he'd have got a gold star. As it was, he was just a thousand year old eight year old kid. So I sighed – again. "Like, Q." CG must have heard blank was in style this season. I sighed for a third time. "You don't get to see too many movies, huh? Never mind. Forget it."

This time CG sighed. I guess he figured it was his turn. He opened a drawer, and reached in for a file. "So. You've done your homework I take it? Here's how we're going to do this…"

The slam was loud. Louder than my Glock. But then you can't put a silencer on a drawer. CG likely should have been screaming, the way his hand was mashed inside the drawer I'd slammed shut on it. On the other hand my Glock was probably making the whole screaming thing kind of hard, the way it was filling his mouth. I pushed it in a little deeper. "Look. Don't get me wrong. I mean, I actually kind of like you. Well, I might if the whole idea of liking an eight year old kid didn't feel quite so weird. But don't get the wrong idea. Even Mom stopped trying to tell me how to do my jobs a long time ago, and you're not Mom. So your file stays in your fucking drawer, and I tell you what I need. Then you get it for me. OK?" The bitch about the Glock is, it's hammer-less. So you don't get to make a point by tightening the trigger and watching their eyes as they watch the hammer go back. So you do it with *your* eyes. If the mark can't see the hammer there, and the certainty of a whole lot more trouble if they don't do exactly what you want, then you're in the wrong job. I pulled my Glock out of CG's mouth, but slammed the drawer on his hand again. "We clear, pretty boy?"

"You can't - I mean - look, you have to..."

CG clearly wasn't happy. Whether it was because he was probably going to have to stop whimpering long enough to magic himself a new right wrist, or because I wasn't interested in whatever was in his file didn't really matter. What did matter was how people have no idea how much they give away with non-verbal language, like maybe a flickered eyeball. So I didn't bother looking behind me. "Fuck off, Mom. I'm working." Mom's heels got to clip on the floor, the way she hadn't let them when she sneaked in, and CG got to look a bit more scared. Probably not by anything I was saying – more by all the things Mom <u>hadn't</u> said. Things like "Do be a good girl and take your gun out of his mouth, darling." Stuff like that. "OK, CG. Stuff. Not stuff as in 'we don't do it that way.' Stuff as in 'Maya needs'. As in 'Yes, Maya. Right away, Maya.'" I blew him a kiss, just to show I wasn't really mad. Then I stuck my Glock under his chin, just to show we were still working.

"Oh." I could feel his gulp in my trigger finger. Lucky for CG, I'm good with my fingers. If he got real lucky, he might find out just how good one day. "Right. Of course. So, er, how do we do this, boss?"

I had a feeling the 'boss' wasn't a hundred percent sincere. Which was fine by me. I knew I wasn't pointing my Glock into anything actually CG-ish. But it got my point across. "OK. So the gig is, I get to travel in time, I get to make sure Little Miss Maggie doesn't buy a lottery ticket, and I have to keep it loud, but invisible. Good so far?"

"Good so far. And, um, can I have my head back? Please?"

I slipped my Glock back in my thigh holster, making sure CG had some solid distraction while I did. He didn't distract, which was good. It showed we were both working, not just me. "Right. So I need some stuff."

"Stuff. Could you possibly be a little more precise? Do I get a colour, or do we play twenty questions?"

CG's ass was getting smart again. I figured I could smack him down, or let him run. But guys are kinda sensitive like that, so I let him run. "I need the building security duty list for the night before she buys her ticket, and for the next day. Oh, and I need a hat-rack"

"If you hadn't been more interested in breaking my wrist, you'd have seen they were in the file I had for you."

"Great. So unless you want the other wrist breaking too?" I waited. He opened the drawer – with his left hand – and gave me the file. The duty lists had pictures, which helped. Names can be confusing. Like that time in Caracas, and Kim... but that's another story too. I ran my finger down the roster. "Great. The security passes I can take care of. But I'm going to need a glamor..." CG blushed. "Gutter, CG. As in mind. Like, get yours out of. So I'm going to need a glamor ring for this guy, and another one for the hat-rack." Tony Warren was one of the two on the night shift. The hat-rack was a guy called Sam. Because Maggie's job was to keep the 'in' in insurance. As in, the money in, and not out. So when some poor sap made a claim, her job was to find some reason not to pay. Which was pretty bad news for the saps, but good news for me. Because it had made it pretty easy for CG to find someone with a grudge. Sam was ex-military, and a small-time crook. He also had a dead wife, who he'd actually given a damn about before she'd been on the wrong end of a T-bone on her way to work. The Insurance Company weaseled the deal, and Sam didn't get a penny. He was going to fit my hat just fine.

"No can do."

CG seemed almost happy. Me, I wasn't happy about him making me unhappy. "Why not?"

CG sighed. "Look. Just because it's magic, that doesn't mean it's easy. Hell, it's mostly harder. I have to find the right demon, which means finding what your guy's got that some demon might want. That means..."

"So who cares? Time travel, right? We can take as long as we need." The 'magic' thing was getting easier, so long as I didn't stop too long to think about it.

"No, we can't. You're a virgin."

I laughed. "Only in my left ear." I remembered Caracas – and Kimmie, and her trick with... I stopped remembering. I was working. "OK. So not even my left ear."

CG blushed. He was getting good at it. "No. Not that. I mean, time travel. The further back you go, the more careful you have to be." CG blushed again. "Well, or so they tell me."

I was curious. "Who tells you? Demons?"

For a moment, CG looked scared. And I could tell he wasn't the kind to scare easy. "Demons? I fucking wish... No. Others. Just – others. So we have to move fast, so you only trip as short a ways back as we can get."

"CG. I need that ring. Isn't there any other way?"

"Well, sure. All we have to do is get some... well, some... Look, I need to get a lock on his soul, so I need..."

"Blood? Is that all? Why didn't you say so? I'll..."

"No. No, not blood exactly. See, blood's OK, but for real power I need something..." CG blushed a third time. "Well, another kind of, um, personal fluid."

I laughed. "Oh! That's all right then. For a moment, I thought it was going to be something hard." I laughed again. "Though hard may just come..." CG was blushing redder than a brothel on sale night. I giggled. "... hard may just come into it after all."

* * *

"You have <u>got</u> to be kidding me." Tony was snoring gently. I hadn't got round to untying the leather straps from his wrists and ankles before I called CG, and it was a good job he was sleeping, because what he had in his mouth would have made talking difficult. But I'd made damn sure he was exhausted before he drifted off. He had a smile on his sleeping face to prove. it. I shrugged. "All in a night's work, CG. And trust me..." I grinned "... it was real <u>hard</u> work." True to form, CG blushed. "Anyway. I needed his uniform, so I figured I might as well enjoy getting him out of it." I handed him the rubber. "That what you needed?"

CG blushed again. "That... will do nicely, I'm sure. It should only take me about an hour or so."

"Then I'll meet you back at base in maybe two. I've got Tony's pass – now I need to pick up a sample." CG looked blank. I shook my head. "Sample, CG. SAM-ple. There's this new invention – it's called a sense of humour. You should look into it. Oh, never mind. I'll drop it by the office when I'm done. Oh. And bank details. I'll need them. Terry and Sam. OK?" I moved for the window. I've never really been a door kind of girl if I can avoid it.

"Er, Maya?"

I stopped. Yes, CG?"

"Shouldn't you put some clothes on first?"

I sighed. Details. They'll kill you every time.

Sonata
Sviluppo - Secondo Movimento

Washington D.C. - 350 And Down

"So memories are souls."

The man in the black leather duster didn't look up from the gun he was loading, even though he could have done it with his eyes shut. "That's about the size of it, P."

"So memories are souls, and you don't have one. Or if you do, it's not the kind of soul that holds you down, so you can 'feel' other souls, and..."

"That's not quite what he said, P. He said..."

Prowess sighed. "Shut up, Jack. I'm thinking. Damn, Jack. Why don't you have a piano here?"

"Why would I want a piano, P?"

"So I can think, of course. Don't be silly." Prowess' flowed, and a rather fleshy baby Grand Piano, bigger, or rather smaller, on baby than Grand took shape on the floor. Two arms morphed from the front of the piano, and the notes of Dragonstar drifted into the air.

The man in black leather loaded his gun. "You know what they say about playing with yourself, P?"

The baby not-a-piano blushed red. Then suddenly, the piano's lid grew a mouth. "Jack! That's it!" The piano's fingers carried on playing. The man in black leather unloaded his gun, then loaded it again. "I said, Jack! That's..."

"I know what you said, P." Jack's fingers twitched, and the gun was gone. "You said 'that's it'. Then you were going to say how you don't play notes, you play the music. How you don't think about the notes, just how all of them fit together, and let your fingers do the notes while your head does the piece. Or maybe you'd have said heart, because that's the kind of thing you say. And then you were going to say how I shouldn't try and feel where the girl was, and try to find her. I should decide I'd already found her, and feel what was different. Right?"

"I didn't know you could read minds, Jack."

The man in the leather duster shrugged. "I can't."

"So how...?"

"You play piano, P. I load my gun. It's the same thing really."

"So you know where, I mean, when, she is? You can feel her soul?"

"Nope."

"So how...??"

"Because I know when *I* am. I can feel the storm. And it wasn't there until I decided I was going to find her." Where the gun had been in Jack's hand, there was something much more dangerous. Jack uncapped the bottle, and the smell of Unicorn horn filled the air. Then he was gone.

The piano smiled at the space that used to be Jack. Then it smiled at the shadow that hadn't been on the wall until it was. "Did I do it right?"

Shadows can't generally speak. So this one didn't. "You did just fine. How did you...?"

The piano shrugged, a clever trick for something without shoulders. "Oh, some subsonic here, some ultra there, a whisper he'll never remember hearing. It's a lot easier when I'm the strings as well."

The shadow that wasn't there flowed from the wall it wasn't on. "So why the hands?"

The piano did its own flowing. Prowess fingers never stopped playing, even though there wasn't a piano anywhere for them to play. The notes of 'Dragonstar' filled the room. "So he didn't ask questions. And because I love to play." For a moment, she looked sad. "Can you wait? I love this part."

The shadow raised an eyebrow it didn't have. "Wait?"

Prowess turned away from the shadow. The last notes of Dragon Star hung on the air a moment longer than they should have. "I mean, before you make me forget again." The shadow on the wall raised a shadow arm, one holding a shadow rod. The rod fell on Prowess' head, but gently. The shadow sighed. "I'm sorry, Lee-Ann." Then the shadow was gone.

Jack unwrapped the Shadow round him and unloaded his gun. He knew neither of them would remember him being there - it happened a lot, and it was just the way he liked it. He used to wonder if that was why The Dragon had chosen him to be a gnat. It came in useful. Now he was beginning to think maybe they hadn't chosen him at all. He reloaded his gun, and took the real flask of Horn from his pocket.

Chapter Ten
Wake Up Yesterday

Whatever Jethro Tull said (OK, so Mom likes weird old music) – this 'livin' in the past' thing wasn't anything to write home about. Getting there, or in my case here, since 'there' seemed to be where I was, was a bitch. Or at least yucky enough my taste buds were seriously considering legal action. I don't know if it's the Unicorn Horn or the Virgin's Tears – but trust me. The stuff in the bottle CG gave me was never going to catch on with the 'do you come here often, and your place or mine' cocktail crowd. Still, either the Organisation had some amazing movie sets, and it probably did, or I was going to have to stop sniggering every time someone said 'magic'. A newspaper I grabbed had a date insisting Steve Logan had a few weeks to walk without limping, and the streets round me weren't downtown Middle of Nowhere. The Apple was Big, and all round me were bits just waiting for me to bite. Hell, I even knew what numbers the lottery machine was going to spit out at the end of the week. CG had made a big deal of reminding me. And an even bigger deal of telling me how much high velocity lead poisoning I was going to get if I did anything quite so stupid as trying to use them. So unless all the livin' I wanted to do in this particular past involved screaming a lot while bleeding to death from a gut-shot, it had better be just another day at the Organisation's kind of office. A day when a file needed the Organisation's kind of closing.

Now. It doesn't matter what you do, but pretty much every kind of work has its own language. Like, I could say I needed some talent to sucker a mark while I reefed his leather. And if you were the type of contact I'd actually say that to, you'd know I needed some cute chick with lots of cleavage and a habit of forgetting buttons to walk by some guy so I could lift his wallet while he was busy looking elsewhere. Or I could say the best way to pop a Bailey cherry was a rim job – but then I'd have to stop your gutter mind dropping below street level and tell you Baily makes some of the best safes in the world, but a good way to crack most of them open is to pack the gap between the door and the walls with epoxy putty, but not so packed you don't leave space all the way round. You leave a little hole at the top, let the epoxy set, and pour in enough liquid nitro to fill all that nice space you left all around the door under the epoxy. Then get a good ways off and light up the nitro. Rim job, see? But it's all just trade talk. So when CG told me Mom wanted this one Loud but Invisible, I knew what he meant. Because Loud meant anyone in the trade would know someone had done something. But Invisible meant even people in the trade weren't supposed to know what that something was. And I had a week.

* * *

One week later

BOOM!

When you want Loud, nothing really beats Semtex. Well, there's Octanitrocubane – but while it looks good in the lab, even the Organisation hasn't actually been able to make enough in one place to put bang in its boogie. So it's still experimental. And there's always HMX – but the military keep a pretty close eye on that. So when a girl's gotta boom, Semtex and C4 are generally the ways to go. Easy to get hold of, if you know the right street corners, stable – and you can mold both of them like play-putty. But Sem's a little tougher for electronics to detect, so it's generally the 'eek' I'm most likely to put in my 'plast'. And it's reliable, as the two storey block of rubble that used to be the eight storey office block Maggie Spencer worked in – and I hoped 'used to work in' - was doing nothing to disprove. But like Mom sometimes says. 'Hope's a dope'. So I grabbed my Emergency Services jacket and ID, and went into the rubble. It wasn't that Maggie Spencer had had a weight problem – but fat or otherwise, I had to make damn sure this lady wasn't going to be singing ever again. Or buying any lottery tickets. Or the whole of the last week would have been wasted – and since the Organisation wasn't big on failure, the next thing to get wasted would probably be me.

* * *

One week ago

If you read just about any military manual on the planet, it'll tell you the most powerful weapon you have is knowledge. Which is fine until you're down a dark alley facing three guys with knives. In that type of situation I'll see any page in the encyclopedia you want to offer and raise you a short skirt, six inches of thigh and a Glock the punks aren't expecting. But by and large, the whole knowledge thing is righteous. So if Jethro Tull wasn't going to have to write some track called 'Gettingyourheadblownoffbyyouremployerforscrewingup in the past', I was going to have to get to know a damn sight more than was in even Mom's files. Which meant leg work, and not the kind I showed guys with knives. It meant tails, stakeouts, hanging out in bars and all the other joys of what we in the trade call being a 'pavement artist'. In Maggie's case, the bar work was mostly optional. I didn't need to grab any fresh DNA, so I didn't have to talk her into any hotel rooms. What I did need was number two and three of the Holy Trinity. Motive I was fine on – most days Mom stopped at 'because I said so'. But if I was going to take care of business, Method, Opportunity and I needed some quality time together.

With wet jobs there are generally two approaches. You can try to get the target on their own – which is what most civilians seem to think is best. And sometimes it's even the right way to do it, though a lot less times than you might think. Or you can do the job while the target's surrounded by people, which is good a lot more often than you might think if you do it right. A nudge on a crowded subway platform and a mark can end up under a subway car without any camera able to prove a thing. Down a dark alley you'd be surprised how often there's the one set of eyes you never planned for. But this job wanted Loud. The subway wasn't going to work. So I needed somewhere predictable, somewhere part of a pattern Maggie wasn't easily going to break. And I was lucky – until Lady M won the lottery she wasn't going to win, she was just another Jane Schmoe at another office desk. An office desk on the fifth floor of an eight storey office block, where she found reasons folk in trouble, who thought they had insurance because they'd been paying premiums like, forever, weren't going to cost the insurance company she worked for a red cent. Hell, even if she hadn't been on Mom's list I might have done her just for fun.

To be honest, a habit Mom had beaten out of me a long time ago, generally explosives are a really bad way of killing someone. I mean, they're pretty good at killing some<u>one</u>. Put the bang into boogie in any building round town, or some car by the side of the road, and there's a pretty good bet the next day's paper will be needing extra copy space for the obits. But when it comes to killing some<u>one</u> – when you've got a specific target who has to go in some place without coming out – not so much. If you do their car, was it them? Or was it the parking valet at their hotel? Or maybe a 'jacker who was gone in a lot less than sixty seconds when they hot-wired the wrong four-wheels-and-Semtex-to-go? If you do a building – their house, their office – was it maybe the cleaner who opened the closet door with the trip wire? Was this the day your mark called in sick, and the infra-red switch in their desk drawer said goodnight Irene, or in this case Maggie, to the office intern and a bunch of collateral nobodies? Could be. Of course, there are ways to make it more specific. Trigger the Sem with, say, the signal from the mark's mobile phone, but only at short range. Or reef their pass card, lift the keycode, and set things to blow just for that particular card. But every one of those runs the risk of there being some little piece of rather too specific circuitry left around for some smart-ass with more curiosity than was good for me picking it up and wondering what it was for. Still, Sem fitted the job too because it wasn't just loud. If I did it right, there'd be a whole bunch of collateral for Maggie to get lost in, or what was left of her at least. So one glamor ring, and 'Sam' made some purchases even Wal-Mart didn't sell. And he went into his bank, and made a transfer of pretty much every cent he had to the account of a guy called Tony Warren. The rest was straight out of the book - Mom's kind of book, anyway. I spent a lot of nights on the roof of Maggie's building. Well, me and the passcard I'd lifted from Tony, or would lift from Tony in a month's time, did. The card and a set of night camo let me scope out the building and the way the guards did their thing. Turned out Tony always did his roof check just before shift change. It looked like an easy job – but I knew something was wrong. Real wrong.

* * *

The night before

Most building security is designed from the bottom up, and the top down. Like, you lock the front door, and you put out rent-a-cops. But you figure most people can't fly, so even if you put locks on the maintenance doors to the roof, and maybe a camera, the cops stay downstairs. Apart from when they're on patrol. And if a camera sees a rent on walkabout – who cares? Especially if you pick your time. See, most building security, the biggest thing they care about is not being fired. And the best way not to get fired, is to make sure the paperwork's done. So every shift change, you got the new crew going over the old crew's reports while the old crew are still busy writing them up. Watching screens? Not so much. And it's really easy to find out when shifts change. I hadn't even bothered to ask CG. Nobody notices one more bag lady on the street, and it doesn't take long to see the handover. Maggie's building, shift change was six AM. So I figured I had from midnight to maybe six thirty. I'd hung out on the roof a few nights, and I knew Tony did his roof check around five AM. That gave me time to pay a last visit to Sam. Of course it was my first as well – but who's counting. I set up an email on his home computer explaining everything. How he didn't want to live no more now his wife was gone, but the fucking insurance company who sleazed out of paying her insurance weren't going to get away with it. I rigged his machine to send the email to the newspapers just before noon. Then I grabbed Sam. I'd already killed him, but he still had a job to do. He had to wear my hat.

Just after midnight I did my best Spider-chick up the side of the building to the roof, courtesy of some monomolecular finger pads fresh from the Organisation's Special Projects Division. They clung to just about anything. That, or they were magic. The walls I'd climbed didn't seem to care, but I was still happier with the building roof under my feet than thin air. Climbing with Sam hanging from a rope under me had been a bitch. The way I had the job laid out, no smart ass Medical Examiner was going to be able to tell he'd been dead a while – not even if they found all the bits of him he'd be in by the time the job was done. But I still needed him as a hat-rack, so he got to play dead-weight in more ways than one. Once I was up on the roof I wired him with a vest, using some of the Sem 'he'd' bought on the street. I rigged the vest with a radio transponder and I put the trigger for the transponder in his hand. It was dead, but it looked convincing and it was going to end up in bits anyway. The maintenance door had a lock my kid sister could break – even if I don't have a kid sister. It popped like a cheer-leader's cherry. I started working the stairs, making sure I stayed out of camera sight. It wasn't time to be seen yet. But I wore Tony's uniform and his glamor ring just in case. The glamor ring made sure any cameras just saw Tony. CG had tried to tell me how it wasn't actually like that. How the glamor ring just put a morphic field on the recording so anyone watching it saw Tony. I told him I didn't give a shit provided they didn't see me. He muttered something about stupid girls, I put a slug in his shoulder. We'd probably have called it flirting if he wasn't, like, eight years old.

When I'd checked over the fire stairs, I went back to the roof. Waiting's always the hard part. Killing time's a bitch – even for my Glock. But eventually the door opened and Tony came out for his roof check. He was right on time. Or rather, he was late. At least he was once I'd put a hole in his head with the gun 'Sam' had bought yesterday in a back-street, no-questions dive. I put Sam's fingerprints on it and dropped it near Sam's body. One glamor ring and uniform later, and 'Tony' went back down the fire stairs. At the bottom, 'Tony' opened the street exit and slipped a plastic shim over the door bolt so it would close, but not lock. Then I made my way to the front desk, and filled in Tony's paperwork for the night. 'Tony' left the building, heading for home. A change of glamor ring, and 'Sam' walked up to the fire stairs street door. I was wearing Tony's uniform, with the cap pulled down over 'Sam's' eyes. I made sure the camera saw me, but not for long, and went in. Up the stairs, onto the roof, one spider-chick down the wall and I was on the street. A glamor ring, a change of clothes, and 'Tony' came back up the street in civvies, heading for the exit door. I let the camera see me, and opened the door. The tapes would show Sam going in, and his 'accomplice' Tony following him, so them both being on the roof would make sense. On the roof I changed back to Sam and worked the stairs. If you can call wiring the length of each one with packets of Sem at carefully spaced intervals 'work'. At every door, under the top of the banister, I put a sensor rigged to trigger when three people had passed it, and added a little secret sauce to the fire alarm. Then I went back to the roof and did another spider-chick down. I still had the feeling there was something I was missing. Something nasty. But good or bad, it was time to boogie.

* * *

BOOM!

The thing with offices is, folk do as they're told. They follow patterns. Round about eleven, the little old bag lady nobody ever notices remotely triggered the fire alarm. The folk on the second floor started to evacuate. The sensor there waited until three of them had gone by, and told the sensor on the third floor to wake up. As soon as the third person passed that one, it woke the sensor on the fourth. Which meant that by the time the sensor on the eighth woke up, the stairway was full. Full, and the fifth floor would be empty, and Maggie still going down. The Semtex wired to the stair rail just changed her direction about a hundred and eighty degrees, even if only for a little while. The radio transmitter sent a signal to the roof, and Sam went all to pieces over his wife. Once the email went out people would stop asking questions about who did it, and nobody would be looking for the girl who was never there. Miss Maggie wasn't going to be buying any lottery ticket on the way home and nobody was going to think of her as anything more than a cheap-side city funeral nobody would go to. Loud, and invisible. It was as close to a perfect job as I'd ever done.

Which didn't explain why something was still nagging me.

I had no idea what it was, but something wasn't right. The little old bag lady hung round where the building staff were gathered, to make sure Maggie never came out, and she didn't. An Emergency Services jacket went in, and I confirmed one particular body was part of the count. I had my head on a swivel, like I was checking for a tail – but I knew I hadn't been followed. I'd been checking my six, five and a few numbers that weren't on any clock you'd find on a wall. I was clean. Definitely. Absolutely.

Probably…

No. The hell with it. It really was a clean job. I was just going field crazy. But no matter how often I told myself that, I still knew it wasn't. Something was fucked, and I had a feeling it was me. Still. Mom was going to be waiting for my report, and waiting is one of the things she's really not very good at. It was time I got horny, and I already hated the stuff. I grabbed my bottle, and I did what any good girl does – I swallowed.

Sonata
Sviluppo - Tertio Movimento

BOOM!

The man in the black leather duster stepped back behind the corner. As jobs went, it was clean. A bit careless – there'd been twice when the girl was scoping the building when she'd been caught by the cameras as the guard while the guard was on camera somewhere else. But Jack had snatched the disks. The guy with the limp had taken care of them, and made sure there was only one Tony Warren, then Jack had put them back. She'd been looking for a tail, which would have been good if she was on Jack's side. She hadn't seen him - which was better, because she kind of wasn't. And she hadn't seen the kid either. Otherwise, the girl hadn't done bad at all. Which meant someone had spent a lot of time on her, because nobody got that good by accident.

Finding the girl had been easy. Jack wondered if it had been too easy. On the other hand, finding her hadn't been the problem. Unicorn Horn took care of the When. The Where – Jack had never had much trouble with the Where when he was Dragon. But that was when he had a soul to track, or at least scraped off bits of one, even if he didn't know what he was doing. This time the target didn't have a soul to scrape. So he didn't look for one. He just looked for the hole where a soul should be, like looking for a tear in a map even when you couldn't read the street names. Finding it had been easy. Two easy – because that's what there was. One hole, and two problems. The hole was the girl. The tail stuck to her butt like used gum coming off a park bench was a different story. Because he had a soul – but there was something off about him. Something wrong.

It had taken a while to see him. Maybe too much of a while. Jack wondered if he was getting old. Sure, the tail had been Shifting. A guy with a briefcase, a kid on a skateboard. But it wasn't a Shifter. Not like P, anyway. Once Jack had caught it, he'd seen the ring thing. So the tail was a mage. And a pretty dumb one – totally fixed on the girl. Never even glanced Jack's way. Which didn't fit – dumb mages didn't last long enough to be a problem. Before Jack could show the mage just why, the girl had used a ring too. Which made the mage maybe a partner – or maybe a contingency plan. Either way, it was too soon. So he watched. He was watching when the dumb-ass mage dropped one of the rings he was switching. So he was watching when the dumb-ass mage turned out to be the kid he'd seen blow the girl's head off after she shot Jack. Which was about three bullets too many, and one bullet too few - the bullet Jack was going to put in the mage's head.

But not yet. Not yet, because the other thing he'd watched was the girl laying the job out. And everything about how she did it was every way Jack would have done it. Because she did it the way Jack had been trained – and that meant Dragon.

Except there shouldn't have been any Dragon way. Not this time. Jack had taken care of that. It just looked like

181

someone, somewhere, hadn't got the memo. Jack figured he'd take care of delivering it. Maybe he'd wrap it round a fifty cal. Hellround. Because someone knew way too much – and maybe the Dragon hadn't been Barbas' idea after all. Or if it had been once, maybe it wasn't now. Jack winced. He could feel a headache coming. Mostly he left those to Haures, but mostly those didn't involve a kid who could put a bullet in Jack's head. Especially one Jack wasn't allowed to kill. No, scratch that. Jack knew he'd get in front of any bullet headed her way himself if he had to – he just didn't know why. And not knowing what was going on tended to have a price. A price people often wanted to be Jack, but one Jack made sure someone else paid. Jack figured it was that time again. He smiled - cold enough to give an ice-berg an inferiority complex. He did it again. It had been way too long since he'd had any fun anyway.

Following the girl had been a bitch. Not so much the following – that was just following a hole where a soul should be. It was the tail made it harder, but it made things easier too. When things got cramped, Jack could drop back and follow the tail instead. That way, if the tail turned out to be a problem, Jack would know exactly where to put his next slug. But the tail never made a move on the girl. All he did was take a glowing red stone out of his pocket every now and then – and talk to it. That was when things started to make sense. Because that made it...

***

May 06, 1937 – Lakehurst (New Jersey), May 06, 1937

The man in the black leather duster tightened the last bracing wire. The wires didn't actually need to snap – they just needed to look like they *could* have snapped. The one he'd already broken hung where he'd left it, the tear he'd put in the hydrogen cell above it on a path the broken wire could have made. He checked he could still see the photographer's flashbulb, wired to a dry cell battery and a radio receiver, tied to the edge of the rip in the gas cell.

The cell had been leaking hydrogen for a good ten minutes or so. It was nearly time.

The landing delay wasn't going to help any. Jack was supposed to be well clear of the ship before the Big got into Bang. It was going to be tight. But landing activity had started, and the rigger should be along soon. Jack clipped a line onto the walkway running under Gas Cell 4, rolled off the walkway and waited. He'd been doing it for three days since he'd sneaked on at Rio. A little more wouldn't hurt. He waited some more. The sound of the rigger's footsteps on the gangway was all he needed. Young Eric didn't know it, but his head was about to make a great hat-rack. As Spehl came under the torn hydrogen cell, Jack triggered the radio transmitter. The battery circuit closed and the flashbulb did its job. Jack crawled back along the gangway, the burning hydrogen playing tag with his heels. As LZ 129 fell from the sky, Jack jumped to the landing gantry and made his way to the rendezvous. He waited some more.

After a while, the Countess' agent arrived, still dressed in her nurse's uniform. "So, Shadow. Let's see how you did, shall we?" She was pissed. She pulled out her file. "First, Spehl didn't die. You were supposed to kill him. I had to take care of it myself. That's twenty points off, right there." The nurse made note in her file.

Jack shrugged. "One more dead body isn't very interesting. You wanted everyone looking elsewhere. I gave him a post-hypnotic suggestion. He was going to write a suicide note confessing. Better headlines."

"You changed the plan?"

Jack shrugged again. "I changed the plan."

"You're not allowed to change the plan! He might have resisted! He might not have written..."

Jack reached into his pocket. The nurse flinched. Jack smiled. The nurse flinched again. She hadn't believed the stories about this trainee. She was beginning to wish she had. Jack handed her a sheet of handwritten paper. She read it – and crossed out the number on her file. "OK. So you're a hot-shot. Not hot enough to see me following you, trainee. That's another..." she looked at the 100 on her file sheet, the 20 points she'd taken off added again. "OK, so it's still twenty points off.. I've been on your ass since..."

Jack sighed. "You got on in Rio..."

"How do you know I got on in Rio? You boarded at Frankfurt!"

Jack shook his head. "Of course I did. I'm a good little boy, and I did as I was told. I didn't get on early, and I didn't see you in your pink Schiaparelli. By the way. That Empress Eugenie hat really didn't work for you." Jack's grin got even colder. "You switched to the Norman Hartnell in Frankfurt. I think you looked better in the night camo, while you were watching me do all the hard work in the gas bag. Oh, here's a list of the contents of your underwear drawer from the Rio run. The second sheet's got the Frankfurt. For the record, you snore. Loudly. Oh, and..." Jack reached into his other pocket and took out a glass vial "... here's the antidote."

The nurse blanched. "Antidote?"

"To the delayed action poison I injected you with last night. In case you..." Jack glanced at the file in the nurse's hands "... turned out to be a hostile."

"So you knew I was there." The nurse's voice was flat. "You knew I was there all along, and you poisoned me."

Jack shrugged. His cold eyes never left the nurse's.

The nurse sighed. "You're a bastard, Shadow." She scribbled over the new 80 on her file, replaced it with a 100. "You're a bastard, but you're ready for field ops, I guess." She raised an eyebrow, and smiled. "So what do you think? Maybe we should celebrate? I'd love to get out of this dumb uniform." She smiled. "And maybe some other things."

Jack reached out, pulled the nurse close. She opened her lips for the kiss. Jack's forehead slammed forward, and he dropped the unconscious woman to the ground. He searched her pockets, and pulled out the flask. He looked down at the nurse. "Well. I could sure use a drink." He took the cap off the flask. The smell of Unicorn horn filled the air. Then he was gone.

* * *

... that made it a training run. He watched the little old bag lady who wasn't a bag lady drink what the wind said was Unicorn Horn. Then she was gone. Jack expected the mage currently Shifted to a traffic cop to do the same. He didn't. He looked round and didn't see Jack, just like all the other times he hadn't seen him. He walked away. Nobody ever saw Jack – or at least, they never remembered seeing him if they did.

Sometimes Jack didn't even have to kill them to help them forget.

Jack followed. As the cop turned a corner, he took a ring from his pocket and Shifted into a teen-punk. The punk walked into a side alley. He checked his six, and Jack wrapped Shadow round himself. The mage who'd shown him how to do it had talked about 'partial-temporal-dislocation'. Jack had called it 'wrapping Shadow', and the mage had limped off, muttering about technical philistines. The punk took a sheet of paper from his pocket, and taped it to the wall. He wrote on it with a thick felt marker, then took a red gem from his pocket. He looked at it, and swore. Which, Jack thought, was also interesting. He'd bet very few people in the current world knew enough Old Saxon to say 'Good Morning', never mind 'shit in a church'. Jack did – but that was just business. He remembered Corfe, and the snap of Edward's arm as Jack pulled him from his horse. The punk swore again. He tore the paper off the wall and stomped out of the alley. Jack followed him. Watched him as he picked his target - another down and out in another alley. Watched him as he pushed the red gem against the down and out's head, as he pushed a knife through her eye and into her brain. The gem filled with a dull red glow. The punk taped the sheet of paper to the alley wall and began to chant. The spell didn't take long – but his scream took longer as a burning fire filled the gem in his hand. Now dull eyed, he held the gem tight. He leaned in to read the sheet of paper, then tore it from the wall. He took a flask from his pocket, and the smell of

Unicorn Horn filled the air. The teen punk drank – and was gone.

Jack frowned. That made two too many people getting horny for Jack's liking. But things were working out. Someone wanted to know if the girl was ready for something. She wasn't. Not quite. Jack was willing to bet the tail had a file. And he'd bet that file had a number in it the girl wasn't going to like. Jack did. That number meant he'd have another chance to find her. To find her, and to find who wanted the girl to be ready to give Jack a 357 blow job. Jack grinned. He and the girl had some talking to do. Talking they'd do Jack's way. He took his flask out – and the smell of Unicorn horn filled the air.

Chapter Eleven
Back to the Future

"Sixty! What do you mean, sixty? I got more than that in tenth grade English! And I'd never even *heard* of Coleridge!"

"Coleridge? What's Coleridge got to do with...?" CG looked down at the clipboard in his hand, then up. Then down again at the numbers on his pad. He was looking like he was trying out for the Confused Olympics.

I didn't give a shit. I was pissed. "OK, smartass. So tell me."

"Yes, Ealdric. Do tell. I'm quite fascinated. AS I'M SURE AGENT MAYA IS. Isn't that right, darling?"

I hadn't heard Mom come in. That wasn't good. Because nobody creeps up on me. I remembered the bug I'd had in my ear during the mission. Well. Probably nobody. So if Mom had, I hadn't been paying attention. That wasn't just not good. It could get me dead. So it was time to stop being pissed, and start being smart. Of course, that wouldn't stop me kicking CG's ass later. Yup, pissed *and* smart. I shrugged. "OK, boss." I looked at CG. "So hit me, C."

"I wish." CG probably thought he'd said that under his breath. Mom winked at me, and smiled. I wondered if that meant she had or she hadn't already dug a hole for me out in the desert. CG turned to look at Mom. "Field report on Agent Maya, preliminary field assessment mission."

Mom raised an eyebrow. "Preliminary?"

CG shrugged. "I regret to inform my esteemed boss that Agent Maya failed to attain a passing grade. Just, I will refrain from reminding my esteemed boss, as I told you she would, boss."

"Don't be a smartass, Ealdric." Mom's voice could have chilled the vodka I wouldn't have turned down right now quite nicely.

CG blanched. "No, ma'am. My apologies, ma'am."

"Boss will do Ealdric." Mom smiled. I wondered what frozen vodka actually tasted like. "Report."

"Yes, ma'... er, boss." CG consulted his notes. "Agent Maya completed the mission as per specification, L. The target was terminated, and the method was indeed suitably loud. However, as a primary issue, she did not detect me following her. So that's twenty points off, right there. Second, she was sloppy with the video files. I know for a fact there were a couple of times the tape showed her on the stairs as the guard while it showed the guard somewhere else at the same time. Mind you..." CG sounded puzzled. "I checked the tape just before she blew the building. It was clean. No twin brother for Mr Warren. How did you do that, Maya?"

"Maybe if you don't know, you should be thinking about that number some, huh?" I grinned. I wasn't as good as Mom yet, but my vodka wouldn't be needing any ice cubes. Problem was – I was faking. I really had missed the tapes. And whoever the hell had fixed them, it sure wasn't me. So if it hadn't been CG, that meant there's been someone else I missed on my ass. Someone who had my back. I wondered what for. I could almost feel a target painted there – I just didn't know who was holding the gun.

"Agent Maya has a point, don't you think Ealdric?" I could tell Mom was amused. "On the other hand, Agent Maya, I really do think you should have detected Ealdric's presence. Don't you, dear?"

I winced. Like always, Mom didn't really care who won the battles. Either way, she knew she was going to win the war. "Yes, Mom. I..."

"Boss will do, dear. We are at the office, after all."

It's hard for a few words to drop the temperature in a room thirty degrees. I swear, Mom's could do fifty and give a dollar change. I winced again. "Yes boss."

CG scribbled on his clipboard. He crossed out the 60, and wrote a neat 70. "There was also the matter of the target. Agent Maya let her go to work, and relied on the explosion to terminate her. She then had to wait, to make sure the target didn't escape the building. While there was no sign of her, and indeed later reports confirmed her termination, in my view it would have been better for Agent Maya to eliminate the target herself the previous evening, and then place her body in the explosion, and..."

I laughed. "And that's why you're Rear Echelon, CG. Not Field." I grinned. I had this one cold. "Mom? Er, boss?" Mom tilted her head, and nodded, very slightly. But she was grinning too. It was looking like I might even get to drink that vodka. "CG, your way, sure. I wouldn't have had to wait for her to come out. But there'd have been too many flags."

"Flags?" Cg's Olympic Gold was looking like a done deal. His voice already had him on the podium.

"Yeah. Flags. Like, the guy she sees on the street every morning on the way to work, walking his dog. The guy she always says hi to. The guy who never saw her that day, and remembers when the cop comes round and ask him questions, because she always gives his dog a treat. Or the lady in the coffee shop she always buys her morning coffee from, who remembers her because she's a lousy tipper, and remembers she didn't come in that day. Or..."

"There aren't any such people! They're not in the file!" CG grabbed the target file and started flipping through it.

I put my hand on his arm. "It's OK, CG. Calm down. They're not there. I mean, I have no idea who they are. There might not be a dog, or a coffee shop. But there's always *someone*. Actually, someone-s. Little people, little things. Things that get missed from the file. Things dumb cops pounding beats they could walk in their sleep find right away. Things that raise questions. Flags. So my way was better." I didn't even look up from CG. "Right, boss?"

"Absolutely, dear." I could hear Mom was grinning. CG wasn't. He scrubbed the 70, and wrote a neat 80. I raised an eyebrow. He crossed out the 80, and wrote 85.

"But you still missed Ealdric, dear. So I think you need another job, before we can – well, before we move on. Something to make sure you know how to remain properly aware of your surroundings. And I think you've given me an idea. Ealdric? My office please. Oh, and do be a dear. There's a book I'd like you to bring. Number 978-1236735959, I believe." She grinned. "And Maya? Well done. Very well done indeed." She smiled. The smile told me I'd been right, Back Then. Something really was fucked. And it was starting to feel even more like it was me.

Sonata
Sviluppo - Quarto Movimento

Washington D.C. - 350 And Down

"So she works for... for someone who wants you dead." Prowess wasn't playing the piano. Mostly, she was hitting things. Anything that <u>wasn't</u> her piano.

"Yup." The man in the black leather duster unloaded his gun. Then he reloaded it.

"So they're training her." Prowess kicked the wall. "Then when she does what they want – they kill her! It doesn't make sense!"

"Sure it does." The click of bullets in a magazine echoed in the room. Then the click of them being removed.

"Not to me!"

"She's me. She's me, and the kid's Jack."

"You? She can't be! And the kid - we left Jack at Baie St Marie! Or... what do you mean, she's you?"

"Me? What are you talking about, P?"

"You said she's you, Jack! And you said the kid's Jack!" Prowess' lips moved as she tried to make sure she had enough Jack's between them and not one too many. Either way, she didn't look as though the ones she had tasted too good.

Jack sighed. "Right. She's me, and the kid's Ruby. Jack Ruby."

Prowess raised her eyebrows. "You know Jack, you have way too many Jacks in your life. She paused, her brow furrowed. "But she doesn't look like any bloody Jack I ever knew. Oh damn. You made me say a Bad Word! You happy now Jack? And if she's you, then who are you?"

Jack sighed again. "Me? I'm John K. I'm the President of..." He paused. "Well, probably not. Be kind of hard being a President nobody noticed. And most everybody noticed John K. No. Even Dallas wasn't <u>that</u> confusing. But she's still me. See, I mean it's like the Kennedy thing. Like Dallas."

"You mean - Jack, did you shoot Kennedy?"

"Me? No. Well, or yes. One of those. See, he was Dragon, Kennedy was. Right through the middle. Dragon heard he was going to get retired. So they sent me to find whoever shot him. Persuade whoever it was not to. Permanently. Thing is, I did."

"You stopped him? Jack, I hate to tell you this – but you didn't. Kennedy was assassinated."

"Oh, I know that, P. No. I didn't stop him. But I found him. Right before he pulled the trigger."

"So you saw Oswald? Why didn't you stop him Jack?"

"Oswald? Who said anything about Oswald?"

"<u>You</u> did! You said you saw Oswald going to shoot Kennedy!"

Jack sighed a third time. He'd obviously had a lot of practice. "No I didn't, P. I said I saw who shot Kennedy. And that wasn't Oswald. Oswald was just a patsy."

"Patsy? You mean Oswald was a girl? Like Nixon? But..."

"Girl? Who said Oswald was a....?"

It was Prowess' turn to sigh. "You did, Jack. You said Oswald was really Patsy. Like Nixon was really Lucy, right?"

Jack shook his head. "Not <u>Patsy</u>. <u>A</u> patsy. See, it was like this...

* * *

Some Where. Some When.

"So there it is, Shadow. Someone's going to give Agent Kennedy a six and a half millimeter headache. A rather permanent one, unfortunately." A faint look of disgust marred the lips of the man with the silver topped cane. "Millimeters, Shadow. I'd ask you what the world was coming to if it wasn't exactly what we were making it." The man with the silver topped cane curled his lip. "Millimeters. If the inch was good enough for Edward the Third, it should be good enough for anyone." He sighed. "But as I said, there it is. And there you are, Shadow. Or you'd better be. Find whoever it is, and get them out of our business. Just remember – forget Oswald. It's the Knoll. We don't know much, but we know that." The man with the cane raised an eyebrow. "So why are you still here?"

Jack didn't look up from the mission file, or the map and photographs spread on the table. He sighed. Umbrellas. Tramps. Magic bullets. OK, so maybe magic bullets. The rest was – messy. Busy. Someone had gone to a lot of trouble to make a mystery – and to make one where no mystery needed to be. Which meant a total amateur – or someone really good at what they did. Which didn't matter. However good they might be, Jack was better. He took the flask from the table, and let Dealey Plaza soak into him. He could almost feel the Paradox Storm round him. He uncapped the flask – and the smell of Unicorn Horn filled the room. Then he was gone.

The cane tapped as the man walked out of the room and up the corridor – a sound not yet the terror of Whitechapel. He turned into a small side room. "It is done." His voice was surprisingly deferential, even scared, for someone speaking to a young boy not yet past puberty.

"Excellent, Jack. Lil... My Lady will be pleased." The man with the cane raised an eyebrow, but said nothing. "Ah. Of course. Your... payment." The boy took a wrapped package from a shelf and opened it. In the box, red gems shone with dull glows. He handed the man with the cane a small notebook. "This will tell you how to use them. You understand, it will hurt a great deal?"

The man with the cane smiled. "There is a price for everything." He turned to leave. His cane tapped a song the streets of Whitechapel would learn soon enough.

*** * * ***

Dealey Plaza – November 22nd, 1963

Just in, a bullet, and out. Another day at the office. The buzz of Dealey Plaza filled Jack's ears. He made his way up Elm Street, heading into the Plaza. Whoever was there would never see him coming. People never did – or never noticed. He heard the sound of the motorcade coming into the plaza – and he saw the figure on the Knoll. The figure nobody was looking at – the figure nobody was noticing. He took his gun from his pocket, and walked towards the man on the Knoll, a bead on the side of the man's head. The figure turned – and Jack froze. He looked at himself, as he smiled, and put a finger to his lips. He looked at himself as he raised his gun – and fired at the oncoming motorcade. He watched himself, as he took a flask from his pocket – and the smell of Unicorn Horn filled the air. Then the him he knew he'd never been – at least not yet - was gone.

*** * * ***

"Only target I ever missed, P. Well, I wasn't going to kill me. So anyway, whoever it was, they'd set Oswald up to take the fall. Hell, he might even have believed he did it. There's ways. Not that it mattered. Two days later, a guy called Jack Ruby put a thirty eight slug in Oswald. Sure stopped anyone asking him any questions."

"So you killed Kennedy – but it wasn't you?"

"Could be, P. Or it might be – but I didn't do it yet."

"So that's why they killed her. To cover their tracks. Like Ruby, when he shot Oswald."

"Could be. That's one reason, anyway."

"What's the other, Jack?"

"Well, P. It's like this. See, it's like, there was this farmer once. And he had a load of sheep..."

"Flock."

"Hey, P. Language! Anyway, you never swear. What's wrong?"

"I did so not swear! I said... Oh. Right. You're teasing. So tell me about the flocking sheep, Jack." P smiled.

"Flocking sheep. Riiight." Jack smiled. Then he stopped. "So this farmer, he has these sheep. Which is great, because he can take them to market, and sell them and get rich, right? But there's this tiger. And this tiger, it likes sheep. So it keeps killing them and eating them. Now the farmer, he doesn't like that. He can see his getting rich getting real unlikely to happen. So he goes to the market and he talks to this other guy, and this other guy, he has him a trained bear. And this bear, it's been trained not to like eating sheep. So the farmer buys the bear, and he keeps it hungry, and then one night, he lets it out near the sheep. And the tiger comes by to get him some sheep, but the bear's there, and the bear might not like sheep, but nobody told him, or maybe it's a girl bear, not to like tigers. So she, the bear I mean, she kills the tiger and eats it."

"Oh. Right. Is that it then? So this girl, she's like..."

"No. That's not quite it, P. See, the farmer, he hears the girl – I mean the bear – and the tiger fighting. And he comes by and he sees the dead tiger, and the bear's eating it. But that bear, it's real hungry. And there's all these sheep, but it's been trained not to like sheep. So it kills the farmer, and it eats him too."

"Oh. So..."

"So if you get a bear to kill a tiger, you'd better think about what you're going to do with the bear afterwards. Before it does it to you."

"So you're the tiger, Jack?"

Jack grinned. It wasn't a warm grin. "Me? No." His hand ran over a lump in his leather duster. "No. I'm a dragon."

"So... so what are you going to do about it, Jack?"

The man in the black leather duster unloaded his gun. Then he reloaded it. Then he grinned again. "What I do best, P. I'm gonna fix it." His grin disappeared. "But there's someone I need to talk to first."

"Talk, Jack? That's not like you. You don't say much, and even when you say something, you still don't say much, right?"

Jack grinned. Or maybe he didn't, and it was just a ghost of the grin that had just died. "Nope. Or yup. Take your pick, P. Or maybe I should say Lee...." As Jack said the word, the name, Prowess froze. Jack nodded to himself.

"That's not nice, Jack." Shadows don't talk. So the shadow on the wall, where no shadow should be, clearly didn't say anything. Which didn't stop Jack hearing it. "You were going to use her old name, weren't you? That hurts her, Jack."

Jack shrugged. "You didn't make me nice, lady."

"Me, Jack? I didn't make you. None of me did."

Jack raised an eyebrow. He shook his head. "I think I'm starting to figure it out. The old guy, he tells the truth in a hundred lies. You, you let someone hear a lie in a hundred truths." He shrugged. "Whatever you say, lady. So who's Lee-Ann?"

"She's someone you knew once. Or someone else knew once, perhaps. One of those. It doesn't matter. Even if it does. So why bring me here, Jack?"

"Answers. Like, I need some."

"Answers, Jack? Don't you have people for those? A Fallen Angel and – well. And."

Jack shrugged again. "Haures would remember I'd asked. I don't think that would be a very good idea. The old guy? He ain't easy to get hold of. Anyway, I didn't have anyone around I could shoot. You spend so much time here, I figured maybe it was time to collect some rent."

"Rent." Shadows don't sigh. So the shadow didn't. The air shivered with the sigh it didn't sigh. "So what do you want, Jack? You know I can't interfere."

Jack didn't grin. The grin he didn't grin would have been a gold medal at the grinning Olympics. "I do? When did I find that out?"

If a shadow could wince, the shadow would have winced. "Damn you, Jack. You really are a bastard. There's only so many times the Universe can be rebuilt, you know."

"I do?" Jack didn't grin. Again. The shadow didn't wince – again. "Amazing, the things I know. Seems like you know what I know before I do. Like it was, maybe, Fa..."

"Don't say it, Jack. Don't be a smart-ass. It doesn't suit you." Jack raised an eyebrow. "OK, so it does. So what was it you wanted to know if you knew, Jack?"

"Souls."

"Souls, Jack? I thought you were more of a jazz man?" It was the shadow's turn not to grin. It did it very well.

"Riiiight." Jack shook his head. "So if Dad..."

"Dad?"

"The old guy. Red and white, and a bad case of 'why me'. I figure Dad's as good a name as any. Whatever I am, he made me. And I'm damned if I'm calling him Boss, Moms."

"*Moms*?"

Jack grinned. "Well, there's three of you, right? And if I drive you crazy, you're supposed to get that from your kids, right?" He grinned some more.

"*Moms*?"

Jack grinned some more. "Dad told me I can Nudge Time because I don't have a soul. So I could probably figure out, that means if someone else can do it, they can't have one either."

"Ah. Logic. I swear, I could bloody murder Apollo sometimes."

"So if Dad made another me..."

"He didn't, Jack." Outside the walls of the room, something very, very large creaked ominously. And loudly. The shadow flinched. "Bugger. Now look what you made me do, Jack. Er – I mean YOU'D PROBABLY..." Outside the walls, the creaking got louder "... ER, I MEAN, YES, YOU'D DEFINITELY KNOW THAT, JACK." The creaking stopped. The shadow sighed. "Did I mention you're a bastard, Jack?"

"... or someone else did."

"Of course, you'd know that's impossible, Jack." The voice the shadow didn't have was flat.

"Right." So was Jack's. "I figured I'd know that. So if I knew that, that it was impossible but it had to happen anyway, that would make it a...?"

"Yes, Jack. It would." The shadow's voice was part sad, part wistful. "Would it be so bad?"

Jack shrugged. "Guess I'll find out."

"Yes, you will."

"So I'll need to..."

"Yes, you will. And I'm damned if I'm telling you how." Shadows can't blush. So the shadow didn't. It was good at it - an egg would have fried on the blush the shadow didn't have.

"And then..." Jack's hand brushed over a lump in his leather duster.

"Yes."

"So I need a dragon."

The eyes the shadow couldn't have were sad. "Not this time, Jack. You could probably guess..." Outside, the Universe creaked. Loudly. "I MEAN..." The Universe creaked louder. The shadow stamped a foot, and a shadow rod thumped the wall of the room. "SHUT UP! DON'T YOU MAKE ME COME OUT THERE!" The creaking stopped. The shadow sighed. "Sorry, Jack. It's a union thing. Where was I? I mean, where were you?"

Jack's hand brushed over a lump in his leather.

"Oh. Right. I can't tell you." Jack raised an eyebrow. "No, Jack. I *really* can't. I mean..." the shadow paused. "How did he put it? Er, will put it? Oh, yes. We don't want to get into any trans-temporal-quantum-irregularity universe fucked up and ending paradox stuff, like might happen if the Fates tried to make sure things didn't screw up beyond all recognition rather than just watching, now do we? Something like that, anyway."

"So how do I...?"

Shadows don't have eyebrows. So the shadow didn't raise the ones it didn't have. "I guess you'd better make sure someone who can tell you, tells you Jack. After they find out, of course."

Jack sighed. "Crap. Oh, well. And then there's the kid."

"Yes, Jack. There's the kid."

"That's one of her names isn't it? Thief?"

"Stealer? Yes."

"So that's where he came from. I guess I'm going to have to fix that. But that means he's got a soul. So if he can... well, if he can, I'd know he'd have to..."

The shadow rod tapped the wall. The shadow waited. Nothing creaked. "Yes. Er, I mean, yes you would, Jack."

"And that would really, really hurt. Right?"

"Yes."

"Good." Jack's voice was cold. "And he'd have to have something to put it..."

"Yes."

"And I bet they wouldn't..."

"No. They didn't. Right up to their last breaths."

Jack's eyes got colder. "Right." The shadow that had never been there faded. Jack slipped the last round into his gun. He waited. After a while, the door opened. The two men in leather dusters looked at each other. Both men grinned, and lowered their guns. The man in the doorway raised an eyebrow. "I thought you'd be taller." Jack raised his own brow. "Me too." The man in the doorway reached slowly into the pocket of his duster, and pulled out a small notebook. He dropped it on the floor. "Let's not do this again, huh Jack?" He pulled a flask from his pocket, and the smell of Unicorn Horn filled the air.

Jack picked up the notebook, and began to read. Eyes that were never warm turned slowly to ice. Prowess looked up. "So... so what are you going to do about it, Jack?"

The man in the black leather duster unloaded his gun. Then he reloaded it. His eyes were ice. "What I do best, P. I'm gonna kill someone."

Chapter Twelve
Xanadu

"You want a <u>what</u>?" Most times Mom asked me to do something for her, it meant giving someone a headache. A permanent one, lead lined. This time, it looked like the head was gonna be mine.

"I said, I want a poem, dear."

"You want me to write you a poem? I didn't get a perfect score on a field test, so you want me to write you a fucking <u>poem</u>?"

"No, dear. I don't want you to <u>write</u> me a poem. I want you to <u>get</u> me a poem. And since we're in the office dear, the correct response is not to whine like a spoiled brat. The correct response is 'Yes of course, Boss.'" Mom raised an eyebrow. She waited.

I sighed. "Yes, Boss. Of course, Boss. What fuc... er, what poem would you like, Boss? There's this thing called the Internet. You might have heard of it. I'll just..."

Mom smiled. It was her shark-screaming smile. With extra teeth. "Oh. Of course, dear. I'm sure you know best. But remember. I want all of it. Now let's see. How did it go? 'In Xanadu did Kubla Khan, A stately pleasure-dome decree...'"

I winced. Mom grinned wider. Somewhere, sharks began committing suicide en-mass, which was kind of clever since they couldn't know French. A bad day was turning out worse - and the Internet wasn't going to help.

Sonata
Sviluppo - Quinto Movimento

Some-Where. Some-When. A biker bar on the edge of town.
The girl on the motorcycle she thought she'd stolen from the brother she thought she had smashed through the window of the biker bar. In mid-air, she hauled the bike upright as it fell to the floor. She twisted the throttle just enough to put kick into the rear wheel as it touched down, and the bike slid neatly up to the bar. She reached out, the cycle still growling, and grabbed a beer bottle from the guy leaning on the bar next to her. She lifted it, drained it, and smashed the bottle on the edge of the bar. She licked a spike of glass sticking out from the bottle neck in her fist, and winked at the guy she'd taken it from. "I hear you're recruiting."

Muscles rolled under the tattered leather vest on the guy's back. The patch with a picture of a dragon head in flames was worn, but well cared for. He didn't look at the girl. "Nice riding. But the bike's more use than you are. Take it, boys." The bikers in the bar stood up. Knives and guns filled hands under eyes that looked like they were used to using both.

The man in the leather duster stepped out of Shadow. He raised his gun, and a single shot rang out. A biker near the girl fell to the ground. The man in the leather duster raised an eyebrow, and waited. A whisper ran round the room as bikers with suddenly blanched faces dropped whatever weapon they were holding. Shadow. Shadow. Shadowshadowshadow...

The lone biker at the bar looked at the girl. He looked at the man in the leather duster. "Ri... er, right." he looked at the dead biker on the floor of the bar. "I guess you're right. We're recruiting." He looked behind him, at the scared bikers. "Someone get the bitch..." He stopped, the spike of the smashed bottle in the girl's hand slowly pressing into the pulsing carotid artery in the side of his neck. He gulped.

The girl smiled – and the room chilled. "I may be a bitch – but I ain't your bitch. It's Rosie." she pushed the bottle spike a little harder, red blood seeping round the tip.

The pack leader looked past the girl at the man in the leather duster. The man in leather smiled. The pack leader winced. "Someone get sister Rosie a fucking patch!"

The man in the leather duster stepped over to the girl. He leaned close to her ear. "Now you owe me."

The girl shrugged. "So what's the price?" She wrinkled her nose as a strange smell filled the air "Hey, what's that...?" But the man in the duster was gone.

Chapter Thirteen
Xana-didn't

Fucking Coleridge. Well, not fucking Coleridge. Not really. Fucking Porlock.

See, school and me - we don't get along so good. It's not that I hate knowing stuff. You want to know where to find C4 in Cleveland, I'm your girl. You want to know why you don't hold a gun sideways like they do in the movies, sure. I can tell you. On the other hand, you want, like, the capital of Nicaragua, unless Mom's got a job for me there I could care less.

But I got an A in English last year. Top of the class. Which was kind of cool, since English was about the only class I went to without a gun to my head.

What happened was, Mom had a job, and she couldn't do it herself. Well, that's what she told me. Now, I wondered if it was, like, try outs for the swim club. Not that I ever tried out for anything. But maybe like Mom giving me the one-last-time to see if I'd fit in the Organisation. Anyway, she said she had this job, and it needed to be done clean. So she asked me if I could do it, and I said sure, and she sent me to... well. Never mind. If I told you on where, I'd have to kill you as well. But the hit was clean, 'cause that's what I do. So Mom got me a little sugar. Like, the English paper I had coming and hadn't studied for because I was putting a 357 headache on - on someone who's none of your business, but who'll never need an aspirin again. I mean, I wasn't gonna study for the damn thing anyway, but Mom got me the English paper, and the answers too.

That's when I met Sammy.

OK. So I didn't actually, like, *meet* him. Not then, anyway. But it sort of felt like it. See, the paper was all about Kubla Khan. Or I guess It wasn't. Not Kubla Khan the guy in history. It was Kubla Khan, the poem. How this Kubla guy built this shit-hot palace called Xanadu, and – well, and not so 'and'. Because it wasn't so much Xanadu, as Xana-didn't. See, Sammy, that's Sammy Coleridge, he was a junky. Like, they didn't have much to ride on back in the day, but Sammy didn't let that stop him. He liked his poppy, and one night he decided to get on the horse, even if it wasn't, like, horse. And he'd had a wild dream, all about the Kubla guy and Xanadu. So he woke up and he started writing it all down in a poem, because that's how he dreamed it. And it was a really cool poem, like, amazing. Until somebody knocked on the door. I mean, he's writing this, like, mad-cool poem, and some fuck-wit from Porlock, which was just down the road from where Sammy was living, knocks on the fucking door. Probably trying to sell him insurance, or a lifetime subscription to 'Why I never finished writing the best poem of all time'. Because he didn't. Sammy, I mean. He didn't finish it. By the time he got rid of Porlock, he'd forgotten his dream. So all he had was, like, these fifty-four lines, and it should have been hundreds. But I liked it, and I hadn't minded boning on it for the paper. But that was the thing. It was never bloody finished. And now Mom was telling me that was what I had to bring her. The whole damn thing. Which really only meant one thing. And what it meant was, someone from Porlock was about to have a really bad day. And I was going to get to give it to him. Or her – Sammy never really said. Now I was going to be the one who made sure he never had to.

* * *

The British Library, St Pancras, London, England.
"I'm telling you Curator, it was bloody gone! I came in, to make some notes for the next bunch of bloody Philistines I'm getting at Oxford, and it was bloody gone! Just an empty case!"

"Yes, Professor Spencer. I'm sure it was. But it isn't now, so that's all right then isn't it."

"No it's bloody well not! It's not all right! Because I came in again this morning, and there's bloody two of them! And... and one's... I mean, I know it's his bloody writing. But look at it! 'Lucille en la ciel avec diamants'! And look at what's under it!"

"Yes, Professor Spencer. I know. And may I commend you on your memory? It's quite remarkable. Almost nobody remembers.. but no matter. And it's scribbled out, yes? So it doesn't really... I mean, after all, we don't actually have to... Look. Just pretend you never saw the damn thing. Ever. We'll burn it."

"Burn it? You can't bloody burn it! This is... it's incredible! It's... I mean, the implications! And a new work by... you can't! When I make my next presentation at the Coleridge society, this is going to be my center-piece!"

"Ah. Yes. I suppose it would be. I mean, will be. Quite. Well, Professor, I suppose there's nothing else for it. I'll have this wrapped for you. It will only take a few minutes. I'm sure my secretary will get you a nice cup of...

of something. She's just outside my office. Why don't you go and ask her?"

"Ah. Right. Yes – tea. Of course, Curator. Tea. Thank you."

The office door closed behind the straggle haired academic. The Curator sighed, and picked up his telephone. "Miss Clark? Yes, I'm afraid it's another one. Coleridge this time. And the Professor... Yes. He does seem a little excited, doesn't he? No, Miss Clark. I don't think he's the type to forget easily. Tell Doctor Bailey we won't be needing him and his flickering lights. We'll have to... Yes. Indeed. Would you...? Ah, the brake line on his car? An excellent idea Miss Clark. I can see you'll go far. Ah. Very droll, Miss Clark. No, I wouldn't go far in the Professor's car either. But let's make sure the Professor does. We don't want anything too close to... Very good, Miss Clark. You'll take care of it? Thank you." The Curator put his down his telephone, picked up one of the two manuscripts on his desk – and lit a match.

* * *

From The Times Obituary Column.

It is with deep regret that we must report the death of world renowned Coleridge scholar Professor Wilberforce Spencer. Professor Spencer was returning to Oxford from studies at the British Library when his vehicle lost control while...

* * *

The Coleridge Museum, Nether Stowey, England.

"But... but it's impossible, sir!"

"Well, Mrs Wilkinson. I'm sure it seems impossible. But..."

"But it's fresh, sir! I mean, it's clean! And it's <u>new</u>! Well – some of it is."

The Museum Director looked down at the lock of hair on his desk. He looked up at the Museum Manager in front of the desk. "Mrs Wilkinson. This is a lock of Samuel Taylor Coleridge's hair. It would be rather difficult for it to be new. Mr Coleridge has, after all, been dead for..."

"But it is, sir! It is! I... well, sir. I know it's not really proper. But first it disappeared, and then it came back, but it was – well, it looked wrong sir! There was too much of it! When I saw it in in the cabinet – well, I had to know, sir! My grand-son, he's at Southampton University, sir. So I sent... well, just some hairs..."

The Museum Director sighed. Clearly, today wasn't going to be a good day. Now he just had to find out who it wasn't going to be good for. "You sent him some hairs, Mrs Wilkinson? Without asking me first?"

"Well, yes sir. I just... I needed to know, sir!"

"And do you, Mrs Wilkinson? Was your son able to – to help?"

"Well, his girlfriend is studying Forensic Psychology sir, and..."

The Director sighed again. "I see."

"Yes, sir. And she took them to the lab, sir! The hairs, I mean. And some of them - they're _new_, sir! Not all of them – just some. Which means – well, I don't know _what_ it means, sir! It's incredible, isn't it?"

"Absolutely, Mrs Wilkinson. Quite – incredible. But we have to be careful with these things. So I have to know. Have you told anyone else? Apart from your son, I mean. Well..." The Director made some notes on the pad in front of him "... and his girlfriend, of course."

"Oh no, sir. I came right to you."

The Director nodded. "That's good, Mrs Wilkinson. Now, it happens that the Curator of the British Library is a friend of mine. I think you should show him your... your find. And it would probably be a good idea if you took your son and his girlfriend as well – so he can get the whole picture, you understand."

"The British Library sir? The _Curator_? Oh, sir! That would be wonderful! I'll call my son right away!"

"Yes, Mrs Wilkinson. You do that."

As the door to his office closed behind his Museum Manager, the Director sighed for a third time. Then his picked up his telephone, and dialed a number. "Ah. Miss Clark. May I speak with the Curator? Oh. I see. Well, if you could tell him I've sent someone to see him. Well, three someones actually. I'm afraid it's Coleridge. Yes, I know Miss Clark. Someone's been rather careless. Oh, you'll take care of it? Thank you, Miss Clark."

The Director hung up the telephone, and took out a file. He sighed for a fourth time. He hated interviewing for new staff.

* * *

From The Bridgewater Mercury.

It is with regret that we must report the death of local historian Florence Wilkinson of Nether Stowey. The sad victim of a road traffic collision, Mrs Wilkinson was killed when her vehicle lost control as a result of a burst tire, despite having recently been serviced. The accident also claimed the lives of her passengers – her son Robert and his friend Alice Drake...

* * *

Mom was pissed. I could tell – mostly by how much she was smiling. So I wasn't really surprised when I went to CG for a mission pack and he said she'd told him not to give me one. So I asked him how the fuck I was supposed to lock on to Sammy Coleridge and he said it wasn't his fucking problem and how Mom had told him it was *my* problem. Which was when he patted my butt and told me to be a good little agent and get on with it. And if he hadn't been only eight, plus a thousand years or so of not being nine, we might have gone somewhere and talked about my butt some more. But he was, and if Mom was pissed, I was pissed-er, so he shouldn't have been surprised at what happened next. I mean, I don't think I broke *too* many bones.

OK. Maybe I did.

Still, I felt bad when I stormed out of the office and finally felt what he'd slipped into my back pocket while he was patting. The guide to the British Museum was interesting, especially the big black circle round their exhibit of 'probably the original manuscript of Coleridge's Xanadu'. And the pamphlet for the Coleridge museum seemed to want everyone to know about their lock of Coleridge's hair. Then I thought about it, and decided it was all Mom's fault anyway and CG would just have to look after himself. Because without a mission pack to tell me how to get when, and when, I needed to be, I needed something else – and the first something else was a plane ticket.

Sonata
Sviluppo - Sesto Movimento

October 18th, 1797. Ash Farm, between Porlock and Linton.

The man in the black leather duster clapped his hand over a mouth for the eighth time. A twist, and bone snapped.. The kid hadn't done a bad job on the team covering the door, but he figured she was supposed to. She'd missed the cover team – also like, it looked, she was supposed to. Jack dropped the body, and dug the dull red gem fragment from its forehead. He'd seen that trick before. Jack slipped the gem fragment into his pocket to join the other seven, and picked his way through the six dead bodies of the decoy team.

The door to the farmhouse was open. He wrapped Shadow around himself. This was going to be tricky. He checked the loads in his gun again, and the thing in his pocket. Then he stepped through the door. The two of them were where they were supposed to be.

* * *

In a place that didn't actually exist, an old man in a blinding white vest and red overalls chuckled. The shadow hanging on a wall that wasn't actually there - didn't. "What the...? The Idiot! Was this your idea? Is he going to...? But he can't do that! I mean, I couldn't do... It's impossible!"

The old man shrugged. "Ah. Impossible. So if he does it then, that's, like, a Paradox?"

The shadow not hanging on the wall that wasn't there sighed. "You know, you really are a bastard."

The old man shrugged again. "Well, someone has to be."

Shadows don't smile. So the shadow that wasn't really there didn't. Widely. "Idiot."

The old man grinned. "Always."

The shadow sighed. "So? Are we going to help?"

The old man raised one eyebrow. "You mean cheat?"

The grin the shadow didn't have got even wider. "I won't tell anyone if you don't."

The old man's grin couldn't have been wider. "That's my girl."

Shadows don't blush. So this one didn't – bright pink.

* * *

Jack concentrated, wrapping Shadow round the two figures in front of him. Then he raised his gun, and pulled the trigger. The Sig P239 stopped pointing at the back of the girl's head and fell to the floor. The man who'd been holding it clearly thought the gun had the right idea and followed it down. The girl spun on her heel, her hand going under her short skirt. Jack figured he was supposed to be distracted. The skirt rode up, mostly because of the Glock in the girl's hand. Jack's gun fired again, and the Glock flew out of the girl's hand. Jack grinned. "I saw that in a movie once. Always wanted to try it."

The girl spat. "Bastard! You just killed Coleridge!" She spun on her heel again, her foot slammed into Jack's head in a perfect ushiro geri. Or it would have, if Jack's head had still been there.

Jack slid one step sideways. The heel of his palm slammed under the girl's chin, snapping her head back. His other arm curled under her unconscious head, cradling it with an odd gentleness. He lowered the girl to the floor. "Yeah" he whispered. "We should talk about that." He ran his hand up the inside of the girl's thigh. His hand stopped. He nodded to himself, his eyes cold. He took a flask from his pocket and opened it. The smell of Unicorn Horn filled the air.

Chapter Fourteen
Calendar Girl

So I know what you're thinking. It's, like, hey. The girl can travel in time, go any-place she wants, any-when. So why does she need a plane ticket? Like, even if she doesn't have a case file, she can make a good guess. And if she gets stuck, she can always come back and try again, right?

Guess what. It's not that easy.

One of the first things CG warned me about was flying blind. Like, as in not doing it. Ever. Which is why the Organisation does the whole case file thing. Because a bad signpost is worse than no signpost at all. Like, if my target is, say, Santa Claus. And I figure I don't need no steenkeen' case plan, because everybody knows you can find Santa any day before Christmas Eve, at the North Pole loading up his sleigh. So I get me some Horn on, and I send myself to last Christmas Eve and the North Pole, so I can have a nice little chat with Mr S about the pink jumper I somehow got and not the new pink bō shuriken I was <u>supposed</u> to be getting.

Bad Idea. <u>Real</u> bad.

See, I hate to break it to you, but there ain't no Santa Claus. So even though there is a North Pole, Christmas Eve or Labor Day, he isn't going to be there. But the Horn, it doesn't care. I do anything quite that dumb, it's going to send me *some* damn place. I've got no idea how the damn stuff works, and from what CG said, neither does anyone else. But it's like it's alive or something. Or maybe it just opens you up to the Universe, and the Universe is alive. With a really fucking warped sense of humour. Because if I was dumb enough to try the Santa Claus thing, the Horn, or maybe the Virgin's Tears, they'll latch on to something else I was thinking of. Or maybe something else <u>someone else</u> was thinking of, or to atmospheric conditions, to shoes, to ships to sealing wax – to any damn thing it finds. And it'll send me <u>somewhere</u>. Some<u>when.</u> But not to any-place or any-when <u>I</u> wanted. Which isn't likely to be good for me, or for anyone who gets in my way when I get there. And I know. I can hear you, even if you're not saying anything. Like, so I just get more Horny, and I come back, right? No. Not right. See, I get back because I know how I got <u>there</u>. Even if I have no idea how it works, I still somehow know, CG told me. But if I don't know where I am, I don't know how to get back. Like, you live in New York, and one day I snatch you and dump you some place. And you wake up and you have no idea where you are, and the people speak some language you don't know, or there's no people, and you know where you came from like the back of your hand, but you still can't click your ruby slippers and take one step back home – because you don't know which way to step.

Remember that Bad Idea thing up there? Well, there aren't many worse.

But Bad Idea or no Bad Idea, I still had to find Sammy C. And I didn't have a case file. Which was entirely what Mom wanted. Like, an initiative test. First I figured I could pound a file out of CG. But I'd already pounded him for the butt thing, and the Organisation infirmary has locks to give Houdini nightmares. So I was stuck with the whole initiative deal, and that meant I had to make one. A case file, I mean. And CG, because maybe he wasn't so bad after all, and maybe we should take some time to talk about my butt when I got back even if he <u>was</u> eight-going-on-a-thousand, had given me some damn good hints. But to do something with them I needed to be some places I wasn't. So yes, a plane ticket. But there isn't much you can't do with an Organisation credit card, which is why the British Library was now short one original manuscript, and the Coleridge museum was down what I was hoping was actually Coleridge's real hair. I'd seen the look in Mom's eye, and I knew that Mom or not, I was either coming back with Xanadu or I was going to get a terminal case of lead poisoning. Or a mind wipe, which might be even worse. Because to her, it wasn't like she'd be losing a daughter. It was like she was going to be getting rid of a fucked-up waste of her time. Either way, I'd be ex-Organisation.

So I'd got me my plane ticket, and I'd danced some night-fandango at the Library. Then I'd come here, to the Coleridge museum. It didn't matter that I'd taken their prize exhibits. If things went well, I'd put them back. I grabbed an imaginary eraser and scrubbed out the imaginary 'if' in my head. <u>When</u> I was done, I'd put them back. Now what I needed was the right date to aim at. Which was a problem. Because nobody seemed to know exactly when Xanadu was actually written. Just possibly smart guesses. But the Mission position's no place to be guessing. Because where there's a will, there's a history book, and a visit to the Coleridge Museum in broad daylight told me all I needed to know.

* * *

January 14th, 1798. Shrewsbury High Street.

I watched Sammy come out of the church. Five foot nine, or near. Pale, wide mouth, thick lips. Long, half curled black hair. Good enough. I slid back behind the alley wall and let him almost-pass. Then I took him from behind, my knife at his throat. Of course, I wasn't going to kill him, but he didn't need to know that.

"I have little coin upon me, if that is your..." For a man with a knife at his throat, he didn't seem very scared. Something was wrong. He reached back. What is it about guys and butts? "That's leather! Who...? Oh. It's you again." His voice was different. I was right. Something was more than wrong. I slapped his legs from under him and dropped him. But I kept him face down. Whatever was wrong, I didn't need it getting worse. "Xanadu. Kubla fucking Khan. When?"

His leg kicked, and it wasn't random. Sammy C couldn't possibly know Muay Thai, but apparently his leg did. "Look. I've got the bloody books. I'll tell mommy you were a good little girl. Now get the fuck off me before anyone sees you."

This was bad. Worse than bad. Badder than a very Bad Thing on a very Bad Bay. Either Mom was even more pissed than I thought, or there was a new player in the game. Either way, I needed a date, and whoever was under me was the closest I had to a Plus Two. I twisted my knife on his throat. "Xanada! Now!"

He chuckled. He fucking laughed! "Oh! I get it! You haven't done it yet! You're the before, not the... Oh. Right. They told me not to say anything about that. Spoilers, they said. Hell, you're good. Maybe even as good as She says you are. OK. October seventeenth. But play nice – no hit..."

I smacked his head hard enough to stop him being a smart-ass for a while, then grabbed my flask. I was already fucked, and nobody had bought me dinner. Someone was going to pay for that, whether I did or not. I pulled the flask from the pocket in my skirt.

Sonata
Sviluppo - Settimo Movimento

Washington D.C. - 350 And Down
The man in the black leather duster checked the cuffs on the girl's ankles and wrists. He looked up at the woman playing a duet with herself on the piano in the corner. None of her four arms and hands missed a note as she nodded.

The man in black leather stepped back carefully, and pulled up a chair, out of reach of the girl's arms or legs even if she got free. Suddenly the piano player's head came up, and she stared at the girl. "Jack! She's..."

"I know, P." The man in the black leather duster unloaded his gun, then loaded it again. But he never took the live round from the chamber, and if he wasn't exactly aiming it at the girl, he wasn't aimless either. "It's dead. Or not alive. One of those."

"No, not the demon, Jack! She's... it's..."

"I know, P. I know." Jack looked at the girl locked in the chair. "So you gonna stop pretending you're asleep kid?"

The girl's eyes opened, piercing blue and cold. She said nothing.

Jack grinned. IT was a shame there wasn't any vodka around needing ice cubes. "So what's it going to be? Dislocate your thumb and pull your left wrist out of the cuff? Then grab your gun, the one you think I was dumb to leave in your thigh holster? Oh. Right. The thigh holster I'm not supposed to know you have, right? Then you're going to kill me." Jack's vice was flat, and his eyes never left the girl..

The girl's eyes widened. "How...?"

Jack shrugged. "Because it's what I'd do. Difference is, I wouldn't be where you are. Anyway. You did that already. Well, killing me, anyway. And I hate repeats." Jack stood up. He stepped over to the girl and unclipped her wrist. He reached under her short skirt, and pulled the Glock from the thigh holster. Then he put the Glock in the girl's hand and stepped back. As the girl pulled the trigger, once, twice, three times, there was a flash of red and white light. He pulled the three petunia blossoms out of the Glock's barrel and tossed them at the wall behind him. Three cracks echoed through the room and three bullet holes opened in the wall. He looked at the girl and raised an eyebrow. "I think Jimmy's a bit too dead to be putting on weight, kid." Jack sat down in the other chair. "So let's talk. About keeping you alive - even if it kills you."

Chapter Fifteen
Piano Girl

October 17th, 1797. Ash Farm, between Porlock and Linton.
There's a lot of things I'd rather have in my mouth than Unicorn horn. Hell, just about anything, and not just what you're thinking. But the bad taste I had in my mouth this time wasn't the Horn. Mostly it was the six guys in Kevlar armour seventeen-ninety-seven shouldn't have known a damn thing about. The ones I was guessing I wasn't supposed to have noticed before I went skipping up to the door of the farmhouse to tell the nice Mr Coleridge not to answer the door to any insurance salesmen from Porlock. The ones with their eyes glued to long sights covering every approach to the farmhouse door. Sights set on top of four hundred and fifteen millimeter barrels able to throw five rounds of thirty-nine-millimeter-you're-fucked every three seconds at any target they saw inside three hundred and fifty meters. Right now I was wishing Mickey K had stuck to fucking poetry.

Poets. You just can't trust them.

Still, where there's a will, there's a way. Or in my case, where there's a piano wire garrote there is. Because whoever put these guys out, they hadn't given them overlapping fields like the kind of books Mom gave me to read when I was six say you should. See, that way if someone's creeping up on you with, like, the piano wire I mentioned, one of your buddies (or two if they're laid right, and I'm never against a guy's buddies getting laid) is half looking at you as well as the kill zone. Like that, the chick with the piano wire, assuming there is one, gets introduced to some real bad news even if she gets you. The way these guys were laid, they weren't going to get laid ever again, at least not by the time I was done with piano practice. But that still left me with a problem. If I cleared the meat, it wasn't going to be as quiet as making it meat in the first place. Sammy was likely to stop the scribbling he'd better be doing right now and come see what the racket was. If I left it where it was, then any passing insurance salesmen might see it. And that was apart from the other thing. The thing I'd missed. I had no idea what it was, but I knew there was something. Because there's <u>always</u> something. That was one of the first things Mom made me learn, and made me learn all over again every day. The time you think you covered everything, the time you think you didn't miss a thing? That's the time you're dead. So I dropped back down the track to the farmhouse, and I kept on dropping. I stayed in cover, but I kept moving. The only thing any insurance salesman was going to need was life-insurance, and the good news was he wasn't going to have to worry about making any more payments. Of course, that was the bad news too.

Or he wouldn't have had to. If he'd existed. Because there wasn't one. In fact, there wasn't anybody. Porlock or Poughkeepsie, this was starting to feel like the wrong Sammy. Like, less Coleridge and more Beckett (some stuff at school wasn't all bad). Because nobody came, and nobody went and nothing happened. All night. Which might have been just fine for Estragon and Vladimir, but not for me. See, I was here to fuck-up history, not get fucked by it – and somebody who might or might not have been an insurance salesman from Porlock was supposed to be dead by now. I had a feeling something was wrong, and the feeling was starting to feel like a friend with benefits. Like, one way or another, I was screwed. It was like a really bad game show, and I had to choose a door. Thing is I only had one and I didn't know if opening it or leaving it shut meant game over. I tossed a coin in my head, and it came down wondering what Sammy C would say to a girl in black leather at his door. I ran back down the track to the farm door – and I knocked.

Sonata
Sviluppo - Ottavo Movimento

Washington D.C. - 350 And Down

The man in the black leather duster sat back in the chair facing the girl. "I'd tell you that you get used to it, but you don't. Not really. You just stop noticing."

The girl's eyes were cold. She said nothing.

The man in black leather raised an eyebrow. "Please yourself. But right now your head hurts like hell and you don't know if it's Thursday or Christmas. Even more than usual I mean. Because you get that a lot. The memory thing, right? Or rather – the not memory."

The girl darted a glance at the four armed woman at the piano. The woman didn't look up, but four hands slid gently into 'Rhapsody in Blue'.

Jack shook his head. "Nothing to do with P. You just got Nudged."

The girl spat. "Nudged? Whatever you hit me with, nudge isn't the half of it. You like hitting girls you bastard?"

"You're lucky, dear. You should have seen what he did to the Countess." The piano player's hands slid into 'El Diablo Cojuelo'.

"Countess? What Countess?"

Jack shrugged. "Long ago, and far away. And besides, she's dead. She bloody well better be, anyway." Jack's eyes went colder than the girl's. "But then, you know all about that. Or Maggie Spencer does, right?"

The girl's eyes narrowed. "Fuck. I <u>knew</u> I missed something. I could feel it. So CG wasn't the only one. I guess Mom's even more pissed with me than I thought, right? So what happens now?"

Jack raised an eyebrow. "Now? Right now, your soul knows you jumped a guy in 1798. Thing is, it knows he got dead in 1797 too. Or rather, it doesn't. Because you don't have one, do you?"

For the first time, the girl grinned. "I don't know about soul. I've always been a jazz..." She stopped. On her face, scared danced with puzzled, and it looked like both had two left feet. "Anyway. Fuck that! And fuck Mom too. Whatever this is, it's on you! You fucked up my mission!

Jack sighed. "Your mission. Yeah, you had a mission. You've always had one. Just one. Want to see?"

"See? See what?"

Jack shrugged. "I don't remember. Not yet, at least." He pulled a bottle from his pocket, opened it and drank. The smell of Unicorn Horn didn't fill the room. "You know how some folk drink to forget? This doesn't do that. This makes you remember. Even things that never happened." He held it out. The girl locked her eyes on his – and nodded. Jack stood up and stepped over to the girl. He tipped the bottle to her mouth. "P?"

The piano player got up, and came over to the two of them. Two hands settled on Jack's head, and two on the girl's. Her fingers sank into their skulls.

Outside the room, the Universe screamed.

Chapter Sixteen
Dead Man Talking

October 18th, 1797. Ash Farm, between Porlock and Linton.

When you're an eighteenth century poet, and you open your door, and there's a gorgeous chick dressed in tight black leather with a pink gun pointed at you standing there, there's a way things are supposed to go. Like, maybe you say whatever the eighteenth century version of 'what the fuck?' might be. Or maybe you don't say anything at all, and your jaw makes a dent in the floor. Or maybe you figure you're still flying on the poppy you did last night, so it's, like, normal. What you don't do is use one arm to knock the chick's gun hand up to the ceiling, then slide your arm up hers to grab her wrist twist and twist it just right to make her drop her damn gun. And you certainly don't step back past her leg and do a perfect Kosoto Gari and put her flat on her back. And even if you do all that, you don't lean over her, and you don't fucking wink and you don't fucking grin and you don't say 'Hey, Maya. You're late.'

I didn't have to ask why the grin looked familiar. Somewhere, I knew some real badass sharks were screaming for their mommies. And some-when, I could almost see my own Mommy Dear with my file, scribbling out Maya and writing in 'Patsy'. So I kicked up, and I hooked my leg over the throat of Mr I'm-not-Sammy-C, and I smacked his head on the floor hard enough to make him forget next Thursday. I'd have blown his head off, but he had to live at least long enough for him to tell me to come back here tonight. Whatever he'd meant about books, I knew what he'd meant about Mommy. Because if nothing else made any sense at all, one thing did – I'd been set up. I was here for something, but it sure wasn't Xanadu. And wherever the real Sammy C was, he probably had a hole in his head that meant a lot more than Xanadu wasn't going to get finished. Or, like, started. I grabbed the bottle in my pocket, opened it – and swallowed.

* * *

Some-When. Middle-of-Nowhere, USA.
"You set me up!"
"Boss. Or ma'am."
"What?" Mom didn't seem fazed by the pink Glock I was pointing at her. Some other time that might have been because of the number of times I'd shot her with it without so much as a bruise on her after. This time it was more likely because I wasn't pointing it. I'd left it on the floor in Ash Farm and didn't have it to point. That wasn't good.

"Boss. Or ma'am. You see dear, this isn't the part where you're my daughter, and we laugh, and you tell me you'll do better next time. This is the part where you work for me, and you remember who's in charge. Although perhaps 'work' is a little bit of an exaggeration for the mess you just made of a perfectly simple task. And I suppose you'd feel more comfortable if you hadn't dropped this, hmm?"

It wasn't a whole lot pink any more, and the rust and years hadn't left it a whole lot of Glock, but it was a whole lot of mine. I caught it from Mom's throw over to me. "OK! So I dropped my gun! So sue me! But..."

"This isn't the type of employer who sues you when you mess up, dear."

I couldn't remember if I'd ever heard Mom's voice so cold. "Mom – OK, so boss – like, the job was already screwed. That wasn't Coleridge. He was one of yours! So how the hell could I get Xanadu off him? I figured I'd come back and tell you he'd..."

"Tell me what, dear? That he'd killed Samuel Coleridge, and you were going to fail English because you knew a whole lot of poems he was never going to write? Surely if he was one of mine I already knew that, brat."

Something was wrong. Mom had called me a whole mess of things in our time, but brat wasn't one of them. I worked the slide on the once-a-Glock. It snapped in my fingers.

"And the mission was never about Xanadu, you pathetic child. It was to see how you handled the unexpected. Which, it appears, you didn't. Not quite as bad as last time, but still – oh, to the Hells with it. I can work on that. A little less obstinate, and a lot more biddable next time, child. And if raising you is always so tedious, at least I get to kill your mother again. Ealdric? Do be a dear?"

They say you never hear the one that kills you. CG must have been using sub-sonic loads, because I almost did. Then the bullet ploughed into my hea....

Sonata
Ricapitolazione – Primo Movimento

Washington D.C. - 350 And Down

"She killed me!"

Wherever the three were, it wasn't quite the room they'd been in. The piano player's fingers stayed deep inside both the man in black's head and the girl's. The man in black leather shrugged. "Could be. Might have been. Might be. One of those, anyway."

"My mother! She fucking killed me!"

Jack shrugged again. "Your mom. Riiight. We should probably talk about that. Just – just not yet. See, thing is, you messed up, kid. She figured you weren't up to the job she needed doing. So she started over."

"Started over?"

"Yeah. Like I'm figuring somebody did to me. Started over. So maybe you wouldn't mess up next time. So maybe you'd be ready."

"Ready? For what?"

"Let's find out." The man in black leather nodded, and the piano player's fingers flexed inside two heads.

* * *

"You know they can't do this either." Shadows don't speak. So the shadow on the wall didn't say anything to air in the room.

"Why not?" Words don't have colours. So the voice wasn't red and white. Even if it was.

"Because it's impossible, of course."

"I thought we'd been through that?"

"Right. But that was just him. Not the piano-player. You know I can't let you do that." A shadow arm reached out, a shadow rod poised to smack down on the frozen man's head.

"Guess not. So you'd better stop it then. Of course..."

"Of course what?"

"Well, you remember it. Remember this, right? So it has to happen. That's how it is, right? Like it's Fa..."

"Don't say it! You know I can't... I mean, trans-temporal-quantum-irregularity universe fucked up and... what is that noise?" The shadow didn't drift off the wall, and it didn't open the door, and it didn't shout at the screaming Universe. "Oh, do be quiet. Don't make me come out there!" Whatever the shadow hadn't done, the Universe decided it didn't want to make it do it again. It fell silent. Since the shadow had never left the wall, it didn't return to it. "OK. So they can't possibly do it. But I remember it. So it must have happened. Just like it did before. Just like it will again." Shadows don't sigh, so the shadow didn't. "You know, I'd be having a headache if it had been invented yet. Has it?"

"Oh, I think so. It was probably my fault." If a red and white laugh could be pink, the air in the room blushed.

"Then I supposed we'd better make sure they can do the impossible again, hadn't we dear?"

The shadow wrapped the room's air close round it, and reached out to the three frozen in the middle of the room. Outside, the Universe thought about screaming again.

Chapter Seventeen
Ash Wednesday

Washington D.C. - 350 And Down
"You know this is impossible, Jack?"
"What is, P?"
"Showing her. Showing her a future she never lived. One **we** never lived."

"**You** didn't, P. Not this time. But **I** did. That's how it works. I remember. Everything. Even the things that didn't happen because they got fixed. Because I fixed them. So take it from me."

"Oh, I believe you, Jack. It's just..."
"No, P. I mean, take it from me. My memory."
"But I can't, Jack! I can't read you! It's impossi... Oh. Right."

"Right, P. See, it was like this. Or it was once..."
October 18th, 1797. Ash Farm, between Porlock and Linton.

When you're an eighteenth century poet, and you open your door, and there's a gorgeous chick dressed in tight black leather with a pink gun pointed at you standing there, there's a way things are supposed to go. Like, maybe you say whatever the eighteenth century version of 'what the fuck?' might be. Or maybe you don't say anything at all, and your jaw makes a dent in the floor. Or maybe you figure you're still flying on the poppy you did last night, so it's, like, normal. What you don't do is use one arm to knock the chick's gun hand up to the ceiling, then slide your arm up hers to grab her wrist twist and twist it just right to make her drop her damn gun. And you certainly don't step back past her leg and do a perfect Kosoto Gari and put her flat on her back. And even if you do all that, you don't lean over her, and you don't fucking wink and you don't fucking grin and you don't say 'Hey, Maya. You're late.'

I didn't have to ask why the grin looked familiar. Somewhere, I knew some real badass sharks were screaming for their mommies. And some-when, I could almost see my own Mommy Dear with my file, scribbling out Maya and writing in 'Patsy'. So I kicked up, and I hooked my leg over the throat of Mr I'm-not-Sammy-C, and I smacked his head on the floor hard enough to make him forget next Thursday. I'd have blown his head off, but he had to live at least long enough for him to tell me to come back here tonight. Whatever he'd meant about books, I knew what he'd meant about mommy. Because if nothing else made any sense at all, one thing did – I'd been set up. I was here for something, but it sure wasn't Xanadu, and wherever the real Sammy C was, he probably had a hole in his head that meant a lot more than Xanadu wasn't going to get finished. Or, like, started. I thought about grabbing for the bottle in my pocket, and somehow it felt wrong. For a moment, it was like the whole universe shivered. But running home to mommy didn't seem like a good idea at all. Mom wasn't big on 'fair' – mostly she was big on kicking my ass for whining.

I'd smacked Mr probably-not-Sammy-C pretty good. It was going to take him a while to wake up, so I took the time to check the farmhouse. The probably-used-to-be-Sammy-C was proving 'the way of the third eye' mostly translated as 'some bastard shot me'. Mr Kosoto Gari had left him lying on the bed, like I was meant to find him. So I went back downstairs. I could tell he was behind the door waiting. So I put on my best sucker-smile and let him get behind me and put his gun to my head. Whoever had taught him hadn't told him that getting close to your target was a bad idea and I knew I could drop him easy if I had to. But first I had to find out why I was really here. "Damn, slick. You got me. So what's the deal?"

"That's better, kid. You're good, but maybe not as good as your Mom thinks you are. Didn't they tell you how you come in a room that might have a gun in it?"

I figured I could either tell him the twenty – I thought a moment – twenty three ways I could have killed him dead, or I could carry on playing a while. Guys tend to be big on size, so long as it's ego and not anything a girl can actually have fun with, so I let him gloat. "Like I said. You got me. So what's a you? I guess that's the real Sammy C upstairs with lead poisoning."

"You catch on quick, kid. What this is, is retirement."

I flexed a muscle or three, just in case. "Retirement?"

"Yeah. The Organisation, well. It can't have people who used to work for it anywhere they can be a problem, or let them drop out of sight. So this is what they do. Some plastic surgery, some language training, a bit of history, and some kid brings me back down the line. 1797 with a bullet, and I get to be Samuel Taylor."

"And the guys with Uncle Mikhail's finest outside?"

"Oh, your... Mom... decided she wanted to see how you handled a hot LZ."

I didn't miss the hesitation. When I didn't say anything, I felt the gun on the back of my head relax. That made the hesitation important. Like, I'd just passed some test, but maybe only because I'd failed. I figured it could wait. "So you get to come back here and live out your life as one of the greatest poets of all time? Beats a pension, I guess."

"Not quite. Or not yet, anyway. See, there's a problem. I mean, I tried his poppy. Good stuff, it is. But this is the best I got." Not-Sammy put his gun away, and I turned round. He handed me a piece of paper. On one side was as far as Sammy had got before somebody very not-from-Porlock had interrupted him. On the back of it... well, I could tell you, but then I'd have to kill you. It's cheaper than the lawyers' bills – and copyright's a bitch. I looked up at Mr not-Sammy. "Your French is lousy."

"Right. And so's your headache."

"Headache?"

"Yeah. The one your Mom told me you'd be having about now."

Thing is, he was right. My head was pounding like John Henry's hammer.

"See, right now, you know all the poems a certain Mr S Coleridge wrote. The ones you learned to pass that English paper your Mom told me about. Thing is, there's a dead body upstairs that isn't going to be big on poetry for the rest of my life, and the best I have is Lucille there. So all that stuff you know he wrote isn't going to get written. And you're going to have to remember it that way too. Because you'll never forget, even if nobody else knows what you do. Because they won't."

"Oh, I forget all sorts of things." And I do. Not important things, like where to get C4 and how to make everything near it C-used-to-be. But things like Coleridge? Hell, I could... I grabbed by head. I could use a fucking Excedrin. Maybe a hundred. And I could use my Mom tied to a table and a whole bunch of red hot needles, that's what I could... "Oh, hell. So what's the catch?"

Not-Sammy-C shrugged. "Your Mom said that was your problem, not mine. So what's it to be, kid?"

I grabbed my Glock. And I grabbed my bottle. I had a headache to get rid of, and no amount of Excedrin in the world was going to get rid of it. But I had an idea for something that might.

***

See, that's the thing with Mom. Whether it's boss-Mom or Mom-Mom, she's not interested in whiners – just winners. She knew I'd figure it out. A trip back home gave me a chance to put Sammy's hair back in the museum. I'd dropped the lock I'd stolen, but not-Sammy and a pair of scissors had obliged. And a visit to a few bookstores soon got me what I needed. I took the big pile of books back to Ash Farm, to Soon-to-be-Sammy. He got a twisted look on his face, and he asked me if, since I'd brought the books back to him already written, and he didn't know a damn thing about poetry, even if he copied them out, like I told him to, on the dates the book said – who the fuck wrote them in the first place? I told him to enjoy his headache – and to get writing. Because if I got one hint of a headache, he'd better hope I was bleeding, or I'd be back.

***

Some-When. Middle-of-Nowhere, USA.
"You set me up!"
"Boss. Or ma'am."
"What?" Mom didn't seem fazed by the pink Glock I was pointing at her.
"Boss. Or ma'am. You see dear, this isn't the part where you're my daughter, and we laugh, and you tell me you'll do better next time. This is the part where you work for me, and you remember who's in charge. And 'work' is looking like just the word I wanted, dear. I've no idea how you did it, but as far as the world is concerned, Mr Coleridge is just the same as he always was. Well done!"
I had a feeling something was wrong. It was a feeling that was getting way too familiar. See, Not-Sammy had said people wouldn't remember. But Mom clearly did. I slipped my Glock into my thigh holster. "Yeah. Well, I saw

your little setup, and went back another day, and I waxed your guy before he could do whatever..." As kites went, it was weak. But it was maybe worth seeing which way Mom's wind was blowing.

"No you didn't dear." Mom took a paper from a file on her desk and read it. She looked up. "You took out the shop-window team. You see? I told you piano lessons would come in useful one day. And you came back and found my former Accountant all he needed to complete Mr Coleridge's work. I have no idea what you did to the backup team, but they were expendable anyway." Mom waved the paper at me. "A friend of mine gave me a full report. In between headaches, of course." Mom smiled. "And don't try and be clever, dear. Do that again, and I might have to think harder about your... long term... employment prospects." The smile was warm. The eyes were cold. I figured the eyes had it. "But an excellent job. Are you ready for another?"

I wondered who her friend was with the headaches. I looked over the desk at the paper. The H at the bottom was very ornate, and burned red - none of which helped. What helped even less was the backup team, and how I'd taken them out. Mostly because I'd never even seen them, never mind taken care of them. And If I hadn't, somebody else had. Somebody I hadn't seen. Which was another feeling that was getting far too familiar. I thought about asking Mom about the Somebody. Then I stamped on the thought and made it wish it had never been born. Mom didn't like questions, only answers. And I didn't have any. Apart from one. "Another job? Sure, boss!"

Chapter Eighteen
Double Date

Some-When. Middle-of-Nowhere, USA.
"You want me to kill <u>Kennedy</u>?"

It's one of those questions old farts ask each other. Like, 'where were you when Kennedy died?'. Organisation players don't get to be old farts much, but I wondered what would happen, if I ever got to be old, if someone asked me that question and I said 'looking over the sights of a Glock'. Hell, I probably wouldn't even have to kill them afterwards – the heart attack would do them nicely.

"No, dear. Well, and yes, of course."

Mom could be like that sometimes. Like, she'd be trying to work out what we should have for dinner, and she'd be, like, 'Well, I could do steak. With tomato sauce. On the pasta. If we didn't have steak, I mean.' Me, I got to eat a lot of pizza. Especially pizza Mom hadn't cooked.

"No. I mean, yes, do kill him, dear. He's been – or rather, he was being – rather a naughty little boy. Skimming from Organisation accounts is perfectly fine and understandable. So long as I'm the one doing the skimming. Otherwise, we tend to have a review of the agent's retirement plan."

"Huh? Kennedy was *ours*?"

"Only indirectly, dear. Marilyn was the brains. We had such plans for her. But oh, did that girl love her knives... '43 we just wrote off to high spirits – enthusiasm. But after that thing in '47 – she'd even got herself her own silver topped cane! We just had to move her to Special Projects. But then Bobby... Well. He never liked her. Clumsy, though. We had to wipe the whole room down. Poor Marilyn. Still, we took care of dear Bobby. He wasn't our man. Or girl..." Mom did her shark-grin. "Never forget, dear. The Organisation looks after its own." Her eyes went cold. "Unless I tell them not to, of course."

"So you want me to kill Kennedy?"

"As a favour, dear. Since you'll be in the area. But no. He's not your target. There's someone else." For a moment, Mom sounded almost scared. "He's going to try to stop you. I want you to look him over, make sure you'll know him when you... But I'm getting ahead of myself. Just make sure you know him, dear."

Sounded, hell. Mom *was* scared. And nothing scared Mom. *Nothing*. "Mom – er, I mean, boss - he sounds like Bad News. With a capital 'fuck him'. Why don't I just take him down too? Since he's going to be there anyway?"

Mom grinned. But for the first time, I didn't hear sharks screaming. She was faking it, and I wasn't even a guy. "First, darling, because he works for me. Or rather, he will be working... I mean, was working..." Mom's lips moved, like she was trying to work out whether they were hers or not. "This time thing you humans... I mean, we humans... I mean, it's so confusing! Never mind, dear. You can't kill him then. He has things to do. For me. No, I just want you to make sure you'd know him again."

"You mean, while this shit-hot baddass is trying to kill me, while I'm trying to kill Kennedy, you want me to ask him to hold off a minute while I take his fingerprints?" Sometimes Mom isn't so big on the planning part of things. She just tells people to get things done – the how is their problem.

"Darling, I know you think you're clever. And really, sometimes you almost are. But – how do you children put it these days? You don't know jack? Well, you really, really don't. But don't worry dear. I've thought about that." Apparently, this wasn't one of those times. And whatever it wasn't, what it was, was a Really Really Big Deal. Because Mom didn't call me stupid very often – but when she did, she didn't kid. And all of a sudden, I could hear sharks screaming again...

* * *

Dealey Plaza – November 22nd, 1963

Just in, a bullet, and out. Oh – and a kickass-badass to check out, but not to 'check out', so I'd know him some time to be defined later. A badass Bad enough to scare Mom. Who, like, *never* scared. Just another day at the office, without an office to be in.

The buzz of Dealey Plaza filled my ears.

November 22nd, 1963. It's one of those dates. If you're old enough for it to mean anything at all, it means pretty much everything. Hell, I'd barely needed CG to run up a case file. There were more web sites, more pictures, more precise diagrams and who-what-whens than you could shake a poison flechette firing umbrella (I kid you not – it's out there) at. So it hadn't been hard to make sure the Horn landed me on the grassy knoll. Or rather, not me. That was what Mom meant. Because CG had some rings for me. One was a neat glamor ring, without any lace or stockings required. It didn't make me invisible, but it made folks not want to look at me, or if they did, to just catch me out of the corner of their eye. And not even me, because that was other ring. It made me into not me. It made me into – well, nobody. I put it on, and I checked a mirror. Whoever he was, he was nobody. He had one of those faces you could forget while you were still looking at him. Not cute, not ugly – like, nobody.

There was only one problem. I knew him. Like, <u>knew</u> him. And something was busy telling me I'd be a lot better off if I didn't ask Mom why.

The stuff I'd read had all said the same thing. Johnny-boy went down to a 6.5x52mm brass Carcano. Now, I'd do a lot for the Organisation. Mostly because I was pretty sure they'd blow my damn head off if I didn't. But lugging a Carcano 91/38 carbine round with me wasn't my idea of smart. So I talked to the shop back at the ranch, and they did some work on a couple of Glock 9mm pieces. Not mine – nobody touched my Glock but me. But even though they'd only fire once, I had two slugs ready to rock. And like I told CG – I don't miss. One would be enough. So here I was, and I could hear the car coming. Which was when I turned, and saw him. The figure nobody was looking at – the figure nobody was noticing. He walked towards me, his gun out and a bead on the side of my head. And it was like I was looking in that fucking mirror again. Because the guy with the gun was the guy I'd seen back at the ranch. And I figured, of all the targets he was going to kill – he wasn't gonna wax himself. So I reached out, and I tried to 'feel' him, like I could feel pretty much anyone near me, a tail, a target – and I couldn't. Because there wasn't anything there. Not a damn thing. Just – empty. And it started to make sense. Because I'd bet he wasn't from here. Not here-here, and not here-now. I'd bet any penny I had, and all the ones I could steal off anyone who hadn't nailed them down, if I was a Horny bitch, he was a Horny bastard. So as he stood and stared, I smiled, and put a finger to my lips. I raised my gun – and fired at the oncoming motorcade. And he watched me as I took my flask from my pocket – and the smell of Unicorn Horn filled the air.

* * *

Some-When. Middle-of-Nowhere, USA.
"It's done."

"I know, dear. Otherwise, all sorts of people would have forgotten how dear Johnny died. Which they haven't. So you managed that part, at least. And what about the real mission?"

"He was there, Mom."

"And you'll know him again?"

"I'll know him, Mom."

"Ah. Good. So he still doesn't wash often enough. Isn't that right, dear?"

That's when I put three rounds in Mom. A nice group, right in her chest. They didn't do any more than I expected, which meant they didn't do a damn thing. But I was pissed. "No, Mom. There wasn't a fucking smell." Three more rounds. "It wasn't any damn thing." Three more. "Because he wasn't fucking there. Even though he was. I was busy forgetting what he looked like while I was still looking at him. And I couldn't <u>feel</u> him, Mom. And you knew! You..." six rounds "... you fucking knew!"

"Yes, dear. He's like that. It's what made him so – useful."

"He's one of <u>ours</u>?"

"Mine, dear. Not ours. Let's not get too far ahead of ourselves, shall we? Yes. Or no. One of those. I know he was one of ours – mine, I mean. But there was... I mean is... I mean was... I think there was something I... we... a plan. And I can't remember! And I <u>always</u> remember! And whatever it is, it's his fault. Even if it isn't!" Mom was pacing. Mom was shouting. Mom was – well, whatever it was, it wasn't any Mom I'd seen before.

I waited. Then I waited some more. After a while, nothing happened. "Er – Mom?"

"Yes dear? Oh. Back already? Is it done?" Mom raised an eyebrow.

Whatever was going on, I was pretty sure I wanted it to be going on with someone else. <u>To</u> someone else. "Yes, mom. It's done."

"Excellent. Then I have another job for you. Do it right, and there's a bonus in it for you, dear." Mom smiled. I realised I knew how the sharks felt. The ones I always heard screaming. "Job, mom?"

"Yes, dear. Go talk to CG. He's got all you need."

I went. He had. And after he'd finished telling me, there was only one thing left to do. So I checked my Glock – and I drank.

* * *

December 1475, Near Bucharest

I could hear the battle from behind the tree. Steel blades. Men dying. The men, I could care less. But the screams were useful. They'd probably cover any small sounds I made. After a moment, the air shivered, and he was there. I could tell it was him – mostly because I couldn't tell it was anyone else. He laid a gun-sack on the ground, unzipped it, and started to put the Barrett M82A1 together. If nothing else, he had great taste in guns. He set up, and steadied his sight on the target. I could tell he hadn't noticed me. Of course, nobody ever did. Just like, I bet myself, nobody ever noticed him. That raised some questions. Questions I didn't think were going to get answered. At least, not by him. I stepped from behind the tree. At the last possible moment, he turned, his eyes locking mine. Which was flat out im-fucking-possible. Nobody *ever* saw me coming – *nobody*. I grinned. Well, apart from Sven and Maria. Not that it made any difference. Impossible or otherwise – he was toast. My trigger finger tensed – and a 357 slug hammered into his head. The Barrett fell, and he slumped over it. I slipped the Glock back into my thigh holster. I moved in, to clear the site. Mom would be real pissed if there was so much as a scrap of evidence. That was when CG stepped from behind a rock, gun in hand. I grinned some more. But this was my Queen Victoria grin. Something was wrong, and a grin was as good a cover as any. I started to reach for my Glock. "Hey, CG! I didn't know you were riding shotgun!"

He shrugged. "It's a good job I am, I guess. We've got a problem."

Crap. Crapcrapcrap. This wasn't just Bad. This was Badder than a Really Bad Thing on a Really Bad Day. For some reason, I wished the guy in the black leather duster wasn't busy being dead. For some reason, I knew he'd have fixed things. "What problem? I don't miss. Like, ever. He's dead, CG."

CG shrugged. again "That's the problem, M. Or rather, you are. See, you're supposed to be dead now too. Or gone. Or never here. One of those. But we can fix that." His gun came up.

They say you never hear the one that kills you. CG must have been using sub-sonic loads, because I almost did. Then the bullet ploughed into my hea...

Chapter Nineteen
Dead girl talking

Washington D.C. - 350 And Down

So let's recap. I was dead. Twice. Because my mother killed me. Or had me killed. Twice. Which, apparently, didn't stop me being tied to a chair in a room with a shapeshifting piano player who could stick her fingers in my head, and a guy who was just as dead as I was, because I'd killed him. And I wasn't sure which I was supposed to be more worried about. That I remembered killing him, even if it hadn't happened yet, or that *he* remembered. Because that didn't just mean he was like me. It meant it *had* happened. To him. It meant I was going to kill him some time in his past - and he wasn't putting a bullet in my head right now to make sure I didn't.

Time travel. It definitely had its down sides. I was having a real bad day, and I was starting to think maybe it wasn't the first time I'd had it. I could feel the headache coming, and it wasn't the two slugs Mom put in my head.

But if I had no idea why I wasn't dead, one thing I was sure of. I was pissed. "She killed me! I mean, she killed me again!"

The piano player's fingers eased out of my skull. The man in black leather said nothing.

"My mother! She fucking killed me! Twice! OK. It was CG. But he wouldn't have unless... My mother! She fucking killed me!"

The guy the piano player called Jack shrugged. "I see. So your Mom – we really should talk about that – your Mom killed you. Then she killed you again, because she didn't kill you the first time. Which is why you're here. Talking. Because you're dead. Right?"

"No. That's not it. Well, it is, but…"

"But?"

If this was a movie, about then I'd have been doing a backflip in the chair and the chair would break. Then I'd slip the cuffs and beat the crap out of everyone in the room. Of course if this was a movie the Bad Guy with the gun would be so busy watching me, he'd forget to pull the trigger and kill me. Or in this case, kill me again. Or even, counting Mom's two tries, again-again. But it wasn't a movie. It wasn't a movie, and the guy in black leather had that look. The look that said he knew the chair thing, and he knew I could do it, and he didn't give a shit. Because if I tried it he wasn't going to forget he had a gun in his hand

and he wasn't going to miss. I knew that look, because it's exactly the look I'd have had if he was the one cuffed to the chair. And I knew he wouldn't miss because I knew in his place *I* wouldn't miss – and if I didn't know why that was important, I knew it was.

The guy in black leather shrugged. "Thing is, she didn't."

"What?" If this had been a movie, I'd have been calling my agent to sue the script writer for assault-with-a-crappy-script. But it even though it still wasn't a movie, somehow I seemed to have the shitty end of the script stick.

"Your Mom. She didn't kill you."

"Well since I'm the one with a bullet in her skull – actually, make that two..." I wasn't going to remind anyone with a gun about the one I'd put in his own head in a hurry "... I'm pretty sure she did." As snappy repartee went, it wasn't going to win any Academy Awards. But I figured maybe I'd let the script writer live. Especially as he didn't exist.

The guy in black leather shrugged again. "Oh, she killed you. She just didn't kill *you*."

I wondered if any of CG's files might have addresses for non-existent script writers. Of course, if they did, it would give me a problem. Like, whether to kill CG before or after I smoked the guy with a keyboard. I raised one eyebrow. It was only fair – leather guy had done it enough to deserve some competition. "Right. So my Mom killed me – twice – but it's OK. Because she didn't kill *me,* she killed – well. Me." I raised my other eyebrow, in case the first one was getting lonely. And to stop it twitching from the headache I was getting. "Oh. And I remember her killing me because I'm still alive. Or something like that." I looked over at the piano player. "Is he always like this?"

The piano player didn't miss a note, but she shrugged. I guess it was her turn. "Well, there *was* the time he raped a Countess."

"He what?"

"Well, to be fair Jack didn't know. If he was a virgin, I mean."

"He didn't know if he was a virgin. So he raped a Countess." I made a mental note to check the Organisation stores for extra eyebrows when I got back. Times like this, a girl needed more than two. Then I made another note – because after what Mom had done, maybe going back wasn't such a good idea.

The piano player shrugged again. "You had to be there." she shuddered – but she still didn't miss a note.

"Nope. Nothing like that." Probably-Jack put his gun down. I wondered if it was time for a backflip.

"Jack! Do we have to? There's got to be another way…" The piano player sounded scared.

Pretty-Certainly-Jack "shrugged. "Only two, P. Only two."

The piano player sighed. "You're a bastard, Jack. I hate it when you're right."

I didn't know what worried me more. A scared piano player – or that Pretty-Certainly-Jack didn't think he needed his gun. Either way it was time to buy some time, and I was kind of short on negotiable currency. "Look. Let's not rush anything. I know you kidnapped me, but we can..."

"No I didn't."

"What do you mean? I sure as hell didn't volunteer. And I'm here, aren't I?"

"No. you're not." People who try to sound scary don't scare me. Whoever – or whatever – Jack was, he wasn't trying. And that scared the shit out of me. "You can't be. After all, you don't exist. See, it was like this..."

Chapter Twenty
Beta-Jacked

Washington D.C. - 350 And Down

Shadows don't have eyebrows. So the shadow didn't raise the ones it didn't have. "I guess you'd better make sure someone who <u>can</u> tell you, tells you Jack. After they find out, of course."

Jack sighed. "Crap. Oh, well. And then there's the kid."

"Yes, Jack. There's the kid."

"That's one of her names isn't it? Thief?"

"Stealer? Yes."

"So that's where he came from. I guess I'm going to have to fix that. But that means he's got a soul. So if he can... well, if he can, I'd know he'd have to..."

The shadow rod tapped the wall. The shadow waited. Nothing creaked. "Yes. Er, I mean, yes you would, Jack."

"And that would really, really hurt. Right?"

"Yes."

"Good." Jack's voice was cold. "And he'd have to have something to put it..."

"Yes."

"And I bet they wouldn't..."

"No. They didn't. Right up to their last breaths."

Jack's eyes got colder. "Right." The shadow that had never been there faded. Jack slipped the last round into his gun. He waited. After a while, the door opened. The two men in leather dusters looked at each other. Both men grinned, and lowered their guns. The man in the doorway raised an eyebrow. "I thought you'd be taller." Jack raised his own brow. "Me too." The man in the doorway reached slowly into the pocket of his duster, and pulled out a small notebook. He dropped it on the floor. "Let's not do this again, huh Jack?" He pulled a flask from his pocket, and the smell of Unicorn Horn filled the air.

Jack picked up the notebook, and began to read. Eyes that were never warm turned slowly to ice. Prowess looked up. "So... so what are you going to do about it, Jack?"

The man in the black leather duster unloaded his gun. Then he reloaded it. His eyes were ice. "What I do best, P. I'm gonna kill someone."

A tentacle flew over Prowess' piano, wrapping tight on Jack's gun hand. "Jack! You can't! She's just a girl!"

"She's a bit more than that, P." Jack didn't seem worried about the tentacle. "She did kill me, after all."

"Yes. She did. How did she do that, Jack?" Prowess sounded thoughtful, but her tentacle never left Jack's gun.

Jack's finger tapped idly on the notebook in his hand. "Because she's more than she should be. And less than she has to be."

"Jack, you're not making sense. Not that that's particularly unusual. What do you mean?"

"I mean its time."

"Time?"

"Time we asked her who she wants to be."

"So you're not going to kill her then?"

"Nope. Well, not unless she doesn't."

"What?"

"It's like this, P. And hold on – it's going to get kind of bumpy..."

* * *

Washington D.C. - 350 And Down

"So is this the real was it happened Jack? This time, I mean?"

"They're all real, P. It's just this one's the one that going to stay real."

"Don't you ever get headaches, Jack?"

"Not really. Mostly I give them to other people. Permanently."

*"Are you going to give **her** a headache Jack?"*

"I guess so, P. Or I guess not. One of those. Or maybe neither. That's her choice, P. Or it will be..."

October 18th, 1797. Ash Farm, between Porlock and Linton.

The man in the black leather duster clapped his hand over a mouth for the eighth time. A twist, and bone snapped. The kid hadn't done a bad job on the team covering the door, but he figured she was supposed to. She'd missed the cover team – also like, it looked, she was supposed to. Jack dropped the body, and dug the dull red gem fragment from its forehead. He'd seen that trick before. Jack slipped the gem fragment into his pocket to join the other seven, and picked his way through the six dead bodies of the decoy team.

The door to the farmhouse was open. He wrapped Shadow even tighter round himself. The Shadow Tunnel back to 350 stretched away behind him. This was going to be tricky. He checked the loads in his gun again, and the thing in his pocket. Then he stepped through the door. The two of them were where they were supposed to be. He concentrated. "You ready P?"

"You know this is impossible, right Jack?" Prowess' voice was faint, but clear enough. "And I'll need a new piece. Let me think a while – I hate composing in a hurry. Oh – and you're going to need something powerful to..."

Jack reached into his pocket, and pulled something out. He shook his head. "It's the last one. I knew I'd need it one day."

In a place that didn't actually exist, an old man in a blinding white vest and red overalls chuckled. The shadow hanging on a wall that wasn't actually there - didn't. "What the...? The Idiot! Was this your idea? Is he going to...? But he can't do that! I mean, I couldn't do... It's impossible!"

The old man shrugged. "Ah. Impossible. So if he does it then, that's, like, a Paradox?"

The shadow not hanging on the wall that wasn't there sighed. "You know, you really are a bastard."

The old man shrugged again. "Well, someone has to be."

Shadows don't smile. So the shadow that wasn't really there didn't. Widely. "Idiot."

The old man grinned. "Always."

The shadow sighed. "So? Are we going to help?"

The old man raised one eyebrow. "You mean cheat?"

The grin the shadow didn't have got even wider. "I won't tell anyone if you don't."

The old man's grin couldn't have been wider. "That's my girl."

Shadows don't blush. So this one didn't – bright pink.

Jack took the emerald out of his pocket and concentrated, wrapping Shadow round the two figures in front of him. Then he gently touched the back of the girl's head with the emerald. "Now, P!" The Shadow Tunnel echoed with the sound of a soaring piano, and an impossible surge of power ran through it. As the power pulsed, the emerald glowed bright green. Jack let the Shadow Tunnel collapse, pulling him back to 350. He put the emerald on the empty chair in the middle of the room. "OK, P. She'll need a memory if she's not going to flip before we're ready."

Sonata
Ricapitolazione – Secondo Movimento

Washington D.C. - 350 And Down

"I'm a *copy*?" The emerald on the chair pulsed bright green.

Jack shrugged. "You pretty much know the rest. Well, apart from the not-being-real thing. But..."

"I'm a fucking COPY?" The girl shackled to the chair struggled, wavering between girl and emerald.

Jack shrugged again. "OK."

The emerald pulsed. If green could be angry, it was one pissed off gem. "OK? O-fucking-K? Up until ten minutes ago, I was a highly trained, gorgeous, drop-dead or I'll kill you assassin-chick. Now I'm a lump of fucking beryl, with traces of, like, chromium. Or maybe vanadium. Either way..."

Jack raised an eyebrow. "Beryl? And – what was the other thing, P?"

"She said – well, the, er, lump of – can I say a bad word, Jack?"

"Well, you're not really saying it, P. Just quoting her. Well, quoting the lump of fucking beryl. So I don't think it counts, P."

"Ah. That's alright then. Well, the lump of fucking beryl said she had bits of chromium in her. Oh, or possibly vanadium."

"Right. Beryl and..."

The emerald pulsed. "I *am* still here, you know."

Jack pulled up another chair, and swung it round so it's back was to the emerald. He sat in it, facing the gem. "I guess that's the question, isn't it?"

"Question?" Green is a colour. It can't be curious, and it can't be pissed off. So whatever colour the gem pulsed, it was neither. Which didn't stop it being both.

"Yeah. The question. Like another question."

"What's that?" The pissed off the green of the emerald couldn't be was losing out to the curiosity it couldn't be either.

"Well, maybe it's 'how do you know emerald is beryl?'"

"It's not just beryl. You need the chromium. Or vanadium. Or it isn't green. And even I listened *sometimes* in..."

"In what?" Jack wasn't raising any eyebrows and he wasn't shrugging

"OK. So whoever I'm a *copy* of listened sometimes. In, like, class."

Jack sighed. "OK. Whatever. Isn't that what kids say? Whatever? When someone's being stupid, and doesn't get it? OK, P. I guess we're done here." Jack started to get up.

"Fuck you!" The girl shackled in the chair did a back flip. The chair flew backwards, and shattered. She slipped the cuffs, and launched herself at Jack, one leg swinging in a roundhouse kick.

Jack grinned. Then stepped to one side, and swept the girl's braced leg from under her, dropping her flat on her back. He leaned over her. "You know, that's a pretty good trick, even for a... what was it, P?"

The piano player looked up. "A highly trained, gorgeous, drop-dead or I'll kill you assassin-chick. I think that was it."

Jack grinned wider. "Right. Yeah, that was it." He looked down at the girl. "So if it was a pretty good trick for a highly trained, gorgeous, drop dead or I'll kill you assassin chick – what kind of trick was it for a lump of fucking beryl?"

The girl looked up at him. "I..."

Jack put his hand over her mouth. "Right. You just stop there. 'I'. Because right now, you got a choice. You got a choice because right up until I told you different, you were a girl. Because you believed it. So you can either be a lump of rock, or you can be you. You can be real. Because this room we're in? It's special. In this room, you're whatever you decide to be. Whatever you believe. So what's it gonna be? Rock or a hard case?"

* * *

I was flat on my back. I was flat on my back, and a guy who put me down without raising a sweat was asking me what I wanted to be, and telling me it's my choice. Now normally I'd roll to my feet and kick his ass, or maybe pull a knife and check the colour of his blood. Or better yet, let my Glock do the talking. But the thing was, I didn't have my Glock, and I didn't have a knife, and I was pretty sure if I tried to kick his ass I'd lose. Which was bad, because I'm not used to losing. But it wasn't the baddest. Because the baddest thing was? Well, apart from the guy in the leather duster, the baddest thing was, he might be right. I mean, when I came round, I knew I was, well, me. I was me, and he'd snatched me and he'd killed Sammy C and I was locked in a chair. And even if all those memories were for shit, I for sure wasn't an emerald. And I wasn't an emerald, right up until he told me I was. And then? Then I was a lump of green rock. As bad days went this one was right up there. But unless I was figuring on changing my name to Balboa, it looked like I had a decision to make. And if the choice really was mine, Sly wasn't getting a look in.

I looked up at Jack. "So you wanna give a gorgeous hard-ass assassin-chick a hand up?" He reached down, and

I reached up. I took his hand, and he pulled – not that it seemed like any effort. I figured he wasn't bad, not for an old guy at least. Then as he was pulling me up, I looked closer. I looked closer, and I thought how maybe he wasn't so old. Or at least – not *too* old. It wasn't the muscles – though he had those. It was the eyes. Eyes that seemed to say, 'whatever it is? Forget it. It's fixed.' And I had no idea how I got there, but I was up against his chest, and my heart was pounding like not even Sven made it pound.

"Some things never change." Behind me, the piano player snickered. I wondered if I should kill her. I looked up, and Jack was blushing. I had a feeling he didn't do it much. I mean, I knew for sure he wasn't a virgin – not after the Countess thing. There had to be a story there. I made a note to myself to get him to tell me sometime – ideally over some rumpled bed sheets. Because he really wasn't *that* old.

"Well, I can't read her Jack. And she's not even wearing a hat. Which is interesting, don't you think? But I don't have to, to see what she's thinking."

I couldn't tell if the piano player was jealous, but I decided she had to go green. I just needed a compost heap. I ran my fingers over Jack's chest, just to see him go even more red.

"It's not going to work, dear."

I was waiting for the piano player to start sounding possessive. Not that it would matter. Like I said, I'm not used to losing. But she wasn't. What she mostly sounded was like she knew something I didn't. I'm not used to that either. So I grinned. "Oh, it won't be work, honey. All I need is time."

"Time. Of course." The piano player laughed "You don't know Jack. He's always best when he's got time on his side."

The words echoed through my head like an AK on full auto. 'You don't know Jack.' I remembered the last two times I'd heard them. The only times I ever heard my Mom sound scared. Back then I thought I knew what she meant. Now I started to wonder if I knew a damn thing. I looked up at the man in the black leather duster. The piano player was right. It really wasn't going to work and I really didn't want it to. I just wished I had the first idea what I *did* want. Mostly, I didn't want to say what I knew I was going to say next.

So I said it anyway.

"Oh fuck. Hey, Dad. Sorry I killed you."

The room filled with piano notes – strong, but somehow gentle. Behind me, the piano player caressed keys. "Do you like this?" I could hear the smile. "I think I'm going to call it 'Shadow Child'."

Chapter Twenty-one
Double Down

Washington D.C. - 350 And Down
"OW!"

I think I was seven when Mom first taught me how hugs were really just a good way to pat someone down without them knowing. Or for them to pat me. Or for someone to get close enough to start breaking things I'd rather keep in one piece. So me and hugs didn't spend much time together. Apparently, wherever my Dad came from someone told him much the same thing. But if hugs aren't really your thing, what *do* you do when you meet your Dad for the first time? In my case, I got to say 'ow'. Like, a lot. Because if hugging was out, a little hand to hand practice definitely wasn't. Think of it as being like hugging but lot more honest.

"OW! So why didn't you just – OW!" I looked up at the ceiling for what felt like the hundredth time. Let's be honest – though that's something I normally try to avoid. I'm good at what I do. *Damn* good. And that includes doing painful things to people even when I don't have my Glock. Or, like now, putting them flat on their back and showing them I can break their arm. So I'm damn good – but apparently my Dad was better. Like, a lot better. I got up. Again.

Dad grinned. "You were saying?" That was something else it was taking some time to get used to. The only time Mom grinned, or smiled, sharks screamed. It meant she'd put something over on someone – sometimes me. Like, maybe I'd forgotten to check my morning coffee before I drank it. Which, if Mom was grinning, meant I was going to be running to the washroom every five minutes just so I'd remember what bad guys - or Moms - could put in it when I wasn't looking. Dad grinned, well, just so he could grin. It was like he didn't do it often, and now for some reason he felt like he could. And I had no idea if I was the reason, but I knew already I kind of hoped I was. And even hoping gave me a flutter in my stomach Mom never had – well apart from the time she had five guys jump me in a dark alley. Of course, that time the flutter was their knife – the one I had to pull out of my gut to waste them with.

"I was saying – OW!" I got up. "I was – OW!" I got up again.

"Yeah. I heard that bit." My Dad reached down and pulled me up. Halfway up, he kicked my legs out from under me. I hit the ground again.

I bit my lip. Licking the blood off, I tried to tell myself the bite was on purpose, so I didn't yelp again. Somehow yelping and 'gorgeous, drop dead or I'll kill you assassin' didn't really seem to fit together, and it was starting to feel like yelping had the edge. I reached up. As my Dad reached down, I kicked up, my foot slamming right between his legs. Well, that was the plan.

Dad raised an eyebrow and looked down from where he'd stepped sideways. He grinned again. I told myself I was imagining the number of times I'd seen the same grin in a mirror. This time I didn't get up. "I was saying, why didn't you just snatch me? I mean, the other me? The real Maya. I mean, yeah. I can see she'd be useful. But me? A fuck-all use recording called Beryl who can't even leave this room? I don't get it." Dad had told me how the room was special, and if I left it I'd just be a lump of rock. Of course, he could have been lying, like he could have been lying about a lot of things. But something else I'm good at is telling when people are faking. And even if Dad was better than me at that too, testing it didn't seem a good idea given what would happen if I was wrong. Dad grinned again, and reached down. I raised an eyebrow. He grinned some more, and shook his head. So I figured, hell. If I couldn't trust my Dad, who *could* I trust? Of course, thinking about Mom and the twice she'd already killed me, the best answer was probably 'just about anyone *not* family.' But I reached up anyway. After all, a girl's gotta start somewhere, especially when it looks like everything she thinks she knows might be for shit.

The guy in the black leather duster – I mean, Jack – I stopped. No. That wasn't it. And even if the way I knew it 'wasn't it' was just something he'd had Little Miss Tinkles at the piano put in my head – I didn't want it to be. Fuck that. Even if I didn't know how, I *knew* it wasn't. Because I knew the guy in black leather wasn't just a guy in black leather. I knew it in a way I'd never really known Mom was Mom. She just *was* – because she'd always been there, and because she said so. Dad hadn't even said he was my Dad – but I knew he was. Or if he wasn't – he was sure as all shit *something*. Like, him and me. Me and him. That was just how it was. Like somehow it had always been that way, and it had just taken me a while to see it. So – and even in my head, for a moment I wanted to savor it while it was still new – he grinned. *My Dad* grinned. "Nope. Couldn't do that. Remember that neat thigh holster She gave you?"

I could hear the capital. "You mean Mom?"

Dad grinned again. This time it had more lemon than smile. "Yeah. We should talk about that. Well, that's why."

"Because of my thigh holster?"

"Yeah. Well, and no. More because of the demon inside it."

"Demon. Of course. You do know there's no such things, right?"

"Well, I guess a smart kid like you knows more than an old guy like me. So you're right. There ain't no demons, like there ain't no magic, and there ain't no time travel."

"Right. At least we've got that..." Magic. Time travel. And most of all, double negatives. Chemistry wasn't the only class I sometimes listened in. English as well, and not just Lit. "Demons?"

Dad shrugged. "Back in my day, they used mages. But that was The Dragon."

"The Dragon?"

Dad shrugged. "I used to work for them. But they pissed me off, so I quit." I'd have bet large lumps of $Be_3Al_2(SiO3)_6$ Dad quitting, or getting pissed off, was why I'd never heard of any Dragon. Why nobody else was going to either. "They used to track us with mages. For you, She used a demon. So She'd know where you were, or where your holster was. You ever go anywhere without it?"

"No! Of course not!"

"Ever wonder why not?"

"Because it had my fucking Glo...!"

"Or why you swear like a hell-cat?"

"I don't fucki...!"

"Or why you always did what She said, and never questioned Her?"

"Because she's my Mom!"

Dad sighed. "Yeah. We *really* gotta talk about that. But no. Not. Not because you think she's your Mom. Hell. you're a kid. That's normally a pretty good reason on its own to do the exact opposite of anything your Mom says. No. It's growing up with a demon on your thigh. Of course, you needed something. To remember for you."

"OK! So I forget stuff! That doesn't mean..."

Little Miss Tinkles looked up – but her fingers never stopped moving. "Yes it does, dear. Because souls – which way is it, Jack? I keep forgetting. Souls are memories, or memories are souls?"

Dad shrugged. "Pretty much both, P. But that's the thing, kid. She needed you to think what She wanted you to think. So She gave you something to remember things Her way - a demon. Whispering every day into the place your soul should be – the soul you ain't got."

"Yeah. Well, I've always been more of a jazz girl I guess." Behind me I heard the piano player miss a note. In front of me, Dad's face said he heard it too, and didn't believe it either.

"Yes, dear. Me too." The shadow on the wall hadn't been there before. Of course, it couldn't be there now, since there was nothing to cast it. And shadows don't talk, so there was no way I was going to admit to myself this one had. Then the shadow that couldn't be there was gone – which made it easier to pretend it had never existed.

"Bloody Shadows. You're all the same." Dad's face said piano-gal didn't swear much either.

"Er – dad?"

"Yeah?"

"I was just imagining there was a talking shadow on that wall, right?"

"Yeah."

"That's OK then."

"Yeah. That was Fate. She was born triplets, so she gets confused. She just pretends to be a shadow."

"Er – dad?"

"Yeah?"

"There's no such thing as Fate."

"And the longer you keep thinking that, young lady, the better." The shadow that couldn't be on the wall didn't reach out from the wall with a shadow of a rod in its hand. And it didn't hit me on the head with the rod. Which didn't really explain why my head suddenly hurt like fuck.

Dad sighed. "You know, was a time I came here to be alone."

"NO JACK. I mean, no Jack. You just thought you did." The old guy in the white T shirt and red overalls vanished as quick as he'd appeared. Which was good, because I had no idea where he'd come from. I thought about telling Dad how old guys in red and white were impossible too – but somehow my heart wasn't in it.

Dad sighed again. "Family. Can't live with them, can't kill them. Where were we?"

"You were telling me why you made a half-assed copy and didn't snatch the real thing, and I was having hallucinations. At least, I hope I was."

"Oh, right. So you're – what did she say, P?"

"She said she was a half-assed copy. Oh, and a fuck-all use recording. Can I say that Jack? Because I'm quoting her again, so it doesn't really count does it?"

"Yeah. You can say it. So I guess I messed up, P."

"I suppose you did, Jack. What do we do now?"

"Well, I guess we..."

"I *am* still fucking here, you know." This time I didn't miss. My right slammed into Dad's jaw. He went down hard.

Dad didn't just grin. He flat-out smiled! "Not bad. For a half-assed fuck-all use recording."

"Well, that's what I am!"

"If that's your choice – sure you are." Dad got up.

"My choice? What other choice is there?"

"That there's some dumb-ass bitch out there in your body – and she's about to get your head blown off."

"So what if there is? What the hell can *I* do about it?"

"I guess you're going to have to kill yourself – before She does it for you." This time I knew damn well I'd seen Dad's grin before. Because I'd seen it in a whole lot of mirrors. It meant someone was about to have a real Bad Day - and whoever was grinning was the Bad they were going to have.

This time, one way or another, or maybe even both – it was going to be me.

Sonata
Ricapitolazione – Tertio Movimento

Somewhere, Somewhen

The truck's lights speared the night.

"Charlie!" The woman in the passenger side of the cab grabbed for the wheel, her foot stabbing for brakes that weren't there. Speared in the eighteen wheeler's lights, the man in the black leather duster made no attempt to get out of the way.

Charlie sighed. He jammed down the gears, slowing the rig. There was no way any driver could stop the truck in time. But this was The Road, and Charlie wasn't any driver. As the truck eased to a stop beside the man in the black leather duster, Charlie rolled down the window. He leaned out. "So. It's you. Figured you'd be taller."

The man in black leather shrugged. "Figured you'd be shorter."

Charlie leaned over, and unlatched the passenger door. He swung it open. "You got a visitor, Ro'."

The woman sighed. "Guess so, Charlie." Her hand twitched, and one end of a long black chain slipped from her arm, wrapping round her wrist.

Charlie leaned over. His arm reached out towards the door latch. At the last minute, the arm slipped round the woman's shoulder, pulling her close to him. He kissed her. "Everythin' got a price, Ro'."

The woman flushed bright pink. "You're an Idiot, Charlie." The chain in her hand whipped out, wrapping round Charlie's neck. Rosie tugged – and her own lips found Charlie's. "Just don't you stop being my Idiot." She looked deep into his old eyes – eyes that never aged. "Is it worth it, Charlie?"

Old eyes suddenly weren't old at all. "Hell, yeah." Charlie kissed her again.

"Kharon Kharopos! You hold right on to that thought. 'Cos I'll be back, and we're gonna talk about this, you can bet!"

"Oh, so it's just talkin', is it? I guess you're too laid back for doin', huh?"

The woman blushed again. "Laid back, Charlie? I guess we can talk about that too. And you'd better be up for more than talking!"

The woman swung out of the cab. "So. It's time?"

The man in black leather said nothing.

Rosie shook her head. "You don't say much, huh? Just like him." She jerked her head at the dark figure in the cab.

"Yeah. I'm starting to get that." The man in black leather looked up into the cab.

"So what do you need?"

"Not me."

"So who?"

"There's a kid."

"*Kid?* You the cradle type?" The black chain in the woman's hand snaked and grew spikes like bitter teeth. It span out and wrapped round the man in black leather's throat.

"Yeah. I guess I am." The man in black leather didn't seem concerned about the chain tightening round his throat. "Now I got to get this one out of hers. So she needs something."

"What she needs is you dead, pretty boy." Rosie tightened her hand, and the chain wrapped tighter round the man in black leather's neck.

"Maybe so. And if that's what it takes, it's hers. Any time she needs it." The sound of a single gunshot cracked the night. The chain fell from the man in black leather's throat, one lone link shattered from the end and falling to the Road. The man in black leather slipped the gun back into his pocket. "But not this time."

Rosie stared at her broken chain. "You – you can't – that's impossible!"

The man in black leather shrugged. "I guess so." He bent down and picked up the broken link. "But she needs something to remember you by. So I did it anyway." He handed Rosie the broken link.

"To remember me by? What... Oh. Oh, fuck. You mean she's...?"

The man in black leather shrugged.

"Where? And when?"

The man in black leather handed her a sheet of paper that looked like it had been torn from a notepad.

Rosie read the note. She sighed. "I'll be there." She looked at the man in black leather. "Jack? You gonna be good to her?"

The man in black leather shrugged. "You tell me."

Rosie smiled, wistfully. "Oh, I think you'll do OK." she walked back to the truck, and swung up into the cab. "Charlie?"

"Yeah?"

"Take me to Paradise?"

Charlie grinned. "Thought you'd never ask."

The truck's lights speared the night.

Chapter Twenty-two
Sister...

Washington D.C. - 350 And Down
"Daaaaad?"

Dad grinned. He'd been doing that a lot recently. So had I – just not right now. "Whining? They teach that to kick-ass assassins these days?"

I flushed. "Kick-ass? You mean that?"

"Well, I *did* have to cover for you with the tapes on that building you blew..."

"Fuck! I *knew* someone was... I mean, er, thank you daddy dear." I smiled. If you look in the dictionary, you can find it – right under 'winsome'. Though the look on Dad's face said maybe 'sickly' would have been a better heading. "Anyway. That wasn't whining. See, whining is, like, 'Daaaaad!' That was wheedling. Like, 'Daaaaad?'" I grinned at the piano player. "He's kind of new at this parent stuff isn't he?"

"Yes. Or no. One of those. Unless it's both." Miss Tinkles didn't miss a note.

"I am still here, you know."

This time Dad wasn't grinning. But I could see the only reason he wasn't was because he was trying hard not to. So

I did it for him. It felt good. "Girl talk, Dad. No boys allowed. You'll get used to it. Anyway. Where was I? Oh. Right. Er - Daaaaad?"

Dad sighed. "No. You don't have to kill her."

"Great! So you'll do it for me?"

"Thought you were a kick-ass assassin?"

"I am! OK, so I messed up on the tapes. I *said* thank you! But this isn't killing some fucking mark, Dad. You want me to kill – well, *me*!"

"Nope."

"What? But you said... OK. That's alright then."

"You want to stay a rock on a chair, in a room that isn't really real – that's your choice. You'll die anyway. I mean, the other you will. Your boyfriend'll take care of that."

"He's not my fucki...!"

The piano player coughed. If she'd been wearing glasses, the look she gave me would have been over them.

I sighed. "I mean, he's not my boyfriend! He's only eight, for a start! Anyway. The only way his ass is going to be mine is because I'm going to put a bullet in his head. Which just means I'll have to aim at his fucki... I mean, shoot his dick off." The look the piano player gave me this time suggested she wasn't sure which she was looking at me for – my language, or my knowledge of anatomy. I sighed. Again. "It's, like, a glamor spell. Without lace and stockings. Blowing his head off wouldn't work."

The piano player laughed. "I don't know, Jack. You and kids. At least this one doesn't sing. Or breathe fire."

"What?"

"What?"

The piano player ignored both of us – but her fingers switched to the tune she'd called 'Shadow Child'.

Dad shrugged. I sighed. The piano player – well, I guess she piano-ed.

"So it's her or me?" Some days, the only choices you got are all bad.

"NO. Er – I mean, no. It's neither of you – or it's both."

"What? Where...?" Wherever the old guy in a white T and red overalls had come from, it wasn't the door.

The old guy in red and white didn't answer. Mostly because he wasn't there. Which meant I could go on trying to believe he'd never been there at all.

"Jack? Don't you think you should introduce Maya to Prowess? I – I mean, she keeps calling her 'the piano player'."

Shadows on walls don't talk. So obviously the shadow that couldn't be on the wall, because there was nothing to cast it, didn't say a word. Then it was gone. I didn't know if that made things simpler – or more complicated. "Er – Dad?"

Dad sighed. "Kid, this is Prowess. She's a concert pianist. And a shape-shifting empathivore."

"Empathi...?"

A tentacle wrapped round me – but it felt like a hug. I wondered if Not-Miss Piano was frisking me. "Empathivore, dear. I feed on emotions. They're sort of like life-force, but more important."

"Er – didn't you have a piano a moment ago, Miss... er, Mrs..."

"Prowess will do nicely, dear. And no. More that I *was* a piano a moment ago." The tentacle unwrapped from round me, and went back to being a piano. The notes of 'Shadow Child' filled the room. Or I guess they would have, if the room was actually real. I was starting to get why Jack scared mom. I just didn't get why he didn't scare me.

"Because that bitch *isn't* your mother. She's... Oh, fuck. Trans-temporal-quantum-irregularities really are a bugger dear. Because he *is* your father. Well. Or he will be. In a way. Even if he isn't. Because he's... Oh, never mind. Because. OK? Because!" A hand that wasn't in my head didn't reach up and smack the inside of my skull with a metal rod. Which didn't stop my head hurting like fuck. Then the shadow that couldn't have been inside me was gone as though it had never been there. I had a feeling my life would be easier if I could convince myself it hadn't been. I had another feeling my life wasn't meant to be easy. And I had a third feeling. That what Dad was really saying was whether I had a life at all was going to have to be my choice – even if it killed me. Because whatever I chose, I was going to end up dead – or never alive. I sighed. Fuck. I was even starting to *sound* like Dad. "OK I get it. So what's the plan?"

Sonata
Ricapitolazione – Quarto Movimento

The Paradise Lodge, Mount Rainer
"You want *what*?"

Rosie sighed. "Heffy. She'll need *something*. The demon will be gone, and she's not got a soul so – hey, Charlie? How come I've got a soul? I mean, I can ride the Road too, so..."

"No, I get that bit. Not that that link'll be worth shit. That was someone else's penny, an' it's only on loan. No, I'll take your penny, an' hammer it flat. A few elder runes, some ether enriched adamanti..." Heffy sighed. The two blank faces in front of him were clearly not new. "OK. Magic-man makee magic-metal-gem for memories." He sighed again. "Not *that*. That's the easy bit. The other thing. I mean – *pink*?"

Rosie grinned. "Yes, Heffy. Pink. With, like, extra pink." She grinned some more. "Hey, Heffy? Could we talk about my chain?"

"What? Your *chain*? No. Not a chance! Absolutely, definitely, *categorically*..."

Rosie smiled. She'd always liked winsome – it was much better than lose-some. "Heffeeeeee?"

Chapter Twenty-three
... Pact

Washington D.C. - 350 And Down
"Ready?"

I grinned. I didn't mean it, but I didn't have anything else. The easiest kill of my life was going to be the hardest – and I still didn't really know if I could do it. I just knew I had to. "Ready, Dad."

"Jack?"

"Yes, P?"

"I still don't understand. The Paradox Storm is already raging. So nobody can get in, and nobody can get out. Well, unless... but that's a summoning! So how are we going to get there?"

"I don't have to get in, P. I'm already there. So's Maya. And you're not going. You're staying here. I'm just taking 350 with us. OK?"

"I suppose so."

Dad shrugged. His black leather duster settled on his shoulders. I could feel him concentrating. He took a flask from his pocket and uncapped it. I opened mine. The god-awful smell of Unicorn Horn filled the air.

"Let's do this, kid." We drank.

* * *

December 1475, Near Bucharest
"Why can't I kill him, dad?" I could feel the Shadow wrapped tight about us, and the tunnel stretching back to Dad's place. "I want to fucking kill him!"

Dad shrugged. "OK. So kill him."

"And then what?"

"Then you're a lump of rock forever, I'm dead, and your mom, who isn't your Mom and we really should talk about that, wins. Or maybe you never exist. It's kind of a grey area. I could ask Haures, I guess – but he'd probably say he had a headache."

"Haures?"

"Oh, right. You didn't meet him yet. Fallen Angel. Well, not really Fallen. It's complicated. He knows everything that ever happened. Says I give him a headache."

"A Fallen Angel."

Dad shrugs.

"My Dad. And you know, like, Fallen Angels. Like, Servants of Satan. Who everybody knows..."

Dad sighs. "Doesn't exist. Right. We should...."

I grin. "We should talk about that. Right. Like we should talk about mom." I shake my head. "And you give this Fallen Angel headaches. Yeah. I bet." I sigh. "So I can't kill him."

"Sure you can."

"But you said...!"

"You just can't kill him *yet*." My Dad smiled. This time I didn't have to worry about sharks. This time, if Mom saw it, *she'd* be screaming. "You ready?"

"Ready." I watched – well, I watched me. I watched me step from behind the tree. At the last minute, the guy in a black leather duster looked up from the Barrett he was aiming, and turned, his eyes locking on my other eyes. Not that it made any difference. My - her - trigger finger tensed – and a 357 slug hammered into my Dad's head.

The Barrett fell, Dad slumped over it. The me-who-wasn't-me slipped her Glock back into her thigh holster. She moved in, to clear the site. She looked up as CG stepped from behind a rock, a gun in his hand. "Hey, CG! I didn't know you were riding shotgun!"

CG looked round. He shrugged. "It's a good job I am, I guess. We've got a problem."

The me-who-wasn't-me looked puzzled. "What problem? I don't miss. Like, ever. He's dead, CG."

CG shrugged. "That's the problem, M. Or rather, you are. See, you're supposed to be dead now too. Or gone. Or never here. One of those. But we can fix that." His gun came up. There was a single crack, and the me-who-wasn't me slumped to the ground, surrounded by a red mist.

Dad concentrated, and stretched the Shadow tunnel so it just touched the me-who-wasn't-me. He called back to 350. "Now, P!" A long tentacle flew down the tunnel, and settled on my head. Another tentacle flew past me, and settled on the other-me's head. The shadow tunnel kept it from appearing in the real world. I could feel the – what? Emotion? Life? *Me*? Whatever it was, I could feel it, running out of me, and into, well, me. The other me. Keeping me not-quite dead.

CG walked over to the not-me, and looked down. He lifted her skirt and ran his hand up her thigh. He sighed. He found what it was looking for and pulled. My – her - thigh holster came loose from my – her - leg, dripping blood. He drew a crystal dagger from the sheath on his leg and kissed the blade. For three minutes his lips moved, his words a harsh whisper on the wind. When he was done, the dagger blade glowed a sickly yellow. He cut into the thigh holster, slicing it open. Red gem fragments fell into his hand. He put them in a box. He looked over at the dead version of Dad, and shook his head. He pulled a sheet of paper out of his pocket, and wrote on it in thick black marker. Then he pulled a red gem, filled with a dull red glow, out of his other pocket and held it tight. He began to chant again – then to scream. As he screamed, the red gem began to glow brighter. Eventually he stopped screaming. I could see his eyes were dull and dead. He took a flask from his pocket. I could smell the Unicorn Horn filled the air. He drank – and he was gone.

"Now!" I grabbed me. I grabbed, and I held me like I'd never let me go. As Dad let the Shadow tunnel collapse, I heard the sound of a motor-bike, roaring like a demon from hell.

* * *

Washington D.C. - 350 And Down

"Fuck!" I staggered. I could barely hold me. Maybe I should go on a diet.

The floor of 350 squealed as the woman on the motor-bike wrenched it into a suicide turn before she hit the wall. She looked at me. "Hey, kid. I'm Rosie."

"I don't know how long I can keep this going. Can we skip the formalities?" Prowess was gasping, her tentacle twitching on my head. For a moment, everything blurred, and I could see the same tentacle wrapped round an emerald Dad was holding against not-me's head.

"You're going to need this." Whatever a Rosie was, this one tossed something to Dad.

"And you're going to need this." She threw something towards me.

I didn't waste time trying to work out how a rock could catch it. I caught it anyway. It slipped into my hand like even my Glock never had. "Damn! That's a neat piece! This is what my Glock wants to be when it grows up! And pink! What's it load? What the fuck is it? Where can I get one?"

Rosie blushed. "Call it a birthday present. I got a - a friend of mine to make it for you."

Dad reached over, and he held my shoulder. "It's now or never, kid." he held whatever Rosie had thrown him against the far side of not-me's head.

I put the gun Rosie had thrown me against my side of her. My finger tensed on the trigger. Then it stopped. Because like it or not – it was me. And I could kill anyone in the world – but not me. I looked up. "Dad! I – I can't!"

* * *

December 1475, Near Bucharest

My trigger finger tenses – and a 357 slug hammers into the guy in the black leather duster's head. The Barrett falls, the guy slumps over it. I slip my Glock back into my thigh holster and I move in, to clear the site. I look up as CG steps from behind a rock, a gun in his hand. "Hey, CG! I didn't know you were riding shotgun!"

CG looks round. He shrugs. "It's a good job I am, I guess. We've got a problem."

I'm puzzled. "What problem? I don't miss. Like, ever. He's dead, CG."

CG shrugs. "That's the problem, M. Or rather, you are. See, you're supposed to be dead now too. Or gone. Or never here. One of those. But we can fix that." His gun comes up. He fires. I feel the slug plowing into my thigh holster – then another in my head. I fall. I know I should be dead – but somehow I'm not. I can feel something wrapped round my head, and it's like there's just enough 'me' flowing out of it, and into, well, me, to keep me alive. CG walks over to me, and looks down. He lifts my skirt and runs his hand up my thigh. He sighs. Fucking guys. I bet I know what he's thinking. He finds what he's looking for, and pulls. It hurts like fuck as my thigh holster comes loose from my leg, dripping blood.

And I feel it. I feel it because, for the first time since I remember, if I even remember anything at all, it isn't there. It isn't there, and it isn't whispering to me, back in my skull where I don't even know I'm hearing it. The fucking demon my Mom – no. not my Mom. The fucking demon She put in me, so She could own me, control me – use me for the one thing She couldn't do. Kill my fucking father.

Then CG draws a crystal dagger from a sheath on his leg and kisses the blade. For three minutes his lips move, his words a harsh whisper on the wind. When he's done, the dagger blade glows a sickly yellow. He cuts into my thigh holster, slicing it open. Red gem fragments spill into his hand, the ump Mom said would be the last thing I'd ever need. He puts it in a box. He looks over at the dead guy and shakes his head. Then he pulls a sheet of paper out of his pocket, and writes on it. He pulls a red gem, filled with a dull red glow, out of his other pocket and holds it tight. He chants – then screams. As he screams, the red gem begins to glow brighter. He stops screaming, his eyes are dull and dead. He takes a flask from his pocket. I can smell the Unicorn Horn in the air. He drinks – and he's gone.

"Now!" I hear someone shout. Someone grabs me. I hear the sound of a motor-bike, roaring like a demon from hell – and I black out.

* * *

Washington D.C. - 350 And Down

Someone's got a gun to my head. Which is kind of funny, because I'm dying. So why shoot me? I want to laugh, but I can't.

"Dad! I – I can't!"

I look up, to see who it is who can't kill me. I want to tell them all they have to do is wait. It'll take care of itself. Then I see. I see who's holding the gun. And it's me. Which is when I know it can't wait.

* * *

I could kill anyone in the world – but not me. I look up. "Dad! I – I can't!"

"Fu... fucking wimp." I – not-me – she – Maya opens her eyes underneath me, and she smiles! She fucking smiles!. "It's getting louder. Can you hear it, sis?"

I'm not even used to having a Dad yet. A sister? But she's right. What else can we be?

* * *

I know I have to make her understand. And I know we don't have much time. I want to cry, because I want to know her, to tell her – fuck. To tell her what? What can I tell her she doesn't know already? Where have I been that she hasn't already gone? Then I realize. That's it. Because it's not where we've been. It's where we have to go. It's not who we are, what we were – it's who we have to be. Or the bitch is going to win, and that's not going to happen. So I smile. And it's hard to talk, but talking's all I got now. ""Fu... fucking wimp. It's getting louder. Can you hear it, sis?" Sis. I never knew my Dad – not until I killed him. And now I've got a sister, because what the fuck else can she be, this Maya leaning over me? And it's loud. It's so fucking loud. I wonder if she can hear it. I wonder if she can hear me, because I'm not sure I can – not sure how long I've got to tell her. And what do I tell her? Do I tell her what the bitch is? Who She is? Do I tell her I wish things had been different? Do I tell her... "Damn, girl. I love you."

And the best I can manage is a whisper, but I hope it's enough.

* * *

And she looks up at me, this Maya I'm not – this Maya I might have been. She asks me if I can hear it. She tells me it's getting louder. And I know what it is. I know what it is, and I know she knows – and I can't tell her, because all I want to do, me the kick-ass assassin, is cry. And she looks up at me, and she smiles. She smiles, and her lips move. I can barely hear it – but it's there.
"Damn, girl. I love you."

* * *

And I lie here. I lie hear, and it's hammering. My heart. And I want to laugh again, because it's like a fucking bad movie – the assassin with a heart. But I can't. I try, and all I get is the taste of blood. My blood. My hearts hammering like an AK on full auto, and every round brings it closer. The silence. So I lift my hand, and I put it over hers – my other heart. My sister's heart. And it's hammering too, like mine. And her hand closes over mine.

* * *

And she looks up, and she tries to laugh. But she can't, and all that happens is the blood seeps faster from her lips. the blood is starting to seep from her lips. And she lifts her hand, and she puts it over my heart. And I put mine over hers – my hand on my sister's.

* * *

I can feel my hand. It's getting cold. And I can feel my sister's. And it's so warm. And I can see now. I can see it all. Who we were. Who we can be. And the bitch who... I cough, and I know it's red. But there's so little time! And I know I have to tell her, but I know she can't know. Not yet. And if I talk, it'll just be more red. So I don't. I take my hand from hers, and I reach up, and I wrap it round her neck. Then I pull. I pull, and I do it. I kiss my sister. And I whisper again. "I love you."

* * *

Her hand is getting cold. I wrap mine tighter round her, willing her my warmth – my life. But she pulls her hand from mine, and reaches up to my neck. She reaches – she pulls me down – and she kisses me. Not a Sven and Maria kiss. Because she kisses me – and it's me. She kisses me – and I hear her whisper. ""I love you." And I can taste it. Her blood on my lips.

* * *

I kiss her. I kiss me. And I know what I have to do. What *we* have to do. And it's hard – it's so fucking hard. But I smile. I smile, and I whisper. "No you. No me. Just us, sis'. Just us – always." I smile again. "So fucking do it, bitch." And I smile. I smile, and as I hear the shot I kiss me for the last time.

* * *

She kisses me. My sister. My me. She kisses me, and I feel her lips move. She whispers, and I can barely hear her. But I do. "No you. No me. Just us, sis'. Just us – always." she smiles again. "So fucking do it, bitch." And I see her smile. Or maybe I see me – and I don't care which anymore, because there is no which. No her, no me. Just us. So I do it. I pull the trigger, my gun against the emerald, against me. I pull the trigger, and the bullet ploughs through her – through me – and into whatever Dad is holding on the other side of my sister's head. I pull the trigger – and I kiss me for the last time.

Chapter Twenty-four
Two...

Washington D.C. - 350 And Down

I look up. There's a pile of shattered emerald at the side of my head. Dad puts something in my hand, and for a moment I can feel it. Feel her. Feel *us*.

Dad's fingers trace the filigree of the black star. I can't tell if its metal or gem. "To remember by." Dad doesn't grin. Somehow, it's even more warming than when he did. "To remember *her* by."

"And you?"

Dad takes my hand and puts it on a lump in his leather duster. "A present. From... from an old friend."

For a moment, we're silent. But I can't leave it like that. "Dad?"

"Yeah?"

"Do I have to lose you too?"

"Do you want to?"

I want to cry. So fuck it. I do. "No. No, Dad. Not ever."

My Dad wraps me in his arms. "Me neither, kid. I'm never losing you either." He kisses me. He grins, but he's not trying to hide his own tears. "So shall we go fix me?"

I look up. "Well, that might be a problem."

"Problem?"

"You know. Bullet. Brain. Um – twice. Does the second one count? Was it really a bullet?"

"I'm betting not." Dad looks up at motor-bike chick. "I'm betting I'd know the maker's mark on that piece, right?"

Biker chick smiles. "Could be, Jack. Could be. Anyway. We square, Shadow?"

"Yeah. We're good."

"Great. Be seeing you, Jack."

Dad winces. "Not if I can help it."

Biker-chick winks. "You know how it is, Jack. What's gotta be..."

Dad sighs. "I almost feel sorry for him."

Biker chick grins. Me, I raise an eyebrow. "Him?"

"Never mind."

"Er – Jack?"

"P?"

"The second one – it was hellfire, but it was still a bullet. I'm keeping it out of her cortex, but it really needs to come out."

Dad looks at me. "It's up to you, kid."

"What is?"

"Whether you trust P."

"You trust her, dad?"

"Second most in the world, kid."

"So who's the most."

Dad blushes. My Dad. My been there, done that, kicked its ass Dad *blushes*. And I want to cry again, I'm so happy. I look up. "Miss Prowess?"

"Just Prowess, dear. Or P. After all, you're Jack's family."

"P? I kinda don't wanna die right now."

"Then let's take care of that, shall we? And...." Now it seems it's a shapeshifting empathivore's turn to blush "...well, would you mind if *I* gave you a present as well? After all, it's a bit like your birthday, dear."

"What present, P?"

Prowess smiled. "You'll see. Come here, dear."

I get up, just, and I walk over to Prowess. She – well, flows is pretty much the only way to describe it. She flows, and she wraps round me like a great, huge blanket. As everything goes black, I wonder how I'm going to breathe.

"Don't worry, dear. I'll take care of it." The voice isn't in my head. It's in every part of me. And it's not a shadow. It's Prowess. I black out.

I wake, and the notes of Shadow Child are in the air. I touch my head, where CG's bullet killed – fuck it. Killed *me,* even if it wasn't my head at the time. There's not a mark, and I feel – I feel great! "Wow, P! How did you...?"

"Oh, I stole some of your life, dear."

"WHAT?" My new pink not-a-Glock is in my hand, and it's pointed at P's head. She doesn't miss a note.

"I stole some of your life. Not anything you were going to miss. It's from a long way off."

"But..."

"She had a choice, kid. You could be dead now, or dead maybe a bit sooner than forever – but not now. You rather dead-now?"

"But..." I try to work out what comes after but. Thing is, there really isn't anything that makes sense. "I'm sorry, P. Thanks – I guess."

"Oh, don't mention it, dear. By the way – that's a really nice gun you have pointed at me. Very – pink." P looks at biker-chick. "Pink? *Really*?"

"Never argue with a girl who's got her pink on, lady." Biker chick twitches her hand, and a long chain slides from her body, whipping round her head. As chains go, let's say it isn't black. Like, very not-black.

Prowess grins. "I suppose not." She looks at her piano. "Jack? Do you think...? Oh, never mind. We can talk about that later. No, I meant it must be quite difficult to carry a big gun like that round with you, dear."

I shrug. "Not really. I just keep it in my..." I stop. My gun hand drops, and lifts my skirt. My not-a-Glock slips neatly into the thigh holster I shouldn't have, because CG tore it off me.

"At least there's no demon in this one, dear. It's all – well, it *was* all – me. It's Shifter skin, dear. Like your old one, but given willingly, not flayed from a screaming prisoner and stitched on with..." Prowess spits. "I'm sorry dear. I knew what it was as soon as I saw that evil little brat tear it off you. Would you mind killing him for me?"

"It will be my pleasure, P."

"Thank you, dear. Anyway. This one's a gift, so it's rather better part of your – well, your you. You'll heal quicker, and even if it won't stop bullets all over, you won't have to worry about anything that hits it. And it will move wherever you ask it to, if you think nicely at it. And it matches you perfectly, with a direct link to Shifter-space, so nobody will ever see your gun. Oh – and one more thing. Jack? May I?" Prowess holds out a tentacle. Dad drops the filigree star into it. "Thank you." The tentacle whips over to me, and down between my legs. It caresses my holster. "There dear."

I run my hand over my holster. I can just barely feel the star under it.

"It will – well, think of it as a memory jogger, dear. I did the same for your father."

"Dad?"

"Of course." Prowess smiles. "Where do you think he got that rather nice leather coat? Now. Do run along."

Dad scoops up the shattered pieces of emerald. "Can you do it, P? He's got to be me, but he can't remember..."

Prowess gives Dad a dirty look. "Do I ask if you can load your gun, Jack? Come here." A tentacle snakes out, and settles on Dad's forehead. Then another sits for a while on the shattered emerald pieces in Dad's hand. "There. Don't worry. The leather will know what to do. And..." Prowess picks one of the shards of emerald out of Dad's hand "... if you crush this under his nose, so will you. Er – he. Well, one of those. Or is it both?" She looks at me. "Let's try not to do this again, shall we dear?"

I raise one eyebrow. "Again? But this is the first..." I look at Dad. "Er – dad? What does she mean, 'again'?

This time it's Dad giving Prowess a dirty look. I wonder how many times I've died, so I can live at last.

Dad pulls some chalk from his pocket. He scrawls what would be a pentacle on the ground, if pentacles weren't just hokey spiritualist shit. The leopard-man appearing in the pentacle makes me wonder if I needed to re-think my views on spiritualist shit as well.

The leopard man looks at Dad. He looks at me. He clutches his head. "Shadow! You can't..." He looks at me again. "Oh. You can. Er – you did. Right. At least we're not going to have to do this again."

"Er – Mr Leopard? About that 'again'?"

Leopard guy looks at me. He clutches his head again. "Never mind. I mean, really Never. Ow!" He rubs his head.

Dad raises an eyebrow. "Haures?"

"Ow! Yes, you can make a one-time disposable Summoning Pentacle. Yes, it will vaporize as soon as it's used. Yes, it will... OW! YesitwillsummonanythingevenintoaParadoxStorm! OWOWOWOW!"

Dad sighs. "So how do I..."

"Left pocket! It's set for Barbas. And I hope it bloody chokes him, so there! Ow!" Leopard guy clutches his head harder.

Dad takes something out of the leopard guy's pocket. Which is a pretty neat trick, given the pockets leopards don't usually have. Dad scrubs a line of the chalk pentacle with his toe, and leopard guy vanishes. Dad looks at me. "OK. This is where it gets tricky, kid. Timing's everything."

I grin. "Great sex, great comedy and war. Timing's always everything. So what's new, Dad?"

Dad grins too. "New is, this time I don't die."

"*This* time?"

Dad shrugs. "It's complicated."

I raise one eyebrow. "Riiiiight. I bet."

Dad takes a bottle from his pocket. "We have to get there just before you drag – well, before you drag you out, but not so close you see you. Got it?"

"No."

"Good. That way you won't try to over think it." Dad tosses me a flask. We drink – and we're gone.

Sonata
Ricapitolazione – Quinto Movimento

Washington D.C. - 350 And Down

"Did you do it, Lee-Ann?" Shadows don't speak. Not even shadows with nothing to cast them. So this shadow didn't ask Prowess anything at all.

"Yes. I did it. It's in there. But it's not fair! I didn't really steal it! It was just a tiny piece! And I only wanted to know why he... why he didn't want..."

"It's alright, Lee-Ann. She didn't mind."

"You can't know that!"

"Of course I can."

"How? How can you know?"

"Because I said so. That's how."

"Oh. Right." Prowess fingers wandered slowly over the keyboard. "Is it... is it worth it? Really?"

Shadows don't smile. So this one didn't. "Oh, yes. It's worth it."

Prowess smiled, and even if the smile was weak, it was real. "Good."

The shadow that couldn't have been there wasn't there any more – because it was gone. And the room echoed as Shadow Child drifted into Dragon Star – and back again.

Chapter Twenty-five
... into One.

December 1475, Near Bucharest

As we appear, I can feel, well, 'us' leaving. The Paradox Storm is burning over us. Dad's next to me, but he's also slumped over his Barrett, dying. "Dad!"

Dad-next-to-me raises an eyebrow. "Me or him?"

"You. I mean, him. I mean – you're fucking dying!"

Not today, kid. Not today." Dad runs over to – well, to Dad. He takes the emerald fragments out of his pocket, and lays them on his jacket. The fragments sink into the leather. Dad slips the pentacle he got from leopard guy into his - - well, the other 'his' – pocket. Then he picks up the Barrett. He aims – and fires a single shot. On the battlefield, one man falls. Dad nods, like he's satisfied. He picks up the spent brass, then he crushes the last emerald fragment under 'his' nose.

Fuck. I hate time travel. I have an idea I know why leopard guy gets headaches.

"You ready, kid?"

"What for?"

"To quit your job."

"To quit my....? Oh, Right." I check my not-a-Glock in my thigh holster. "Fucking A... er, I mean, damn right, Dad. Where to?"

"Wherever your old holster is, kid. Think you can manage that?"

"Oh, yeah. Ab-so-fucking-lutely, Dad."

We take out our flasks – and we drink.

* * *

Some-When. Middle-of-Nowhere, USA.

As we appear, I can hear the echoes of CG's scream. I see the gem crumbling in his hand. But it's not enough that's he's hurting. He killed me. And not just me. I pull my not-a-Glock, and I don't even have to aim. I squeeze off a round. It hits his head, and burning fire explodes from the hole it leaves behind as it smashes into the mirror opposite. CG falls, and I know he won't be getting up. It should feel good – but it doesn't. The speaker crackles. "Maya! So good to see you, dear. And I see you brought me a present! You do remember you were supposed to kill him, don't you? Now be a dear. FINISH HIM!"

I look at Dad. He shrugs. I look at the cracked mirror. "Fuck you, Mom. I quit!" I squeeze the trigger. Red fire and white lightning burn each time I hit the mirror. I look at Dad, one eyebrow raised.

Dad grins. "Hellfire. Direct from Hell. With some added extra – from the other place."

I keep pulling the trigger. "How many loads?"

"It depends. Sometimes? As many as you need."

I keep firing. The mirror shatters.

"YOU PATHETIC BRAT."

Long black hair. Burning eyes. A really shitty complexion. Wings of fire and feet of – I look – a chicken. My big- scary Mom has chicken feet. I want to laugh – but I pull the trigger instead. "You need some fresh blusher, Mom."

"MOM? HOW DARE YOU! I AM LILITH! I AM THE NIGHT-OWL! BRIDE OF SAMAEL, MISTRESS OF ILLUSIONS! I AM THE ONOKENTAUROS, BUT IF YOU TELL ANYONE THAT ONE, I'LL BLOODY WELL SUE! AND I'M *NOT* YOUR FUCKING MOTHER, BITCH! I KILLED YOUR MOTHER AND STOLE YOU, FOR I AM LILITH, THE STEALER OF..."

"You're a loud-mouth." Dad isn't pissed. I think he'd be less scary if he was. His voice is flat, and he's calm. And he's loading his gun. "And I killed Vlad. So don't bother looking for him."

"YOU KILLED – MY TALTOS? MY LORD OF WAMPYR? I SHALL REND YOU! I SHALL FLAY YOU! I SHALL – FUCK! THAT HURT! STOP BLOODY DOING THAT!"

Dad isn't loading his gun any more. He's firing. And his bullets burn red and white too. And he doesn't miss. Not-mom starts to bleed – smoke black and icky green. I start aiming for the holes Dad's slugs have left.

"LOOK. I SAID STOP BLOODY DOING THAT! I OFFER YOU POWER, SHADOWS! POWER OVER – I SAID STOP THAT!"

I want to grin. I want to laugh. I want to cry, for the Mom I thought I had, and the Mom I did. But I don't do any of them. I just pull my trigger.

"YOU HAVEN'T SEEN THE LAST OF ME, SHADOWS. EQVAM ITUL-QAT ATKIOS!" Not-mom scrawls a pentacle on the wall behind her. She steps through it. Or she would, if she didn't mash her nose on the wall. "I SAID FUCKING EQVAM ITUL-QAT ATKIOS! NOW OPEN THIS BLOODY DOOR!" She sighs, and looks at us. "YOU JUST CAN'T GET THE BLOODY STAFF THESE DAYS. WHERE WAS I? OH. RIGHT."

Not-Mom spits. "YOU HAVE NOT SEEN THE LAST OF ME, SHADOWS! NOW EQVAM ITU... OH. AND ABOUT TIME TOO." Not-mom steps through the wall – and she's gone.

Dad shrugs. "Oh, well. Next time." He looks round the shattered mirrors, the burning walls. "You quit pretty good, kid."

I grin. But I know my heart isn't in it. "I guess. Dad?"

"Yeah?"

"Who was my Mom?"

Coda
Secondo Movimento

1971, Washington D.C.

The White House is one of the most secure residences in the Western world. That had become even more so under Richard Milhous ('Lucy' to her friends – not that she had any) Nixon. There wasn't a door could be unlocked, never mind opened, without lights somebody was always watching starting to blink, and alarms someone was always listening for starting to ring. Which didn't seem to bother the owner of the hand unlocking this one. He twisted the pick – and the lock released. Somewhere in a distant room, lights didn't blink and alarms didn't ring. He might have grinned, but he wasn't big on grins. This wasn't fun. And this time – it wasn't just another job.

He stepped into the room, followed by the figure behind him. The sleeper was extremely well trained, her senses fine-tuned and her reactions hair-trigger. She was good. Better than good. But the man wasn't just good. He was the best there was. He stepped silently over to the sleeper's bed. His hand didn't seem to move, but now it had a gun in it. From behind him something wrapped tight round his arm, pulling it down. Or trying to. "Do we have to? There's got to be another way…"

The man shrugged. "Only two, P. Only two." He waited.

The tentacle released from his arm. Not that it would have made any difference. The gun hadn't moved from its position over the sleeping woman's mouth. The second figure sighed. "You're a bastard. I hate it when you're right."

Jack Shadow's gun settled on the woman's lips.

"If you were going to kill me, you'd have done it already. So I guess you want something from me. And since I pressed the silent alarm, but the room isn't full of men in grey suits and sunglasses firing guns, I guess you know more about this place's security than the guy who designed it." The woman didn't open her eyes, or try to get away from the gun. "So what do you want?"

"I..." the man in the black leather duster blushed. The shade of red showed he hadn't had a lot of practice. "I want to get you pregnant."

"You – *what?*"

The door opened again. A young girl came in, about sixteen. "Hey, mom."

* * *

"So let me get this straight. You're going to – we're going to – you know, I think I'm getting a headache."

The girl grinned, half sad, half happy. "Yeah. Dad does that to people. Well, and not people too. There's this Fallen Angel..."

"Fallen Angel. Like, Angel. Like, Fallen. Like, Servant of..."

"It's OK. I already did that bit, Mom."

"Riiight. So you're going to – we're going to, like, *to*. And Maya here's what happens. And a demon queen is going to kill me, to steal her, so she can train her to kill you. Because not even a demon can do it – only your own kid can get close enough to take you out. Because she doesn't have a soul. Which she does. She kills you. But you want her to be born anyway. And that's supposed to makes sense – because?"

The man in black leather shrugs. "Because I'd rather be dead with her, than alive without her."

"Dad!" The girl hugs the man in black leather. She's not very good at – as if she lacks practice.

"And I'm supposed to believe you."

The girl looks sad. "No, mom. Not supposed to. You *do* believe him. You believe him because something's telling you every word is true – and even if you don't know what it is, you trust it."

The woman sighs. "You too, huh?"

The girl shrugs.

"Perhaps I can help." Tentacles snake out from the other woman in the room. One settles on the girl's head, the other on the woman's. After a while, the tentacles fall.

"Fuck." The woman's eyes fill with tears.

"Damn, Mom." The girl's eyes are equally full.

"Thank you. Whoever you are – thank you." The woman smiles through her tears.

"Thanks, P. Really." The girl smiles too, though her tears still fall.

The man in black leather raises an eyebrow.

"Oh, I just gave them the years they could have had. If – well, if they weren't them. And I showed them what She'll do if they aren't. Aren't them, I mean."

The woman in the bed rubs the tears from her eyes. "And I guess I can't remember this either? Or the bitch will know you know she's coming?"

The man in black leather shrugs, his eyes sad.

"Oh, well. I'm sure your – your 'friend' can take care of that. I guess you lose some..." The woman looks at the girl. "... but I sure won some. Or I will."

The girl's eyes fill with tears. "Mom!"

The woman in the bed shakes her head. "It's OK, Really, really OK. Of all the things I ever do – you're the best. Always remember that."

The girl smiles. "I will, Mom."

The woman grins. "Now get your ass out of here. Your Dad and I have some fucking business to attend to."

* * *

From The Times Wedding Announcements.

We are delighted to report the recent marriage of Florence Wilkinson and renowned Coleridge scholar Professor Wilberforce Spencer.

Professor Spencer and Mrs Wilkinson first met when Professor Spencer attended Mrs Wilkinson's appointment as Director at the Coleridge Museum in Nether Stowey, after the unfortunate death of the previous incumbent. Professor Wilkinson was present in his capacity as the new Curator of the British Museum. The former Mrs Wilkinson was attended by her son Robert and his friend Alice Drake...

* * *

Washington D.C. - 350 And Down

Jack sighed, and put down the pen. Bloody field reports. They were supposed to be history – he grinned – after he quit The Dragon. He looked at the kid, sleeping in the camp bed. He shook his head. Complicated wasn't the half of it. Not now, not ever. But tomorrow was tomorrow's problem. Right now he had to deal with yesterday. He closed the notebook and took a flask from his pocket. It wouldn't be possible anywhere but 250. After all, how hard could it be for something that didn't exist once to not exist twice? He drank – and was gone.

The Shadow cleared. Jack pulled his gun, just in case. He opened the door that didn't really exist. The two men in leather dusters looked at each other. Both men grinned, and lowered their guns. Jack raised an eyebrow. "I thought you'd be taller." The man on the other side of the door raised his own brow. "Me too." Jack reached slowly into the pocket of his duster, and pulled out the notebook. He dropped it on the floor. "Let's not do this again, huh Jack?"

He pulled a flask from his pocket, and the smell of Unicorn Horn filled the air.

Epilogue
School's Out

My Daddy's a Shadow. My Mom was a Thief – even if she wasn't my Mom. And I spent a whole long time learning a bunch of shit I'm going to spend a whole lot more time making the bitch wish she never taught me. Because I'm pissed – and my Dad's pissed-er.

So sit down.

Put your head between your knees.

And kiss. Your pasts.

Goodbye.

The End

Also by Graeme Smith, from Books We Love:
JACK SHADOW

About the Author

This is me. Graeme Smith. Fantasy author. Mostly comic fantasy (which is fantasy intended to make you laugh, not fantasy in comics).

Having Graeme Smith as my pen name is convenient, since it also happens to be my real name. Although sometimes I think it isn't. Sometimes I think I'm just a remote set of hands for a keyboard. So maybe Graeme Smith is my keyboard's name, not mine.

When I'm not writing (well, or editing my writing. Or re-writing. Or editing my re-writing. Or... Quite. You get the picture), I'm doing other things. Maybe things involving mushrooms. And knitting needles (but the less said about my cooking the better). Maybe things like online gaming (If you know Bard Elcano, you know me. If you know a grumpy old dragon called Sephiranoth, you know me. If you know a tall, dark, handsome but brooding vampire, charming witty and brilliant - we never met. That's someone else.)

So there you are. Graeme Smith. Keyboard in disguise. Short, fat, bald and ugly (fortunately my wife has lousy taste in men). Time was, I worked on a psychiatric ward. Now I write about people who believe in magic and dragons, and who live where the crazy folk are the ones who don't.

If you want to find me electronically, you can find me here:

Web page: https://www.graeme-smith.net
Facebook : https://www.facebook.com/Graeme.Smith.Author
Twitter: @Graeme_Smith_

Books We Love Ltd.
http://bookswelove.net

Read on for the first chapter of Shadow Dance Book 3, coming in 2016

Shadow Kill
Chapter One
Kitty

Vondelpark, Winter 1941.
Annelies watches the older girl as she skates on her own, her skates kicking clouds of crystal from the ice as she turns. Annelies wonders why she is on her own, when so many skate together. She digs in her skates, and slides over to the older girl. "Hello."

"Hello." The older girl skates on, turning slow circles.

"I'm Annelies."

"Hello, Annelies." The older girl spins her slow circles on the ice.

"What's your name?"

"I think – I think it should be Kitty. I like cats."

"I like cats too. But does that mean Kitty isn't your real name?"

"I – I don't know. Does it matter?"

"You don't know your name?"

"I think – I think I've forgotten it."

"Oh." Annelies starts to skate alongside the older girl, their skates kicking up ice crystals. "Are you lonely?"

"Lonely?"

"Well, there's nobody with you."

"People – people don't see me very often. And mostly – they don't like it when they do."

"I can see you! You're nice!"

The older girl smiles. "Thank you."

"I'll get my friends! We can skate together!"

"Oh, they won't want to."

"Yes they will!" Annelies skates over to her friends "Come with me! I have a new friend! We can skate together!"

"Who's that, Annelies?" Annelies' friend Jacqueline looks round.

"It's Kitty! She's over there!" Annelies points at her new friend.

"Annelies – there's nobody there."

"But... but..." Annelies sees Kitty smile sadly. Then the older girl skates into the rising mist – and is gone.

* * *

Near Merwedeplein . June 06, 1942.

Annelies stares into the store window.

"Hello, Annelies."

Annelies turns round. "Kitty!"

People come and go. Nobody seems to notice Annelies friend.

"What are you doing?"

"It's my birthday soon. My daddy wants to know what I want him to get me."

"Ah. Birthdays must be nice. I think I'd like a birthday."

"Don't be silly. Everybody has birthdays, Kitty!"

"Not when you're dead."

"Dead? Are you – are you dead, Kitty?"

"That's why people don't see me. Or they don't like it when they do. Like your friends, at Vondelpark."

"I'm sorry."

"Oh, it's alright. You get used to it."

The two girls look into the window.

"What would you like, Kitty? If you had a birthday? For a present?"

"Oh, I don't know. What do people give you, Annelies?"

"Mostly things I don't really want. But you have to pretend you do, so they don't get sad. That's why Daddy said I could choose this year."

"I think – I think I'd like a letter."

"A letter? That's not a present!"

"Oh, it would be for me. It would mean someone still cared – someone still noticed me. Nobody does really – not when you're dead."

"Well, I could send you a letter! But I wouldn't know where to send one to a dead person."

"Oh, you wouldn't have to send it. Just to write it. I'd know if you did, and I could read it while you were writing it."

"But that would scare Mommy and Daddy! Because you're – well, you're dead."

"Oh, they wouldn't see me. You only get so many times you can be seen after you – well, after. This is my last time."

"So I'll never see you again?"

"No. But it's alright. You'll forget me soon anyway."

"No I won't! And I *will* write to you, Kitty! Every day! But I need something to write in. I know! That's what I'll ask Daddy for, for my birthday! A book to write letters in!"

"But won't he think it's strange if you write letters but never send them?"

"Oh, I won't ask for a letter-book. I'll ask for – what about that one?"

"Which one?"

"The red and white one – there!"

"But that's an autograph book."

"Right! So nobody will know I'm writing you letters! Kitty? Kitty? Where did you..."

* * *

Near Merwedeplein . June 09, 1942.
"That one, Daddy! Please can I have that one?"

* * *

Washington D.C. - 350 And Down
"We could have saved her, Dad."

"No we couldn't."

"Because then the world would be different? More Her world?"

"Right."

"So a little kid had to die, so we could beat Her?"

"Nope. A little kid had to write a diary nobody would have likely read if she lived – but millions of people read because she didn't. Because it made some of them – even just a few – better people after they read it. It made why she wrote it just a bit less likely to happen again."

"I'm not sure I like this job, Dad."

"Me neither. I just like what happens if we don't do it even less."

"OK. So what's next?"

"Next? Next – we take Manhattan."